CW01394942

PRAISE FOR L

'Vivid and beautifully written, Li
Sarah M

'Beautifully descriptive, unashamedly romantic and evocative,
Liz Fenwick has nailed the sweeping escapist read'
Veronica Henry

'A wonderfully evocative story, packed with secrets and emotion'
Judy Finnigan

'Pure escapism at its best'
The Sun

'With a gifted storyteller's talent for crafting compelling
characters and putting them in alluring locations, Liz Fenwick's
books invite readers to open the covers and explore a dramatic
terrain of love, family, and friendship . . . These are tales that
draw you in and keep you engaged until the last page is turned'
Deborah Harkness

'Full of warmth, wisdom and compassion . . . Liz Fenwick's
writing is vivid, satisfying and descriptive'
Daily Express

'A warm and feel-good romance that will have you
pining to feel sand beneath your feet'
Woman's Weekly

'Evocative and compelling, a glorious tale of the choices
women make for love. I adored it'
Cathy Bramley

'Full of emotion and mystery'
HELLO!

'Sweeping, romantic and gorgeously evocative of Cornwall'
BEST

Called 'the queen of the contemporary Cornish novel' by the *Guardian*, **Liz Fenwick** is the author of eleven books, including *The River Between Us* which won the Popular Romantic Fiction Award from the Romantic Novelists' Association. She lives with her husband and two mad cats near the Helford River in Cornwall. When not writing Liz is reading, painting, knitting, plot walking, and procrastinating on social media.

You can find her on X @liz_fenwick, Instagram @liz_fenwick, Facebook @liz.fenwick.author and TikTok @lizfenwickauthor.

For more information or to join her mailing list visit lizfenwick.com.

Also by Liz Fenwick

The Cornish House
A Cornish Affair
A Cornish Stranger
Under a Cornish Sky
A Cornish Christmas Carol
The Returning Tide
One Cornish Summer
The Path to the Sea
The River Between Us
Delivering Christmas
The Secret Shore

The
SECRETS
of
HARBOUR
HOUSE

Liz Fenwick

ONE PLACE. MANY STORIES

HQ
An imprint of HarperCollins*Publishers* Ltd
1 London Bridge Street
London SE1 9GF

www.harpercollins.co.uk

HarperCollins*Publishers*
Macken House, 39/40 Mayor Street Upper
Dublin 1, D01 C9W8, Ireland

This edition 2025

4
First published in Great Britain by HQ,
an imprint of HarperCollins*Publishers* Ltd 2025

ISBN: 9780008608743

Typeset in Sabon Lt Pro by HarperCollins*Publishers* India

Printed and bound in the UK using 100%
Renewable Electricity at CPI Group (UK) Ltd

FSC
www.fsc.org

MIX
Paper
FSC™ C007454

For more information visit: www.harpercollins.co.uk/green

For Brigid Coady
She is simply the best!
And she always wanted a story for Rory.

I would venture to guess that Anon, who wrote so many poems without signing them, was often a woman.

　　　　—VIRGINIA WOOLF, *A Room of One's Own*

Prologue

28 March 2003

S. W. Barton Auctioneers was empty as Dad and I entered the building and walked through the artwork-lined hallway and past a Louis XIII chest of drawers tucked under the stairs. I loved these Sunday mornings when Mum was volunteering and it was just the two of us in the auction house. This was the routine he and I had fallen into ever since he'd first brought me here on a Sunday when I was six. We'd been doing it for five years and it was always an adventure.

'Well, Kerensa, what shall we do?' he asked as we bypassed his office and went into the showroom. Paintings covered the dividers and walls. Sometimes there were three or more hung above each other and sometimes just one large one, like my favourite abstract picture all in blues. It was like the sky on a summer's day.

Dad picked up a strange still life off the top of the display case. Everything he'd chosen in the past had come with a story. It could be a tale of exotic origins, previous owners, even murderers. The more stories an item held, the more interesting for me and the more value to Dad. I think he secretly wanted to run a museum rather than be the person selling on these things. He'd told me stories about a ruby from a scorned lover,

I

a handbag from a minister's mistress, a self-portrait of an artist who hated themselves, and my favourite, a stuffed rabbit that had inspired a children's tale.

He held out his other hand and together we went to the biggest room upstairs. There was an old sofa against the wall that had been sold but never collected. It was covered in a fabric that looked like a Turkish carpet. We sat down on it and he handed me the funny painting.

'What can you tell me about this?' he asked, like he always did.

The first thing I noticed was it was heavier than I expected. It was of a vase with red roses in a slim gold frame. 'Why does it weigh so much?'

He took off his glasses and polished them. 'You tell me.'

'It's not like that Russian painting all done with a palette knife and so much paint.'

'True.' He leaned back.

I loved this game we played. We never rushed it. My favourite time had been with an Easter egg covered in bright green enamel and coloured jewels. Its story had been sad but it held a small chick, which chirped loudly when the egg was opened. I'd so wanted to keep it, but like all these things, it went to sale. Dad said that was how we became part of the object's story. I'd rather have kept it.

'Well?' he prompted.

I turned it over like he'd taught me. The canvas was a bit scrappy, with uneven edges. It distracted from the stretchers that made the canvas taut. 'The wood of the stretchers is different to the usual.'

'How so?'

I studied them. 'They're a darker colour and the grain of the wood is denser.'

'Good.' He watched me with a big smile on his face.

'There's no writing or mark to say it's been sold through an auction house.'

'Well remembered.'

I made a face at him. 'Why wouldn't I remember? You only told me to look out for that last month.'

He laughed.

Normally I figured out the story quickly, but with no marks and no signature, this was hard. I flipped it over again. It was a boring painting, and I couldn't see what was important about it. Or had I missed something? He'd told me that many times the back of the painting could be more interesting and more important to us Bartons than the front. By looking closely, we could see what others had missed. This meant we could tell a better, more complete story about the object, which would increase the interest in it. I hadn't understood this at first, but now I did. The more intrigue in the story around the piece, the more it was worth. He'd explained it was like the Duchess of Windsor's jewels. Without her ownership they were simply diamonds and emeralds. But because they were hers, they had extra glamour, history and value. The story made all the difference.

I balanced the canvas in my hands. One side was heavier, and one half of the back was dirtier. I peered from the canvas to Dad before I turned it over again.

'This is like the ones they sell on the park gates in London. There's nothing special about the artwork,' I said with more confidence than I felt.

'You have a very good eye.' He looked at me over his glasses. He was so clever. This auction house was all his – well, his and Uncle Stephen's. One day I'd be the owner of S. W. Barton's and I'd be clever like Dad. 'So why is it here?'

It was a terrible painting and it was unsigned. I bit my thumbnail and studied it again.

'You've told me half the story.'

I put it down between us in frustration. 'It looks like the roses you see at petrol stations, the ones with no smell. Not like the ones in our garden.'

'I agree.' He removed his glasses and cleaned them.

I picked it up again and turned it over one more time. Looking more closely, I saw the canvas had empty nail holes. It must have been put on different stretchers. Also, on the right-hand side, the lighter side, the canvas had been bent away from the wood. It was creased. 'If it's nothing more than a street painting, why did the owner replace the stretchers?'

'Why do you think?'

'There has to be a reason.' I huffed. He'd never given me something so tricky before. He raised an eyebrow, and I ran my fingers carefully along the wood so as not to get a splinter. There were no woodworm holes either, and I'd been told with furniture that usually meant a hardwood. 'The wood looks like the table Uncle Stephen was so excited about.'

Dad smiled. I was on the right track.

'There has to be something special about this painting or we wouldn't be auctioning it.' I looked at the back one more time. Lifting the canvas on the dirty side, I saw a small indent. I slipped my finger in and wiggled it, but nothing happened. I thrust the painting at Dad. 'It's there but I can't do it.'

He turned the painting top to bottom and with his right thumb he popped the piece of wood open.

'Smuggling!' I clapped my hands. This was good.

'Well done. It was used to smuggle diamonds and other gems.'

'Clever.' I could imagine it all, the glistening stones tucked inside, making the weight equal. 'Was it used by a bank robber?'

'No, something far more interesting.' He polished his glasses again. 'A woman used it to move jewellery out of Germany just before the war for her Jewish friends.'

'That's great, but she had bad taste in paintings.'

Dad laughed. 'Not bad, just different.'

I made a face. 'No one would want that.'

'Exactly.'

An ugly painting being good made no sense, no matter how I twisted this around. I waited while he put his glasses back on. Only then did he speak. 'The painting was carried in and out of the country like a souvenir.'

'Is that why it's of boring roses?'

'Indeed.' He held it up for me to look at again. 'Customs officials took no notice of it.'

'Why are we selling it?' I looked from the painting back to Dad.

'It tells a story.'

I shrugged. 'Who wants to be part of this story?'

'That is what we will find out.'

'Who gave you the painting to sell?' I needed to know.

'Correct question to ask.'

I smiled. 'Provenance.' I'd heard this word so many times. It was the god of auction houses, according to Dad.

'Indeed, and that is why you will run this company one day.' He ruffled my hair.

'I want to, but that's a long way off.' The thought of this place of stories being mine filled my dreams.

'True.'

The painting was so ugly I kept looking at it. 'Who gave you the painting to sell?'

'The artist who painted it, Sheba Kernow.'

I pulled my chin in. 'Why would she own up to painting

this?' It was oil paint but so thinned it looked more like watercolours.

'Because Sheba needs money to fix the roof after the big storm we had two weeks ago.'

That made sense. I knew all about the damage big storms could do because I'd heard my best friend Tash's mum complaining about the cost of fixing the garden room on their house. It was a lot of money, but I didn't think that even with an interesting story this ugly painting would pay to fix a hole in the roof.

PART ONE

They shut me up in Prose –
As when a little Girl
They put me in the Closet –
Because they liked me 'still' –

Emily Dickinson (445)

1

Penzance

The northerly wind was brisk as it rushed past me on its way to the harbour. March sunshine made no difference to the bitter temperature, and I pulled my coat tighter. The bare trees lining the car park seemed to be holding their breath, waiting for a moment of warmth to bring forth their leaves still clenched in tight bud.

Eight years had passed since I'd last stood here. Back in 2014, I'd promised never to cross the threshold again. Brash words from my twenty-two-year-old self, who never envisioned this day would come. The building in front of me was a hotchpotch of bricks, cement, glass and metal, like I had put it together with wooden blocks and glue as a child. There was no aesthetic beauty about the warehouse-like space. S. W. Barton Auctioneers had been extended as the business grew, but without any of the style or beauty of the items that had been sold on its premises.

Once I had known every inch of the place, but now I was a stranger. I pulled my shoulders back, took a deep breath and walked towards the entrance. The sooner I went in, the sooner I could resolve my father's estate and return to my life in London.

My phone rang. Paul. We'd spoken ten minutes ago as I'd left the house. He was worried about me, but I couldn't postpone this any longer, so I didn't answer. With each step I took towards the main door, I reminded myself that I had every right to be here, even if I didn't want to be.

'Hello, love.' Marcia Williams stood and embraced me in a big hug that defied her petite size. When I pulled back, there were tears in my eyes as well as hers. She was the glue that held the auction house together.

She blew her nose, then asked, 'Still take your coffee black, no sugar?'

'Yes, thank you. Well remembered.' Her office was lined with past catalogues filed neatly in glass-fronted bookcases that had first been used in some solicitor's office in the 1930s. It added an air of authority to the place.

She put the kettle on. 'Not used to this.' She waved her hand around. 'He was always here when I arrived, unless he and your mother were on holiday in the Scillies.'

Dad's boat would have to be sold. One more item on the list of loss.

'I'll bring the coffee; you go to the office. I haven't touched anything since . . .' Her voiced trailed away.

I swallowed a lump in my throat.

This place felt timeless. The corridor was lined with paintings for the next fine art sale in two weeks' time. I clenched my hands and counted to ten. Breathe. Function. Move forward. This was only temporary.

The door to Dad's office was slightly ajar. Inside, nothing had changed. I wanted it to be different somehow – not as it always had been, with files stacked on the bookcase behind the desk, the tall clock that had never kept time occupying the corner. My father had loved the chimes. As if on cue, it struck eleven, but it was not yet nine. When the sound stopped, I closed my eyes and listened – Marcia's voice on the telephone next door, the rumble of traffic on the road, and loudest of all, the pounding of my heart.

I circled the desk, not ready to sit in my father's chair.

My phone beeped with a message from Paul. He loved me. I held that to me, for I would need his love, especially today. I touched the locket I wore. He'd given it to me on the first anniversary of our being together, eight years ago.

'Kerensa.' Marcia set the coffee on the desk and sent me a look. I stood by the window. 'I know this is hard, but he always believed in you.'

I closed my eyes for a moment. Eight years ago I had made a huge mistake by being extremely cautious listing a painting as Impressionist school after Cézanne rather than the real thing. Even just thinking about it made part of me shrivel.

'I believe in you too.'

'Thank you.' I turned to her. 'That means the world.'

'There's no time like the present to sit down and get your feet under the desk.' She took my hand and led me like a child to the chair. I sat obediently.

'His password was love1992.'

I looked down at my hands.

'No caps, all one word.' She pulled the door closed as she left.

My name, Kerensa, meant 'love' in Cornish, and 1992 was the year I was born. I didn't know where to look, let alone what to do.

'Pull yourself together,' I said aloud, putting my hands on the top of the desk. If I treated this as a research project, it would be simple. It was a job, nothing more than another task to accomplish, even though it meant being here.

The phone rang. I stared at it. Who used landlines these days?

'Hello. Barton's.'

'Ren.'

'Paul?'

'You didn't answer my call or my text. I'm worried about you.'

'Thank you.' This was so much harder than anything I could have imagined, had I ever pictured this day.

'Darling, I just wanted to tell you I love you and you can do this quickly. Then you can come home and I can look after you.'

'Once probate is done.'

'But you won't have to stay there until probate is done, especially with all the delays now since the pandemic. Just find out the lie of the land, then hand it to the solicitors.' He spoke slowly, as if I needed clear instructions. Maybe I did. Losing Dad so suddenly had shaken me.

I hoped that the task of selling my mother's and my share of the business would be that simple. My father had been somewhat organised, so my role should be nothing more than box-ticking.

'I've lost you.'

'Sorry, I'm distracted and I haven't seen Uncle Stephen since the funeral. He won't want me here.'

'Don't be silly. You own twenty-four per cent of the business now that your father is gone. Your uncle can't kick you out.'

'I'm not being silly.' Not at all. Stephen had done just that eight years ago. Paul had been my rock since then, when my world fell apart and I broke down.

'OK, not silly.' He paused. 'Be quick, though.'

'I miss you too.' I thought of the ease of our life in London. Everything was arranged to help me manage my anxiety.

'Love you.'

'Love you too,' I said, and put the phone down. When I looked up, Stephen was standing in the doorway.

'I won't say welcome, but I hope you can at least be useful while you're here. We're a man down,' he said bluntly, as if I didn't know why I was here. Like me, he was dressed in black, but maybe that was what he always wore. Today it was black trousers with a black polo neck.

He dropped a folder on the desk. 'Your father was working on this, and you can be useful by finishing it.'

'I'm not here to do this.' I tapped the file.

'If I could give it to anyone else, I would. But it's an easy enough task, even for you.'

Before I could reply, he was gone.

The beige folder sat in the centre of the desk.

It was a challenge.

My uncle had placed it there as if he was handing out an exam paper. Perhaps that was exactly what it was, a test. My bodily responses were identical to the many exams I'd sat. My heart sped up and drummed louder, blocking out all rational thought.

I couldn't do this. I wasn't good enough.

The walls closed in on me. I shouldn't be here, but this was exactly where I was supposed to be. It was where my father wanted me to be, where my mother needed me to be. But the last place I wanted to be. My uncle didn't want me here either. We could agree on that at least.

Outside the office window, seagulls cried. The fields were filled with unpicked daffodils oddly shouting joy when I was still dressed in black. It had been three days since my father's funeral, and despite my mourning clothes, I still couldn't process it. He couldn't be gone. But he was, and I was sitting at his desk.

A pile of papers, an old inkwell, a family photo and a totally out-of-place Mac computer covered the surface. Even he had been pulled out of the early 1900s into computer use for the ease of research and communication with clients both buying and selling. I touched the keyboard to bring the screen to life, and wished I could do the same for him.

The smell of mould rose from the slightly damp file in front of me. The whole building was filled with the scent of beeswax, varnish and decay. The latter was everywhere, from foxing to woodworm to crumbling paper. The dust of the ages hung in the air and covered every surface.

The first sheet of paper in the file was in my uncle's handwriting. It declared it was the estate of two distinguished ladies, Bathsheba Kernow and Vivian Sykes. The names rang a bell: artists possibly. They had died four years ago, in 2018. The house and all its contents were to be sold by order of the court. What was the story behind this? Four years? Even allowing for the pandemic, that seemed a long time.

It wasn't my problem. My father's estate was. I wasn't here to work, for I was a liability. That had been agreed eight years ago.

Yet I couldn't help it, I was intrigued. The file would have to wait, though. First, I needed to find the company accounts and then locate my father's private ones. Mum had no idea of their whereabouts. Tonight I would have a closer look at the women's estate. Before I shut the file, I turned one more page to find Dad's handwritten notes. He had the worst writing, but I could read it, or I had always been able to in the past. The blur of words in front of me now were like a foreign language. Had it been that long since I'd read anything he'd written, or had his handwriting deteriorated since I'd left?

Preliminary visit to Harbour House scheduled for 8/8/2019
Bathsheba Kernow – painter
Vivian Sykes – sculptor
Artwork – WB
General contents – SB
Postponed on 7/8/2019 and client to advise on new date

I closed the file and put it in my bag. First things first, my father's estate. That's why I was here.

* * *

The long clock in the corner chimed eight; it was 6.15. I couldn't linger here any longer. Mum would be waiting for me. I put the large set of keys for the artists' house into my bag. Tomorrow morning I would go there and assess the time required to make an inventory.

In the corridor, I paused to listen to my uncle on the phone, then glanced at my phone. Another message from Paul.

I need you here. Nothing is right without you.

As if I wanted to be here. London was home and here was not. No one, especially not my beloved father, had planned for him dying in a bicycle accident while he was out for an evening ride. At fifty-eight, he was fit and loved to indulge in his passion for cycling and sailing. My poor mother was a different story. A little over a year ago she had suffered a stroke, and her recovery had been slow. My father's death wasn't helping.

Outside Marcia's office hung a black and white photo of the premises in 1920. S. W. Barton Auctioneers had been founded by my great-great-grandfather in 1902. Ever since, there had been a family member driving the gentlemanly business through both good times and bad. The company had made a name for itself with the many artists who had flourished here in Cornwall. My father had been an expert on the works of the Newlyn and St Ives schools. My uncle was more concerned with furniture, porcelain and the bottom line. When I'd asked to see the accounts, he'd said he didn't have time today and would get them to me tomorrow afternoon.

'When are you heading to Harbour House?' he called from the end of the hallway, where he was leaning on the door frame of

15

his office. Tall, handsome and bitter, he was five years younger than Dad, and in this moment looked five years older.

'Most likely tomorrow morning if all is well with Mum.'

He nodded, with a sour expression on his face. 'None of the furniture has any value; it can go straight to a general sale. You'll need to inventory it immediately.' He turned and closed his office door.

I'd tried all day to have a proper conversation with him, but he'd done nothing except issue orders as if I was the junior in the office. Back when I had been just that, he'd been more fun, or at least I'd thought so at the time. Maybe my memory was failing a bit, like Mum's. I could put hers down to her stroke and the stress of losing Dad, but I wasn't impacted in quite the same way. I had lost my champion, but not the love of my life and the centre of my existence.

I waved goodbye to Marcia.

'See you in the morning,' she said.

'I'll head to Harbour House first thing.' I tapped the folder in my bag.

'Good luck with that one,' she said.

I stopped. 'Why?'

She shrugged. 'Nothing's been done for years because of missing wills and a dispute over who inherits.'

'Oh. How many heirs?'

She closed her eyes for a moment. 'Two great-nephews, I think. And all rather complicated because of their living situation.'

'As two distinguished ladies?' I raised an eyebrow.

Marcia nodded. 'Quite.'

Such antiquated language, but that suited my uncle, who never said anything directly if possible. Down the corridor, his voice droned on.

2

I stood on the footpath and tried to think of this house as home, but couldn't. This bungalow was nothing like the home I'd known all my life, but after Mum's stroke my parents realised that they would need to move to something more practical. Maybe if Dad was here, it would feel different. It was a sorry fact that until he'd died, I hadn't set foot inside their new home. There hadn't been time, I'd told myself, but I'd lied and made myself believe it.

They'd moved in three months ago. Paul and I had been down the month before that to help with getting rid of a lifetime of collecting. Paul had been brilliant with Mum while I weeded through everything with Dad. We'd laughed and we'd cried as we carted stuff to the charity shops and to the auction house to sell. Mum's mood had been so variable that long weekend. Paul jollied her along. With me she was sharp one moment and loving the next. I put it down to the stress of selling the house she loved and leaving her garden.

I should have come back down to see their new house after they moved in, and that truth was hard to swallow especially when I couldn't fix it. If I was honest, I hated the thought of coming to somewhere that wasn't home, but that was a terrible excuse. Part of me had been mourning the old house. I always escaped to that house in my dreams when I was stressed. It had been such a haven growing up. As a child, I'd practised walking down the curved stairs pretending I was a bride, and I'd imagined my own children playing in the huge garden. But a wedding wasn't going to happen, because Paul didn't believe marriage was necessary. So it didn't matter that the old Victorian pile was being torn down and five new executive homes were going to be built on the plot. Could you grieve for a house? I'd thought so until I'd learned what grief really meant. My gut twisted at the reality that I saw daily in my mother's eyes.

Meg Pascoe, who helped Mum during the day, waved and left the front door ajar for me. When she reached me on the path, she tapped my arm in a motherly fashion. 'It's been an OK day.'

What did that mean? Mum's recovery from her stroke had been steady, but she needed help, which I had witnessed since Dad died.

'She dressed, ate lunch and spoke to the gardener.' Meg pulled her keys out of her bag.

'The post?' There were hundreds of letters of condolence from all over the art world, which I hoped would help comfort her. Replying could be a problem as Mum was left-handed and that hand still hung limply at her side. Maybe we could tackle them together in the evenings.

'Hasn't touched it, dear.' Meg sighed and went on her way.

From the front hall I could hear Mum chatting to someone. Her voice sounded too bright, too forced. It was normal to be down when you'd lost the love of your life. She didn't have to appear fine when both she and I knew she wasn't. Dad would know how to help, and that was the worst part.

In the hallway, I paused. The paintings were familiar and I saw my father in each of them. The washed tones of a Maddie Hollis watercolour and the bold shapes of a Peter Lanyon. These had been purchased long before their value had been recognised. He hadn't collected them for their potential gain. No, he'd wanted them for their beauty and the moments they captured, reminding him of his favourite places with my mother. I stopped in front of the painting of Frenchman's Creek by Jaunty Blythe. That was where he had proposed. He'd planned it all. It was Mum's favourite book. Dad was romantic and strangely precise.

My mother's laughter rang down the rugless hallway. No trip hazards allowed.

'Oh, I'm doing fine, Paul.'

I froze. It was so kind of him to check on her. But she was telling him she was fine when I had told him the opposite this morning.

'No, she's . . . been great, and . . . I know how you miss her, but she shouldn't be too long away.' Her speech had returned, but it was slower and with the odd pause.

The truth was my mother wasn't getting out of bed in the morning unless Meg Pascoe or I helped her. She was as far from fine as it was possible to be, and gripped by grief.

I hurried into the kitchen to see her leaning against the counter, her stick propped beside her.

'Take care, Paul, and thank you for letting me know.' She put the phone down and picked up the kettle with her right hand. With slow, awkward movements she poured water into a mug, then stared out the window. It broke my heart to watch the effort it took her to do simple things.

She looked over her shoulder. 'Oh, you're home.' She smiled, then winced.

I grabbed the milk from the fridge to save her a few steps, then noticed there was no tea bag in the cup, so I added one to the hot water. She wasn't sleeping well but hated the decaf ones, swearing they tasted awful. Maybe she should try a herbal tea.

I added a camomile one to another mug for me. My sleep hadn't been great either.

'How was today?' I asked with as much brightness as I could muster.

She didn't reply. I placed the mug on the kitchen table for her, and leaning heavily on her cane, she made her way to the chair. I so wanted to help her but didn't have a clue where to begin.

'I went through the paperwork on Dad's desk,' I said to start a conversation.

She raised an eyebrow.

'Stephen handed me an estate to value.'

'Dear, you know you can't do that.' She glared at the tea.

I drew a breath. It was dire when even your own mother didn't believe in you. But she had every reason to say that after what had happened. Still, she had never been so direct or so pointed. This was new. Was it the stroke that had changed her, or something else? 'Well, whether I can or I can't, it's down to me to do it.'

'Silly man.'

I couldn't argue with that, but it was clear she thought I was useless. Her words stung, and I swallowed the resentment I felt. Why was she acting this way? Was it grief? Her face gave nothing away except her exhaustion. It didn't lie. I heard her crying in the night.

'What did you do today?' I tried again.

She lifted her left hand an inch and it flopped to her side. 'What do you expect me to do?'

'I thought you might look at the letters of condolence.' I gave her an encouraging smile. 'As you always said to me in the past when you wrote to someone, it might help with the grief.'

She pushed her chair back slowly, the scraping sound on the tiled floor saying far more than she would voice. Then with a heaving sigh she stood and shuffled out of the room.

I put my head in my hands, knowing I'd made things worse. The tea in my mug looked like watered-down whisky. Tea was not what I needed right now. A strong drink would be a better choice. But instead of drinking either, I went to the freezer and pulled out a shepherd's pie a neighbour had made. Once it was in the oven, I rubbed my temples and tried to clear my head before I called Paul. It would be good to talk things through with him. He was so good at helping me sort my thoughts and calm my anxiety.

I tried three times, but his phone went to voicemail. My father was dead, my mother wasn't coping and my uncle was being passive-aggressive at best. Talking about all of this would help. I tried one more time, but there was still no answer. There was one other person who would understand. Tash. Speaking to her would help, but still I hesitated. I really needed to talk to Paul. My temples throbbed. I picked up the tepid tea and knocked it back. Dinner in the oven smelled delicious. Hopefully a good meal would help both my mother and me. God knows something needed to.

* * *

As I cleared the dishes, I heard the television in the other room. We'd eaten dinner in silence. Exhaustion had filled the space between us, or at least that was what I was putting it down to. From the theme music I heard, I knew Mum was watching reruns of *Midsomer Murders*.

My phone rang.

'Hi, baby,' I said with as much energy as I could muster.

'Sorry I missed your calls earlier.' He sounded contrite.

'That's OK,' I replied.

'I was out with Charles and Susie. We missed you.' He paused. 'But they understood why you couldn't make the party. They send their condolences.'

'That's so kind.' It had totally escaped my mind that tonight was the launch party for Susie's latest book on the Tudors. I flicked the kettle on, then turned it off. I didn't want more tea. 'How was the rest of your day?'

'Worked through a PhD student's thesis. Dire stuff.' He huffed.

'Sorry about that, but I'm sure with your guidance it will come up to scratch.' I knew how hard he was to please. My unsubmitted master's thesis was in a box in the room I was sleeping in.

'Not so sure.' He coughed.

'Anything else?' I paced the kitchen, longing to chat about my day.

'No, simply exhausted.'

'You had a chat with Mum.'

'Did she tell you I rang?' he asked. 'I called to check in on her. I know this is hard for both of you.'

It was a thoughtful gesture. He was good like that.

'She was on the phone to you when I came home.'

'That's not your home.'

'You know what I mean.' Only the paintings, the books and a few antiques were familiar, home-like.

'Your home is here with me.'

'True.' I pictured the immaculate flat. Everything in its place and neutral colours all chosen to soothe. He'd taken so much time to make sure there was nothing there that would trigger me. I was such a mess when I moved in with him. My thesis was due, the press were hounding my father and my uncle, and it was all my fault. I cracked under the pressure and Paul helped me. He made sure nothing distressed me while I recovered from my breakdown. No social media, no busy places and few responsibilities. He even helped me find the job I love. As Dad always said, love is more about what you do than what you say. Paul was always looking out for me.

The phone beeped.

'Look, that's Louis. I need to take the call,' Paul said. 'Chat tomorrow. Love you.'

The line went dead. That was not the conversation I'd wanted or hoped for. There was no sense in dwelling on it, though, for there was too much to do.

I scrolled through my emails and found one from Tash's father, Jack Thomas, who was Dad's solicitor. In it he laid out the key steps to sorting probate and the big-picture stuff. Dad had left me a ten per cent share of the business, adding to the four per cent my grandfather had left me and the previous ten Dad had given me when Stephen had sold it to him to fund the purchase of his beloved cottage on the cliffs. Dad's remaining shares would go to Mum along with everything else bar a small Hepworth sculpture. I'd been with him when he'd bought it. It didn't feel real that he was gone, yet the evidence was all around me.

* * *

It was near midnight when I had finally convinced my mother she needed to sleep, and so did I. Time disappeared helping her with things, so I hadn't even glanced at the file on Kernow and Sykes.

I opened the folder and found Dad's notes. God, how I missed him, but I focused on the task at hand. It wasn't for me that I was doing this; it wasn't even for him. It was for Mum. These weeks since Dad died had shown me how bad things were. She needed help, and help wasn't cheap.

Bathsheba Kernow, painter, born 1914, died December 2018
Vivian Sykes, sculptor, born 1920, died December 2018

23

I paused, struck by them dying in the same month. Which one had died first?

Harbour House, Newlyn
Inventory, value for probate, and sell by January 2020

January 2020 was struck through and a series of further dates added and deleted. The latest was written in my uncle's sharp script.

Ordered by the court to be completed no later than June 2022

It was now the end of March. Not much time.
I turned the page and saw that he had added another note.

No item of furniture is worth more than a hundred pounds. All to be included in a general sale. I doubt the art, books or papers are worth a sale in their own right, but to be included in a sale of Cornish artists' works.

On a separate notepad I began a list of questions.
Why had the sale been delayed?
What prices had been achieved for their previous works?
What schools or universities might be interested in collections of artists' papers if any were discovered?
A search of the sale of artists' papers revealed disappointing results unless they were well known. These two were not. Hardly any of their work had sold in years. That could be down to their ages. Kernow was one hundred and four when she died, and Sykes was no spring chicken at ninety-eight. As both women had

lived in Cornwall, maybe Falmouth University might want them. Of course, I was getting ahead of myself. I hadn't been to the premises. How long had they lived at Harbour House?

I closed my eyes and in my mind travelled the short distance along the coast from Penzance, through Newlyn and on towards Mousehole. The house sat just off the road, and I'd always admired its Georgian bones, with a garden that presented itself to the roadside. It had the look of being uncared for at first glance, but explosions of colour shouted careful planting.

Opening my eyes, I saw my father's study, which was a bit chaotic. It was so him, and had been me too, but now, at the age of thirty, I'd learned my lesson. Everything in my life had a place, and God help me if it was even the smallest bit askew. Untidiness did my head in. I straightened the pens on Dad's desk.

As I did with every artist I researched in my job for the television programme *Fake or Fabulous*, I typed Kernow's name into the search engine to see what, if anything, was known about her and her work. Google always threw up the most obvious and the most sponsored, but sometimes it also gave me an idea of what sort of job was in front of me.

Both women had achieved some degree of success, but I suspected not anything like they deserved. Female artist after female artist had been seen through the lens of who had taught them, who their lovers had been and who their family were. I'd hoped by this point in my life to have made some impact on this imbalance, but I hadn't. Maybe I could with these two.

Kernow had a Wiki page, but my jaw clenched as I read it.

Bathsheba Kernow, daughter of painter Francis Kernow and his wife Rebecca, née Arthur, was born in St Ives in 1914 just before her father served in the First World War. Francis Kernow's experiences on the battlefield changed his style of painting. Pre-war he had been influenced by the nearby Newlyn school, but his style became less classical post-war. He had major exhibitions in London, Paris and New York and was part of the St Ives school. He is well known for his encouragement of many of the younger artists like Patrick Heron and Peter Lanyon, helping them to forge their more modern approaches.

'Fascinating, but what about Bathsheba?' I muttered.

Bathsheba Kernow trained with her father, then, after travel in Europe, studied at the Slade in 1935, working with Derek Thompson, who became renowned for his abstract work.

I slapped my hands on the desk. 'Bloody hell, does it never end?' I said aloud. It was the same story I saw over and over again in my studies of women artists. The same pattern, the repeated telling of the men who'd fathered, taught or even loved them. Little or nothing of the artist themselves. It was simply so wrong.

It was a sad fact that until the twentieth century, if a woman hadn't been born into an artistic family, she stood little chance of becoming an artist. Women were denied so many opportunities that men took for granted, like life drawing. It was thought improper for a woman to draw nudes. That was why Dame Laura Knight's 1913 self-portrait with Ella Naper was ground-breaking. She had put herself in the painting with a nude, and on a large scale. I remembered my father explaining all this to me on a trip to the National Portrait Gallery.

It had begun my passion for putting women back into the history of art and not simply researching who their families were or who had taught them. Of course, all that work sat in the box in the bedroom, not forgotten but not good enough. But I still championed women artists in a small way in weekly posts to Instagram, the one social media I allowed myself. In each post I would highlight one artist and her work. This I could do. It didn't take convincing arguments, simply pictures of their art and some facts. It didn't change the world, but it highlighted the lives of female artists one square on the grid at a time. Doing this for so many years had gained me a large number of followers. But I hadn't had the heart to post since Dad died. I must return to it.

I touched the blurry photo of Kernow on the screen. She appeared out of focus, wind-blown, with her long hair wrapped about her neck and face. 'Bathsheba Kernow, if I do nothing else in this project, I will make sure that when we sell your work, we will sing your praises and not those of your father or your teachers.'

The biography of Vivian Sykes was no better. It spoke of her father and brothers and the men who'd taught her, with one mention of her sister, also a sculptor. Every time I thought the world had moved forward and women could be looked at in their own right, I was proved wrong.

I stood and closed my laptop. Looking at Wiki had been a bad idea. Sadly, I doubted the art market press would be any better. I clenched my hands, accepting that to maximise the publicity and possible value of the work for the sale, some of these facts about the women's families and teachers would increase interest. But I was determined to find out more about the artists themselves to make them shine in their own right. The first step would be to discover more about their deaths, details that should be readily available.

3

1 April 2022

Newlyn

I picked my way along the garden path to the red door. The front of the house was covered in an ancient wisteria, which would be divine in a few weeks. Daffodils bloomed where they chose, appearing like random pockets of happiness. They were under the oak tree, in a rose bed, in the middle of the lawn and in tubs. I couldn't help but smile, loving the chaos of it. It would drive Paul to distraction. But nature was like that in gardens, my mother had taught me years ago. She would plant something in one bed to find it preferred another. Rather than fight it, she would enjoy the fact that the plant was happier.

A shiver ran across my skin as I reached the door. Too many memories of having appraised the contents of houses with Dad over the years settled on my shoulders. We'd had such fun poking into other people's lives. Always respectful, of course, but in a way, by naming me as the executor of his estate, Dad had asked me to do the same with his things, his life. I wasn't up to the task for so many reasons. The first one being that I was out of practice. Possibly my uncle had handed me this to remind me what to do, but that could be giving him too much credit.

A magpie cried and landed on a ground-floor windowsill. He was alone.

'Morning, Mr Magpie.' I bowed my head in greeting. He tossed a look over his shoulder and flew away. Sorrow. Must not dwell on the past and must focus on the task at hand – the estate of two distinguished ladies.

I found the key for the front door and pushed it open with more force than necessary. It swung wide with a thunk. The house had the musty smell of unused, unopened places. I left the door ajar to clear some of the stagnant air. Dampness wasn't good for houses or their contents, and especially not for paintings.

'Who's here?' a gruff voice called.

I swung around. 'Ren Barton, from S. W. Barton Auctioneers.' I squinted at the person who was silhouetted in the doorway.

'That's all right then.' The voice softened on the last word. After cleaning her feet on the mat, the woman walked in and towered over me. 'I'm Tilly, the gardener.' She held out a hand.

As I shook it, I felt the calluses and noted the stained skin. She had the look of someone who enjoyed her work.

'I've been keeping an eye out as people know there's no one living here.'

'Sensible.'

'The place shouldn't be empty. They would hate that.'

I tilted my head in an unspoken question.

'They were both private people, but the best people, and it wasn't their plan that the place should be picked apart and sold off.'

'Oh.' I thought of the notes in the file. They were clear. Catalogue, value and sell everything.

'I'll leave you to it.' She slipped back out the door before I could ask anything else. *It wasn't their plan.* What *had* their plan been?

I put my queries aside and placed the folder down on a mahogany table in the vestibule. It looked to be George III. Furniture wasn't my strength, but my uncle was wrong about this piece at least.

After years of declining values for brown furniture, as it was called these days, it was seeing something of a revival thanks to environmental concerns coming to the fore. Reuse and recycle. Running my hand over the dusty surface, I knew that this table had a value of more than a hundred pounds, so what was my uncle's game? Was this a test?

I opened the notes app on my phone and began an inventory.

> George III tripod table – single-piece tip-up top supported
> by a turned column and three carved legs with spade feet

I used the measurement app on my phone to fix its rough dimensions.

> 1 metre diameter

Then I added the next item.

> Arts and Crafts coat rack stand – oak, eight turned knob
> hangers, carved wheel design on back and drawer, 195 cm

Waxed jackets still hung on it like the occupants of the house would arrive at any moment and slip them on before venturing into the garden.

> 1 gilt mirror – Victorian, with scarred glass
> 1 oil on board 50 cm by 100 cm – landscape in greens
> signed Sheba

Sheba? Bathsheba. The work looked like what I'd seen online last night.

I noted the Turkish carpet under my feet before I left the entrance and went into the hallway, where a sweeping staircase dominated the space. I looked up its curved lines and there my gaze stopped.

The wall was owned by a large portrait of a woman dressed in black. She was beautiful, with big luminous eyes and pale, slightly flushed skin. Her gaze met mine and I shivered. Longing and sadness plus intelligence. Blue-black hair cut into a 1920s bob highlighted the defined bone structure. Her beauty took my breath away. She wore a bias-cut evening gown that draped and pooled around her as she reclined on a chaise longue. The material looked lightweight and only served to highlight the feminine body beneath. Sexual power and yet innocence radiated from the work, but mostly I felt the caress of every brush stroke on the canvas. I climbed the stairs to get closer.

Intoxicating. No one could look at this painting and not feel the passion the painter had had for the subject. There was a sense of witnessing something very private. I couldn't look away. It was in her expression. A chill ran across my skin and the hairs on my arms lifted. Fear or desire, or both.

There was no signature on the front of the canvas. It was far too large with its ornate frame for me to take off the wall on my own. The style of her clothing told me it was likely painted in the late twenties or early thirties. The background wasn't England. The quality of the light in the distant view was very different. I could be wrong, but the glimpse of water, the drapery behind the woman and the shape of the arms on the chaise reminded me of Venice. In fact, it reminded me of John Singer Sargent's painting of Lady Helen Vincent. But it was better.

I stared at the woman. What was her story? Who had painted her with a nod to Sargent and Philip de László?

The front door slammed and I jumped.

'Hello,' I called out, wondering if the gardener was still about, but only the sound of a branch tapping on a window answered me. With my phone I took a picture of the woman then made my way back to the ground floor. Opening off the hallway were five doors. The first to my right led to a book-lined room where watery light filtered in through the grime- and salt-covered windows. But even through filthy glass, the view of Mount's Bay was breathtaking.

I should be taking the inventory, but instead I looked through the varying titles on the bookshelves. Spines with worn gold lettering on leather sat next to old Penguin paperbacks. Eclectic. I could spend days in here delving into each volume, and with my valuer hat on I sensed there were many first editions on the shelves. The sofa under the window was Victorian and covered in faded red velvet. Not to everyone's taste, but striking. It looked like it should belong in a grand home in London rather than a house on the coast. Due to the bookcases lining two and a half walls, there was only one painting in the room, which hung above the fireplace. It was unsigned but looked like a Lamorna Birch. My father would know, but he wasn't here and I was. If there was some magic I could intone, I would use it to bring him back. But I had only the modern witchcraft of my phone. I took a quick snap so I could research the painting later.

Back in the hall, I entered the sitting room. Like its neighbour, it was dusty, and weak light filtered through the half-closed curtains. The threadbare carpet under my feet had once been a riot of colour but now only hinted at past glories. The sofas were covered in throws and colourful cushions. There was a striking bronze cat stretched out in front of the fireplace. The walls were lined with bright canvases representing so many of the artists who had made Cornwall their home. Bathsheba – Sheba – would have known many from her childhood and her life here in Newlyn.

Across the hall, a study faced north and smelled of mildew, which given all the paperwork and photographs lying on the desk and almost every surface was not ideal. Everything I touched was damp, including bills and other correspondence.

The bust of a woman's head sat on the desk. Was it Sheba? The picture I'd seen on the internet had been too low a resolution to get anything more than just a sense of the woman. Whoever the sitter, she was handsome, with large eyes and a strong nose. So many questions, but that was always a good starting point for any project. I wanted to know more about the women, and not just for the sale. The things they had chosen to have in their home, especially the portrait above the stairs, had captured my interest.

I opened a few of the desk drawers. They were stuffed full of paperwork. It would all have to be searched for receipts and the like to provide provenance for the many works in the house. This would be time-consuming but essential.

I didn't linger in the study or even in the kitchen, but went to the outbuildings, imagining that this was where they both worked. The larger one would be Vivian's at a guess, but maybe Sheba worked on vast canvases. It took a few moments to work out which of the many keys would let me in, while the wind whipped about my legs.

The situation of the house right above the water was idyllic and I was certain the place would go for a pretty penny, even though it was almost untouched since the early seventies judging by the Formica countertops I'd noted in the kitchen. But it also meant that its Georgian bones were intact. Was it listed? It would be awful if someone bought it who wasn't interested in the architecture of the house, only its location.

The door to Vivian's studio opened towards me and the light from the north-facing windows and skylights flooded the space. A large piece of marble sat in one corner and a half-finished sculpture in the middle of the room. It pulled me to it. A twisted trunk of a scrub oak was still half covered in bark and the other half was smooth and sinuous. Sensual and sad. A figure seemed to merge into the tree rather than emerge from it. I swallowed. Sorrow. Loss. It called to the grief animal that lived in the centre of me at the moment.

I turned away and viewed the other pieces – some finished, many only partially so. On the sill of one of the windows sat a cat sculpture. It was incredibly lifelike, similar to the one by the fireplace. I wanted to stroke it, but as I stepped forward, its head swivelled and bright orange eyes viewed me with disdain.

'How did you get in here?' I asked, holding my hand out so the feline could sniff. Then it leaned its head over for a scratch. Some of its semi-long black fur was bleached and told me it wasn't young. There was also a grey tuft near its right ear.

'That's where she is,' a voice from behind me said.

I jumped. 'Yours?'

Tilly, the gardener, walked to my side. 'No, belonged to Sheba and Viv.'

'They've been gone four years.'

'Tried to bring her home with me but she won't stay. Kept finding her back here so gave up trying to tempt her away.' She shrugged. 'Now I just make sure she's OK and has enough food, but Bastard's a real mouser so she won't go hungry for long.'

'Bastard?' I asked.

Tilly laughed. 'Yes, that was Sheba. She found the kitten abandoned by the harbour and called it a poor bastard. And it stuck, even when they took Bastard to be neutered and discovered she was a girl.'

Bastard sent me a look, daring me to call her anything different, except maybe Queen of the World or Empress of All. She reminded me of the cat I'd had as a child. I'd longed for one since, but Paul had jokingly said I could barely take care of myself so how could I look after an animal? And more importantly, it would scratch the furniture.

Bastard leaned in with her chin for a rub and my heart went with my fingers.

'She's taken a shine to you,' Tilly said. 'More prone to take your eyes out, but you must be all right.'

'Cat lover,' I said in my defence. I'd never met a cat I didn't adore, even those that had scratched me. I paused. 'Is the other shed Sheba's?'

'Right mess it is. They wouldn't let me touch anything but the garden.' Tilly pushed her hair back, revealing a pretty freckled face. 'Thought I might pinch something.'

I frowned. 'Who?'

She harrumphed. 'The court-appointed administrators. No one can find the wills. Think there are two great-nephews, one each, but never seen them. Not sure my ladies had either. Just doesn't feel right.' She drew a breath. 'I'm off now. Make sure you lock up, and you can feed Bastard tomorrow.'

I opened my mouth to say I wasn't sure if I'd be here tomorrow, but she was gone.

Bastard jumped down and weaved her way through my legs, marking me thoroughly. After I'd taken a few pictures of the studio, I went to Sheba's with the cat close by my heels. Tilly was right. The place was a disaster. Despite the glorious light, how could any work have been created in this chaos? There was no order at all. It looked more like someone had tried to burgle it. I stopped. Was that what had caused this mess? Had someone been looking for something specific? There was no way to know what had happened unless Tilly decided to enlighten me. She gave off the vibe that information would come only when and if she felt I was worthy. But I had passed the Bastard test.

With the studios locked, I went back into the house, and Bastard followed before slipping past me straight up to the first floor. All the doors upstairs were shut bar one, which was where Bastard headed to.

This bedroom faced the sea. The curtains were open and the grime that covered the windows was not as thick as on the ground-floor ones. I stood and almost breathed in the view. To wake to this every morning would be bliss. Paul's flat faced the Thames, which was nice, but this was heaven. It reminded me how much I missed the sea air and the light. I'd convinced myself that being beside the Thames was enough, but it wasn't. Here my lungs expanded and I felt lighter.

Bastard jumped down from the chest of drawers with a thump and flattened a silver picture frame. 'Be careful, Bastard,' I said, righting the frame. It was a picture of a woman standing in St Mark's Square, Venice. The black and white image was sharp and captured the woman's almost conspiratorial smile. Her hair was pulled back off her face in the style of the thirties and she was dressed in trousers. Under her arm was a paintbox. Was this Sheba? She was young and beautiful in a tall, angular way. Her eyes looked directly at the camera. She knew the person taking the photograph. I'd say she knew them well. The photographer understood composition. Behind her was the column bearing the lion of St Mark, and the Grand Canal with its gondolas was just visible. But none of it distracted from Sheba. She was like the column in her posture, yet she was fluid somehow. I took my hat off to the skill of the person behind the camera.

Without overthinking it, I opened the back of the frame.

Written in pencil on the reverse of the photo was *St Mark's, June 1934*, and initials that had faded too much for me to see in this light. I took a picture of it, hoping the phone was better at picking up the faint marks, and made out the letters *TK*.

One thing I had learned in my years doing research for the television programme was that artists frequently congregated together, and this could have been taken by someone of note. But TK didn't ring any bells.

Bastard sat on the corner of the carpet and yowled. I ignored her and studied the painting hanging between the windows. It was Sheba's work, yet different from the others of hers I'd seen, though I couldn't pinpoint how. After a final glance about the room, I left and peered into the other four bedrooms and the two bathrooms. It was a beautifully proportioned house, yet cosy. The artwork, in abundance, softened the lines. There was never one picture where more could fit, and I liked their style. In fact, I liked these women, and their cat, who stayed right beside me.

On the main hallway stairs, I stopped to study the portrait and noticed other paintings around it. When I'd first walked in, it was as if they hadn't been there, but now I realised that the woman was surrounded by Sheba's signature abstract landscapes, mostly of West Penwith from what I'd read.

Downstairs, I checked the kitchen door to make sure I'd locked it, and then went back to the hall. Bastard had disappeared. I couldn't lock her in for the night, so I did a quick search. She wasn't in the library, sitting room or dining room. That left the study, and sure enough, there she was, sitting in one of the drawers I'd opened but hadn't closed.

'Comfy as that drawer is, Bastard, we have to leave.'

She licked her paw and began to clean her face. I knew enough to know that if I picked her up, I would finish with scars. To interrupt such a regal creature during her toilette was a crime.

But time was running on and I had a meeting with my uncle that I needed to attend. Being tardy wasn't an option.

With my sleeves pulled down, I quickly scooped her from the drawer and ended up with some paperwork too. I had no choice but to continue out of the study. Only then could I put the cat down. Bastard was not impressed. She cast me a look and sauntered out the front door.

I glanced at the papers I'd lifted from the drawer. One was an old train ticket. Paris to Venice, Simplon Orient Express, 24 May 1934. Images of the various adaptations of the Agatha Christie novel appeared in my mind. How exciting and glamorous. What a fascinating life Sheba had lived. It must have been her ticket, as Viv would only have been fourteen at the time.

The other sheet of paper looked like a letter at first glance. But as I scanned it, I realised it was a poem. Probably a first draft, as there were annotations all over it.

Sunlight is blessed
It can touch you
I cannot
Water is lucky
You frolic in the sea
It beads and rolls across your skin
Where I would linger

I stopped reading. It was almost too personal, and in a strange way, vaguely familiar. It reminded me of something I'd studied for my English A level, yet I couldn't quite place it. It would come to me, but time was flying. Quickly I put the items back in the desk, collected the file from the vestibule and left, making sure I'd locked the front door properly. Tomorrow was Saturday and I wasn't needed for the auction preview that was taking place, so

I could spend more time here. And as I looked over my shoulder, I knew I wanted to. My father would have loved this work.

My shoulders fell. I wasn't him. This job was too big for me. These days I researched one item at a time and had experts to work with. I rarely had to leave the flat. What if I failed again? So much for my bravado in the small hours of the morning. Sorry, Sheba and Viv. I was the wrong person to set the record straight. I hadn't even recognised an original Cézanne when it had been in front of me. The worst thing was that I should have. I had done my undergrad thesis on his early work. I could still hear my father's voice saying that I had been right to be cautious as Cézanne was one of the most forged artists of all time.

Bastard sat on the garden wall watching me. She slowly blinked, and I returned the message. The cat liked me and she needed to be fed tomorrow. That I could do. I'd have to find someone to help me with Harbour House. This wasn't a simple job like my uncle had implied. There were a hundred paintings in the house alone. God knows how many in the studio. Then there was the sculpture work. I took a deep breath. I'd take it up with him when I reached the office.

'See you tomorrow, Bastard,' I called to the cat, which earned me a stern look from an older woman walking past the drive on her way into town.

* * *

My phone rang as I pulled into the car park at Barton's. I turned the engine off and answered. 'Paul?'

'Just checking on you.'

I glanced at the file on the passenger seat. 'Thanks. I've just come back from an initial assessment of Harbour House.'

'Did that belong to your father?'

'No.' I tapped the steering wheel. He was right. I was not here to work. Playing with my locket, I tried not to think of why I *was* here. 'It belonged to two artists and Dad was working on it when he died.'

'And?'

'I'm about to go and have a meeting with Stephen.' A seagull shat on the bonnet of the car. I bit my lip in frustration and looked to see if my water bottle was to hand so I could wash it off.

'Don't let him walk all over you. You're too kind and he will take advantage.'

'True.' I found the water. 'Thank you for the reminder.'

'Always. Of course, it's selfishness on my part. I love and miss you.'

I climbed out of the car with the water and poured it on the guano. 'You could come down. It's almost the Easter holidays.'

'You know I have the deadline on the paper.'

'Sorry, I forgot.'

'Your father's just died. I get it.' His voice softened. 'Just come back to me.'

'Love you,' I said, then slammed the door closed, already thinking of the meeting ahead.

'Be quick,' he said before he hung up.

Easier said than done. I must not forget to ask my uncle about the furniture at Harbour House. There was nothing really high-end that I saw during the walk-through, but it wasn't charity shop either. Had my father done a preliminary viewing? If so, where were his notes?

Pulling the main door open, I hoped that Stephen would have the accounts ready for me to look at. Only then could I call Jack Thomas and begin making things happen quickly as Paul had asked.

'How was Harbour House?' Marcia looked up from her computer.

'Fascinating.'

'I bet.' She grinned. 'Always wondered what it was like. It's in such a stunning location.'

'Gorgeous, if dated on the inside.' I paused. 'It's a bit of a time warp of early- and mid-century furnishings, with a few fine earlier pieces and more art than seems possible.' I glanced at the wall clock above the bookcase. 'Is Stephen in his office?'

'No.' Marcia pushed back from her desk.

'No? He said he would have the accounts for me.'

'He never mentioned it to me.' She shook her head. 'He went off to check his warehouse. Something about a broken pipe.'

'His warehouse?'

'Yes, he bought it a few years ago. He's been doing up furniture in his spare time, I think.'

He was passionate about furniture, which was why I was surprised about what he had said about the contents of Harbour House. 'Do *you* have the accounts?'

'No, that's his territory. Never lets anyone near them.'

'Oh.'

She looked at the clock. 'He'll be back later, or if not then, tomorrow morning, as he has an appointment with Mrs George.'

'During the preview?'

Marcia nodded.

I hadn't planned to come here tomorrow, but needs must. I sent Marcia a smile and tried not to let frustration overwhelm me. Without the accounts, I couldn't move forward. It would be tempting to go into Stephen's office and look for them, and once I might have done that. I was part owner too and I had a right to know the state of the business, but up until this moment I hadn't cared. That wasn't true. I cared a lot. In fact, it broke me.

In my father's office, I sat down and typed Bathsheba Kernow's name into his computer. After the Wiki entry there was a piece from the Hypatia Trust on Cornish women of note, with a short obituary but no mention of the exact date of death. Next, I put in Vivian Sykes. The Trust had a brief article on her too; in her obituary, only the month she died was mentioned. I printed both articles off and went back to Marcia.

'Here are the obits for the two ladies, but there's no date of death.'

Marcia blinked. 'Oh no, there isn't one.'

'What?'

'They'd been dead for at least two weeks, maybe more, when the gardener found them on her return from holiday.'

'Ugh.'

'Exactly, poor woman.'

'How did they die?'

'Old age, I imagine.' Marcia tidied the pens on her desk.

I threw my hands up. 'More detail, please.'

'Well, apparently I heard they were in bed together, wrapped around each other.'

'Suicide?' I was happy that they had been together, no matter what had happened.

'Apparently not.'

'So that's why there's a problem.' I sat on the corner of Marcia's desk. 'They can't tell which of them died first.'

'Yes, and it's such a shame because they were both so lovely.'

'You knew them?' I asked.

'Wouldn't say that, but every so often they would come and sell something.' She paused. 'They were both very private, making sure never to draw attention to themselves.'

'Was there a reason why?'

'Today two women living together as a couple is normal, but back in the forties, it would have raised an eyebrow or two.'

I drew a breath. 'True.' The world had made huge leaps in accepting diversity, but there was still a long way to go.

Marcia made a face. 'I want to say there was some scandal.'

I opened my eyes wide, waiting.

'Not scandal exactly, but something that made people talk.' She clasped her hands.

'And what was it?'

'Before my time.' She shrugged.

'Dad knew them?' I asked. A memory came back to me and that was why Sheba Kernow's name seemed familiar.

'Oh yes, he thought they were super.'

'That smuggling frame?' Even now I remembered the feel of it in my hands.

'Yes, that's it.' Marcia smiled. 'Miss Kernow said that in many ways it was her finest work.'

'Even though the painting was terrible and nothing like the ones that fill her home and studio.'

'Her friend, a writer, had used it to smuggle jewels out of Germany as Hitler's grip was tightening and Jewish families struggled to leave.'

'A wonderful story.'

'The best part was . . .' Marcia paused. 'The painting went to one of the people who benefited from the jewellery.'

'I'm not sure I ever heard the result of the sale.' That Sunday long ago with Dad in the room above was like a different lifetime. A wave of grief hit me. I pushed it away. Now wasn't the time.

'There was quite a bit of news coverage, but Miss Kernow wouldn't be interviewed by the press.' Marcia drew a breath. 'She did talk to the buyer, though.'

'Do you remember who it was?' I picked up a porcelain bowl that was on top of one of the cabinets. It was a fine pink lustre piece with a house depicted on it. It reminded me of the collection my mother used to have, before it was sold.

'It will be in the sale records.'

I headed to the filing cabinets.

'Why do you want to know?' Marcia came and opened the right drawer.

'That is a very good question, and my answer at the moment is pure curiosity. I want to know who this woman was who lived such a quiet, private life, died in her lover's arms and called her cat Bastard.'

'Bastard? Really?' Marcia handed me the file.

'A regal feline that Bathsheba Kernow saved.'

Marcia laughed. 'An interesting woman indeed.'

'And as Dad always used to say . . .'

'It's all in the story,' we finished in unison.

'And the first step in telling a good story is asking the right questions – and, of course, research.'

I pulled out the paperwork on the sale from that auction all those years ago. It might lead to nothing, but it was worth a try. The house had whetted my curiosity, and it was quickly shifting to something of a compulsion to discover more with each new piece of information about the artists.

4

Paris

Train stations are overwhelming. Even the one in St Ives fills me with fear. Everything at the Gare de Lyon is amplified. So many people, all rushing. Noises, colours and smells. My head is swimming. The train to Venice leaves in an hour. Winifred speaks to the porter in French. Slowly I translate, but by then we are walking to a platform. Steam belches from the engines, filling the air with the bitter scent of coke.

I want to become invisible. In Cornwall that isn't possible because everyone, and all they do, is known. But here in Paris, aside from Winifred Nicholson, no one knows me.

'Are you sure you'll be fine on your own in Venice?' she asks.

'Yes,' I lie. I'm unsure of everything right now and have been for months, maybe longer. Things came to a crisis a few weeks ago.

'Well, your mother was.' She sends me a sideways glance. 'She did return pregnant with you.' She pauses, looking around. 'I always thought her marriage to your father in Venice was so romantic.' She takes my hand in hers. 'I know you miss her, and so do I, but I also know she would be so proud of you.'

Even now, having read all her journals, I can't accept that my mother was like me. In Venice she found my father, and somehow the city transformed Rebecca Arthur from a freak into a wife and mother. I hope whatever magic she discovered there still exists, or I might never be able to go home. My stepmother's words – *deviant* and *pervert* – still echo in my ears. But as hard as it was hearing those words from her, it was far harder to hear them from my closest friend, Nellie. I went to her for support, but she just made fun of how I'd felt all those years ago when she'd practised kissing on me. That had been life-altering. Her recent words brought all that self-loathing to the surface, reminding me I wasn't like other girls. They like boys. I am unnatural, a freak.

I have always sensed that I'm different. First, I'm tall, and second, I have red hair. It is impossible to be invisible when I look like this. Then, for whatever unknown reason, my parents gave me the name Bathsheba and called me Ba or Baba. The times I was taunted at school with Baba Black Sheep, or more correctly, Baba Ginger Sheep. With that name, I was never going to blend in. How could I as the only child of two upper-class artists in a local school in St Ives?

But I also didn't fit in with my cousin who had gone to boarding school, as my parents had. Now I'm a person of no place. I always thought Cornwall was my home, that I could be happy there, but Nellie corrected me in no uncertain terms. Unless I wanted to live in relative seclusion in Lamorna like the other lesbian artists, Cornwall wasn't the place for me. In her words, St Ives was for normal folk, and I couldn't expect that people would understand. I'm not normal, but Nellie is. She married three years ago and has two children. The gap between us has never been wider.

'Right, I'll leave you here.' Winifred lets go of my hand. 'The porter has taken your bags and is putting them on the train.' She points to them. 'Write to me. Go to the Biennale and tell me how my paintings look.'

'Of course,' I say, trying to imagine having my own work on display at the Venice Biennale.

'Things have a way of working out,' she says as she gives me a hug. She is separated from her husband, who is currently living with Barbara Hepworth, the sculptor. If that is 'working out', I'm not certain I want that either. 'It seems hard to believe,' she nudges me into the queue, 'but things do happen for the best.'

Feeling like a child of ten rather than a woman of twenty, I retrieve my passport from my bag and watch Winifred walk through the crowds. Only when she is out of sight do I pay attention to the people in front of me. Passengers are boarding the midnight-blue carriages. The guards' uniforms are very smart. This will be nothing like my trip to London or the one here. My grandfather insisted I travel first class. He wouldn't hear of me making the journey any other way, despite the fact that I insisted I had my own money. He smiled and said, 'Allow me to help, Bathsheba, humour an old man.' He was so like my mother in his kindness that I couldn't deny him this.

Yet as I look at the woman in front of me, I wish I had. My trousers and jacket are more functional than fashionable. The woman wears a Chanel dress and coat. Last week Winifred showed me all the smart places in Paris and encouraged me to sketch what I saw, to record everything. It would be good to do that right now to pass the time. The curve of the woman's neck is visible below her bobbed hair, which is the colour of coal. Even in the smoky atmosphere it glistens with her every move.

The man beside her fusses with his jacket and the papers in his hand. He is handsome and they make a beautiful pair, but there is something about his eyes. They are out of proportion, too small, ruining the balance of his face. It does make him a more interesting subject, though. In a portrait I would emphasise the jut of his chin, and his hands, which have very short fingers.

He marches up to the *chef de train*, who is having an animated discussion with another man. 'Is there a problem?' His voice disappoints me. It has no musicality to it. It is brisk and rude.

'*Sì, sì.* I need to be on this train tonight, for I must be in Milano tomorrow to meet Il Duce, as he has poetry for me to read.' The Italian waves his hands, shaping out his problem. His rotund shape is wrapped in a belted grey tweed jacket. His appearance is fussy, but his eyes are kind.

'Poetry? Mussolini writes poetry?' The man leans closer. The woman with him turns away with a look of distaste on her face. She is the most exquisite beauty. Her skin is pale and unmarked. Her cheekbones are high and more notable for her fringe, which also highlights her huge eyes. My fingers touch the sketchpad in my bag. As soon as I reach my compartment, I will draw this woman, particularly the line of her neck, which is wrapped in pearls. I take a deep breath and catch the scent of rose and vanilla.

'We have no room for an additional guest, as I have said repeatedly, Monsieur Rossi.' The train captain waves his hand. 'Now I must attend to Monsieur and Madame Forster, and the woman behind them, I believe, is Mademoiselle Kernow.'

Mr Forster turns and assesses me from my uncovered head to my sensible shoes. I'm dismissed as I have been many times. Mostly it stirs anger, but this time I don't care. He is ridiculous in his tweed travelling suit and fussy moustache.

'Surely *she* can wait until tomorrow,' he says.

'Darling, that is so rude. If anyone should give up their berth, you should offer ours. One more night in Paris will not matter to our arrival in Venice, surely. The poetry competition is not for weeks.' Her voice is of the upper classes. She smiles at me in what seems to be an offer of friendship, or at least understanding.

'Monsieur Rossi, these people have tickets, you do not,' the train captain says. 'There is nothing I can do.'

Mr Forster's face goes puce as he looks from the captain to me. He sees me as less than him, less than the Italian man without a ticket. This is not a new experience for me. But he knows nothing of who I am . . . I could be the Queen of Sheba, after all. I swallow my mirth. It is best to face this with humour if I can. It will make everything easier.

'There are no berths available?' he presses on, in spite of what the train captain has already said. He wins for persistence.

'There are no available berths because I cannot put a man in with Mademoiselle Kernow,' the train captain explains slowly.

So yet again I'm the problem, and so is my sex.

Mr Forster looks from me to the Italian. I have a valid ticket and he doesn't. Mrs Forster studies me, and a slow smile spreads across her face.

'Darling, I know it's not what we planned.' She touches her husband's sleeve. 'But what if I share with Miss Kernow, if she doesn't mind, and you share our compartment with Signor Rossi? It *is* only one night.'

Mr Forster sends me a dismissive glance. 'But darling . . .' His voice trails away.

'Oh, Signora Forster, you would make me and Il Duce so happy.'

Mr Forster draws a deep breath and pulls his shoulders back. 'If it would make Il Duce happy, and it is for the sake of poetry, then needs must.'

'*Bien.*' The train captain looks at me. 'Mademoiselle Kernow, will you accept Madame Forster in your cabin?'

'Yes.' I shrug. As she said, it is one night.

He nods and begins to sort the paperwork. Mrs Forster extends her gloved hand towards me. 'Thank you, that is kind. I'm Katherine Forster.'

'Sheba Kernow.' I take her hand.

Her eyes meet mine and linger. Warning tingles run along my skin.

'Sheba? As in Bathsheba?' She still holds my hand.

'Yes,' I manage to say.

'How wonderfully biblical.' Her eyes gleam. 'Are you from Cornwall?'

I nod, for my voice has disappeared altogether.

'I've visited the Isles of Scilly,' she says.

'A beautiful place, I'm told.'

'You've never been?' Her large eyes open wider, and I'm close enough to pick out the sap green and lemon yellow in the ultramarine.

'I haven't.' On a clear day I have peered out from Land's End to the horizon, imagining the islands beyond just visible. 'I'm from St Ives.'

Mrs Forster looks down at my hand in hers. 'You're an artist?'

'Yes.' I don't need to ask how she knows. There is cadmium red under my fingernails, though the rest of me is as tidy as can be. I checked my face before leaving Winifred's apartment, making sure there wasn't the normal telltale smudge of charcoal on my cheeks or paint in my hair. Travelling on the Simplon Express meant that I needed to be respectable. I even packed an evening dress, but it is for Venice and my desire to go to the opera at La Fenice. In her diaries, my mother spoke of it with such detail and passion, it was almost as high on my list of things to see as the Gallerie dell'Accademia. The diaries are safely in my bag. They are the closest thing to having my mother with me. Her untimely death three years ago made me so much more than motherless.

After I hand over my ticket and passport, the sleeping car attendant appears and beckons for Mrs Forster and me to follow. Mr Forster is engaged in conversation with Signor Rossi and doesn't notice his wife's departure.

We walk down the platform towards the rear of the train.

'This is excellent. We won't have to listen to the engine,' Mrs Forster says as she slips her arm through mine and pulls me to her side. 'It will be like being back at school. Girls together and chats into the night.'

I laugh awkwardly. This is not what I expected. Already my plan of staring out of the window at the changing scenery is fading away. It is clear that Mrs Forster's school was very different from mine. Mine was one room of forty children. Far from a boarding school, although I recall that fraught conversation between my parents years ago.

'We must send Baba away to school,' my mother said.

'No, she will only be like you. It would encourage it with all those girls.'

My mother laughed. 'Is that a problem?'

'She may not be as lucky as you,' my father said.

I heard them kiss.

'She could go to the one in Penzance and still be close.'

'No, it would be a waste. She has no need for that type of education.'

For years I never understood what my father had meant. Now my eyes are wide open. My mother loved women as I do. What I wouldn't give to be able to talk to her about this. How did she fall in love with a man?

5

The attendant helps us onto the train and I'm struck by the beauty of the interior. It gleams. The corridor is panelled in wood, with intricate marquetry depicting flowers and birds. Even with all this beauty about me, though, I can't stop watching Katherine Forster. She moves with grace while I'm clumsy, all arms and legs. The attendant stops and opens the compartment door with a flourish. Our overnight bags are there already. The compartment is tiny. It would have been ample for me alone, but for two it will be like dancing on a matchbox to move around each other. Maybe it is like a girls' school, as she mentioned.

'How marvellous.' Mrs Forster turns to me and grins. 'May I have the top berth?'

The current arrangement with a sofa does not show the top berth, but I can picture it. 'Yes,' I say, almost falling onto the small table with a lamp by the window. In the mirror on the door to the next compartment, I see my reflection. I don't belong here. Katherine Forster does. From the pearls around her neck to the gloves on her hands she is elegance personified. The jaunty little scarf at my neck, which this morning I thought was chic, looks tired and trite.

The attendant opens a door to reveal the washbasin. Everything is functional and beautifully made. The small space is maximised by toiletry holders and a mirror fixed to the wall above the basin.

'Your dinner reservation is at nine,' he says. 'And I will prepare your beds while you are dining, if that is acceptable.'

'Of course,' Mrs Forster replies. He bows and backs out, closing the door behind him.

'Well, this is going to be fun.' She throws herself onto the sofa, slips off each glove and sighs. 'All we need now is a drink.'

I don't need a drink but I could do with a bit more space so I can be further away from her. It's too intimate, but as much as I don't want to be, I'm entranced.

'You do drink, don't you?'

'Of course.' During my stay in Paris I developed a taste for red wine and champagne. So different to the cider I would normally choose. My father used to enjoy wine, but since my mother's death he's turned to whisky and beer.

'Excellent. Then we shall have a blissful time relaxing, reading and sipping cocktails without talk of Il Duce and Mr Hitler. I am quite done with all that.'

I try not to stare. Nellie's husband is quite taken with both leaders. He is particularly fond of the fascist view that women must stay in the home. I don't agree with that, and it isn't just because Nellie has changed so much since she married him. 'Your husband is a fascist?' I ask. Nellie never looked any further than marriage, but this woman in front of me is so sophisticated that surely her life isn't bound so tightly.

'He leans very strongly that way and it's so boring.' She pulls the pin out of her hat and removes it. With graceful movements of her fingers, she fluffs her hair. 'We must make ourselves respectable for dinner.' She glances at the watch on her wrist. 'We have just over half an hour to transform ourselves into fascinating creatures of the night.'

I think of the green silk blouse and black crêpe trousers I packed to wear in the evening on the train. Mrs Forster probably has chiffon and diamonds with her.

There is a tap on the door and I assume it will be her maid from second class, although I did not see one while we were waiting to board the train.

'Come in,' says Mrs Forster.

The door opens and a waiter stands there holding a bucket of ice with a bottle of champagne and two glasses.

'Monsieur Rossi sent this as a small gesture of thanks.'

I take a step back.

Mrs Forster claps her hands. 'I like this Signor Rossi.'

'May I open it, madame?' the waiter asks.

'Of course,' she says, giving him a warm smile.

A resounding pop fills the air just as the train pulls out of the station with a jolt. He pours two glasses and hands them to us, then with a flourish takes a piece of paper from his breast pocket, handing it to Mrs Forster. 'From your husband,' he says before disappearing, closing the door behind him.

She leans back and takes a gulp of the champagne. Only then does she open the note with a sigh. I can't look away as she reads. Her face is so expressive and so beautiful. My fingers burn to touch it, and as I can't do that, I long to sketch it. Instead, I take a sip of champagne. The bubbles tickle my nose.

'Well, that is simply the best news.' She folds the letter.

'What is?' I ask, looking into my glass rather than at her.

'Simon will be dining alone with Signor Rossi. Apparently it's proving too difficult to alter the planned seating for dinner at such short notice.' She takes another gulp before she continues. 'He also says that Marlene Dietrich is on the train. How divine.' She tilts her head and studies me. I try not to flush. 'You remind me of her in a way.'

I cough. I've been compared to many things in my twenty years, but a famous film star is not one of them. I sink onto the banquette and give up trying not to study her. She must be thirty or so. There are fine lines around her eyes, but her actions strike me as younger, much closer to my age.

She stands and opens a garment bag. 'Now, which gown should I wear this evening for my dinner with you?'

'You would look marvellous in anything,' I practically stutter.

'Thank you.' She looks over her shoulder at me as she pulls out a cerise satin gown. 'This suits my mood.' She drains her glass and refills it. Her glance at my still full glass is disparaging. I take a large sip, hoping it won't rise up my nose. My weeks in Paris haven't changed me into a cosmopolitan woman; I remain a country girl. Not that my parents didn't educate me, but unless we were visiting my grandfather in London, we lived simply. Fancy things are not me. The call of the quayside and the pull of the cliffs are what hold my attention. Only art and words take me away from these things. In my work I focus on the everyday, if one can call the beauty of Cornwall everyday. But it is, for those of us who live and work there. My time in Paris has pushed me to look elsewhere for the mundane. The back alleys, the docks along the Seine and the bars at night. I would sketch, watch and listen. It has been another type of education. My eyes have been opened.

Mrs Forster tops up my glass. 'You are too tall to call a mouse, too pretty, too.' She strokes my cheek and winds a strand of my hair around her finger. I can't breathe. 'The colour is like gold caught in the sunrise, tinged with orange.' She closes her eyes and I try to compose myself. No one has ever spoken to me this way. I drink more of my champagne. Already the alcohol fizzes in my head.

She peers into my bag. The green blouse is visible. 'This

colour is perfect for you,' she says as she pulls it out and gives it a shake. 'Oh, it's only a top.' The look she sends me is full of disappointment.

'I didn't think I'd need proper evening wear on the train.'

Mrs Forster purses her mouth. 'Darling girl, Marlene Dietrich is on board. What chance have we of being noticed if you are dressed . . .' she pauses and takes out my crêpe trousers, 'like a man . . . or a mouse.'

'I try not to draw attention to myself.'

She laughs. 'That is obvious, my dear, but you are beautiful and young, and quite frankly the world needs to know this.'

'Do they?' The question spills out of my mouth.

She bends down to look me directly in the eyes. 'They do. Beauty fades, so embrace it while you have it.' She stands straight. 'It may be all you have to hold on to.' Her left hand, bearing a large ruby, lies flat against her heart. Drama or real feeling I'm not sure, but I am entranced.

She takes another gown out of her bag. 'I think this will do. We are about the same height, and the colour will set off that glorious head of hair.' The dress she holds is all the shades of a peacock feather. I've never seen anything so beautiful. My mouth dries.

'I couldn't.' I vigorously shake my head.

'Of course you can, and you will.' She glances at her watch. 'We have fifteen minutes.' She pulls the blind on the window. 'I'm so pleased I left my maid behind. We can help each other. This will be so much fun.'

I only met her an hour ago, and now she is removing her clothing in front of me. Without a pause, she pulls her dress up and over her head, and I look down. The pattern in the carpet repeats every three inches. It would be too busy if it weren't for the subtle shades of umber used.

'Surely you've seen a woman undress.' She stands before me in nothing more than a garter belt, stockings and pearls. I immediately return my attention to the carpet. 'If I didn't know better, I would say you've never seen a woman nearly nude before.'

That's it. *Nearly nude* makes it so much more. That is what I discovered in Paris.

You are an artist, I tell myself.

But I'm not wearing my artist's hat now, keeping everything focused on lines and angles, shadows and light. This is different, closer and more real.

She picks up her glass and drinks deeply. When it's empty, she carelessly pulls the cerise gown over her head and turns her back to me. 'Would you be a dear and deal with the buttons.'

I cough to cover my nerves. The buttons begin just above her rounded bottom and stop halfway up her back. Her vertebrae are clearly visible on her slender frame.

She steps away. 'Now it's your turn.'

I flush.

'No need to feel shy.' She picks up the champagne bottle and refills her glass, then tops mine up again. 'Dutch courage, you clearly need it.'

I drink it all, then put the glass down and fumble with the buttons on my blouse. My trousers are no easier, but finally I stand in my tap pants and bra. My shape is awkward, with large breasts yet slim hips.

'You'll have to take off the bra – it's not cut low enough for the dress.' She holds the glorious creation out.

Reluctantly I remove my bra and take the dress from her. I step into it with care, not sure how it will fit me. She turns me around and encourages it into place with cool fingers, leaving a tingling where she touches. When she is satisfied, she rotates me so I face her. She smooths the fabric across my ribcage and I lose the ability to breathe. Her touch is like silk caressing my skin. I can't look at her. My face is flushed.

'That is the way it should fit.' She smiles and runs her hands down her sides. 'Oh, Sheba, you've missed a button.' She presents her beautiful back to me. I have indeed missed one entirely and need to undo the top three, revealing a birthmark by her first lumbar vertebra. My fingers graze the rose-coloured mark.

'Ah, you've spotted my flaw.' She laughs. 'Or God's kiss, as my mother always called it.'

'It does look like a kiss.'

'More like a lover's than God's, unless he's Apollo.' She laughs wickedly. 'Simon hates it. He says it shows how bad I am. He thinks it's the evil within seeping out.' She waltzes out the compartment door while I contemplate how he could think such a thing. Mrs Forster has been nothing but kindness.

Focusing on that thought, I race to catch up with her. The air drifting in from the open windows is sultry, or maybe that is simply how I feel watching Mrs Forster weave her way through the carriages.

6

As we enter the dining carriage, all eyes follow Mrs Forster. The way she moves, the fabric of her dress, the texture of her skin and her beautiful face all force people to look. She oozes confidence and I want to hide, to not be the peacock despite the gown I'm wearing. People will look at me too and this is the last thing I want. There is nothing I can do in this moment except get through it. To distract myself, I focus on her spine and think of the birthmark just out of sight. This is madness. I'm here to step away from myself, to learn to be different, to find men attractive, to become normal like Nellie, to live a life that no one notices.

I study the faces – young, old, elegant and interesting. Without the borrowed plumage I wear, I would draw more attention than I do at the moment. Even dressed in her gown I'm no match for her, and I exist in her shadow, which is good. I relax a little.

The sound of voices chattering overrides the quiet clunking rhythm of the wheels moving across the tracks. The crystal, silver and white linen are even beyond what I have known in my grandfather's Kensington house. So many shining objects, but my glance keeps returning to the woman in front of me. She is mesmerising. As we approach, waiters step aside and the maître d' greets her by name.

She looks over her shoulder at me as we reach the table. 'Unfortunately things have changed and we are now to sit with my husband and Signor Rossi.' She forces a smile as she sits.

The maître d' holds out a chair for me as he has done for her. I copy her every move. This is an entirely new world for me, from the decor to the other dinner guests. It is like a film, and of course, there is a movie star on the train.

'While you wait for the gentlemen, may I get you an aperitif?' he asks.

'A champagne cocktail for us both, please.' Katherine beams at him.

My head is already awash with what we drank in the compartment. I don't need more.

'Well, let's hope that Signor Rossi will be lively.' She rests her hands on the table. 'I had hoped it was just us and we could get to know one another.'

The cocktails arrive and Mrs Forster says, 'Let's make a toast to a new friendship.'

I raise my glass and meet her glance. She is more intoxicating than the drink and I'm certain I will never forget this evening, but a friendship between us I doubt. People like me do not feature in the world she moves in. We will have this time on the train and she will never think of me again. With that thought something settles inside me, or maybe it's just the contents of the cocktail.

'Mrs Forster,' I say.

She interrupts, 'Katherine, please.'

I swallow. 'Katherine . . .'

'Here they are,' she says, fixing her expression to a welcoming one that looks like a well-worn mask.

'Katherine, I didn't want to leave you unattended and the maître d' was able to work miracles.' Mr Forster takes his wife's hand and brings it to his lips. She flinches and shakes him off with a shiver.

'Two beautiful women for company at dinner is perfection.' Signor Rossi bows before taking a seat beside me.

Mr Forster engages immediately with the waiter. He speaks fluently in French and I'm only able to pick up a few words. Katherine leans forward, blocking her husband with her bare shoulder.

'Simon tells me he is heading to Venice for the poetry exhibition.' Signor Rossi pauses and adjusts his cuff. 'I know of your husband's excellent work and have been discussing possible translators and publishing.'

'You're a publisher?' She takes a sip of her drink.

'In a way.' He waves his hands. 'I know many people and I have been helping Il Duce prepare his brilliant poetry for publication.'

'Yes, isn't it wonderful,' Mr Forster says as he turns back to the table. 'Il Duce writes and loves poetry.' He is flushed with enthusiasm.

Katherine gazes into her glass, her expression blank, then looks up with a smile. 'This is truly marvellous, darling, and it bodes well for the poetry event in Venice.'

'It does, doesn't it. My work has been so well received in England and the United States, but not yet in Italy, the home of Dante.' He draws a breath. 'Now that would be something.'

'I wish you were stopping in Milano, because in two days' time I have a meeting with just the man to publish you,' Signor Rossi says.

Mr Forster chews his bottom lip, acting more like a child than a grown man.

A waiter appears with a carafe of white wine, followed by another with delicate bowls of consommé. It smells divine and I look down in panic at the massed cutlery, trying to remember the etiquette. I watch Katherine take the outermost spoon and dip it in the clear liquid, pushing it away from her before lifting it to her mouth. It all comes back to me and I relax a bit.

'Katherine,' Mr Forster says, holding his spoon mid-air. 'Would it be a problem if we joined Signore Rossi in Milan and delayed our arrival in Venice?'

Katherine puts down her spoon and takes a sip of wine. 'It might be for Mary. She is expecting us tomorrow evening, and you know how she is. She will have made plans.'

He is crestfallen, as if she has taken his toy away. But only an hour or so ago she was willing to delay their departure. Why has she had a change of heart?

She places her right hand on his. 'What if I continue to Venice to placate her, and you could have your exciting meeting in Milan?'

'Of course, that's just what I was thinking. As always, you've read my mind.' He waves to the waiter and orders champagne to celebrate.

The soup is cleared away and a toast is made to a successful outcome of the trip to Milan. The gentlemen talk of accommodation there while Katherine and I stare out the window at the faded landscape in the twilight. The world outside the train appears less real than the reflection candlelit drama within.

After the main course is cleared, Katherine says, 'Darling, Miss Kernow is an artist, from St Ives in Cornwall.'

Mr Forster blinks for a moment, then looks at Signor Rossi and asks, 'Will we meet Il Duce while in Milan?'

Signor Rossi smiles at Katherine and me. 'The arts, all the arts are so important to Il Duce.' He puts his glass down. 'Miss Kernow, in what style do you paint?'

I open my mouth to reply, but Mr Forster says, 'She is too

young to have painted anything of merit. Returning to my question, will we be able to meet Il Duce?'

Signor Rossi sighs. 'I am not certain. We might, but I do not wish to raise your expectations.'

'I do believe he would appreciate my poetry.' Forster waves to the waiter. 'If only I had some translations of my work.'

Out of the corner of my eye I see Katherine roll her eyes. They are not two people I would put together, despite the endearments they use to speak to each other.

'The great leader can speak English, but it would be best to first show the poems to him in Italian.' Forster pauses while dessert is placed in front of us. 'Il Duce admires the work of Pound.'

'Dear Ezra,' says Katherine with a half-smile.

Her husband frowns. 'Katherine crossed paths with Pound in the early twenties,' he explains.

'He was so encouraging.' Her face falls for just a moment.

'Only because he wanted to seduce you.'

She laughs and finishes her wine, but I'm not sure how to react to this. Forster looks as if he's about to say more regarding Pound. Instead, he gives his attention to the delicate mousse in front of him while Katherine takes only the smallest taste of hers.

'I'd planned to find a translator for my work in Venice, but that will be too late.'

I stare at Forster. His arrogance is astounding.

Signor Rossi sends Katherine and me an apologetic glance. He seems to enjoy Mr Forster's company, but he is aware of his rudeness as well.

'If you have some of your poems with you, perhaps tomorrow we could work together on translating one or two.'

'That is kind of you, Signor Rossi. We are so fortunate to have met you,' Katherine says, placing her napkin on the table.

'Gentlemen, if you will excuse us.' She gives me an encouraging smile. 'It's been a long day.'

Both men stand.

'Of course, my love, you need your beauty sleep.' Forster pulls out her chair and places a kiss on her cheek.

Signor Rossi helps me with mine and I am touched. 'Thank you for your kindness today, Miss Kernow.' He bows quite formally.

I look for the waiter to pay for my meal. Rossi smiles at me. 'I will settle the bill. It is the least I can do.'

I nod, not sure how to reply. I've been thrown into a world where I am completely out of my depth. Despite the fine gown I'm wearing, I'm a fraud simply passing for something I'm not.

The overt attention of the other diners confirms this. Katherine moves with ease while I have to think about how to walk in this gown. Each step is precarious. At the last table I spy Marlene Dietrich, and she studies us as we approach. Her glance lingers on Katherine, and when she meets mine, I see that she knows. I have not fooled her. A hint of a smile appears on her rouged lips. She understands the act of being someone else. It is a skill I must learn, like transferring the image I see in front of me into lines and colour on a page.

7

It is a relief to return to the compartment. Tiredness oozes out of my every pore. Nothing has happened as I imagined it would, from the moment I stood on the platform in Paris to now, when there is a knock on the door. I open it to find an attendant holding a tray with two snifters of brandy.

'Madame Forster, as you requested.'

'Thank you, Antoine.' She takes the glasses from him and hands me one. 'It should help with the indigestion caused by my husband's conversation.'

There is nothing I can say. Her husband is a pompous bore. Never have I heard a man so full of himself, and I've heard men from all walks of life. What I can't figure out is what could have possessed Katherine to marry such a man. But as I look at her, it hits me that I know nothing about her except that she has a kiss for a birthmark. We stand there watching each other. There is no place to sit as such because the sofa has now been converted into an upper and lower bed. The atmosphere is too intimate.

'Do you mind if I sit on your bed?' she asks.

'Please do.' I perch by the pillow and she at the foot by the window.

'May I open the blind and the window?'

'Of course.' A gust of cool air eases the atmosphere in the room. The sky still holds some light, though it is now near eleven. The shapes of buildings and, in the distance, hills rush past. Without thinking, I reach for my sketchbook in my bag, but stop myself. Charcoal couldn't capture the brilliant colours of Katherine. I will have to remember them, as well as the sensuous shape of her reclining, cradling the brandy glass.

'How long have you been an artist?'

I run my fingers over the book's cover. 'I think I've been one since I could hold a pencil.'

'Wonderful.' She turns the glass in her hand, looking at the golden liquid. 'To be so certain of who or what you are.'

'Aren't you?'

She laughs bitterly. 'I am nothing.' She takes a sip of the brandy. 'And we were discussing you and your certainty.'

Am I that certain? The small table lamp with a pink silk shade casts a diffused light, softening everything including the shadows on Katherine's face. She looks weary.

'Well, my parents are, or were in the case of my mother, artists, so it feels natural or even the only option.'

'You've lost your mother?'

'Three years ago.' The loss is still sharp. It feels it will never ease.

'Painful, isn't it.' She turns the glass in her hands. 'You feel . . . rudderless for a while.'

'That's true.' I think of my mother's diaries and hope they can guide me. I would rather have her with me, though, and from the expression on Katherine's face she still feels her mother's absence too. 'How long?'

'Oh, years now.' She closes her eyes for a moment.

Years have passed, but in this moment it is clear that the loss of her mother is fresh. My mother has been gone three years. I was seventeen and I imagine that Katherine must have been a bit younger than that.

She dips her finger into the glass, tapping the surface of the liquid. She pulls it out and runs her fingertip across her mouth. I can't take my eyes from her.

There is another knock on the door.

'Enter.' She puts her glass down.

'Excuse my interruption. I require your passports, for we will cross the border in the early hours of the morning.'

'Of course,' says Katherine. 'You'll have to ask my husband for mine.'

The conductor bows his head in acknowledgement.

I extract mine from my bag and hand it over.

'Thank you, mademoiselle.' He backs out of the room.

Katherine stares out of the window with her hand pressed flat against the glass. Without warning, she rises and digs in her bag, pulling out a leather-bound notebook, and scribbles across the page. Squinting, I can just make out the words.

Prison walls
Of glass
Escape only possible
From glass
Bird stuffed and displayed
Under glass
All coo and proclaim beauty
Of the dead living
Beneath glass

She snaps the book shut, pulls the shade down and takes out the diamond clips holding back one side of her hair. With deft hands she removes the pearls about her neck and lets the long strand puddle on the table. She sheds her gown and slips into a sheer lawn nightdress, which she covers with a crimson silk dressing gown. Once she has secured it at the waist, she slips her feet back into her shoes.

'The only thing I dislike about the train is the distance to the lavatory,' she says, and heads into the corridor.

For a moment I stare at the closed door, stunned. Then I force myself into action, changing from Katherine's gown into a pair of boy's pyjamas. My mother noted in her diary that they were far easier on train journeys. If there is an issue in the night, one is dressed to deal with anything.

With care I hang up the gown I wore and the one Katherine discarded. She is not used to a life without a maid, and the compartment is so small it is essential that everything has a place. I straighten the notebook she scribbled in. It takes all my willpower not to open it. She is a puzzle. I pull the shade away from the window. Her handprint is still visible on the glass. I place mine on top of it. It is cool like her touch, but provides no insight into her or her words, only greater confusion in my mind.

* * *

Sleep hasn't found me and I'm not sure I want it to. The darkness and the gentle motion of the train provide me with permission to let my thoughts go where they choose to.

'You,' I mouth silently as I stare at the straps that suspend Katherine above me, letting the dialogue I want to have with her play in my mind. 'Since our meeting only hours ago I can think of little else but you. Your birthmark haunts my thoughts. Your ghastly husband looms large.'

The train jolts and Katherine moans. I hold my breath until the normal swaying rhythm returns and her breathing softens again. Below there is the sound of metal against metal. Alike but different. The friction speeding up and slowing down as the train slides into a curve.

Curves.

Yours.

Shapes.

Empty spaces.

Between us and around us.

If I could paint it in negatives and positives. Three feet of empty space between Katherine and me. She turns over and sighs.

Footsteps in the corridor pause outside the door. I still both my body and my mind, waiting for the knock, but it does not come. The steps fade away and I force my thoughts on to details. Passports, tickets, accommodation and supplies.

Eventually I sleep, but I wake with a start and am struck by the stillness. The soothing noise of the wheels over rails is gone. I hold my breath, focusing on the silence. Only then do I hear her gentle breathing, the distant sound of voices, and I smell cigarette smoke. To clear my mind, I rise and grab my dressing gown. Moving slowly so as not to make a noise, I slide on my shoes, slip out of the compartment and peer out of a corridor window. Dawn is not far away, and on the platform I watch crates being loaded into the restaurant carriage. Our breakfast has arrived. I roll the window down and lean out, breathing in the morning air. My head is still cloudy from the unaccustomed quantity of alcohol.

'May I be of assistance, mademoiselle?' asks Antoine, the cabin steward.

I'm about to say no, then change my mind. 'Would it be possible to have some tea, please?'

'Of course.' He turns and walks away.

The men on the platform scatter and the train lurches forward before the steady rhythm returns. At the far end of the carriage a man stokes a coal fire. I shiver in the fresh morning air as I wait for the tea. A large lake surrounded by mountains comes into view. This is more like a dream than reality.

* * *

'Good morning.' Katherine stands by my bunk. 'I thought you were never going to wake. It's gone nine and breakfast will be finished shortly.'

'Sorry.' I push myself up. She is dressed, looking very chic, with her pearls back in place. I swing my feet out of the bed. 'Why don't you head to the dining car, and I'll meet you there in a few minutes.'

She places her hand on the door handle. 'Coffee or tea? There is evidence that you have already had the latter.'

'Coffee, please.'

She leaves me, and with more haste than care I wash in the basin and dress in trousers and a white blouse. It is not a glamorous outfit like Katherine's, but the items are clean and not too travel-creased. The mirror above the washbasin highlights the shadows under my eyes, which almost resemble bruises. I am not cut out for the life of a socialite if it means drinking and late nights. There is nothing I can do to fix my face; only sleep will do that. After doing what I can to tame my unruly hair, I dash out to join Katherine.

The dining carriage is empty except for an elderly couple. The gentleman is reading the *International Herald Tribune* while the woman holds a guidebook to Milan. We will reach Milan at half past eleven.

'What happened?' Katherine asks, pouring coffee from the pot into my cup.

I send her a questioning glance.

'Your fringe?'

I slap my hand to my forehead. I did my best, but in the walk through the train it has gone its own way, curling up and away. I must look an absolute fool.

'With your glorious curls I think you may need to use a hair oil.' She pauses. 'The curls are sweet but not sophisticated.'

I laugh. 'I've never been sophisticated.'

She studies me over the rim of her cup. 'You are so striking with your rich red hair, pale skin and luminous eyes. It wouldn't take much to—'

A waiter places toast down. 'May I take your order now?'

Katherine says, 'I'll have two poached eggs and some smoked salmon. And please thank them in the kitchen for making an exception for us.'

He nods and turns to me. 'And you, mademoiselle?'

I swallow. The toast would be sufficient for me, but it might seem rude. 'Two soft-boiled eggs, please.'

As the waiter leaves, Forster arrives.

'Darling, will you be all right without me?'

Katherine schools her expression. 'Of course. I shall miss you, but it's only for a short time.'

'That's not what I was referring to.' He glances at me, and I turn to look at the passing scenery. 'It's the arrival in Venice and finding your way to Lady Bosworth's palazzo. You know there are unscrupulous foreigners about who would take advantage of you.'

Out of the corner of my eye I see Katherine's knuckles whiten as her grip on her cup tightens.

'Thank you for the concern, but I'm sure Mary will send her boat to meet us.' Her voice is sweet, too sweet, like an overripe berry.

'Of course, I'd forgotten that.' He pulls out a chair.

'Don't you have some details of your time with Signor Rossi to work out?'

'Yes, yes, I do, and I have written a new poem.' He hands her a sheet of paper. 'I think you'll approve.' His voice changes and the hairs on the back of my neck rise.

'I'm sure I will.' She pauses. 'When should I return it to you?'

'Before half ten,' he says, but not politely. It's an order, and it doesn't give her much time, as it's nearly ten now.

'Fine.'

I don't look at Katherine until he has gone. She scans the contents of the page with her mouth tightly pursed. Whatever is written there, she doesn't like it.

The waiter brings our breakfast, and she turns the page over and smiles at me. It is like the sun has come out on a particularly dreary Cornish day, transforming what looked bleak into the most perfect scene ever.

'How long have you been an artist?' she asks, buttering a piece of toast.

I blink and look down at my hands, flexing my fingers.

'I asked that last night, didn't I?'

I glance up at her. 'Yes.'

'What did you say?'

I close my eyes. Everything is clear, even though I was drunk.

'Difficult question?'

I could express my hurt that she has forgotten my words, but instead I say, 'I want to say I have always been one.'

She arches an eyebrow.

'I know it sounds pretentious, but growing up as the daughter of two artists, my hands were always dirty with paint, or charcoal, or even plaster.' I tap the top of one of my eggs. 'I was always creating.'

'I like that.' She sits back in her chair. 'Art is like talking or even breathing for you.'

I nod, relieved I've made myself understood.

'What is your preferred medium?'

I pause and think hard before saying, 'Oils.'

'Thick impasto or watery, almost watercolour-like?'

'Both,' I reply.

'How so?'

I shrug, thinking of the last work I did in Cornwall before my world changed. 'Well, it depends on the subject.'

'Do you have a style, are you part of a school?'

I laugh. 'I was raised in St Ives, so the artists there were my early teachers.'

'Interesting, but you haven't answered my question.'

'No, I haven't.' I put my spoon down. 'I'm trying everything until I find the style that portrays my soul.'

'I like the idea that your style can portray your soul.' She eats a piece of salmon. 'What colour are you?'

'Do you mean what is my favourite colour?' I pick up my coffee cup.

She shakes her head. 'Your personality. You could be a fiery magenta, or even puce. Or you could be a cool green or vibrant chartreuse.'

'That's difficult.' I fuss with my napkin. 'To be only one colour feels like a corset that restricts your breath and your thoughts.'

'So your soul is a rainbow of colours.'

'I can't think of anything better. The rainbow is so joyful when it appears, when the sun has dared to show itself in the face of the thundery clouds.' I must sound like a fool. Here is this polished, educated woman, and I'm rabbiting on about rainbows and clouds.

'I think my soul is a purple so dark it's almost black.' She runs a finger around the rim of her cup.

How can I respond to this? There is such sadness in her eyes I could weep. What could have caused such pain? 'I see you more as a spring lilac, with hints of white and yellow.' I glance away from her direct gaze.

'Thank you.' She rests her hand on mine. My breath catches.

She stands. 'If you'll excuse me. I have some editing to do.'

I watch as she leaves, then pour myself more coffee and gaze at the passing scenery. It should hold my attention, but all I can think about is her hand resting on mine.

8

When I return to our compartment, it has been converted into its daytime arrangement. Katherine is by the window, totally engrossed in her editing task. I dig out my sketchbook and settle on the banquette sofa by the door.

Inspired by the wooden inlay of flowers on the wall, I sketch a more realistic version of the same bouquet. I long to paint in bright colours how they feel rather than how they appear. Every time I look up, Katherine is scribbling furiously across the page that her husband has given her. When the pencil stops, she goes completely still except for her mouth. It moves as if speaking. Her eyes are closed, and it is clear she is somewhere far, far away.

Suddenly she opens her eyes and sees me staring. 'Sorry, I have been terribly rude.'

'Not at all.' I was the rude one, staring.

'I have, but this is almost done and then I would love to see some of your work.'

I swallow and fight the urge to hide my sketchbook. But it isn't right to feel this way. I'm an artist. I need to overcome this feeling of exposure each time someone studies my work. Especially if I want to sell my art.

'Of course,' I say, loosening my grip on the pencil.

'Good. I'll just return this to my husband.' She carefully folds the paper and puts on her jacket, then leaves the compartment.

How would it feel being edited? Over time I have become used to more experienced artists adding the odd line, or suggesting the addition of a colour, but nothing that would stop the work from being mine. Maybe poetry is different. I wouldn't know. I recall a few poems my mother loved by Robert Frost, but I have never studied them. I simply enjoy the feelings they bring forth in me. I imagine most casual viewers of art are the same. But I could be completely wrong. People experience art and poetry in all sorts of ways.

I flip through my sketchbook to take my mind off Katherine and her husband. It is not something I need to spend time thinking about. As soon as we leave the train in Venice our paths will never cross again, and the only reminder of her will be the few sketches I made of her this morning when I couldn't sleep. My mouth dries. She can't see those. What on earth would she think? But as I reach those pages, she walks back through the door. There is no time to rip them out.

She holds out her hand and I close the book and give it to her. How can I explain? What will her reaction be?

She settles by the window and begins on the first page, which contain sketches of the poorer side of Paris. I wanted to capture it all. Seeing it from this distance, it looks chaotic, even messy. But Katherine's fingers trace the various vignettes of life.

'Paris fascinated you,' she says without taking her eyes from my drawings. Each page is flipped and studied. She strokes the work as if trying to absorb it through her fingertips.

The scenes change to the prostitutes of the night. These are mostly done in watercolours and are very fluid. My time there opened my eyes. I knew of these things but to see them was different. At first I was shocked, but after chatting haltingly with some of the women, I looked at their roles with new eyes. They didn't judge anyone, including me.

'You are talented.' She looks up from the book. 'You enjoyed the underbelly of the city.'

I smile. 'I guess I did.'

'Is this the sort of thing you painted in St Ives?'

I pause. 'Yes, and no.'

'That's not really an answer.'

'If I'm painting people, I'm drawn to those who occupy, as you say, the underbelly, but in Cornwall I'm equally pulled to the landscape.'

She glances at the page and then back to me. 'Do you ever combine them?'

'Rarely do you see the people I'm interested in painting standing on a stunning cliff admiring the view.'

'That's a shame.' She returns her attention to the book, and I'm jealous of it. Every page is devoured with her glance. Each brush stroke or pencil mark is noted. I almost forget my worry of her finding herself portrayed, but then she reaches the sketches. She looks up at me, then returns her focus to them. Her fingers caress her birthmark. I can barely breathe. The compartment is suddenly too warm, and I'm trapped. My fascination is exposed, hanging in the air between us.

'It's always interesting to see how you are viewed by others,' she says so quietly I almost miss it. 'You have drawn me differently to your ladies of the night, and yet there is something . . . something that has carried over.'

I blush and hope she doesn't see my desire. She wouldn't understand. I don't either. Despite wanting to be normal, I am captivated by her.

My breath returns when she reaches my drawings of the train carriages and the compartment. These are more like journal entries recording my trip. No interpretation, only what I see. Not photographs, but not far from them.

'I would love to see some of your finished work.' She closes the book.

'I've shipped the work I did in Paris back to Cornwall.'

'To a dealer?'

'Definitely not.'

'Why not?'

It is a valid question. I'm an artist, and selling my work is part of that, but aside from a few small paintings done for visitors, I haven't offered my work further afield. 'I . . .' I stop and look at my hands.

'Yes?'

'I haven't worked out what my style is yet, so everything is scattered, and to launch my career I would need to have a body of cohesive work.'

'That makes sense, but I wonder . . .' she touches the cover of the sketchbook, 'if it's more than that.'

I push myself back into the cushions and cross my arms. She is too insightful.

'You will have to share your work to fully become the artist you are and to embrace the glory of your skill.'

My skill, at least at this point, is more that of an apprentice than a master, but I can't say that when she has been so kind about my work.

'Now, I must go and wish my husband *bon chance*, as we are nearing Milan.' She smiles. 'Why don't you come and say farewell to the charming Signor Rossi?'

I don't know how she endures her husband. He is handsome in a conventional way, so that aspect is understandable, but it is his personality that makes me angry. He brings out the harpy in me and I wish I had the right words to put him in his place, for he has clearly put Katherine in hers. She is different when he is around, and I much prefer the Katherine who is beside me now. By the time we reach him she will be altered, almost like she becomes an entirely new person. How can anyone be that much of a chameleon and live with themselves?

We sway with the train's motion through the dining carriage and walk towards the front. The engine slows and outside the scenery has changed from rural to industrial. Even so, there are residential pockets, with bright geraniums adorning every balcony. They are strangely joyous amongst the warehouses.

The two men are standing by the window opposite their cabin. Signor Rossi smiles in greeting, but Forster frowns.

'Katherine, you are five minutes late, and you know how I despise tardiness.'

'Sorry, Simon.' She lowers her eyes demurely.

'Here's your passport and other papers. Don't lose them.'

I open my mouth, then shut it. She is not a child.

'At least you are in time for Serafino to tell you his thoughts on my latest poem.' He holds out a sheet of paper. It is freshly written. I glance at Katherine. Her face is blank.

'Simply brilliant.' Rossi waves his hand. 'The imagery and use of words. Genius. You are lucky to have such a talented husband. You must continue to do everything to keep him so creative, so passionate.' He pauses. 'Yes, that is what powers the poem, the restrained passion bubbling below the surface.' He brings his gathered fingers to his mouth and kisses them. 'I look forward to reading more of his work. I feel . . . invigorated, and longing for love.'

Forster hands me the page to read. In clear black ink the words of the poem flash at me. It is about the last flight of the day before finding a roost high above the ground. The mingling of two birds, alone and safe for this moment in time. The wings touch, the beaks nuzzle . . . I see it all, and not just the words. Longing, love and . . . lust. How can such a man, an insensitive man, write with this finely tuned feeling? I look up from the page, seeking Katherine. She glances out of the window and only turns to look at me as the train slows further.

'What do you think, Miss Kernow?' Forster asks.

I draw in a deep breath and decide to judge the words and not the man who wrote them. 'Exquisite.'

'Even a simple painter sees the worth of my work.'

'Darling,' Katherine says quietly. 'Miss Kernow is an accomplished artist.'

He waves his hand in dismissal and engages Rossi in conversation. The train comes to a stop at the station and he and Katherine step off.

'It has been a pleasure to make your acquaintance, Miss Kernow. I hope our paths cross again in the future.' Rossi takes my hand and bows over it very formally before he too steps off the train. Out of the window I see Katherine kiss Forster's cheek. Her expression is unreadable.

Unsettled is how I feel in this moment. Something I can't name or place is gnawing at me. Restless, I head back to our compartment without waiting for Katherine. On the way, I pass Marlene Dietrich with barely a glance. Once there, I open my sketchbook and draw the most frightening caricature of that buffoon of a man. Why does she put up with him? Surely she doesn't have to stay with him? Is it only because he is a genius with words? As I scratch the words *The pompous poet* under the figure, Katherine walks through the door. She looks at the sketch on my lap.

'You've captured him.' She picks up her bag and places her documents in it, then leaves again before I can say anything. Have I offended her? The sketch is a way for me to put my thoughts and feelings somewhere outside of me. I have encountered many men like Forster. Some who are tolerated, even lauded for their genius. He must be one of them. That must be why she stays with him.

But Katherine is different, though I can't define how. I stand and look around for the notebook I saw her write in last night. I long to understand her. I find it in her hatbox, under the table by the window.

There are notes, phrases, lists, images, and searing moments of exquisite emotion. In the front of the book there is a poem, 'The Artist', by Amy Lowell:

Why do you subdue yourself in golds and purples?
Why do you dim yourself with folded silks?
Do you not see that I can buy brocades in any draper's shop,
And that I am choked in the twilight of all these colors.
How pale you would be, and startling—
How quiet;
But your curves would spring upward
Like a clear jet of flung water,
You would quiver like a shot-up spray of water,
You would waver, and relapse, and tremble.
And I too should tremble,
Watching.

Murex-dyes and tinsel—
And yet I think I could bear your beauty unshaded.

Is Katherine a student of poetry? Is this how they met? Hearing footsteps in the corridor, I put the notebook back and return to sketching. Where has she gone? It is only hours before we arrive. I must pack. It will be good to reach Venice and breathe different air. It might help, as nothing on this journey makes sense. Maybe my mother felt the same way at the start of hers.

9

Verona

Katherine returns and the door clicks closed behind her. Without a word, she flings things into her bag. 'Sorry to have abandoned you. I've been chatting to Marlene Dietrich. We attended the London premiere of her latest film, *The Scarlet Empress*, earlier this month. I didn't have the chance to meet her then, so it was good to make her acquaintance properly.' She turns her back to me and puts her notebook in another bag, then sends me a smile over her shoulder. Her glance falls on my sketchbook. 'I hope you've been productive.'

I fight the urge to hide it. Page after page is filled with drawings of her as I try to work her out. She appears to be a shallow socialite, but I'm not certain. Nothing about her adds up, which intrigues me even more. On the surface, she is a beautiful model wearing the latest designs and jewellery. But what is behind the mannequin? Nothing? Or does the costume hide something deeper, richer?

'That's done.' She closes the bag. 'I'll meet you for lunch in the dining car in five minutes.'

Before I can reply, she has left, and I'm staring at the closed door.

I pick up my mother's journal and place it safely in my satchel.

This whole journey is a chance to change, to become normal. Yet I feel far from it, and glancing in the mirror, my eyes appear large and overbright.

'Who are you?' I ask the reflection staring back at me from the glass. With more force than needed, I close the door to the wash cupboard and leave the compartment.

Katherine is already at the table as I enter the dining car, and her face lights up. My steps falter, but the maître d' captures my arm and leads me to the table for two.

'I haven't ordered, as I didn't know what you wanted, but I couldn't resist ordering you this delicious concoction.' She points to a glass on the table.

I nearly collapse into my seat. Katherine is different yet again. Will the other diners notice the change? Energy radiates from her like heat from the sun. Although she is sitting, nothing about her is still. I'm fascinated.

The maître d' hands me a menu, saying, 'Today the chef is recommending the sea bass, as it arrived straight from the Mediterranean this morning.'

Katherine wrinkles her nose. 'I would like the foie gras to start, followed by the filet of beef.' She looks up at me. A quick glance at the menu and I'm overwhelmed. She sees my discomfort but doesn't intervene.

'I'll have the sardines to start, followed by the sea bass,' I say eventually, putting the menu down.

'Very well.' The maître d' turns to Katherine. 'Wine?'

'Of course,' she says, and points to one on the list.

'Excellent choice.' He bows.

'You'll join me, of course,' she says, then grins at me. 'This will be fun.'

I take a sip of the cocktail and nearly cough. It is strong. I can't make out what alcohols are in it.

'Have you been to Venice before?' Katherine asks.

'Before April I'd only been as far as London.'

She tilts her head in the way she does frequently. I'm not sure what it means. 'For an artist, that is a small world.'

'There is plenty of life and landscape in Cornwall.'

'I won't deny that, but the world,' she spreads her hands wide, 'offers many wonders, and such varied people and views.'

I take another sip, thinking. 'The people frequenting the pubs in St Ives or Penzance or Newlyn are little different to the ones I watched in Paris.'

'Characters like that I imagine are the same the world over. Do you intend to spend your time in Venice lurking in the dark and watching the less fortunate?'

I nod.

'That would be a waste. Did you not go to the Louvre while in Paris?'

'Of course I did, and I will visit the Accademia and other museums in Venice, as well as the opera.' I want to follow every footstep my mother recorded. This trip is my chance to change.

'Good. You are too talented to stay in the dark.'

'Thank you.' I play with a fork. For the moment, I don't want to be in the light.

'You can of course pick your time to shine forth.' She glances out of the window. Tall cypress trees stand like sentinels along the track. 'I will be staying with Lady Mary Bosworth, who has been living in Venice since her divorce. Simon doesn't really approve, but she is well connected, and through her he has been invited to the poetry competition.'

'Is the competition part of the Biennale?' I ask.

'Connected somehow.' She smiles as the wine is brought to the table.

'Will mademoiselle have a glass of wine now?' The waiter

clears my empty cocktail glass. I nod, feeling the power of the drink running through my head. I don't need more alcohol.

'Venice will be marvellous,' Katherine says.

'It will be,' I agree, but I doubt my reasons for thinking that are the same as hers.

'Where will you be staying?'

'A pensione in San Cassiano.'

She holds her glass in mid-air. 'Is that safe? Isn't that where the prostitutes used to display their wares, so to speak, on the bridge . . . the Ponte delle Tette?'

'Safe?' I lean back in my chair. She hasn't seen the places I visited in Paris. Venice can't be any worse. 'I'll be fine.' My mother managed to live there without problems, so I will do the same, I'm certain.

She sighs. 'How long do you plan to stay?'

'I'm hoping for at least six months, but I will see how things go.'

'What things?' She pauses while the first course is delivered. 'You seem to be on . . . something of a pilgrimage.'

'I suppose I am.' I taste my wine, which is dry and makes my tongue roll.

'A painting pilgrimage, or one of faith?'

'Painting and learning.'

She spreads her bread thinly with butter. 'There's something you're not telling me.'

This is true. I haven't revealed the purpose of my journey to anyone.

'Ah, your silence says I'm right.'

I shrug and focus on my food. The reasons for my pilgrimage are mine alone; no one else needs to know them.

'As you aren't answering, I shall run through a list of possible reasons for you to have left Cornwall, which you clearly love from all you have said about it.'

I will not rise to her provocation.

'You have been scorned by a lover.'

I look her directly in the eyes. I have been kissed a total of five times in my life. There have been no lovers. But I do not say a word.

She turns her wine glass in her elegant fingers. 'You caught your parents in affairs with other people.'

My father with his current wife comes to mind. She was a model for both of my parents, and I know my father had an affair with her. Yet my mother was untroubled by it. After my mother's death, it was my father's indecent haste in inviting that woman into our home that angered me, and still does.

'There is something in that,' she says before finishing her foie gras. 'But something else is firing your furnace for this journey.'

I try the Gallic shrug I witnessed so often in Paris, but it doesn't work.

'I know.' She grins.

She can't know.

'You are on a journey to find yourself.'

My glass nearly falls out of my hand, for although that is not the reason, it is a little too close. I must become better at concealing my thoughts.

'It should have been obvious. You are twenty, and I was much the same at that age.' She holds her empty glass out and a waiter comes rushing to fill it.

'How were you the same?'

'My mother had died. I was angry with life, with my father, and all the men were broken, especially the one I loved.' She gazes out of the window. 'I lived, God did I live fully. Nothing was off the agenda.' She looks back at me. 'I'm the daughter of a Swedish aristocrat and an English academic. My behaviour was beyond the pale. I left Sweden and wouldn't speak to my father,

87

but alas, he had control of my money, my mother's money, and in the end that won.'

'Won?' I ask. Surely she could have found employment of some sort. The world had changed after the war.

She laughs bitterly. 'I was pregnant, and my father insisted I marry.'

'You're a mother?' I can't keep the surprise out of my voice.

'You don't think I'm fit to be one.' She takes a large gulp of wine. 'That says it all.'

'That's not what I said. It's just that most mothers talk of their children.'

'Ah.' She smiles sadly. 'Mine was born dead.'

The waiter appears with our main courses and the bottle of red wine Katherine ordered. As he pours the wine for her to taste, so much makes sense to me, particularly the drinking.

Once the waiter has departed, I say, 'I'm so sorry.'

'Not as sorry as I am. In a way, my daughter abandoned me, and I couldn't blame her. I was unfit, and I was stuck married to the man you have met because of her.'

I open my eyes wide. 'He was not her father?'

'No, he was the husband of my father's choosing.' She stares directly at me. 'By the time I knew I was pregnant, the man I loved was dead of an overdose because of what he had seen on some field in France.'

I swallow. 'I . . . I'm sorry . . . which is a hopeless and useless thing to say.'

'But you have acknowledged the loss, which is more than many do.' She cuts into her filet. 'I was a social pariah for having lost a man and then a child.' She stops cutting. 'I received what I deserved.'

'No!' The word is out before I can stop it. Even in the few short hours I have known this woman, I know she has not received what she deserved.

'Oh, but I did. You see I didn't know I was pregnant, and when he died, I did anything I could to help me forget.' She looks down. 'I'm sure that what I took harmed my child.' Her words are whispered, and I only just catch them.

'Many things can cause a stillbirth,' I say. I knew of some that happened in St Ives, in the artist community and among the local working folk. The babies weren't viable for many reasons. I never saw it as the mother's fault.

'Yes, they can. But you see, I both wanted my daughter more than anything and also hated her because she tied me to Simon.' She laughs bitterly. 'And now I live the life I do because I am evil.'

'You are not.'

She slowly shakes her head. 'I like the way you see me.' The corner of her mouth lifts, and in that moment, it is clear she understands how attractive I find her.

The waiter hovers and pours us more wine. My head is swamped from the alcohol and her revelations.

'Please don't let what I've said trouble you.' She glances at the view again. 'I have made my bed and I lie in it.'

'But you could leave him. How long have you been married?'

'Almost sixteen years.' She sips her wine. 'On what grounds could I divorce him? He is faithful and he needs me.' Her mouth twists and a bitter sound escapes from her lips.

The waiter clears our plates and asks about a sweet course. I shake my head, but Katherine asks for truffles and another glass of wine. She drinks to live her life, but Simon isn't here right now and she doesn't need to be drunk with me. I want to take her by the hand, pull her off the train at the next stop and tell her to forget the past, but instead I accept the chocolate she offers me. I'm no match for her sophistication, nor for the attachment she has to a man who belittles her. I am merely a twenty-year-old artist trying to find my way.

* * *

There is a tap on the door and the attendant speaks my name. He knocks with more force. 'Madame Forster has sent me with tea. May I enter?' he asks. His voice is muffled, or maybe it's my hearing.

I must have fallen asleep. 'Come in.'

'I shall put the tray on the table.' He doesn't look at me. 'It is four o'clock.'

My head throbs and my mouth is parched. As I pour the tea, I notice that Katherine's things are gone. A note is propped against the lamp.

My poor dear little bird,

I have broken you. I am sorry. Take the two tablets once you wake. I added the peacock gown to your bag. It suited you so. You shall embrace your plumage one day, for you could never be a little wren.

K x

My heart stills. Is this her farewell?

I scan the room and spy my bag. On the top is my sketchbook, which I had tucked away. My face flames. It might be just as well if she has left. She knows how I feel about her. I slap my hands to my face. Oh God, what does she think of me?

I sink onto the sofa and drink some tea, looking at the two white tablets, which I assume are aspirin. I swallow them. This is not how I wanted to arrive in Venice. Outside the window the countryside is beautiful, but looking at it passing by turns my stomach.

The train is full of noise as passengers prepare for arrival. Another knock on the door.

'Enter.'

'Mademoiselle Kernow, I shall take care of your bags. Do you wish to go to the dining car to watch as the train comes into Venice?'

I almost say no, but I nod, taking the small bag holding my documents with me. In the corridor, I hesitate. What if Venice doesn't work its magic on me? What will I do then?

'Pardon me,' a man's voice says in an accent I don't recognise.

I step aside, then walk towards the dining car, hoping to see Katherine. Her tablets are working. My headache is going but my stomach is still a bit hollow. She is not there, but Marlene Dietrich is. Her glance meets mine. I hesitate, but she smiles and beckons me. I join her at a table by the window. Soon we will be crossing the lagoon and the train will arrive in Venice.

The quality of the light changes as we begin to cross. On the right-hand side the new road bridge runs parallel. In my head, I hear Forster telling me that Mussolini opened it last year. I push his intrusive voice away and drink in the scenery. It reminds me a bit of home. Something to do with the water and the sunlight creating a different palette of colours. Here, though, the sky is more phthalo blue, unlike at home, where if it isn't raining it's mostly ultramarine.

'Where is she?' Marlene asks.

I shrug and close my eyes for a moment. When I open them again, the lagoon is filled with boats, both sail and motor. I don't know where to look and want to burn the view into my mind.

'So, you are scorned.'

I blink, not sure how to respond.

'There will be others.' She rises. 'We have come to the station. May Venice dazzle you with her beauty and fulfil your dreams.'

'If only,' I say as she takes my hand.

'Be careful what you wish for,' she says, and heads towards the front of the train.

I walk in the opposite direction, uncertain how this will all work out. As I reach the compartment, the train comes to a stop. The attendant opens the door and helps me off.

'One moment and your bags will be here,' he says.

I scan the platform for Katherine, but I can't find her. Part of me is relieved, but the other part is desolate. She is so bright and everything revolves around her, especially when that dreadful man isn't about. He flattens her and hides her light.

But I mustn't think on that now. I'm in Venice, and that is what is important. My mother wrote of her first sight of the city, and I wait almost breathlessly to lose my heart to it. Images from her sketches in the diary fill my head. My fingers curl, longing to create my own, even though the city is a complete mystery to me.

This is not the journey I imagined, but it is one I will never forget. Further along the platform I see Katherine being embraced by another woman. She appears different yet again. I could never alter myself that much or as frequently. I'm simply Sheba Kernow, once known as Baba. I am the black sheep, stealing away.

'Mademoiselle Kernow, shall I ask a porter to arrange a boat for you?'

I consider the cost, but then look at my easel and other awkward items. This is one time when spending money makes sense.

'Yes please,' I say, smoothing my sweaty palms down the legs of my trousers before handing him a tip. He has a few words with a porter, and before long we are out of the station. On the threshold, I pause, taking a deep breath. It is not the smell I expected. Dead fish, drains and something else I can't pinpoint. The early-evening sun beats down relentlessly. I will need a hat and some cooler clothing. It will only become warmer as the days progress.

While the porter and I wait for a boat, I catch sight of Katherine in a gondola heading to the right. In a city like Venice, I doubt I will ever see her again. My chest tightens and tears threaten. I pause and blame the emotion on too much drink at lunch. But as her boat disappears from view, I know I'm lying to myself.

PART TWO

But words, words! How inadequate you are! How weary one gets of you! How you will always be saying too much or too little! Oh to be silent! Oh to be a painter!

Virginia Woolf

10

Penzance

Paul's morning pep talk about being firm with my uncle was wearing off as I walked through the showrooms, noting the large number of people on this Saturday morning who had come to the viewing. It was Stephen's success that had brought them here. He'd kept the business afloat while Dad had slowly rebuilt the reputation of the fine art side of the business after my mistake had trashed it.

Local and national papers had had a great time with the story. Family auction house misses genuine Cézanne. The client had bought the painting at a car boot sale for a tenner. Even to this day I remember telling him it shouldn't go in the upcoming fine art sale. It was good, very good, but I wouldn't say it was a Cézanne without any provenance. He wanted my father's take on it, but he was away in Australia on holiday with Mum. The client was impatient and wouldn't wait. Under pressure from both him and my uncle, I agreed to list the painting as Impressionist School, after Cézanne. The hammer price was twelve thousand pounds, well over the estimate of five. He was initially very pleased, until the new buyer did what I'd asked our client to do – to take the time and have the painting assessed by an expert. Only a year later, it sold for a million. Barton's reputation was destroyed, I had a breakdown while trying to finish my thesis, and the client sued. We won, but at the cost of our good name.

Stephen's voice carried as he wished Marcia good morning. I wanted to catch him before his meeting with Mrs George. The accounts were vital to selling my mother's and my shares in the business and resolving my father's estate. Every time I thought those words, I stopped breathing for a moment. It just wasn't real, but it was. There was nothing more I wanted in this moment than to talk to my father. How would he handle my uncle? He could also tell me how best to help my mother. Her behaviour was odd, even accounting for her grief.

When we were sorting the old house a few months ago, she'd made some strange comments that I'd put down at the time to the disruption of the move. Now she was struggling with the loss of the love of her life. It was hard to be without your partner. I missed Paul, who had made it lovingly clear where I should be, and it wasn't Cornwall. Twenty minutes ago, saying goodbye to Mum and Meg, I'd agreed with him. But in this moment, with sunlight filling the showroom and glinting off the polished surfaces, I wasn't so sure.

Stephen walked towards his office and I dashed after him. He swung around. 'What are you doing here?'

I flinched at his tone, but I wouldn't be put off. 'I'm here to review the accounts.'

Marcia scooted by with Mrs George in tow, ushering her into Stephen's office.

My uncle pushed past me. 'Unless you're bringing money or clients into the business, I have no time for you today.'

Mrs George gasped so loudly I'm certain everyone in the building heard. The sooner this was sorted the better. But Stephen wasn't making it easy. He stuck his head back out of his office. 'By the way, your partner made it clear that you're vulnerable at the moment. Go and have a spa day to treat your nerves.' He closed the door with a thud.

Paul had spoken to Stephen. No doubt he thought he was helping, but in one act of kindness he had taken away any remaining credibility I had. My uncle's words had been heard by Marcia, several potential clients and two of the men who worked shifting the items for sale.

The clock in my father's office chimed. Time was rushing past me and I was doing nothing. I went to his desk, picked up the phone and called my best friend. 'Tash.'

'Ren, hold on a sec.' I heard her say something in muffled tones. 'Right, your god-daughter was trying to put every stuffed animal in her room into her suitcase.'

'Are you off somewhere?' As soon as I asked the question, I felt like an idiot. It was the holidays.

'It's Easter break and the in-laws beckon.' Her voice dropped away.

'Oh.' On the wall hung a print of my father's favourite Laura Knight, *At the Edge of the Cliff*. The title could describe my life right now.

'What's up?' Tash asked.

'Doesn't matter,' I said quickly.

'Don't give me that crap.'

She wouldn't stop asking if I didn't reply. I knew that from our years of friendship. 'I was hoping you were free and could give me a hand today at Harbour House.'

'The one in Newlyn, the Georgian beauty?' Her voice lifted in excitement.

'Yes, that one. I need to do a full inventory for a sale.'

'You tease, you know I can't resist poking into old houses.'

'True.'

'Just today?' The noise in the background was getting louder.

I bit my thumbnail. I could lie, but that wouldn't help me. 'If you could give me a day, that would be great, but realistically I think it will take longer.'

'Hmm, let me have a word with himself and I'll call you back.'

It was a big ask even if we had been talking to each other regularly, which we haven't been. We'd been best friends since nursery school and had lived through bullying, braces, bras and boys. Boys had been the big thing. After Tash's fiancé was killed in the Gulf eleven years ago, I didn't leave her side until I knew she was strong enough to go on. But now I didn't know what was happening in her life, and part of me died inside at this thought.

Her help with Harbour House would make the task more fun, and importantly much quicker. In our teenage years we used to work for Dad in the summer holidays doing just this sort of thing, and it would be good to spend some time with her again. It had been too long, partly because Paul didn't like her. In his words she brought out my immature tendencies. But he was fifteen years older than us and I imagine we did appear that way to him when we were together. He was such a calming influence on me. His sense of humour was sophisticated and his charm with people like my mother was fabulous. I envied his ease. I'd become so awkward and reclusive since the breakdown, but he ensured that I met interesting people to stimulate me in the right way. He made it plain that if Tash was in London, he didn't want me to see her, and he certainly wouldn't. I never understood, because I loved them both. I could count on one hand how many times I'd seen my best friend and my god-daughter in the past few years. This filled me with sadness. It wasn't like they lived on the other side of the world.

My phone rang. It was Tash calling back.

'Right, he's agreed to go without me. Which means I am blissfully free for the next week at least. Can you swing by and pick me up, or shall I meet you there?'

'You're a star.'

'I know.'

'I'll be there in ten.'

I heard her laughter as I hung up. As I gathered my things, Stephen was escorting Mrs George to the door. He sent me the filthiest look. I smiled, then waved to Marcia before I fled.

* * *

'I'm all yours.' Tash plonked herself down in the passenger seat. 'Thank you for saving me from the in-laws.'

'You love them really.'

'I do, but I love them best at a distance. And it will give Gareth time alone with his parents, and with Annabelle.' She clicked her seat belt on. 'He's been so busy lately that down time hasn't existed for him.'

'Every doctor is overworked these days.'

'Too true, and paediatric consultants are no exception.' Tash opened the sun roof and warm light flooded the car. Something like happiness filled me for a moment. My phone beeped. It was a text from Paul.

'So I take it Meg is with your mother today?'

'Thankfully, as I wouldn't be able to do this otherwise.'

'My mum saw yours the other day. She thought she was good considering.'

I turned out onto the road. 'Things are getting worse not better with her. I don't know what to do.' I drew a breath. 'When I was home four months ago, she was low because of the house sale but she seemed to be improving physically. I asked Dad about it then and he sort of brushed over it.' I stopped to let a pedestrian cross. Dad had looked like he wanted to say something at the time, but he didn't. I'd put it down to him having so much on his mind. 'Since he died, when people come to visit she perks up and puts on a convincing act, but as soon as the door closes, she collapses.'

'Must be hard to see.'

'In those moments she goes from something like her previous vivacious self to an old woman.' How had my father coped? I should know, but I didn't. That was the most awful thing. He never said and I hadn't asked. Why hadn't he mentioned it?

Tash put her hand on mine briefly. 'I'm here for you, always have been.'

I swallowed hard. 'True.'

She fiddled with the car radio until she stopped on a tune I hadn't heard since we were sixteen. 'God, I love BBC Cornwall for the way they keep pulling out these oldies.'

As we drove along the waterfront, we both bellowed out the lyrics to Katy Perry's 'I Kissed a Girl' at the top of our lungs. Neither of us could carry a tune, which was why at school we were always made to paint the scenery or sort lighting for any show that was being put on. It cemented the close bond between us that I thought would never be broken, and yet I hadn't been there for her brother's wedding or her grandmother's funeral. I had missed these important things in her life and that left a hole inside me.

Yes, I texted regularly, but it had to be a year since we last had a good catch-up. Every time I planned to do something with her, luck would have it that Paul needed me for an event or help with a deadline. But I did know what was going on in Annabelle's life. We wrote to each other the old-fashioned way. It all began after a school project when she had to write a letter and I was the lucky one. I replied, and the exchange continued, so I knew all about her love of horses and dogs, and her biggest disappointment. She was not allowed a puppy because Gareth was allergic. But I hadn't had a letter in a while. Maybe Annabelle had grown too big to write to her godmother.

Out of the corner of my eye, I saw the joy on Tash's face and knew that I hadn't had that feeling in a very long time. What *was* joy? The answer might just be singing badly at the top of your lungs to a banging tune.

'I love that song,' she said when it ended. 'Do you remember when we both had the hots for Tommy Gooden and made a deal that neither of us could have him because it would break us apart? And then we had to watch him go off with Amy Sale.'

'It was awful. It would have been easier if it had been you, then at least I would have known all the details.'

'I would have embellished them for you.' She grinned.

'You're good like that.'

Tash pretended to shine her halo. 'I know.'

I pulled into the drive of Harbour House. Bastard was waiting.

Tash looked at my phone as another message flashed up on the screen. 'Does he always text like that?'

I squinted at it.

Come back now. I miss you. I'm lost without you.

It pinged again.

Love you.

Tash raised her eyebrows.

There was no point in defending Paul to her. She didn't like him and nothing I said would change that. Plus I had so much to do. This was all a lot harder than I'd thought. Nothing was straightforward and I needed to talk to Tash's dad. I'd found a lasting power of attorney for Mum in the paperwork that had been in a file on the top of Dad's desk. This puzzled me because she was only in her late fifties but they must have done it after her stroke.

Tash was already out of the car and heading to the house. The air smelled of low tide, and gulls screeched overhead. From her perch on the windowsill, Bastard looked up at the birds before turning her gaze on us.

'Whose cat?' Tash asked.

'Bastard belongs to the house these days.'

'Bastard? That's a bit cruel. Did he scratch you?'

I laughed. 'That's her name.'

'Good God, how glorious.' Tash bent and said, 'Hello, Bastard.'

The cat didn't budge until I reached the door. Then she jumped down and brushed up against my legs while I let us all in.

'Right, Ren, what's your plan?' Tash stopped in her tracks in the hallway. 'Holy Mother of God.' She sounded just like her Irish gran. 'Who is that siren?'

'Beautiful, isn't she?' There was something about the woman in the painting that I still couldn't pinpoint.

'Stunning and so sexy.'

I sent her a look.

'Seriously, whoever painted it was in love with her. Look at the brushwork.'

I studied it again. 'It's not signed on the front, so I have no idea who the artist is.'

'Right, a mystery.' She rubbed her hands together. 'Your father loved a mystery. Remember that time we helped him on a probate valuation and found the bronze cat?'

'The cat that was too hot to touch by the electric heater.'

'Bloody Tutankhamen's cat.' She laughed.

'Yes, that did rather well.' The story had even made the

national papers, putting our little auction house on the map in a good way. Now here I was doing it all again, but this time I was wiser and had no plans to make Barton's my life. No, my life was in London with Paul, researching for a TV programme. That suited me just fine. We lived in Docklands in a beautiful new building, and I had a partner who loved me.

As if on cue, my phone pinged again.

'Paul?' Tash asked.

I pulled it out of my pocket to check, then slipped it back in. 'Yup.'

'Does this happen all the time? It's so distracting. How can you think? Doesn't he have anything else to do?'

'Of course he does. He's just worried about me at the moment.'

She cast me a sideways glance and I bent down to stroke Bastard, who complained that I hadn't yet fed her. Without responding to the unspoken questions rolling off Tash like a thick sea fret moving to shore, I went to the kitchen and refilled the food bowl I found there. Bastard brushed against my leg on the way to her meal.

As Tash followed me into the kitchen, my phone went again. I pulled it out and turned it to silent, which I didn't often do now because of Mum. If it kept pinging, Tash would press on with her questions and thoughts, and that was the last thing I wanted. Paul's texts were a bit excessive, but it was because he loved me, and that was good. Even if he did interfere too much sometimes, like talking to Stephen. Tonight I would make it clear that he couldn't do that again.

'OK boss, where do you want to start? The big painting?'

'We'll leave that until last. Let's begin up in the bedrooms.'

'Cup of tea first?'

Tash took off her backpack and pulled out a packet of biscuits and a box of Earl Grey tea bags. A rush of memories and love for her almost overwhelmed me. While studying for exams, we'd lived on digestives and tea. Back then that was 90 per cent of our body composition. With the remaining part being cider and Rich Tea biscuits. God, those days felt so close right at this moment.

'Thank you,' I said.

She looked over her shoulder from where she was filling the kettle, and stuck out her tongue.

'I've missed you.' I leaned against the counter, enjoying the warmth of the sunshine and her friendship.

'I know you have.'

'Oi.'

'I've missed you too. It felt like my left leg was missing.' She jiggled it about.

I swallowed. The truth was, I felt the same, I'd become accustomed to being one-legged, but now to have both somehow felt even worse.

She opened her arms and I fell into them. Tears began to fall, and before long her shoulder was damp. When I finally pulled away, it was to locate some kitchen roll to blow my nose.

'Sorry,' I said once I'd dried my face.

'No need to apologise for crying. You've lost your father, your mother isn't coping and needs help, and your partner isn't here to support you. You have every reason to cry and cry and cry.'

I shook my head, because I had no right to tears or self-pity. I had so many things that others didn't, and I needed to pull myself together for my mother. Paul needed me too, I reminded myself as my phone vibrated in my back pocket.

'You know, turning it to silent won't stop his texts. Only he can do that, and you need to tell him to stop.'

I shook my head.

'If he misses you that much, he could get his ass down here. It's not term time, for Christ's sake.'

I glanced out at the harbour. The sky was blue as only a Cornish sky could be. Not a cloud to be seen. The sea was calm, and it felt more like summer than summer often did. 'He has things he has to do.'

'What's more important than supporting his partner after the loss of her father?'

'Research and a deadline.' I looked away from her to an abstract landscape on the wall. It was one of Sheba's. There was so much honesty in it, from the undulations of the greens to the burst of raw umber.

'Ha, that's only because you're not doing it for him.'

I looked down. Tash had been my flatmate in London when I'd started dating Paul, and I couldn't deny what she had seen. She also hadn't approved because he was an associate professor in the art history department. In her words, he was too old for me and shouldn't be shagging a student.

'It's different now.'

'What, now that he's a full professor and can ask some poor PhD student to do his research for him?'

I took a step back. She had never made her dislike of Paul so obvious. I knew he wasn't her idea of heaven, but after Tommy, we had never liked the same boy again. She had gone the rugby player route, while I went for the artistic, academic types. She'd said they all needed a good meal and a walk in the park to get some colour in their cheeks and meat on their bones. We'd argued over Paul almost from the first moment, and it was a relief when he asked me to move in with him. Meanwhile, Tash had met Gareth Lugg, a rugby-playing medical resident, while taking Scottish dancing lessons in preparation for the ceilidh at our friend Sue's wedding. It had been love at first twirl for her. And I'd been so relieved that she'd found love again after losing Mark three years before.

Knowing we had a lot to do, I climbed the back stairs from the kitchen to the bedrooms. Bastard sat in the middle of the landing watching as Tash joined me. An awkward silence stretched between us. She knew Paul was everything I wanted – clever, funny, good-looking and totally into me – so I wasn't sure what the problem was. Yes, he was intense and wanted all of me, but that was good. Maybe during the course of this week I could win her over.

'OK, let's start with the single bedroom.' I entered the room and immediately went to open the window. This house cried out to be lived in, and without fresh air it was musty.

'What a gorgeous bed.' Tash ran her hands over the headboard. It was French at a guess, and it would be perfect for a child, especially if freshly painted.

Using my phone to take measurements, I added the item to the spreadsheet I'd made last night on my tablet. Covering the bed was a crocheted white cotton bedspread that was a work of art.

'That took someone some time.' Tash lifted a corner. 'Heavy, too.'

I added it to the list.

After I'd photographed the paintings on the walls, I noted the dimensions. There was a glorious oil seascape of the cliffs near Land's End. It was signed by Charles Naper and must be one of the few paintings of his that still existed. He had burned most of his work. Also hanging in the room was a work of Sheba's with her distinctive broad swathes of colour. There was joy in just looking at it. It was simply framed so that nothing distracted from the image.

Tash peered at a small watercolour of a child. 'This is exquisite.' She lifted it off the wall and handed it to me.

I turned it over, looking for a signature or signs that it might have been in a sale somewhere. The work had been done quickly, and a few strokes had captured the essence of the child, who looked to be around two. The location was hard to pinpoint. It was a sketch, not a finished painting, and it was interesting in that it was beautifully framed.

Tash had moved on and was holding an old teddy bear. 'He's been well loved.' She stroked the bald patch on the bear's stomach.

I smiled. 'Any maker's marks?'

She shook her head. 'Might have been home-made, looking at the stitching.' She turned the bear upside down. 'Beautifully done, but not from a factory.' She placed it back on the chest of drawers. 'This feels like it was a child's room.' She spun around. 'But the house belonged to two women.'

'Maybe it was for one of the two great-nephews?'

'Nothing about it shouts boy's room to me.' She pulled a book from the shelf and handed it to me. *Ballet Shoes*.

'You're right. A niece, then?'

Tash began to look more closely at the books, and I wished I had a phone number for the gardener. She seemed to know a great deal about both the artists. Not that that information was important to the task today. We were cataloguing everything and marking out certain pieces that might be of higher value. As lovely as the collection of framed Christmas cards by Robert Borlase Smart and Patrick Heron were, I didn't see them making much for the estate. Although many painters lived and worked in Cornwall, only a few had made it into the big time. Barbara Hepworth being one and Stanhope Forbes another.

'There's a copy of *The Secret Garden* here. It says, "To Isabella, love from Sheba".' Tash slipped it back on the shelf. 'Sheba?'

'I think it was what Bathsheba called herself.'

'I'm not surprised. What on earth prompted her parents to lumber her with a name like that?'

I frowned.

'You never paid attention at Sunday school.' Tash wagged her finger at me. 'King David had the hots for Bathsheba because he watched her bathe.'

'Really?'

'So the Bible says. He sent her husband to the front line of the battle so that he would be killed.'

'Charming.' I shivered at the thought. It was just so creepy.

'Then he married her.'

'Yuck.'

'Exactly, so I'm with Sheba. Best to leave Bathsheba behind.'

'Agreed,' I said, walking out of the small bedroom.

Bastard was sitting on the table on the landing. She looked almost like a statue next to a beautiful porcelain vase. The landing was also home to fifteen paintings, one stone statue and one bronze, as well as a bookcase and an armchair. I left the furniture for Tash and began with the largest painting. It was a seascape, one of Sheba's. Her distinctive use of colour and shape really stood out, with vivid turquoise and cerulean for the water and the sky, and bright greens for the fields. It was stunning, and so vital. Joy and energy sprang from the canvas. But it wasn't everyone's taste. Looking at the date on the back of the canvas, I saw that it was one of her last paintings, dated 2017. Having searched the market to see what her work had been achieving, I'd been disappointed. It deserved more attention and certainly more value.

'Look at this book of poems.' Tash held out the volume, with the dedication visible.

To Sheba, a young artist who shows so much promise.
Simon Forster
Venice, June 1934

'We studied his poems at school,' she said.

Memories of staring out of the window instead of focusing on the task at hand came rushing back to me. 'We did.'

'They were quietly sexy.' Tash grinned.

'Yeah, not John Donne, but in their own way they were intense.'

'Do you remember Mrs Baker?' she asked.

'How could I forget? Her rendition of the poems was dire, but she made the history around them interesting.'

'She did. When we learned that Forster stopped writing after his wife died during the war . . .' Tash placed one hand on her heart dramatically, with the other on her brow. 'God, how romantic we found it.'

'We were so gullible then.' I flipped the pages and saw some annotations. Sheba must have read the poems carefully. I didn't have time to study them now, so I placed the book on the top of the console table to have a closer look at later.

We left the hall and entered the master bedroom. Here the view vied with the striking canvas I'd noted on my visit yesterday. It defied definition but stirred something strong. Passion, need and love.

I took it off the wall. It had been signed by Sheba on the front, and on the reverse was the date 1934, but with the 4 struck out and 5 written over it. The colours used were not what I'd call her Cornish palette. Where was she in 1935? Still in Venice?

Tash lifted an old quilt off a small chair. 'Gorgeous colours.'

I nodded, but what caught my attention was the chair itself. 'I think this is a Chippendale.'

'Really?' She squinted at the black-painted piece.

'Yes.' I stroked the curved arm. 'I'll double-check with my uncle. Strangely, he said there was nothing noteworthy here.' To be fair to Stephen, I hadn't noticed the chair when I'd done the walk-through, as the quilt had covered it. As much as I didn't care for him, I had to admit he had kept the business afloat with his furniture sales.

Tash put the quilt on the bed where it belonged. It was hand-stitched, and the autumnal colours matched the landscape above the bed, which wasn't Sheba's but her father's.

She stood back. 'I wonder if there are any other valuable pieces in the house.'

'Not that I noticed yesterday.'

'Too struck by that portrait, I imagine.'

'True.' I scratched Bastard's head as she bumped my legs. 'And by Bastard.'

'Ah yes, the ghost cat that haunts the house.'

'More like the cat that sees ghosts. She watches things that we can't see. Like right now.'

Bastard was sitting on the edge of the carpet staring at the corner of the room. It was empty, not even a spider to be seen. Just an old metal plate covering what might have been an electric socket at some point.

'Cats are like that, though.' Tash dropped her notebook onto the bed. 'I'm going to put the kettle on again and have a quick peek at the rest of the house.' She stepped over Bastard, who remained fixated on the corner.

As she went downstairs, I made notes about the other paintings in the room and the abstract sculpture on the chest of drawers that might be an Arp. There were so many things to follow up on, especially my uncle missing a Chippendale chair. This wasn't a straightforward inventory at all. Was he setting me up to fail again?

11

On the wall of the back staircase hung an oil sketch of a nude by Laura Knight. It was breathtaking, and I had a hunch that it featured the same woman, Ella Naper, who had appeared in Knight's groundbreaking self-portrait. Knight's work had been a passion of my father's. Had he seen this? Grief hit and I almost doubled over with it. It didn't feel like he was gone, yet he was. The grief was followed by a flood of intense anger. This surprised me but I'd been left with a mess. Why was I having to fix this? I couldn't even fix myself. I needed to grow up and get a grip. No one prepared you for this. Maybe it wasn't possible. I was a head-in-the-sand – or in my case, a head-in-the-research – type of person, ignoring the world and all its problems. But that wasn't possible now. I loved my mother and wanted to help her. It was only a matter of working out how to.

My phone vibrated. Paul. Tash was right. This was distracting. Right now I had a raft of problems, including Stephen. I shoved the phone back into my pocket and walked into the kitchen. Tash handed me a mug of tea and a biscuit. 'I think the bookcase in the study is another Chippendale piece.'

'Really?' I dunked the biscuit.

'Ye of little faith.'

I flinched.

'Sorry, Ren.' She reached out to me, but I pulled back. 'I didn't mean that. Furniture isn't your thing and paintings are.'

'Well I don't do too well with those either.'

'Hogwash.'

'Tash.' I looked at the ceiling, seeing discoloration where water or damp must have come through at one point. It had been repainted, but it couldn't completely cover the mark. That was me. I tried to move past my error and yet I kept seeing it no matter what I covered it with.

'We all make mistakes.'

I laughed bitterly. 'Not ones that cost so much.'

'True.'

'It took years to fix too.' I looked around. Why was I here?

Tash threw an arm across my shoulder. 'You were young.'

'I was stupid.'

'Cautious.'

I drew a deep breath. 'I know, but . . .'

'It's history. As they say, let it go.' She waved her arms dramatically.

'Ha, easier said than done.'

Bastard appeared, then darted off. I jumped, and bumped into the wall, disturbing a painting.

Tash righted it. 'I love Sheba's work, and I'm not into modern stuff.'

I laughed. 'Yes, you always preferred the photographic type of art.'

'I do like me a bit of Monet too!' She placed her hands on her hips.

'Ah yes, the poster of the water lilies in your uni house.'

'Don't say I don't do culture.' She grabbed a biscuit.

'Never!' We had always disagreed on art, and on books too.

She liked fantasy and I preferred a good old romance. But I supposed both of us liked to be swept away somewhere else. What saddened me was that I no longer knew what she was reading. Or if she read at all. Annabelle was coming up to seven. Tash had said in the early years that sleep was rare and concentration was harder. I had commiserated, but part of me was jealous. Children were not on Paul's agenda. He'd said we would wait until I could look after myself. I'd been devastated at the time, but he was right and he'd only been thinking of me. When all of this was done, I would talk to him about it again. Neither of us was getting any younger. I was thirty and he was forty-five.

My phone vibrated and I smiled. He must have sensed I was thinking of him. His text said he loved me. Tash shook her head.

'I'm going to take a look at this bookcase,' I said.

'Don't believe me?' She stared at me all wide-eyed and innocent.

I laughed. 'I don't believe even I would have missed a Chippendale bookcase.'

'Fair,' she said, grabbing another biscuit.

Bastard was waiting for me by the main stairs. She kept close to my side as I stopped to view the portrait again. Together Tash and I should be able to take it off the wall and see if the reverse of the canvas would reveal its origin. But in the meantime, if there was a Chippendale in the study I needed to know, and if Tash could recognise it why hadn't my uncle?

I flicked the light on. The switch was an old Bakelite one. So much of this house was in a time warp, including the electrics. The only modern things were the later works of art, and Bastard. When I was in this room before, I'd been drawn to the desk. Tash had tidied all the paperwork into neat piles. With a clear view of the bookcase, I could see she was on to something. If it wasn't an original, then it was a damn fine copy. The piece was painted in what was called japanned decoration. The shelf height was adjustable, and what looked like doors on the bottom was actually a drawer. Pulling this open, I found it stuffed with notebooks and piles of letters. It was chaos. Had the women left it this way, or had someone been looking for something? There was a great deal of paperwork to be sorted.

'Am I right or am I right?' Tash leaned against the door frame with her arms crossed.

'I suspect you're right.'

'I know I am, because I saw its twin at the V&A two months ago.'

I raised an eyebrow.

'School trip.'

'Long way.' She hadn't let me know she was in London.

'We were there overnight and took in the V&A and the Science Museum.'

I looked at the piece, blinking. It stung that she hadn't been in touch.

'I messaged you.'

I turned to her, seeing a challenge in her eyes. 'I didn't receive it.'

'It said read. Both Annabelle and I were upset. I think she still is.'

'I would never hurt her.'

'I didn't think so, but she so wanted to see you.'

I pulled out my phone and scrolled through Tash's messages. 'When was the trip?'

'October.'

I kept going through until September. Nothing. I handed her my phone.

She scrolled and shook her head, then pulled out her own. She found the text in seconds.

Hi Ren, Chick and I are in London for two days with school and we'd both love to see you.

There were two blue ticks. I shook my head. 'I don't know what happened.' I hadn't read it, that much I knew. A sinking thought occurred that perhaps Paul had and hadn't told me. If he'd seen it first, he could have deleted it. But he wouldn't do that, even though he didn't like Tash. There must be another explanation.

'I'm sorry.' I looked her directly in the eyes. 'I will make it up to Annabelle.'

Tash nodded. I needed to be more engaged with the world. My life had become too small and I relied too much on Paul. We lived in his circle of academics, with only the crew of *Fake or Fabulous* for light relief. But by missing the text, I had failed Annabelle, and that cut through everything else. It was why I hadn't had a letter or a postcard from her.

'Apology accepted. But you'll have to negotiate with Annabelle yourself.'

'I will.'

'Good, now this.' She tapped the bookcase.

'It appears we may have two Chippendale pieces, and that means that this is not simply a small house clearance.'

'Did you think it was?'

I shrugged. Truthfully, I didn't know what to think. My father's notes were minimal, but he wouldn't have missed the Chippendales, let alone the Laura Knight. Something was odd here, and it wasn't simply my uncle's behaviour.

'What do you know about these two artists?' I asked.

'Me?' Tash pursed her mouth. 'You're the expert.'

'I wasn't living here when they died.'

'You don't need to remind me of that.' She played with the paperwork on the desk. 'It made the local papers, of course. Two women dead for at least two weeks.' She picked up a page and scanned its contents. 'Poetry, eh?'

'Yes,' I said, then it clicked. Simon Forster. There was the signed book of his work upstairs. Maybe they had kept in touch.

Tash went on. 'The gardener found them, which must have been horrific, but at least it was December.' Though even in the cold weather, bodies lying around that long couldn't have been pleasant. 'Oh, and Dad mentioned that because of the fire at Jim Fine's old place, they couldn't find the wills.'

'So there were wills.'

'Absolutely, he remembered filing them when he was a clerk there during his training.'

'But no copies?'

She held her hands out.

It was odd, but I wasn't here to solve the mystery of their deaths. I was here to value and sell the contents of the house. The only real puzzle was that of the painting in the hallway.

'Can you give me a hand with the portrait? I need to have a look at the back of it.'

Tash nodded and led the way to the stairs. 'We'll need a ladder.' She stood under the painting.

'I'll look through the outbuildings.'

Bastard followed me and sat patiently while I unlocked the back door. Outside the air smelled briny and of something sweet I couldn't quite pinpoint. A clump of daffodils with white petals and bright orange centres grew out of an old granite trough. One sniff told me they were responsible for the fragrance.

I hadn't noticed a ladder in Sheba's studio but there must be one in Vivian's. Many of her pieces were large. Bastard sat in front of the studio door. It took three goes to find the correct key, then the cat nosed the door open. Light flooded in from the skylights and illuminated a draped object on the left-hand side of the space. Overcome with curiosity, I pulled the dust cloth off and gasped. It was a sculpture worked in wood, not unlike the one that stood in the centre of the room. But this one was much larger, and it was complete. The piece of elm was old and the grain twisted like the sinuous shape of a dancer, picked out by dark threads running through it. It was spectacular.

I reached into my back pocket for my phone to take a picture. But it wasn't there. I must have left it in the study.

At that moment, Tash walked in holding it in her hand. 'Your phone was vibrating, so I answered it.'

I frowned.

'In case it was your mother.'

'Oh.'

Her expression was like thunder. 'Why do you put up with that?' she asked.

'What?' Without knowing what Paul had said, it would be best not to say anything.

'Before I could speak . . . he did.'

I hadn't replied to any of his messages. He must be pissed off. His temper could be sharp, but it was always short-lived. He needed to vent and then it was over. That was how he worked. It was the opposite of me. I held onto things and overthought them until I was tied in knots inside. I stroked the wood of the statue. I didn't want to hear Tash's take on this and it would be better not to know what he'd said to her. 'Have you seen this piece?' I asked.

'I mean seriously, Ren, that is not OK.'

I kept my gaze on the sculpture. 'He's missing me.'

'So he bullies you to show love? That's twisted.'

Her words hurt. Paul was great. Yes, a bit protective and at times needy, but weren't we all. 'He loves me so much, and he needs me.'

'He doesn't deserve you.' She paused, clenching her hands. 'You've changed. Gone is the fun-loving friend and in her place is a frightened middle-aged ghost of the former you. A bloody Stepford wife but without a ring.'

'No.' I felt the colour drain from my face. It wasn't that way at all. I might not do the same things I used to do, but Paul gave me confidence and supported me. 'You're wrong. He loves me and he . . .' I struggled to find the words to stop Tash thinking like this.

'He doesn't hit you, does he?'

'How could you think that?' I spun around to look at her. 'He loves me and he's lost without me. That's all.'

She handed me the phone. 'It didn't sound like love is all I'm saying.'

I took it from her and shoved it into my back pocket.

'When I finally got a word in edgeways, he hung up.'

That explained the current vibration in my pocket. He would text me until I responded. Somehow it would be my fault that he'd embarrassed himself, and it was. I should always have my phone with me. Now I pulled it out again and took several pictures of the sculpture. Tash stood in silence. There was no way I wanted to talk to her about Paul. Nothing I said would change her mind. I'd tried in the past to alter their opinion of each other, but if anything, they had both become more certain they were right.

I watched Tash out of the corner of my eye as she walked slowly around the sculpture.

'My heart aches looking at it,' she said, touching its surface. 'She's highlighted the gnarly bits and the places where the tree had suffered damage but grew on.'

I blinked. I hadn't seen that. Sometimes Tash startled me with her insights. She might be a brilliant accountant, but there was another side to her that I had forgotten. I was the one who had received an A in GCSE art, but she could have done a degree in it. Instead she had chosen the sensible path, while I had for the longest time followed my heart and my gut. No longer. Only when I had hard-and-fast proof did I give my opinion. This was fine, and I was never in front of the camera; I was simply the grunt in the background making everything look good and providing the interesting side alleys and rabbit holes so that they had a narrative to follow. The journey, the story, whether it ended with success or failure, had to be interesting. There must be highs and lows in each episode, but I tried to avoid them everywhere else.

'Thought it was you when I saw the car.' The gardener, Tilly, stood in the doorway with the sunlight at her back. 'Stunning piece, isn't it?'

I nodded.

'It was the last thing Viv did.' She shook her head slowly. 'Sheba had cancer, and Viv knew their time together was ending.'

'Was Viv ill too?' Tash asked.

'Didn't show it if she was.' Tilly stepped into the studio. 'She was as strong as an ox – had to be to work on these large pieces.' The phone in her hand rang. She glanced at it, then walked back out.

'Viv died of a broken heart.' Tash stroked the sculpture. 'She couldn't face life without Sheba.'

I pursed my lips. 'That sounds romantic, but she could have had a massive stroke or something.'

Tash frowned. 'I know what I see in this piece, and it's heartbreaking while still managing to express true love.'

Tash had never been the romantic that I was. What had changed her? She adored Annabelle, of course, and loved Gareth, though their relationship had never appeared on the outside to be a grand passion.

'It's a breathtaking piece, but what people see and feel about it will vary.' I bent to give Bastard a stroke.

'Really.' Tash stood back with her hands on her hips. 'Some art is like that, but this piece . . . it's the real thing. Raw, messy love.'

I studied it again. The wood was sinuous, and I could see what she was saying, but with art I didn't think things were that cut-and-dried. It hit everyone differently and could do so from one second to the next, let alone day to day. Today my impression was that the piece was beautiful and full of pain and loss. There was no love other than that shown by the artist for her materials.

Outside, Tilly's voice carried. What I really wanted to do was press her for details about these women. I needed to create a narrative around the artists to ensure we received maximum interest and price. Heading back to the house, I stopped in the brilliant sunlight. Something inside me wanted to make their work shine.

'Ren, where are you off to in such a hurry?' Tash was dragging a ladder.

I shook my head. 'Sorry, I forgot the reason I went in there in the first place.'

'Hmm.' She made a face. 'Take the other end, please.'

I did as I was told, and we manoeuvred the ladder through the kitchen and into the hallway. We could have used Tilly's help, but I heard a car leave and realised it would be up to the two of us to do this.

Tash looked from the ladder to the stairs to the painting and back again. The ladder was long, but it would still be too far away from the painting to safely take it off the wall.

'This isn't going to work,' she said, balancing it against the stairs.

'I can see that.'

'It's good you can see something.'

I sent her a look. That was a very sharp comment and had nothing to do with the task at hand. I wasn't sure exactly what she was referring to.

My phone vibrated away in my pocket. I whipped it out ready to shut it off, then saw that it was Mum's number.

'Mum?'

'It's Meg. Your mother has had a fall. We're at the hospital.'

12

I brought mugs of tea into the living room and handed them to Meg and Tash before sitting down. Mum was spending the night in hospital for observation. It wasn't clear if she'd simply misstepped and fallen, or had another stroke. Meg looked shaken. I was so grateful she'd been with her. This had underlined the fact that my mother couldn't be left alone, but how would this all work now without Dad? My plan had been to stay here long enough to finish probate. But it wasn't going to be that straightforward. In fact, far from it. Unless she improved dramatically, she would need full-time live-in help. Tomorrow I would begin looking at the options, after I'd spoken to her to see what she was thinking and feeling.

Meg cleared her throat. 'I hate to raise this now, but could you check why the standing order for my salary hasn't gone through?' Her glance darted about the room, taking in the antiques and artwork.

'Absolutely.' I gave her an encouraging smile. 'I'll ask my mother for her log-in details.'

She twisted the mug in her hands. 'I did ask her about this shortly before she fell.'

'The fall was not your fault,' I said.

'You had every right to ask that question.' Tash stood and walked towards the wood burner. The day was far too warm to require its heat, but it gave the room some life. Despite the familiar artwork adorning the walls, the house lacked something, and I wasn't sure what. It could simply be that I missed my childhood home.

'Whatever the problem is, I'll resolve it,' I said with more confidence than I felt.

'Right, in that case I'll be off. Call me in the morning when you know what's happening.' Meg rose and left. My spirits sank without her bright presence in the room.

As the front door clicked, Tash turned to me. 'Do you want me to make the first stab at your dad's desk, and also see if he noted down your mother's passwords?'

I frowned.

'It's what my parents do.' She laughed. 'Dad keeps a small spiral-bound notebook with all the passwords in it. Not very security-minded, but needs must.'

'Thank you.' My shoulders fell. She was being an absolute star.

'We've had quite the day, and I seem to recall your father had bloody good taste in wine.' She grinned, and it was clear she was thinking about the time we took a bottle from the cellar thinking no one would notice. But we'd pinched a bottle of Château Margaux and of course he had. The only thing he'd asked was whether we'd enjoyed it. That had been far worse than if he'd told me off, or grounded me, because he knew we hadn't. We'd already been drunk, and the quality of such a special wine had been completely lost on us.

'I'm sure I can find something.' I went to the dining room, where my father had relocated his wine collection, remembering how Paul had come straight here on the one night he'd stayed.

Without asking, he'd taken one of the finest bottles and opened it. He had drunk the better part of it himself, only thinking to offer my mother and me a glass when it was almost finished. When I'd raised the subject as we crawled into bed that night, he'd said he'd needed a drink to counterbalance the loss he'd seen on my face.

It hurt him that I was so broken by my father's death, and the last thing I wanted to do was hurt him. Tash was wrong about him, and about me. Yes, because Paul was older I did different things now, behaved differently, even sounded older. Tash's friendship had pushed me into the fray of life, but I'd always been a bit quiet. Paul brought this out in me and that wasn't bad. She only thought those things because they didn't get on.

My stomach growled. A lasagne would hit the spot tonight and I knew there was one in the freezer, so I looked for an Italian wine that would match it. Landing on a Barolo, I took it to the kitchen and opened the bottle before locating the pasta dish and placing it in the oven.

After I'd dropped off a glass of wine to Tash in Dad's study, I went to my mother's bedroom. Her tablet was beside the bed. If she had a banking app, it would be on this rather than her phone. She didn't keep anything important on her phone since having it stolen a few years ago.

The pile of letters of condolence teetered on the bedside table. I sank onto the bed. How was I supposed to handle this? Should I do it for her? I picked up the top envelope, which was already open. It was their latest bank statement.

The account was five thousand pounds overdrawn.

My hand shook. This made no sense. They'd sold the big house for a tidy sum, and Dad had always been careful with money. Never tight, but watchful.

'Ren, there's something you need to see.' Tash appeared in the doorway, staring at me. 'What's up?'

I held the statement out to her. 'What do I need to see?'

She led me to the study. 'Take a look at that.'

It was another bank statement. I scanned the page, struggling to breathe. Just two days before Dad had died, he'd made a payment of a hundred thousand pounds.

'Did you find any other statements?' I asked.

'Yes, there are large chunks of money going out every month, to the same recipient.'

'It can't be blackmail,' I said with more certainty than I felt. This explained why Meg's standing order hadn't been paid. What the hell was going on? Would there be a way to find out what was happening?

'Over the past year, your father has paid out about six hundred thousand pounds.'

'Seriously? That's madness.' I paused. 'That would be all the profit they made on the house after the purchase of this one.'

'Yup, and according to this,' she tapped the last statement, 'there was only five thousand pounds in the account at the start of the month.'

'The funeral cost a lot more than that.' I pushed my hair off my face. Did he and my uncle receive a salary from Barton's? I'd never paid attention to that type of thing when I had worked there. I'd been paid and that was all that mattered. But my mother needed money to survive and more money to thrive.

My phone rumbled in my pocket. It was Paul. 'I have to take this.'

Tash raised an eyebrow. 'Really? You've just discovered your father has shelled out over half a million pounds over the past year. Do you really need his shit as well?'

I froze for a moment, wanting to say something, but instead I accepted the call and walked into the kitchen. If he was going to shout at me, Tash didn't need to hear it. I didn't need to either, but I would.

'Are you ghosting me?'

I sighed. As if. 'Mum's in hospital.'

'What?'

'She had a bad fall and they don't yet know if it was caused by another stroke.'

'God, Ren, I'm so sorry.' His voice dropped to a soothing level. 'This is such a worry for you.'

I closed my eyes. He didn't know the half of it. 'It is.'

'You haven't replied to Jenny.'

'What?' I shook my head, trying to clear my thoughts.

'She's emailed you and you haven't replied.'

'How do you know?' I hadn't looked at my phone, let alone my emails, for hours.

'Umm,' he cleared his throat. 'She called me, concerned.'

'Really?' It was the weekend.

'Yes, she was checking on when you'd be returning to work.' He paused. 'They're getting ready for the new season.'

'They don't need me until they've chosen the objects.' I didn't need this right now.

'Not so sure. She's very keen about something.'

'OK, I'll call her on Monday.' I paused to prepare myself to ask the next question. 'Why were you talking to my uncle about me and saying I was vulnerable?'

'Darling, I'm worried about you and I thought he might be overloading you.' He drew a breath. 'Being executor of your father's estate is a big enough job already.'

I couldn't argue with that. 'Fair, but please don't intervene on my behalf again.'

'But I love you, and you don't stand up for yourself.'

'Please allow me to.'

'I'm only trying to help.'

It didn't feel that way. It was making everything harder, but I couldn't tell him that right now. 'I know.'

'I'm so worried about you. I miss you, and you need routine.'

I twisted the wine bottle on the counter, then glanced at the corkboard by the door, at the photo of Dad in his cycling gear. *Dad, what were you doing paying out huge chunks of money?*

'Ren, are you listening? Cornwall isn't good for you. Too many bad memories, and with your father gone it will make things worse. Think of your mental health.'

'I'm fine.'

'You're lying. I can tell. You always look after yourself last, and I bet you're paying too much attention to Tash. She sucks you dry.'

Tash had been nothing if not focused on me. Possibly a bit too closely, because I didn't like what she'd had to say about me and how I'd changed.

'She tells lies as well. She doesn't like me and she's jealous of the life we lead.'

'No she isn't.'

'She covers it well.'

I stood up straight. 'Look, I know you've never liked her, so I hardly think you're in a position to judge her and her life.'

'I don't like the way you are when you're around her. You change.'

I closed my eyes. 'I don't change. She simply brings out sides of me that you don't need.'

'That's one way of putting it. I bet the two of you have been drinking.'

I looked at my still untouched glass of wine. 'We haven't.' At least this was true.

'You don't lie convincingly, but that's something I love about you. I can read you so well.'

This was a trap. If I protested, it would tell him I'd lied to him; if I didn't respond, he would assume the same.

My phone buzzed. I glanced at the screen.

'That's the hospital. Bye.' I disconnected and breathed a sigh of relief.

'Ren Barton.'

'It's Dr Helmsworth. I just wanted to let you know that your mother did not suffer another stroke.'

'That is brilliant news.' I picked up the glass of wine. 'Is that something I should be watching out for?'

'Yes, but it's more the falling that could be the problem. If she breaks something next time, her recovery will be long and . . .' The doctor's voice trailed away. She didn't need to finish the sentence. The stroke had felled my mother and she'd turned from fit and fabulous to old overnight. Dad's death had added yet more years to her.

'Check in the morning. She may be able to come home tomorrow.'

'Thank you.' I put my phone down and took a big swig of wine, ignoring the taste of it, just looking for something to numb me a bit. Everything was too raw. This was why Paul didn't like me drinking more than a small glass. I softened and said things that were best left unsaid.

'How's the asshole?'

There was no pretence from Tash any longer. Both of them had dropped the veneer of polite tolerance.

'He's missing me.'

She rolled her eyes.

'The doctor rang. Mum didn't have another stroke.'

'Phew.' Tash raised her glass in a silent toast.

'She may be able to come home tomorrow, which leads to another problem. Paying Meg.'

'Does your mother have her own account?' she asked.

'Not that I know of.'

'Can you cover the bill?'

I drew a deep breath.

'Don't tell me, you only have a joint account, and Paul wouldn't like it if you paid for your mother.'

I looked down at my feet.

'Christ, every woman needs her own account. No excuses.'

I picked up the bottle of wine and topped up our glasses.

'Tonight we will open you an account and change your payment details so your money comes to you first and then you can pay into the joint account.'

'I don't . . .' I twisted the glass in my hands.

'You will not win this one. Don't even try.' She took a sip of wine. 'You are a self-employed contractor and a thirty-year-old woman who is clever enough to be in charge of her own funds, full stop.'

'But . . .'

'No, you used to have your own account and managed just fine.'

I couldn't deny this.

'You paid your rent and your taxes, and your overdraft wasn't that big.'

'I know, you don't need to tell me.'

'Clearly I do.' She took my arm and led me into the sitting room. 'Since you've been with him, I've watched that clever, impetuous, funny woman disappear, to become quiet, bland and quite frankly boring.'

'That's not true,' I said, though part of me agreed with her. I slumped into the sofa. 'My life in London is fulfilling and I live in a beautiful flat.'

'It's his flat, not yours.'

'He's my partner.'

'Is your name on the deeds?'

I pressed my lips together.

'Thought as much. But I bet your money pays the mortgage as well as his.'

'It's like rent.' I crossed my arms, willing her to stop.

'Is it? If you were renting, your landlord would pay for a new boiler, for the plumber, but that's not the case, is it?'

My feet twitched.

'I'm right and your feet prove it.'

Treacherous feet. I placed them flat on the floor. They had betrayed me so many times. If my thoughts were in turmoil, my feet wouldn't stay still.

'OK, you have a point.'

'I do.' Tash stood and grabbed my phone off the side table. She handed it to me along with my mother's tablet. 'First check to see if your mother has an account.'

I took a guess at my mother's password and hit the jackpot. It was a good thing I knew she'd once had a dog called Spot, and my father's birthday was obvious. But there was no banking app on the tablet and no messages from the bank in her inbox.

'So we struck out there. When she comes home tomorrow, you can ask the awkward questions.'

I nodded and opened my phone to find the app for our joint account.

'Right, you have any number of choices for banks. Any preferences?' Tash took the phone from my hands. 'I suggest you *don't* use the same one as your joint account.'

'No?'

'No. I use this one.' She pointed to the third one down on the Google search of online banks. 'If you get stuck, I can help.'

'OK.'

'You've got your driving licence with you?'

I nodded.

Before my glass of wine was finished, Tash had helped me to open a bank account of my own. 'Now you need to transfer in some funds. Fifty pounds will do.' She handed the phone back to me. I stared at it. If I did that, then he would know.

'What's wrong?'

'Can't I simply change the payment details on the invoices I send out?'

'You don't want him to know you've done this?' She raised an accusing eyebrow. 'Good communication makes good relationships.'

I couldn't argue with that. 'Even you have to admit that timing can sometimes be crucial, and also being face to face.'

'I'll give you that.' She opened her own banking app and immediately transferred fifty pounds.

'Tash, what?' I gave her a hard look.

'You can send it back when you've put some money into the account.' She crossed her arms.

'Fine, I'll do the work invoice right now.' I reached for my laptop.

'No, right now we are going to make dinner and drink some more of your father's lovely wine.'

'I don't often drink.'

'Good, it will be even easier to get information out of you.' She led the way to the kitchen.

'You could just ask,' I suggested.

'Ha, you know how to sidestep a question, but when you're drunk, the truth comes out. Do you remember when . . .' She raised her glass in the air.

'Do not go down that road.'

'Why not? It's fun.'

'For you.' I shuddered.

'Well, call it payment for lending you a hand with our two distinguished ladies.' She pulled out two plates and some cutlery. 'I mean, really, couldn't they have said in this day and age that they were a couple?'

'I know, typical of my uncle not to be direct, and also not to give me all the information.' I pulled the lasagne out of the oven. 'How did he miss the Chippendales?'

'That is odd, but then I've always found him shifty.'

I turned to her. 'Really?'

'Yes, really.'

As I put the food on the plates, I thought about Stephen. He was odd and awkward, but he was one of the best in the business when it came to furniture.

'Shall we eat here, or on our laps watching something mindless?' I asked.

'Here.' Tash brought the wine bottle over. My plan to remain silent had been foiled by that declaration. What did she want to know?

'So how's work?'

I blinked. That was not the opener I expected. 'Fine. Thankfully quiet at the moment while they put together the next series.'

'Do you find that it's enough for you?'

This was an even odder question. I studied her. 'I enjoy it.'

'But isn't it true that you could do this research in your sleep and it only occupies a small part of your time.'

That might be correct, but how would she know it?

'What I'm wondering is what you're doing with the rest of your time.'

'What do you think I'm doing?' I countered.

'I don't know, which is why I'm asking you.'

I picked up my fork. The bulk of my time was spent on the donkey work for Paul in his research. This she didn't need to know, because the first question she would ask me was whether I was being paid for it. And of course I wasn't. How could I be when it was just a bit here and a bit there.

'Does he still make you do all his research?'

I didn't answer.

'You didn't think I knew, but I did.'

'That was then.' I filled my mouth with lasagne so I didn't have to add anything further.

'And what about your master's? You'd written your thesis.'

'It wasn't good enough.'

Tash put her fork down. 'How do you know if you never submitted it?'

'I didn't need to.' I wanted to stomp my feet like an angry child.

'Because you were shagging a professor in the department and he told you it wasn't good enough.'

I played with my wine glass. 'What's up with you? Can you just stop?'

'I'm worried about you.'

'I'm fine.'

'Fine isn't fucking good enough. You deserve to be good and brilliant, and be shit sometimes and bloody marvellous other times. But you can't be fine all of the time.'

'Have you taken up psychology?'

'No, but it's not a bad shout.' She filled our glasses again.

'Look, don't worry about me. Let's discuss what I do going forward for Mum. I don't think she can live alone.'

'You're thinking of sheltered housing or assisted living somewhere?'

I nodded, though I couldn't hate myself more for this. But it was the only answer. Paul would never move to Cornwall.

'The activities and other people nearby might help.' Tash took another helping of lasagne. 'Unfortunately, that type of care doesn't come cheap.'

I closed my eyes. Why had Dad been paying out all that money?

I took a sip of wine. 'I need to work out what the business is worth and talk to my uncle.'

'I can work out the value for you.'

'Thanks. I just can't figure out what's going on with Dad's accounts.'

'We'll sort it out.' She pointed to the corkboard. 'I love that picture of your dad with his bike. Who would have thought all those years ago that Mr Tweed would end up a MAMIL.'

'MAMIL?'

'Middle-aged man in Lycra.'

'Tash!'

'Sorry, very poor taste even if true.' She stood, walked to my end of the table and wrapped her arms around me. 'Him dying is totally shit, but at least he was doing something he loved.'

I nodded, unable to speak.

'You have so much to deal with along with the grief.' She handed me a piece of kitchen roll. 'I'll go through your father's accounts and the business's.' She paused. 'But whatever is going on, remember it isn't your fault.'

I blew my nose. I wasn't so sure of that.

13

Venice

My days have developed a routine. I rise early and go out to sketch the fishermen, women doing their washing and children heading to school. I love the colour and activity of the market before tourists like myself appear. With the sound of church bells, the sight of nuns in habits and the aroma of exotic foods, Venice is wrapping itself around me. Each time I spy graffiti it strikes me how similar the less well-off places of the world are. Although the words are different from those in London and Paris, the styles used are so similar. It's as if the same person is creating their thoughts on the walls of the alleyways, or *calle*, as they are called here. Part of me loves that their opinions can be displayed, and the other part cries that the beautiful spaces are altered by them. What would otherwise be a peaceful view of water reflections on an umber wall becomes a dramatic statement of anger and outrage.

Each day I find something new. Some things are less appealing than others. It can be the lettuce leaves and other vegetables floating in the canal or the pickpockets who operate with impunity. Thus far I've been able to move freely, bringing as little attention to myself as possible, including from these thieves. My mother followed pretty much this same routine, as her diary outlined. There was milky coffee in the morning and bitter espresso after lunch. My afternoons are spent in my room, using the sketches for paintings. Each day my work becomes looser and more fluid. The morning sketches are fast but classic, while the afternoon paintings are inspirations and feelings wrapped together. The light in Venice dances off the water like it does at home. The canals capture it and throw it onto walls and washing lines.

I would like to say I think about Katherine less as each day passes, but that would be a lie. I wander the streets longing to have her at my side, to tell her every detail and hear her thoughts. Because I don't have her by me, I have written it all down or sketched it. Not as my mother did, though. I detail everything I think Katherine would love. It isn't a record of what I see but what I want to share with her. I must stop. I used to do the same with Nellie, and possibly I'm simply missing the friendship. In the weeks I've been here, I have not caught sight of Katherine once. This is best. I must forget her and fill my head with Venice, and not a Venice where I think I see the flash of her smile or the glossy crown of her head.

It is now 5 p.m. and the air is cooler, so I head out again. Today I take my sketchpad and watercolours and find myself in St Mark's Square. Of course, I have visited the square many times before, but usually in the early hours. Now it is full of people and pigeons. Locating an empty step, I sit and study the light on the basilica, then begin working furiously. I pencil in lines, then paint wet into wet so that the colours bleed together, catching the movement. Only if I look closely can I pick out the faint sketch of the church and the bell tower. Checking my perspective again, I see Katherine. I still. Sunlight falls on her dark head, turning the black to blue-purple in places. I toss aside the previous painting and paint directly onto a sheet of paper. It warps with the water and the colours slip, but in moments Katherine is looking out at me.

When I glance up, she is staring at me. A glow rises in me. She waves to me and my breath catches. This is what I've dreamed of, and now it's happening. I lift my hand to acknowledge her, but as I start to rise, I hear an English voice behind me.

'Katherine, there you are. Thought I'd lost you in these crowds. I'm desperate for a drink.'

The well-dressed woman joins her and they walk together right past me, Katherine's gaze fixed ahead. My face flushes with shame. I'm invisible to her. She has a new friend. What a fool I was to think she would remember me, a simple girl on the train, a diversion for the journey to make it less tedious.

* * *

The sun is hot and sweat trickles down my back. I have been here for hours. The young boy I've been painting is fidgeting, and I promise him another few centesimi. Someday his beauty will be altered by what happens in his life, but at this moment his face is angelic.

I add a few more strokes and he rises, unable to sit any longer. His hand is outstretched as he examines my work.

'*Bene.*' He takes the coins and runs off. I add a dash of cobalt to his shirt, then glance up to see Signor Rossi and Simon Forster. I look down, hoping they don't notice me. My hair is concealed by the hat I wear to shield me from the sun, so hopefully I am unrecognisable.

A shadow falls on my work. I brace.

'Signorina Kernow, how lovely to see you.' Signor Rossi bows.

'I agree, and I must say that is a fine painting. Katherine said you were talented.' Forster squints at the painting now in the full sunlight. The oils glisten and it will melt if I don't protect it.

'Thank you both.' I see my work through their eyes. It is proficient, but from my viewpoint it is lacking. It is not the type of painting I wish to do, but it was what my mother was painting at this point, just before she met my father.

'I think with such skills you will have many who will want you to paint them.' Signor Rossi notes my concern as I try and shield the canvas, and steps forward to block the strong light.

'Thank you.' I like him.

'Where are you staying so I may put people in touch with you?' He smiles.

'At a pensione near the Ponte delle Tette.' My room is clean and large enough for me to work in.

Forster turns to Rossi. 'Isn't that the area of prostitution?'

Rossi wiggles his hand. 'It is not so bad now.'

'That is not a proper place for an Englishwoman to be staying.' Forster fusses with the brim of his hat.

My hackles rise. 'It is fine, and it is what I can afford.'

He tuts. 'Actually, this could work quite well.' He pauses. 'Katherine and I have taken a place on the Grand Canal and I am about to travel with Serafino to work with Il Duce on his poetry. You could stay with her and keep her company.'

'That is very kind, but . . .' This would be awkward at best. Katherine doesn't want to see me again.

'And I will commission you to paint her just in the style that you have painted this urchin.' He turns to Rossi. 'This might be the answer to Katherine spending too much time with Lady Mary while I'm away. Although charming, she is not the best influence, as you must be aware.'

Rossi looks like he is about to say something, but stops. I

struggle to find the words to halt this madness. I'm angry for Katherine that Forster is trying to stop her from spending time with whom she wishes. But he is not a man to be thwarted and I can't deny my desire to spend time with her. I give in. 'Thank you.'

'Excellent. I will arrange for the collection of your things and you can be with us by this evening. Serafino, you will know just the people to sort this.'

Signor Rossi bows to me apologetically and they are gone. In the distance, I see a group of Blackshirts harassing a man. This sight has become too familiar, and their presence everywhere in Venice is like a pervasive storm cloud ready to wreak damage without warning. Despite the sunshine, I shiver as I pack my things.

The painting in my hands isn't bad. My goal is not to flatter but to paint the feeling underneath. I find I'm drawn more to colour and shape, with less focus on realism. I have tried this before but haven't trusted my work. But there is something about Venice that is opening the locks I set inside myself. Is this what my mother experienced?

* * *

The motor launch pulls up in front of the small palazzo set just back from the Grand Canal. I can't shake my unease. Katherine has had no say in my arrival. She is used to this, but it's not right. The memory of her ignoring me the other day still stings. I'm certain she saw me, yet she didn't acknowledge me. Now I will have to face her daily in this palazzo and paint her. Of course, I have done so already. Those paintings I left behind in the care of the signora who runs the pensione, and her words are still ringing in my ears. 'Bad men. No trust men. No good come from this.' Her English is broken but her concern was real and motherly. It almost overwhelmed me. It is only the desire to see Katherine again, which I can't deny although I want to, that has brought me here.

I tap the boat driver on the shoulder, because I have changed my mind. I must go back. This is wrong. I open my mouth to speak, but Katherine comes through the gate. All clear thinking disappears with her smile.

'I've missed you.' She holds out her hand. I hesitate only a moment before I take it. The fizz of connection between us startles me. It has not gone away. This is a warning.

'Simon tells me he's commissioned you to paint my portrait.' She pulls my hand through her arm, closing the space between us. Rose, jasmine and vanilla, her fragrance.

I have no voice to reply.

She points to the building. 'The villa is divine, with the most delightful roof terrace.' She grins. 'You'll be enchanted.'

My things are swiftly unloaded, and Katherine leads me away, saying, 'Let them deal with it all.'

We leave the water's edge and enter a walled garden facing the canal. Almost opposite is the unfinished palazzo, Palazzo Venier dei Leoni. It appears squat next to its stately neighbours, and the rough edges irritate me, but I can't say why. Even in my short time in Venice I've heard of the extravagant parties with exotic animals that have been held there. Marchesa Luisa Casati has been painted by so many artists, including Augustus John. The palazzo was hers, but things have not gone her way.

'I find this stretch of garden so soothing.' Katherine waves a hand at the roses and the manicured lawn. But it strikes me as odd. Most of the other buildings abut the canal directly, yet this one is offset and is smaller in stature.

'Gabriele D'Annunzio lived here for a while.'

'Who?' I ask.

She laughs. 'Of course you wouldn't have heard of him, but Simon talks of little else. He's an Italian fascist poet, and he had a long-running affair with Marchesa Casati.'

'Convenient location.' I glance over my shoulder.

'True. The poor woman made herself a piece of art and ended up bankrupt, from what I've heard.' Katherine pauses. 'I wonder what will become of the palazzo. I find myself trying to imagine how it would have looked had it been completed as planned with five storeys.'

The one in front of us is only three floors and feels modest. We enter on the ground floor straight into the salon. Instantly it is cooler, and as my eyes adjust, I see painted panels depicting rural life lining the walls, along with blistered mirrors in gilt frames. I catch a glimpse of myself in one. I appear like a soul covered in pox. I shiver and look to the ornate ceilings. Everywhere in Venice I've learned to look up. Sometimes the ceilings are covered in large sweeping murals, and sometimes intricate carved golden squares. I have yet to see two alike.

'On the ground floor you have the main salon, the petite one, the dining room and the kitchen and staff quarters.' Katherine takes my hand and leads me up a marble staircase. My heels echo as they hit each step. She only touches down the toes of her shoes as we climb.

'Our bedroom is here, and Simon uses the one next to us as a study.'

I peer through the doors to their bedroom, but the shutters are closed to keep out the fierce heat of the day. I'm left with the impression of intense reds, gold accents and sparkling glass.

'I've put you in the room above us, which has a wonderful view of the canal.' We climb the stairs and she sweeps open the doors. I gasp. Although not as large as their room below, it is far grander than anything I have ever known.

'I'm glad you like it, but what is truly wonderful is the roof terrace. I will show you later, when it has cooled down a bit.' She flicks on the light switch. The walls are covered in a blue-green moray silk, with the fabric's sensuous warp and weft creating the sense of being underwater. The light from the chandelier dances off it. It is soothing yet intoxicating.

'Tell me what you have done in the weeks since I have seen you,' she says.

'Sketch, paint, explore.'

She casts me a sideways glance. 'No lovely Italian lovers?'

I flush.

'You have.' The corner of her mouth lifts and my heart stills. 'I haven't.'

'What a shame.' She shakes her head. 'The men are ridiculously beautiful, so you should.'

'They are beautiful,' I agree, but only to paint. It is Katherine's beauty that entices me. But instead of looking at her, I study the ceiling. Frolicking cherubs cavort across it.

'It's all a bit overwhelming at first, but you do become used to it.' She takes my hand again. 'If it's too noisy or the light is wrong, do let me know.'

She opens the shutters. Sunlight streams in. Even this high up and set back from the water's edge, light bounces from the canal into the room, reflecting off the gold leaf on the ceiling and hitting the mirrors on the far wall. I don't know where to look. One side of the room is dominated by a large four-poster bed draped in rich purple velvet curtains. It is fit for a monarch rather than a young artist. At the foot of it is a bench, and there are also some gilded chairs and a large wardrobe. The chandelier sparkles and plays with the daylight flooding the room. I'm mesmerised.

'Is the light all right?' She touches my arm.

I nod. It is southern light, which isn't ideal, but with the shutters, I can control it.

She peers out of the window. 'I first came to Venice with my mother when I was ten. It cast a spell over me then and it hasn't let go.' She turns to me. 'Has it cast a spell over you?'

I meet her glance. 'Yes.'

'Good,' she says.

Two men walk into the room carrying my things, with a neat woman following.

'Sheba, this is the housekeeper, Signora Bocca. She looks after us so well. If you need anything, she will sort it for you.' Katherine picks up my hand again briefly. 'This will be such fun.'

Forster appears at the door. 'Ah, good, you've arrived.' He glances at my things and picks up the still wet painting of the boy. 'This is marvellous.' He holds the canvas out to Katherine. 'I wish for her to paint you in this style.'

Katherine glances from me to the painting.

The housekeeper looks as well, then says, 'I shall find something to cover the floor and the furniture.'

I smile my thanks. The last thing I need is to leave traces of my painting here in this beautiful room. It was never intended to be an artist's studio. The room in the pensione was spartan in comparison. Thankfully I left that without a spot of paint or a stray line of charcoal.

'I'm off to meet with Conte Volpi,' Forster says to Katherine. 'I don't know how long I'll be. What time are we due at the Contessa's?'

'Nine.'

He kisses her cheek and leaves.

'Signora, please see that Signorina Kernow has everything she needs.' Katherine waits for Signora Bocca's acknowledging bow, then says, 'I'm going to take a siesta. But do come and find me in an hour.' She slips out the door and the housekeeper and I look at each other.

'Welcome.' Signora Bocca's English is accented but her smile is genuine. 'I will be back.'

Once she is gone, I go to the window and peer out at all the activity on the canal. The vaporetti and the gondolas make it look busier than Piccadilly. Maybe with this new outlook I will find my way through all the things pulling at me. The painting that Forster wants me to copy is old-fashioned, reflecting my parents' work and the painters I spent time with in St Ives. They were wonderful, and the grounding that time gave me was important, but I want to move beyond. My fingers twitch. I long to start now, but I need to unpack.

The noise of the gondoliers calling to each other echoes off the garden walls below. Each day Venice is filling with more and more people as the summer season goes into full swing. I'm excited to attend the Biennale and see Winifred Nicholson's work on display. Although her husband's work is being exhibited there as well, Winifred is far better known and appreciated. However, I'm interested in the new directions both of them are taking. The selection team for the Biennale, I imagine, did not know of their split, or maybe they did and considered that would provide an interesting tension for the viewers.

The housekeeper returns, and between us we cover the floor and furniture with old sheets. The room looks like it is being packed away for the season, but soon all my paints, brushes and canvases are carefully arranged.

The sketchbook from the train journey is the last thing I unpack. My time in Paris and on the train feels distant, and Venice is all I can think about, along with Katherine, of course. Just the fact that she is sleeping somewhere close is unsettling. I go to the window and breathe in. Venice needs to seduce me further so I become immune to her.

14

The heat of the day has begun to ease. Church bells announce the Angelus. Although I'm not religious, there is something about the momentary reminder to pause, reflect and pray that I love. Below, the sounds of Venice soften and a light breeze picks up the scent of the roses growing around the edge of the terrace. Bees move from one lavender head to another with no urgency. The angle of the sun's rays has dipped, but there are still hours until sunset. The view is intoxicating, with bell towers, church domes and grand palazzos.

Katherine pours the contents of the mixer into two glasses. She hands me one. 'Now, tell me all that you have been up to since I last saw you.' She pauses and reads the surprise on my face. She asked the same question a few hours ago. 'You have clearly been hiding away, because I haven't spied you anywhere, and I have been everywhere.'

The memory of her looking straight at me the other day comes immediately to mind, but I choose not to mention it. 'I've been working in places you wouldn't go.'

She tilts her head in that way of hers and studies me for a moment. 'You do like the underside of things, or should I say you are drawn to them.' She raises her glass and her eyes dance with mischief. 'To our new adventure as artist and muse.'

Her words land a little too close to home and I try to swallow my concerns. In a way, she has indeed become my muse. She is always on my mind and now she stands in front of me dressed to join Forster later. The white satin gown slips down her frame. She is thinner than she was just weeks ago. The hollows under her collarbone are more pronounced. I long to trace them with my fingers, but I will sketch them later while she is out.

'What have *you* been up to?' I ask. We are standing side by side looking out on the Grand Canal.

'This and that. It's been a social whirl. The first week, without Simon, was a delight. Mary is fun and naughty, and it was lovely, to be honest.' She turns to me. 'You would have loved it. Girls together.' She sips her drink. 'But Simon leaves tomorrow and we shall be girls alone again.'

My mouth dries and the martini doesn't help.

'You've become quite thin.' She runs a hand down my arm. 'Does the food not suit?'

'I've been watching the pennies so that I can remain here longer.'

'I miss your curves.' She looks me up and down. 'It's a good thing you are here and not paying rent. We will feed you and I will make certain that Simon pays more than a fair price.'

'I'm not destitute.'

'I know, but I can help with some things.'

I begin to speak, but Simon appears. 'There you are.' He walks at us full throttle and I wonder if he'll slow down or go straight over the side, but he comes to an abrupt halt. 'I've written a poem that you must take a look at immediately.'

'But I'm just catching up with Sheba.' Katherine places a hand on my arm.

He glances at me as if he hasn't seen me before. Back to normal invisibility now that I have acquiesced to his plan.

'This is important. I want to have it ready for Il Duce tomorrow.'

Katherine suppresses a sigh and takes the paper he hands her. She smiles apologetically and disappears downstairs.

'You'll have plenty of time to catch up while I'm away, when you are painting my wife.' He pours the remaining cocktail into a glass.

'We will.' I look down, trying to appear grateful but not feeling that way at all.

'The German chancellor will be visiting Venice soon.' His face is flushed with excitement. 'I expect great things from Herr Hitler. Il Duce thinks he will be a true fascist ally.'

How do I reply to this? I have watched the Blackshirts around Venice and I'm no more impressed with them here than I was back home. However, this man is Katherine's husband, so I need to be polite.

'This whole movement is so exciting,' he continues, not needing anything more than an audience. 'It is the way forward, away from the socialists. They do nothing but hamper progress.'

I finish my drink. He presses a bell, and one of the men who sorted my things earlier appears and mixes more cocktails. I don't want another, but if he is going to talk of politics, I need to be intoxicated. In the distance, a church bell chimes.

'If you'll excuse me for a moment,' I say.

'Of course.'

Swiftly I go down the stairs towards the lavatory. I pass an open door where Katherine sits head down as I saw her on the train. From this angle her absorption in her task is evident. She has crossed through every line and rewritten it. She pauses and looks towards the window, mouthing the words, changing them again. Nothing of Forster's work remains. The truth hits me. She is not an editor but the poet.

I sway, reaching for the wall for balance. I'm furious at the way he dismisses her. The woman who has written the words that he is accepting the praise for. I don't know where to put myself or the anger I'm feeling.

Quietly I move on, but Katherine looks up. We both freeze. Her glance meets mine. Something has changed.

'You are the poet, not him,' I blurt out as if she was unaware of it.

She narrows her glance but doesn't say a word.

'You are an artist with words.'

'No.' She shakes her head. 'I dabble and think too deeply.'

'He uses you.' I exhale, angrier than I have been since my stepmother told me to leave.

'I cannot give Simon the child he desires, so I provide an editing service instead.'

'I see what you do. It isn't editing. The only thing that remains is the title.' I step closer and point to the rewritten poem.

She grimaced. 'That was one I suggested.'

'How do you bear it?' I couldn't. I wouldn't live under anyone's thumb, providing my work for their glory. It is wrong.

'Lie back and think of England, dear.' She laughs and picks up the paper, leaving me standing speechless.

In the lavatory, I cool my face with water. Slowly my anger fades. Only when I'm back in control of my emotions do I return upstairs. But Signor Rossi is now with Forster. More cocktails are being poured and the housekeeper brings us some appetisers. The Venetians never serve only a drink. It always comes with a small sandwich, a piece of cheese or spicy meat. I enjoy the balance of the alcohol with the food.

'Signorina Kernow, will you be joining us this evening?' Rossi asks.

I shake my head. 'I need my beauty sleep.'

'You are very beautiful indeed, in such an English way, with your glorious red hair. Very Titian.'

I hide my smile behind my hand. My hair is all that is Titian about me. Serafino Rossi is a kind man, even if I don't like his politics. He is difficult to read yet he reminds me of a friend of my father's who would agree with whatever you were saying as long as it was expedient for him.

'Are you all set to paint the beautiful Katherine?' he asks.

'I need to properly set up my work space and also see where it will be best to paint the portrait.'

'I've been thinking about that,' Forster says, picking up a rolled piece of meat. 'I think the view from our bedroom is just right. You can see the Grand Canal and the garden. It will set off her beauty.'

I nod, but from what he is saying, Katherine would be backlit, which would make the task difficult. If I could paint her up here in the golden evening light, it might work.

'I will have Katherine show you tomorrow.' He turns to Rossi. 'I'm just going to check on her.'

Rossi steps closer to me. 'Have you been to the Biennale yet?'

'Not yet, but I have a ticket for the fifteenth.'

'I think you will find much to admire and stimulate you.' He waves his hands about as he talks.

'Venice itself fills me with inspiration. Viewing other artists' work is energising and at times daunting.' I pick up a small piece of cheese.

'In what way?'

'Well, I love seeing how another artist has interpreted something, be it what they see, feel or hear.' I sigh. 'But sometimes I'm overawed by their genius.'

He laughs. 'I see, indeed I do. You think they have not stood where you are and were always so brilliant?'

'Exactly that.'

'I tell you, Signorina Kernow, it is by striving that we make the great. It is only by pushing ourselves that we attain the higher . . . the higher reaches.'

I can't deny this.

'The painting of this morning was most excellent, but I think it was not the painting of your heart.'

'True.' Technically it is strong, but there is no insight. That requires taking time and risks. The latter is the difficult part. I've always chosen the safer option.

'To be good . . . special, it needs to reach further.' He places his glass down and opens his hands outward.

'It does.'

He looks me directly in the eyes. 'Just remember that as you reach further, you will leave many behind you.'

I frown.

'I mean not only other artists with your skill, but also viewers, those who enjoy the art but do not create.' He waves his hand in the air. 'The more different and unique your vision, your work becomes . . . the smaller the audience will be that will appreciate it.'

I take a sip of my drink, letting his words sink in.

'This morning's work could be sold a thousand times to people as different as they come.' He points to the canal below us. 'The beauty is visible, obvious, but say you paint something like your fellow countryman, Nicholson, then there will be fewer people who will see its value.'

I nod.

'We all have decisions we need to make along our journeys. Do we please the many, or do we travel our own route and possibly please only ourselves?' He picks up his glass. 'I wonder what you will do, Signorina Kernow. You have the skill to be the artist you wish to be, but only time will tell what road you will take.' He nods. 'I for one will watch your journey with interest.'

'I've found Katherine,' Forster calls from the other side of the terrace. 'And it's time for us to set off.' Together Rossi and I walk towards him.

Katherine stands by the door. Her expression speaks of sadness laced with tolerance.

'And bless her, she's located the poem I was telling you about. I'm so pleased to be bringing it with us to Milan tomorrow.' He ushers Rossi off the terrace, not even acknowledging my presence. Part of me is grateful and another part is angry. I'm a human being who should be given some respect. But to him, and men like him, I am no more than someone who provides a service.

With that thought, I top up my cocktail and watch the setting sun. I'm not here for ever and I need to make the most of the time. That includes painting, studying and learning. I will paint Katherine for him so that it will please him. And then I will paint her for myself.

15

Penzance

I ignored my hangover as Tash and I worked through Harbour House. Drinking had not been a good idea. I was grateful Mum wasn't being released until this evening so we could continue here. But the portrait in the hallway would have to wait until I had the right type of ladder to reach it safely. So with a slightly sore head, I looked through the desk for details of paintings purchased or received from friends. Provenance was everything in this game.

In the bottom drawer I found letters and what looked like a manuscript. It was poetry, beautiful love poems. They sounded like the work of Simon Forster. Even with a quick read I knew it was important. The manuscript had no title page or author, so I typed a few lines into the search engine to see if the work was already published. There were no matches, but it suggested other Simon Forster poems.

Leaning back in the chair, I tapped the desk, trying to think. An expert in poetry was needed. The first person to come to mind was Rory Crown, who featured in a series about poetry and literature. I'd never met him, but he was on the faculty of the university with Paul. Paul had been disparaging about him, saying that Crown spent most of his time making the programmes and not doing any proper scholarship.

I picked up the manuscript and went to find Tash, who was in the sitting room, cataloguing the books there.

She glanced up from the floor, where she sat cross-legged. 'You've made tea?'

'No, I bring you love poems.' I handed the manuscript to her. 'I'll go and make the tea now. It might help my head.'

'Don't forget the biscuits, too. Need something to sop up that second bottle of wine we drank last night.'

'Don't remind me.'

'I'll never let you forget.' Her laughter followed me down the hall.

Unlike yesterday's sunshine, today was dull and cold, as if winter had returned. The sea was the colour of mercury. On the horizon, sunlight pierced the cloud, creating a bright white line near the horizon. Below the house, the harbour was quiet.

Tea made, I grabbed the packet of digestives and returned to the sitting room, where I found Tash in tears. 'What's wrong?'

'This.' She held the script open and tapped the page. 'So damn beautiful.'

I shook my head. Poetry had never moved me that way.

'Just read it. It's all about saying goodbye because there is no other choice and how love can't win, not this time.'

She blew her nose and bit into a ginger nut.

Left the unsafe harbour
Sailed the uncharted sea
Have tasted paradise
Have lived hell

Ignorance would have saved me
But experience arrived
Damning me
You do not know
I cannot tell
A choice so bitter

I swallowed a lump in my throat. It was pretty emotive stuff even by my reckoning.

'I thought Simon Forster hadn't written any more after his wife and daughter were killed in the Blitz.' Tash brushed crumbs off her lap.

'He didn't, according to the internet, but what if . . .' I put the script down and picked up my mug. 'I ran a few of the lines through Google, and it appears that these poems have never been published.'

'Well they should be.' Tash grabbed another biscuit.

'Agree, but we need an expert.'

'Have someone in mind?' she asked, getting to her feet.

I perched on the sofa. 'Rory Crown.'

'He's divine, and I could listen to him read poetry to me all day long.'

I laughed. 'Does Gareth read poetry to you?'

She stood up straight. 'Actually, yes.'

'Oh.' That was unexpected.

'Don't sound so surprised.' She pulled out her phone. 'I saw something in the local paper about Rory Crown.'

I frowned. I didn't associate him with Cornwall. He was Scottish and lived in London.

'Here it is.' She held out the phone. 'He's here at the moment launching a prize for historical fiction in the name of his former lover, Hebe Courtenay.'

'Former lover?'

'It's such a sad thing. She died at the age of fifty-four of early-onset Alzheimer's.'

'Fifty-four?' I knew he couldn't be more than thirty-five.

'She bought Helwyn House over near the Helford River, and her niece, Lucy, is running it as an arts centre along with her husband, that hot actor Kit Williams.'

I whistled. Kit Williams was fit, but I'd had no idea he lived in Cornwall. 'How do you know all this stuff?'

'I pay attention to the world I live in.' She sipped her tea.

'Ouch.' I held my hands up, but she was right. My world was very small, and that made it easier and safer.

'According to this article, the launch is tomorrow. Shall we go?' Her face lit up.

'No, I don't have the time.' I sighed. A day out with Tash would be bliss. 'I'll email him.'

'Damn, I'd love to see the place.' She took another biscuit.

'Isn't it open to the public?'

'Sort of, but every time they've done an exhibition or something, I've been busy, and as you know, this week I'm all yours.' She grinned.

Closing my eyes for a moment, I travelled to the Helford. It was a favourite place of my parents', and I'd sailed there when I was small. I opened my list of things to do and checked I'd put 'sell boat' on it. There were so many things going on that I was losing track. 'Let's see what he says when I email.'

'Well, do it now and then get back to work. I've finished all the books in here.' Tash sipped her tea. 'What's next?'

'There's a lot of correspondence and all in a mess.'

She rolled her eyes. 'Will hunting.'

'No doubt. I think we should put it all out on the dining room table and begin to organise it by date.'

She saluted and headed to the study, while I quickly drafted an email to Rory Crown.

* * *

Mum beamed at me when I collected her from the hospital, but as soon as we reached the house, she shrivelled. There was no other word for it. It wasn't my idea of home either, but I could see how it would make things easier than our old house. That had been filled with draughts, character and more staircases with differing levels than seemed possible. God, I missed it, and it was clear she did too. She and Dad had had so little time together in this one to make it theirs, and now it was just hers.

Once I had settled her in a chair in the sitting room, I went into the kitchen and popped another one of the many dishes from the freezer into the oven.

'Would you like a cup of tea?' I called to her, though despite this morning's hangover, I felt something stronger was required. Money was not something my mother and I ever talked about. Now it was clear we should have. There was no putting this discussion off.

'I'd love a whisky,' she said.

I popped my head through the door. 'Really?'

She nodded. Who was I to argue?

Once I'd poured two large measures, I joined her in the sitting room.

She took the glass. 'There's something I need to tell you.'

I sank into the chair opposite and waited. If she had said these words to me two days ago, I would have been surprised. Her life had been an open book of community service, first by teaching, followed by volunteering. Now I wasn't so sure I knew my parents at all.

'I'm listening.'

'Something is wrong.' She drew a breath. 'Two days ago, I called the bank to check why Meg's payment hadn't gone through and discovered we had exceeded our overdraft.'

My phone vibrated repeatedly and I cursed Paul, who was bombarding me with messages right when I needed to focus on Mum. He had to stop. A few texts were supportive, but this was too much. It was becoming a burden, and I had enough going on at the moment.

'I don't understand fully.' My mother took a sip of the whisky and smiled and winced at the same time. 'But the bank . . . explained that your father had been transferring . . . huge chunks of money into some account.'

I nodded.

'You don't think he was having an affair?' She drew a breath. 'Has a love child and was being blackmailed?'

I wanted to laugh, but my mother was ghostly pale and still. It was then that I could see the effects of the stroke on her beautiful face.

'I saw the bank statements,' I told her, 'so I knew something was happening, but the thought of Dad having an affair or a love child never crossed my mind.'

'He was human.'

'True, but never was a person so devoted to another as he was to you. I've been with him when women threw themselves at him, and he just wasn't interested.'

She visibly relaxed into the chair.

'But the money is a huge worry.' Behind my mother's head was her favourite painting. It was a Laura Knight of the cliffs near Lamorna, with a lone woman looking at the view. That painting alone might be worth half a million. Last September her painting of Sennen Cove had gone for over five hundred thousand pounds, becoming the top-selling lot in the sale. The estimate had been for between sixty and eighty thousand pounds. Bonhams had put together a wonderful selection of modern British women artists. Dad had met me in London for the preview. But how could I ask my mother to sell her favourite painting?

'What should I do?' she asked.

I twisted the glass in my fingers. 'Do you have an account of your own?'

'Just an old Premium Bond one.'

'Can you liquidate it?'

She nodded.

'May I ask how much?' I prayed it would be a substantial amount.

'Five thousand.'

That wouldn't last long.

'I'm so sorry you're being dragged into this, darling. I know you want to be in London with Paul.'

I nodded without giving it too much thought. Both London and Paul were far away from my current concerns. The first one was how to pay for Mum's carer.

'We need to talk to Stephen.' For days I'd done everything to avoid talking to him and at the same time trying to. Tash didn't like him, which she'd made clear the other day, but neither she nor I could pinpoint when I'd first taken against him.

'He's all right, you know.' My mother smiled. 'He is an acquired taste, though.'

'One I've never acquired.' I sipped my whisky and let it burn in my mouth before swallowing.

'Not true. You actually loved him when you were little.'

'Funny, I don't remember that.'

'Well, after, you know . . .' She looked down. 'He became a bit unbearable because his side of the business was doing well and it took your father a long time to rebuild.'

I blew out a massive amount of air. I couldn't apologise again for something I'd already said a million sorries for. It was the defining moment of my life. There was the happy Ren before, when she'd had everything going for her, and the reclusive Ren after. I'd settled well enough into my post-fuck-up life. And to prove it, my phone vibrated again.

'Is that your lovely man? Do you need to call him?' Mum smiled encouragingly.

'Right now, you're my focus, Mum.' Not Paul's needs and wants.

The phone rang. I was about to kill it when I saw it was Jenny, the producer of my TV show. 'I need to take this.'

'Go ahead.' Mum leaned back in her chair.

'Hi, Jenny,' I said, walking into the kitchen.

'Where are you?' she asked.

'In Cornwall.' I checked on the casserole.

'You said you were going to be back in London and I wanted you to come into the office first thing. There's an exciting project afoot.'

'What?'

'You emailed,' she said.

'I didn't.'

'You did. I'm looking at it.'

'This is crazy. I must have been hacked.' I put the phone on speaker and went to my emails. 'Which account did it come from?'

'Both.'

I hadn't looked at my personal or work mailboxes in days, even when I sent the email to Rory Crown.

'Can you get into your accounts?' she asked.

'Yes,' I managed to say as I saw at least ten emails that I didn't write. 'I can see the ones to you and I can tell you I didn't send them.'

'You'd better change your passwords immediately.'

'Yes.' But even as I said it, I knew who had sent them. I'd been hacked by my partner. He could access my mail from the desktop computer at home and he'd been busy telling people I was back and would be working from Monday. That was wishful thinking on his part.

'Jenny, I won't be able to work for you for the foreseeable future. Things here are pretty messy.'

'To be honest, I was surprised to hear from you so soon. Delighted but surprised.'

'I'll give you a call next week, when I may have a better idea of my timing.'

'OK. Take care of yourself,' she said.

I thanked her, put my phone down and opened the oven. Did I confront Paul, or did I simply change my password and move on for now? It would be easier to talk to him in person, but I didn't see that happening any time soon.

I dialled his number right away. It was best to sort this now. *Violated* was the word in my head.

'Ren,' he said. In the background I heard voices and music. He was out. 'How's your mother?'

'She's home.'

'That's great.' He paused. 'Look, I'm not at the flat at the moment.'

'I can hear that, but we need to talk right now about my emails.'

'Oh, that. I was just giving you a hand, as I know you have so much to do and you always put yourself last.'

'You should have told me.' I drummed my fingers on the counter.

'You're right, I should have. But when have we had a proper chat? You don't respond most of the time, and if you're doing that to me, imagine how Jenny felt with your lack of response.'

'But—'

'Look, I'm just helping. You weren't replying, which isn't professional.'

'No, but—'

'I've got to go. Talk tomorrow.'

The phone went silent. I stared at it and the picture of us on the lock screen. It was a selfie I had taken in the flat. Did we ever go out anywhere other than with his friends? I scrolled through the pictures. The only ones taken outside of the flat were from my morning run or pictures of women's art that I used for Instagram. Was that my world?

I heard my mother in the sitting room. There were more important things to address right now. Fixing things with Paul would wait until I had helped Mum and found out where all their money had gone.

16

4 April 2022

———————————

The rain pelted down as Tash and I entered Barton's at five the following morning. Stealth was essential, as I needed to delve into the accounts without my uncle hovering. Before I had the conversation with him, I needed the facts. Whatever was going on, he'd make it mine or my father's fault, and maybe it was. But I didn't think so.

As I unlocked the building, familiar smells surrounded me and a wave of grief wrapped around me again. All the early mornings here with Dad, drinking sweet milky tea while I helped him sort through paintings before viewing days, came rushing back. Tash gave my hand a squeeze.

'Point me in the right direction.'

I went into my uncle's office and powered up his computer, then found the keys for his filing cabinet. Many years ago I had seen him write his passwords down in a small notebook that he kept in there. Sure enough, the book was there when I delved to the bottom of the top drawer.

'OK, what's his password?'

In the book I found the last one jotted down and read it to her, then I flicked through the other files. One was labelled *Property*, another *Home*, and so forth. He clearly kept his personal stuff here in the office.

'Have you heard back from Rory Crown?' Tash asked.

I drew a deep breath and opened my inbox. There was an email from Rory that had arrived after I'd spoken to Paul, and there was a reply to it not written by me. How could Paul have done it again after I'd told him not to? Shit. I should have changed the passwords last night, but I'd been focusing on my mother.

Paul's reply was simply weird. Thankfully Rory had included his number on his email, and I almost called but then remembered it was only 5.15 a.m. I took a screenshot of his number, because I couldn't be sure what Paul would do. This behaviour was new. I needed to change my passwords now. One by one I did them, including Instagram. Paul hadn't left that alone either. His posts were cringey and I deleted them all.

'What are you doing?' Tash asked.

Feeling guilty, I looked up. I could lie, but it wouldn't help anything. 'I'm changing all my passwords. Paul has been replying to my emails and posting on Insta for me.'

Her face froze. 'That is wrong, so wrong I'm not sure I have the words for it.'

Not trusting the right reply to come out of my mouth, I nodded.

'In other news, I'm in.' She pointed at the screen. 'Can you make me a coffee and let's see what I can find.'

Leaving her to it, I went into the main office and boiled the kettle. Marcia's desk was cleared and ready for the day. A large calendar on the wall listed preview days, sales and when my uncle or I were out of the office. I could see where Marcia had erased my father's name, and my heart stopped. He should be here, not me.

'Bingo!' Tash called.

'Be there in a minute.' I spooned instant coffee into the cups, added milk to mine then topped them both up with hot water.

'Oh my.' Tash pushed back from the desk. 'There's something very wrong here.'

Placing the mugs down, my hands shook. These were words I didn't want to hear. What I needed to hear was that the accounts were fine and the business was sound.

'What is it?'

'That I can't tell you yet, but I can see that things aren't right. It will take me more time than we have right now to work through this.'

'How much time?' I asked.

'I might need an all-nighter.'

'Well, you have two hours to safely work before anyone will appear. I'll go through things in Dad's office.'

'Your office, you mean.'

I made a face at her, then set an alarm on my phone. I didn't need for Tash to be sitting at my uncle's desk and have him stroll in.

Once the desktop in Dad's office had powered up, I began going through his emails looking for clues to what the hell was going on. I sorted them by topic, and then by date. Nothing jumped out at me, nor did any name look unfamiliar or too repetitive.

How was I going to fix this? My mother was relying on me in more ways than one. With all that needed to be done here at Barton's, she would need help six if not seven days a week. Today Meg was coming in. I'd borrowed the money from Tash to pay her until Mum could liquidate her Premium Bonds later today. Last night I'd helped Mum set up a new account. We didn't need her to put that money into the joint account and see it disappear into the overdraft.

In what felt like no time my alarm went off. Tash and I put everything back just as it had been, including the password book after I'd photographed the pages. That made me feel like a thief, but needs must.

'Hey, isn't that your father's writing?' Tash dug some papers out of the bottom of the drawer.

A quick glance confirmed this.

'Odd that these were sitting under the files.'

'Very,' I said, scanning the pages. 'It's his notes for Harbour House.'

'Jackpot,' Tash said, leading the way to Dad's office, where she began printing off the inventory we had done thus far.

'Someone's keen.' Marcia popped her head round the door.

'Could say the same of you.' I glanced at my watch.

'Couldn't sleep and there is always something to be sorted here.' She yawned. 'Shall I make a proper pot of coffee?'

'That would be wonderful.' Tash grinned. 'This was nothing more than coloured water.' She handed over her mug.

Once Marcia had gone, I rested my head on the desk.

'What's up?' Tash asked.

'I can't do this.' I sat up.

'Can't do what?'

I waved my hand around the room. 'This, all of this, being secretive and, well, Mum and everything.'

'Hold on. You've always done secretive.' She placed her hands on her hips.

'That was ages ago, when we were teens.'

'Still counts, and shows you have the skills even if they are a bit rusty.'

'Throwing my mother a surprise birthday party hardly counts.' I smiled at the memory.

'It does, because you have to be very devious to evade detection. Your mother did not want to celebrate her fortieth.'

'True.' It had been a great party.

'See, you *can* do it.'

I accepted my defeat and a cup of coffee at the same time.

'How's Harbour House coming along? Any surprises?' asked Marcia.

'Plenty,' said Tash, taking her coffee. 'A couple of Chippendales for one, and the list goes on.'

'Are you sure?' Marcia asked.

'Tash is right.' I opened the photos on my phone. 'Here, take a look.'

Marcia whistled.

'I know.' I took a sip of coffee and glanced down the corridor. 'What was Stephen thinking when he said there was nothing worth over a hundred pounds?'

She frowned. 'Maybe he's testing you.'

'The thought had crossed my mind.'

'He shouldn't be stooping to that level.' Tash thumped her mug down. 'Seriously, that is childish.'

Marcia shook her head. 'You were right to be cautious.'

'Thank you.' I smiled at her. 'Your faith means a lot.'

'Your father believed in you too, don't forget that.' She gave my arm a little squeeze and went to answer the phone.

'Something smells decidedly off.' Tash opened a filing cabinet. 'I can't put my finger on it, but trust me, I will figure this out.'

'I don't doubt it.'

'Best not to. Underestimate me at your peril.' She smiled wickedly over her shoulder.

'I'd never dare to, but it's best to keep your estimations low for me.'

'That is utter bollocks.'

I bit back a response.

'Cat got your tongue?'

'I've learned over the years that sometimes it's best not to disagree with you.'

'See, that proves you have sense.' She turned, holding out a file. 'Take a look at this.'

The file contained a breakdown of all the auctions for the last ten years, with the overall sales total, highest-value items sold and profit after expenses. After just a quick glance, and with the exception of the sale of three Stanhope Forbes paintings, the highest-earning auctions were the furniture ones, and many had at least two pieces that had fetched remarkable sums. This totally contradicted the market for these years.

'It's not right, is it?'

'It can't be.' There were a few sales with a pencil dot next to them. The marks looked fresh, like Dad had been working through this recently. I went back to his computer and scrolled through his most recent documents. Sure enough, he had updated this one ten days before he died.

'What do you think is going on?' Tash asked. 'Is someone shill bidding? Is that the correct term?'

'It is, but I'm not sure if that's what we're looking at here.' My heart sank. Shill bidding – falsely bidding to push up the price of an item – was not only reckless but illegal. If someone was caught doing it, reputations could be lost, and if the auction house was found to be involved, it would mean an immediate closure and probable lawsuits. 'I'm just going back to the sales that he's marked in pencil to see if there's anything that jumps out.'

'I'll get more coffee.'

I grabbed a clean sheet of paper and tried to discover what my father had been looking for. By the time I'd reached the tenth sale, it was apparent that certain pieces had blown through the estimates and sold for record-topping amounts. However, there was no link between them that I could see. One was a George III desk, another a set of Regency dining chairs, and another a four-poster bed.

'Well?' Tash put the mug in front of me.

'Nothing immediately obvious, except that if you wanted to sell a piece of furniture and get top price for it, Barton's was the place to do it.' I pointed to the screen. 'The estimate for this Welsh dresser was a thousand pounds. It went for six in the end.'

'For a dresser? Had a celebrity owned it or something?'

'It doesn't say, but roughly every third furniture sale, something went way above the asking.'

'How far above?'

'Sometimes . . .' I paused to look at the screen, 'ten or twenty times.'

'Bloody hell. The business accounts should be in golden shape then, but as we saw this morning, they aren't, and nor is your father's personal account.'

'What's happening here doesn't just smell, it positively reeks.'

'Here early, I see,' my uncle said, popping his head into the office. I covered my father's notes for Harbour House with the inventory. The last thing I wanted was for him to know we had been through his office.

He scowled when he caught sight of Tash. 'What brings you here?'

'Giving Ren a helping hand.'

'Kerensa needs all the help she can get,' he said as he walked off.

I rose from the chair and Tash pushed me back into it. If she hadn't been here, I might have punched him. But why? He was absolutely right.

17

Newlyn

'Hello, Ren Barton.' I answered the phone automatically on the car speaker as I turned into the drive at Harbour House.

'It's Rory Crown.'

Tash poked me in the side.

'Thank you for coming back to me.'

'How can I help?' he asked.

'While sorting through the estate of two artists, I've come across a manuscript of sorts filled with poetry, incredible poetry. From what I can tell it has never been published, but it reminded me of the work of Simon Forster.'

'Interesting. Is there any connection that you are aware of between the artists and the poet?'

'Only a signed edition of one of his books that we've found so far. The paperwork in the house is in a bit of a mess, as people were hunting for wills.'

'You're in Penzance, yes?'

'Yes, although at the moment I'm in Newlyn, at the home of the artists.' Sun broke through the cloud cover and bathed the house in light for a brief moment.

'Will you be there for long? Is that where the manuscript is?' he asked.

'The answer to both is yes.'

Tash gave me a big thumbs-up.

'Great. If you text me the address, I'll be there in an hour.'

'That's wonderful. Thank you.'

Tash looked at me with the biggest grin while I texted the details.

'He is the sexiest man.' She practically swooned. 'He could read the phone book to me and I'd—'

'Stop. He's a professional, we're asking for his assistance.'

'He can assist me with anything,' she said, getting out of the car. 'He's divine.'

I opened my mouth to disagree but couldn't. He *was* divine. Because Paul disliked him, I could only binge his series in peace when I was out of the house, at the library or museum. With his delicious Scottish accent and way with words, he had seduced most of his female viewers. The way he read a poem was enough to have you begging him to take you to bed. I blinked. I must put those thoughts firmly away, especially as he would be here shortly.

'I told Gareth that if Rory Crown ever made a pass at me, I wasn't saying no,' Tash added. 'And *his* one pass is with Margot Robbie.' She grinned. 'Fair is fair. I wouldn't blame him for Margot, as I could quite fancy her myself.'

I burst out laughing.

'That's much better. The whole journey here you looked like death.' She stopped halfway to the door. 'Do you think if we ask he might recite John Donne to us?'

'Probably not, if he doesn't want us in puddles of desire on the floor. But he might read the poetry in the manuscript aloud.'

'That's some pretty hot stuff.'

'It was intense, but . . .' I sent her a look. Had I missed something, or was I just numb from too much going on?

'I couldn't resist reading a little bit more, and it gets quite spicy.'

I raised my eyebrows.

'Trust me.'

I cast her a sideways glance as we entered the house. Despite the grey day, light streamed through the skylight and onto the painting. The woman seemed to be smiling at us today. Bastard walked out of the upstairs hallway and swayed down the staircase like she was a runway model. The cat had a sass and a confidence that I could only be jealous of. When she reached the bottom of the stairs, she leaped onto the hallway table and leaned her head towards me, waiting.

'She's clearly fond of you,' Tash observed.

'I feed her,' I said, stroking Bastard's head.

'I think it's more than that, since she can obviously take care of herself.'

'You are an example of strong womanhood,' I told Bastard, scratching behind her ears.

'Strong, did you say. Bloody warrior woman,' Tash said over her shoulder as she headed to the study.

Before following, I took one more glance at the woman in the painting. 'Who are you? And more importantly, who painted you?' I asked her. I half expected a reply, but she was not giving up her secrets so easily. It was only then I noticed that on the end of the chaise on which she was reclining, there was a sheet of paper and a pen. From this distance there was no way to tell if there was anything written on the page. But it was an interesting detail to contemplate.

Bastard jumped down and walked into the study with me. Tash sat at the desk, pulling letters out of the lower drawers.

'I'm going to see if the writing in any of the letters matches that in the manuscript.'

'Good thinking,' I said, taking out the inventory file, which now contained my father's notes.

I sat down and began to read. Emotion wrenched me. It was like walking through the house with him. He had loved the place, which was no surprise. He had never been here before, although he'd known both artists for years, having sold the odd piece for them.

This house should be kept as a museum.

There are several high-worth items including a Dame Laura Knight, a Lamorna Birch, a Peter Lanyon, a Charles Naper, a Patrick Heron, and many others, plus the artists' own works. There are two valuable examples of Chippendale furniture. It is my recommendation after my first walk-through that we hold a special sale on the estate, including putting together a proper catalogue that tells the story of these two remarkable women.

I brushed my tears aside and blew my nose. He was absolutely right.

'Are you OK?'

I nodded. 'Something isn't right. Stephen is trying to do something underhand. But I'm not sure why.'

'Wouldn't inheritance tax have to have been paid by now?' Tash clutched a pile of letters.

'Normally it would. It's six months. It accrues interest after that point.' I paused. 'I haven't a clue what happens when no one can find a will and no one knows which of the two women died first.'

'I'll ask Dad,' said Tash.

'Thanks.' I put my father's notes into my bag because I didn't want Stephen to get his hands on them again. 'I'm going to catalogue the paintings in Sheba's studio.'

'Good luck.'

I would need it, given the state of the room. But I hoped the overwhelming task would help to push my concerns about the business and my mother from my mind for a bit. Yet at the same time I knew I needed to focus on those or I'd never be able to return to London. Taking a deep breath of the fresh salty air, I realised that not heading back there might not be the worst thing in the world.

As I unlocked the studio, Bastard entered first and weaved through the canvases stacked against the walls. There had to be hundreds, of all shapes and sizes.

'OK, Bastard, where do we begin?'

The cat glanced at me and then walked to a stack facing the wall. She sat and looked from me to the paintings.

'It's as good a place as any.' I turned the first canvas around. It was a study in bright blues and greens. The sea and fields. It reminded me a bit of Peter Lanyon's work, with that same sense of the landscape. Sheba felt it, and because she did, the viewer did too. The more I studied the work, the more I loved it, picking out the lines representing hedges and stones. The perspective was odd, and yet it wasn't. I was above looking down, and yet I wasn't. I was in the scene and in the moment. It was a good place to be.

The two-foot-by-two-foot painting was signed, dated and titled on the reverse of the canvas in pencil. *Penwith 2008, July Moments*.

Bastard scratched the side of the next painting. Fortunately leaving no damage.

'Be careful, my friend,' I scolded her softly. 'These are masterpieces.' And as I turned the next canvas over, I was even more convinced that Sheba's work had been wrongly overlooked. She deserved to be up in the pantheon of the top Cornish painters. This canvas was worked in greys, and I felt the weather riding in off the sea. I could almost taste it. It pulled out the buried longing in me to be here. It reminded me that I was part of Cornwall: earth, stone, air and sea.

I lost track of time and place as I experienced each piece. It was like a spell had been cast over me.

'Ren, Rory's arrived.' Tash stood in the doorway.

'What?' I took a few unsteady steps towards her.

'Rory Crown is here. I thought you'd like to speak to him.'

She moved aside, and standing in a ray of light was the sexiest man I'd ever laid eyes on. He was far more interesting in person than on my phone screen, where I normally watched his programmes. Intelligence was sexy, and this man had it in spades, as well as movie-star good looks. But as he stood there with a smile on his face, I knew he didn't see himself that way at all, which only made him more attractive. Damn him. I hadn't had such an immediate physical reaction to a man since I'd first met Paul, and that had been only half of this. It must be the effect of Sheba's paintings. I couldn't explain how I was feeling.

Forcing myself forward, I left the safety of the studio. 'Thank you for coming.'

'Not a problem. I always love a mystery manuscript.' His eyes met mine and I felt a jolt of desire.

'Good,' I said, hoping I didn't sound idiotic. I might not have finished my master's, but I did have a decent brain, or at least hoped I did. But right now, said brain had gone into hiding and clear thought was proving impossible. Yet I had to say something. 'Follow me.'

'I'll make some tea.' Tash looked back and forth between us and grinned.

'Thanks, Tash,' I said as Rory walked behind me through the house. I held the study door open and he smiled at me. My knees went weak. Bloody hell, I needed to get a grip.

Bastard rubbed up against his legs, and I was jealous as he bent down to scratch behind her ears. 'Gorgeous cat.'

'Bastard is a beauty.'

He raised an eyebrow.

'Not the name I gave her, but from the two artists who rescued the poor bastard from the quayside.'

He laughed. 'I like that.'

The cat leapt onto the desk, knocking off a pile of letters.

'Steady on, little one,' he said, gathering them up and placing them back on the desk. He immediately spotted the manuscript. 'May I?'

'Yes.' I was now jealous of the paper. God help me. I'd bet every woman felt this way around him.

After a few moments he said, 'Yes, you're right about Simon Forster. Same style.'

Tash walked in with a tray bearing a pot of tea, three mugs and a packet of Hobnobs. She sent me a look I hadn't seen since high school, when we both fancied Tommy Gooden. That answered my unspoken question. She'd had the same reaction to him. Which was sort of a relief, but only a bit.

He pulled out a chair. 'Do you mind if I sit?'

'Take a seat,' said Tash, and she turned to me and mouthed, 'He can just take me.'

I swallowed laughter. This was madness. He was an expert and I must act like one too.

'These first three poems echo the ones that were rejected by his publisher after the war. Or maybe it's the other way around. The poems he submitted were only replicas of these poems in this manuscript,' he paused to take a mug from Tash. 'Those rejected works are nowhere near as good as these.' He frowned. 'Thinking about it now, it feels more like he was trying to remember them and he could only produce a pale comparison to . . .' He ran his hand down the first page of the manuscript. 'These poems which are superb, like his prime works.' He looked up with a huge smile on his face. 'This is truly exciting.'

That smile.

'Oh good.' Dear God, surely I could have said something more intelligent?

'Do you have any idea how a Simon Forster manuscript could be here?'

'None at all. There are a few puzzles to be solved, like who is the woman in the painting.'

'Yes,' he said. 'That is truly extraordinary. Do you know anything about the artist?'

'We have yet to get the painting off the wall. That should happen tomorrow, and hopefully it will be signed on the back, with maybe the sitter's name too.' I drew a breath. 'And there is a great deal of correspondence that might shed light on it and possibly the manuscript.'

'What interests me are the annotations in pencil, as well as the poems themselves.' He traced them with his finger. 'It doesn't look like Simon's writing, but whoever made them understood the work intimately.'

'Not his writing?'

'No, when I researched the programme we did last year on his work, I read through hundreds of his letters. But I do recall seeing this handwriting before, just not in such great quantity.'

'Will this manuscript be valuable?' Tash asked.

'Academically, yes, and commercially, possibly.'

'How?'

'Well, Simon died in 1959.' One corner of Rory's mouth lifted in a half-smile that took my breath away. 'It is still in copyright, so his heirs might want to find a publisher, and with the story of a lost manuscript, it might make some money.' He looked at the page it was open to and read out the first stanza.

Your brow is furrowed
You peer at me
Seeing more than
Skin and bone
I feel each brush stroke
I am undone
You glance up
Your face flushed
You know
I am seen
Will I ever be able
To hide again?

Tash and I shared a glance. We were all his. His voice and his delivery of the words were more seductive than a touch. I was light-headed.

'This is powerful.' He stood. 'Have you found anything else?'

'We haven't been through all the contents of the desk yet and there is more paperwork in both studios.'

'You mentioned there was a signed copy of a book of poems?' He looked me directly in the eyes. His were green with flecks of yellow.

'It's upstairs in one of the bedrooms.'

I almost found it a relief to leave his presence so that I could breathe. I paused on the staircase and looked at the portrait.

'Absolutely exquisite,' Rory said.

I nearly leapt off the step in surprise. I hadn't heard him follow me, but that was probably because of my racing thoughts. There was no way I should be feeling like this. I'd been nine years in a relationship with Paul. Recently, though, I'd gone off sex. It was a case of lying back and thinking of anything else but him. He hadn't seemed to notice my lack of enthusiasm. But this man standing beside me had woken up my sexual urges, and they were making my skin tingle with anticipation. Which of course was stupid. He was an expert coming to evaluate a manuscript. That was all. He was a professional and I was not a schoolgirl.

As I put one foot in front of the other, it gave me much-needed space so that normal thoughts could return. I was in a committed relationship. But I would allow myself a little leeway, as I'd had a crush on Rory since he first appeared on screen. His passion for literature had changed my mind on so many works that I had despised while studying for my A levels.

Once I reached the small bedroom, I took a deep breath preparing myself for his arrival in the room. I pulled the book off the shelf and held it in front of me like a shield. It was a good thing he had no idea what was going on in my head. If he did, he would think he had stumbled into a lunatic asylum.

'What a stunning house.' He looked about the room. 'Did the artists have children?'

'No, but there are two great-nephews, so maybe they stayed here.'

He picked up the teddy bear from the bed and smiled. 'Lucky them.' Placing the teddy back, he bent low to inspect the books in the small bookcase. When he straightened, I handed him the poetry book.

He turned to the inscription. 'That's certainly his signature.' He continued through the book. 'These are his best-known poems.' He looked at me. 'Although wonderful, it's his Venetian poems that are his best. You'll long to be there.'

I held my words back, for I longed to be in Venice with him. There was something about the city that said romance. I'd gone with Tash when we were twenty. We'd had ten pounds a day to spend, so it was one museum and no food, but I'd fallen in love with La Serenissima anyway. We had both vowed to return. I hadn't, but Tash had gone for her fifth wedding anniversary.

'We read those poems for A level.'

He laughed. 'You wouldn't have read the Venetian ones, as they are very sensual. I would imagine that you read the ones written in the 1920s, which were filled with the legacy of the Great War.'

I nodded, remembering them. 'Their imagery has stayed with me.'

'Not surprised. It's unusual, which makes it stick.'

He continued through the book, and stopped on the final page. Written clearly in black ink were the words *Not all is as it seems and you are privy to secrets.*

'That's not Simon's writing. In fact it looks like it was done by the same person who annotated the manuscript.'

'If it is, maybe that person knew Sheba or Vivian, which might explain why they had it.'

'Hmm.' He walked out of the bedroom and I listened to his footsteps on the wooden floor. The urge to follow him propelled me out the door, but I stopped when I saw him on the landing, staring at the portrait. He was transfixed, and so was I.

18

9 June 1934

Venice

Despite being in a grand location, I decide to keep the routines that I began in the humble pensione. I rise just before dawn and head out with my sketchbook to capture the city as it comes to life. In St Mark's Square, it is only the pigeons and me until swift, silent nuns appear, flowing across the square to the early service.

My mother wrote of this and drew a sketch of the grey figures in movement with the pigeons fleeing in front of them. I turn to a clean page and rough in the architecture and then the flock of women. Something in me almost merges the grey birds with the nuns in their flowing habits. In their midst is a white pigeon or a dove. By the time I've finished working, the only uncovered place on the page is the dove.

'You are talented.' A man's voice comes from behind me.

I jump.

A priest in full black cassock peers over my shoulder.

'And you have captured the nuns and the pigeons so well.' He laughs. He is American, and dark as any Italian I have seen. His eyes are the colour of coffee beans. 'Father Terence Keeney.'

He holds out his hand. I take it and note that he has a direct look about him.

'You're a long way from home,' I say.

'I am indeed, and I would say you too are a long way from . . .' He pauses and studies me. 'I could be wrong, but I have a friend from Falmouth, so I'll broaden the net and say Cornwall.'

I grin. 'Impressed. St Ives.'

'Land of artists, and they've produced a fine one in you.'

'Thank you.' I look down at my work. It is all the shades of charcoal, with fast lines and edges.

'I'm about to have a coffee. Would you like to join me?' he asks.

The square is already filling with early tourists. I stand and smooth down my trousers. 'I'm not one of your flock.'

'With painting the nuns like pigeons, I didn't think so.' He laughs. 'I know a little place that serves the best coffee and pastries.' He winks, and I collect my things.

Before long, we have dived down several calle and walked through to a campo, where we come to a small place that looks nothing like a café. As soon as we enter, space appears at the busy counter for both of us. Father Keeney speaks swiftly in what to my ear sounds like unaccented Italian. It certainly doesn't retain any of his American twang.

Two steaming cups of milky coffee and two cannoli filled with lightly sweetened cream appear while he has a conversation with the man behind the counter.

'Tony here,' he waves his hand, 'is beginning to doubt I'm a priest because I turn up in the early hours of the morning with a beautiful woman.'

I raise an eyebrow. 'You do this every morning?'

'I try . . . except for Sunday, of course.'

'Of course,' I say, wondering what type of priest buys coffees for lone women in Venice.

'The look on your face says you don't trust me.' His eyes crinkle at the corners.

'It might not lie.'

'Excellent. You shouldn't trust someone just because they wear one of these.' He tugs on his dog collar.

'What's an American priest doing here?' I ask.

'I spent a great deal of time in Rome and an opportunity came up to study here for a bit.'

I take a sip of my coffee. It is indeed the best I've had in Venice. I must remember this place and how to reach it.

'You still look wary.'

I smile, letting that be my answer.

'I'll tell you the truth.' He lifts his cannoli and pauses. 'I'm a spy.'

I laugh uncomfortably, because surely he can't be. And if he is, he wouldn't tell me.

'How's our American film star?' A man walks in and slaps him on the back.

My eyes open wide. Have I been really taken in? Is this man actually an actor?

'My sister can't believe you are really a priest. She is going to mass on Sunday to be sure.'

I stop myself speculating on his vocation and instead focus on his face. It is strong. His eyes are wide apart and deep-set. His mouth is not as full as I first thought. Age might be mid to late thirties. Under the cassock, which he wears with ease, he has broad shoulders. He looks more like an athlete than a priest drawn to Rome.

'Penny for them?' he asks.

'Good coffee,' I say.

'You were not thinking of coffee.' He smiles.

'Mind-reader?'

He opens his hands out. 'Part of the job.'

'Priest or spy?' I counter.

'Both. But what were you thinking of?'

'Drawing you, and that you look more like a sportsman than a man of God.'

'Fair. Love both, but God won.'

I finish my cannoli more puzzled than before. 'Why am I here?'

He laughs and his eyes almost disappear. 'If I wasn't a priest, I could say I've always been fascinated by red hair, but in truth I watched you furiously sketching and was intrigued.' He takes a sip of his coffee. 'And once I saw the result, I thought to myself that this woman is an artist to know.'

I frown.

'You began so traditionally, with the lines and shapes, and people and birds, but by the end it had transcended the actual to a more spiritual plane.'

I shrug. 'It's a quick sketch.'

'Don't dismiss it as such.' He taps my notebook. 'There are layers and meaning there that you may not yet see yourself.'

I shake my head.

'Trust me, they are there, and you will see them, if not now, then in a few years.'

'Are you an art historian or critic of some variety?' I squint at him, hoping it will let me see who he really is.

'Well, the Church owns enough art to require one, but no.' He leans in close and whispers, 'Art is my secret passion.'

'Not so secret.'

'True.' He pauses. 'Now I have been rude. I don't even know your name.'

'It is me who is rude, for I didn't give it.' I look down at my hands. I don't know how to behave with this man. He is mildly flirtatious.

'I need to know, because in the future I see great things for you.'

I snort into my coffee in the most unladylike manner. 'So you are a fortune-teller as well.'

He holds out his hands again in a most Gallic way that doesn't fit with his vocation. 'Never that, but I can spot artistic skill a mile off.'

'An artist yourself?'

'No.' He finishes the last of his coffee. 'A bit of a photographer when I have time.'

The man behind the counter clears away our empty cups and plates. I reach into my pocket to pay, but Father Keeney takes care of that after an argument with the man. I can only gather that the café owner doesn't want to take his money. Finally it ends, and the priest takes my elbow and leads me out into the sunlight.

'Are you off elsewhere, or are you going to take that sketch back to your room and create a painting from it?'

'I'm heading back to begin a commission.' I pause, daunted by the task in front of me. I want so much to paint Katherine, but not for Forster.

We walk together back towards St Mark's. This is a part of the city I haven't yet explored, and I will come back here.

'What is the commission, might I ask?'

'A portrait of a very beautiful woman.' Katherine's image immediately fills my mind.

'That sounds intriguing.'

I frown. 'Yes and no.'

'Explain, please.'

We cross a small bridge where women are hanging laundry out. Joyful colour is reflected in the water below.

'Her husband wants something staid and traditional that will act as an object he can show off, saying, "See, this is my exquisite wife."'

'And you don't approve of the husband?'

'I don't.' There is no need to lie about it to this man of the cloth who I am unlikely to see again.

'Or of his possessive attitude?'

'No.'

'Or is it really the bland painting he is asking for that is bothering you, I wonder?'

I don't reply.

'It is all of the above, I think, but it is the last that is the biggest trouble for you.' He stops in front of a plain door. 'This is where I leave you. I hope to meet you again and I look forward to finding out how you work around his request and make it something extraordinary.' He puts his hand on the door handle. 'You still haven't told me your name.'

'Sheba Kernow.'

'As in Bathsheba?'

I nod.

'Very interesting, Miss Kernow.' He bows his head and leaves, his cassock flowing. Who is he, this priest?

* * *

The whole of the palazzo is awake on my return, judging by the energy and noise. Forster's bags are by the door and he is dressed for travel.

'There you are, Miss Kernow. Katherine thought you had fled in the night.'

'No, I was out sketching.' I search the hallway for her.

He frowns. 'No matter now. I will show you where to paint her.' He marches ahead and I follow, hoping this won't be too awful. We climb a flight of stairs and I know my worst fears will be realised. He flings open the double doors to their bedroom.

Katherine stands silhouetted in the morning sunlight looking more like an apparition than a human. Her white silk nightdress glows.

He drags a chaise longue to straddle the French windows. 'Just here, with the glory of Venice behind her.'

The view he is referring to is almost invisible with the morning light streaming in. My eyes struggle to adjust to the contrast between the dark room and the June sunlight.

'This,' he says, 'is what I want.' He takes Katherine's hand and pulls her to the chaise, positioning her like she is his doll. Once her body is in place, he turns her head so that she is looking at the bed. Her profile is beautiful, with her long neck and sharply defined jawline, but not as beautiful as her face.

'You must let Sheba decide some things, Simon. She is the artist.' Katherine pushes her hair back and glances at me.

'I want you looking away.' He crosses his arms. If he stamped his foot, I wouldn't be surprised.

'Is it really me if people can't see my face?' she asks.

'I don't need people to see you,' he says, leaning down to her. This is not comfortable. I step back.

'I want them to see just your beauty.' His voice is low and threatening.

It's clear he simply needs to own everything about her, even her image. Katherine rises, proving he doesn't control her every move.

'Sheba is the artist. You have chosen the subject and the position. Let her decide the rest.'

He casts a dismissive glance at me. 'She needs guidance.'

Katherine purses her mouth.

'I must dash so that I make the train,' he says, and kisses her before leaving. I have seen my mother kiss my father, my father kiss his new wife, and never have I felt as sick as I do now.

Katherine yawns as the housekeeper enters the room.

'*Buongiorno*, Signora Bocca, please may I have some coffee.'

The housekeeper looks at me and I nod.

'What wonderful things have you been up to in the early hours?' Katherine pulls the sketchbook from under my arm. She flips the pages, stopping on this morning's effort. 'St Mark's Square.' She holds it away from her, squinting slightly as she rotates it back and forth, before a big smile spreads across her face. 'I doubt the nuns would like it.' She closes the book before handing it back to me.

'They'll never see it, so I'm not overly concerned.'

'Not afraid you'll be damned to hell?'

'That's always a possibility.' I smile, thinking of Father Keeney. If all priests looked like him, female attendance at mass would rise dramatically, and the queue for confession for those with lustful thoughts would circle the building.

'That is a very seductive smile. Do tell.' She flops down onto the chaise longue and taps the empty space beside her. 'Sorry for my tedious husband.'

I shrug. She is the one who chooses to live with him.

Looking over her shoulder at the canal, she says, 'It will be awfully difficult to paint me here, will it not?'

'Not my first choice, but if we use the afternoon light, it should be better.' I wave my hand. 'This is not the best light for painting, especially in the style he wishes.'

'How would *you* paint me?'

I begin to speak, and then stop. I can't say I'd paint her nude, from the back, with her looking over her shoulder at me. It is her birthmark that is calling to me.

'I might paint you as they did in the past, standing tall with the tools of your trade about you and in the distance a halcyon view.'

'Ah yes, somewhere I have one of my ancestors painted this way.'

'I would love to see it.'

She shook her head. 'No you wouldn't. He was dusty and boring.'

'What portraits have you seen that you like? What style would you like to be painted in?'

'Hmm, as Picasso does. That could be interesting.'

'You might have to sleep with him first.'

She arches an eyebrow. 'Really? You've met him?'

'He is acquainted with a friend of my father.'

'What was your impression?' she asks.

'Genius, but tricky.'

'Sadly, they frequently are.' She lights a cigarette and offers me one. I wave it away.

'Who else?'

'Perhaps Michelangelo.'

I laugh. 'Don't think he did too well with women.'

'You have a point.'

The housekeeper returns with coffee and some toast.

After she's gone, Katherine says, 'Shall we use what's left of the morning and visit a museum or two?'

I accept the cup of black coffee she offers me.

'It won't take me long to dress.' She stands. 'Last night was such a bore. I should have stayed here with you.' She opens her closet and flicks through it, pulling out a blue dress with a white diamond pattern running through it. She tosses it on the bed before pulling out stockings and a slip. Without closing the shutters, she takes off her nightgown, continuing to chat to me about who was at the party last night. I know none of them, so I let her voice run over me as I make sure to look out the window and not at her while she dresses.

'Can you do the buttons for me?' she asks with her back to me.

I secure them, thankful that her birthmark is hidden beneath the fabric.

'Which museum should we begin in?' She finishes her coffee.

'It's best to start at the Accademia.' I have already spent hours there, but each time I find something new to study.

'Bit stuffy, but fine.' She bites into a piece of toast.

'It's always good to start with the earlier works, then move forward.'

'Yes, miss,' she says, mimicking a child at school. 'Have you had something to eat?'

I nod, not sure I want to recount my meeting with the priest, and that strikes me as odd.

'Then let's go.'

I grab my sketchbook and follow, uncertain what the day ahead will bring.

19

4 April 2022

Newlyn

In the kitchen, I picked up a mug and debated a ginger nut. They weren't to everyone's taste. Tash seemed to have an endless supply of biscuits. Would Rory want one with his tea?

Tash was grinning suggestively at me. 'You've got to shag him and then tell me it was fabulous.'

I opened my eyes wide. 'No, absolutely not.'

'*I* can't, because I'm married.'

'I have a partner,' I said, watching Tash roll her eyes. 'He's your one pass . . . your words, not mine.'

'Sadly, he hasn't looked at me the way he has at you, otherwise I'd be in there.' She thrust the other mug of tea at me. 'Flirt then. It's good for the soul and Paul will never know.'

I glared at her, but took the mug and walked to the study. It had been years since I'd last flirted and I wasn't sure I'd remember how to. No. This was not what I should be thinking about. Just because Rory Crown was here did not mean I had permission to flirt. I stopped. Did anyone need permission to flirt? The last time it had happened, it had led to a very unpleasant discussion with Paul. I didn't need that again.

In the study, Rory had spread the script out over the top of the desk. He was scribbling in a notebook and looked up as I placed the mug down beside him.

'This is brilliant. The poetry is sublime.' He leaned back in the chair and focused on me. Everything froze, including my brain, while I tried to think of something intelligent to say.

'Studying words all the time, don't you become immune . . . inured or jaded even?' God, I could kick myself. Why use one word when you could use three.

'Fair question, but first, does that happen to you with art?' The corner of his mouth lifted and I looked away to refocus my thoughts. I was simply having a fan-girl reaction, nothing more.

'Not really. Art is so variable that I'm never not surprised, thrilled, shocked or at times horrified. Only rarely am I bored, and I suspect that is because the artist was too.'

He stood and pulled up an armchair for me. 'Words – literature as a whole – are the same.'

'I see.'

It was a stupid reply, but he smiled. 'I'm sure you've read *Ways of Seeing* by John Berger.'

'Yes.'

'That sentence . . . "Seeing comes before words." It has always stayed with me.'

I looked at him anew. 'Why?'

'I deal in words. I try and look behind them for insight and meaning.' He ran his hand through his dark hair, messing it up a bit. Suddenly he looked younger.

I took a sip of tea and imagined what it would be like to kiss him, but then banished the thought and focused on what he was saying.

'Only those who cannot see start in a different place. So when I'm looking at words, I think about what the author saw, felt, needed, wanted before they put them down on paper.' He paused. 'Then I also stop and consider what they mean to me, how they make me feel and why they do that.'

How he made me feel and why was something I didn't want to think about.

'I've never looked at words that way, but now that you say it, I can see the connection with art.'

He nodded and picked up a page. 'That's what troubles me about Forster's work.'

'Wasn't he your classic Edwardian who moved into the new age after the First World War?'

'On paper, yes, but his later poems, the Venetian ones in particular, don't fit with the man he was then.'

'Sorry, A-level English didn't cover this.'

'It should have. He was a fascist, and during his Venice trip he worked with Mussolini on his poetry.'

'Mussolini wrote poetry?'

'Terrible poetry, but having read some of the correspondence, I believe Forster positively fawned over him.' He held a page out. 'I struggle to think of a man with his politics and the associated views on women and a woman's place in the world writing such emotive, passionate work. In a way the poetry and its beauty are worth study despite the man behind it. How we read these words today is vastly different to when they were read at the time with another world war looming.'

'I hadn't considered that, and now I feel like a fool.'

'Don't. That wasn't my intention.' He smiled and looked at me. It was clear he saw an intelligent woman, and unless I was wrong, one he found interesting. It took my breath away. I was the grunt who did the research, the professor's partner, and the one who'd messed up. But he didn't see any of those things. He saw the Ren I had been. The one I thought lost.

'The brilliance of art in all its forms is that it is not time-dependent. The themes, the feelings, the meanings are timeless.'

I nodded. 'This house is full of such work. But now I can't get the fact that Forster was a fascist out of my head.'

'I'm sure you've come across artists who were vile in how they lived and acted, and yet created great beauty.'

'Absolutely. So many have a terrible record with women, whether as lovers, fathers, brothers or friends.'

'Yes, I love your Instagram posts.'

I blinked. Surely he wasn't one of my followers. I wouldn't have missed that.

'My friend Lucy Williams, at Helwyn House, pointed out your account years ago. I've been following you since.'

Tash walked into the room wielding a packet of Rich Tea biscuits. She looked between us, then said, 'Anyone fancy one?'

* * *

For the past hour I had been double-checking all the paintings on the inventory and I went into the study to check the details of the painting by Sheba's mother. Rory was straightening the manuscript.

'With your permission, I'd like to take this to Exeter for Tim Pearce to assess. He's the acknowledged expert on Forster. I've already emailed him, and he's keen.'

'That should be fine. I've photographed most of it, so I have it on hand for reference.' I placed the painting back on the wall and took another photograph. Sheba's mother's work was excellent. Not the genius of her daughter, but had she lived longer, it might have evolved even more. I would highlight some of it on Instagram. It would be good to see her profile raised even just a little bit.

'These artists are lucky to have you in charge of their work.' Rory was genuine in his comment, and something grew inside me. It had been a long time since I'd received a compliment outside of work.

'Thank you.'

'I can see your determination.'

I frowned, not sure where this was going.

'Your posts on Instagram are great and your work here at Harbour House demonstrates your commitment to showcasing the work of these women.' He stood. 'Would it be possible for me to have a look at the studios before I go?'

'Of course. Sheba's is a mess, but I don't know if that was the way she worked or the result of searches.'

I led him through the house. Tash was in the kitchen, carefully cleaning the dust off a sculpture.

'Do you want to come with us to have a look through the studios?' I asked, collecting the keys off the counter.

She smiled slyly. 'I have to give Gareth a ring.' She pulled out her phone and walked towards the front of the house. She was lying, but I couldn't call her out.

At the back door, we were met by Bastard. Unlike Tash, she wasn't trying to leave us unsupervised.

I opened Sheba's studio first. Chaos and colour.

'I see what you mean.' Rory looked at the canvases stacked against the walls.

'It was a lot worse earlier, but I've begun to sort them by date where possible.' My eye was caught by another canvas. It spoke of autumn with golds, browns and a brilliant blue. Whether it was sea or sky I wasn't sure, but it didn't matter.

Bastard jumped onto a table and pushed a pencil onto the floor. She still had the heart of a kitten. Rory swooped down to pick it up, and Bastard eyed him before pushing it off again. He played with the cat until she became bored and jumped down, sending a canvas flying. Rory and I both went to catch it, his hand meeting mine. I looked up, startled by the feeling of coming home and the excitement of leaving.

'That was close,' he said, meeting my glance.

'It was.' I moved my hand and he put the canvas back.

'Bastard will have to be more careful.' He looked around for the cat, who was now on a windowsill cleaning her paw, oblivious to the damage she could have caused. She sent us a look of disgust and jumped down, setting off the old radio. The sounds of Vivaldi filled the space.

'You have quite a task in here.'

'I do.' I shut the radio off. 'I'm trying to take it in small chunks.' I pointed to a neat pile against the far wall. 'That's where I was working when you arrived.' It was all a bit overwhelming, and my shoulders dropped.

'When I return from Exeter, I'd be happy to help out.' He placed a hand on my arm. It was meant to be comforting, but there was a connection between us that I couldn't deny. I must be careful.

'Thank you.' I smiled. 'That would be great.' No, no, it wouldn't. He was far too attractive. It wasn't simply his good looks, it was his personality too. Quiet, clever and kind. It was dangerous.

'Would you like to see Viv's studio?'

'I'd love to.'

I looked around for Bastard, but she was already sitting outside in a puddle of sunshine, waiting impatiently for us. I locked Sheba's studio and went to Viv's. Dust motes hung in the still air of the large space. It felt other-worldly. The statue on the left-hand side of the studio haunted me now that Tash had pointed out what she saw. Rory was silent, almost reverent, as he walked among the works.

'How is it that her work isn't hailed as genius?'

'I'm coming to the conclusion that neither of them sought fame.'

'That in itself is interesting, and begs so many questions.' He glanced from me to the haunting sculpture. 'You can see so much joy and movement in her pieces, but this one . . .'

'I know. Tash thinks it's grief.'

He turned to me. 'What do you think?'

'I don't know. It's almost too raw to put a name to it.'

'Love.' His gaze didn't leave mine. 'Loss.' He touched the gnarled wood. 'She has captured both, and the twisted wood, the dark and the light, says more about the experience than could ever be put into words.'

I swallowed. 'I'm sorry.'

'I was lucky to have Hebe's love.' He paused. 'I'm still devastated at losing her.' He looked up from the statue. 'Until this moment, I had never seen anything that captured that feeling . . . There is love, there is loss, but there is beauty and hope.' His glance met mine.

'Yes.' I couldn't move. Hope.

20

—————————

Venice

At 4 p.m., Katherine takes me to Harry's Bar. I've heard about it, but it is beyond my means. She waltzes in and I follow in her wake. Immediately she is greeted by name and led to a table.

'Signora Forster, a champagne cocktail today?' a man in a short white coat asks.

'No, I think a pink gin for us both.' She smiles and nods to a gentleman sitting in the corner on his own. As soon as the waiter leaves, she pulls the notebook from my charcoal-covered fingers.

'Why don't you visit the ladies' while I look at what you have done today.'

I hesitate, but she waves me away. It is so exposing to have my work examined in this manner, and it has happened twice in one day. Nonetheless, I climb the stairs and do as I'm told. Looking in the mirror, I am a wild-eyed woman whose hair is in disarray, with a smattering of freckles covering my face. It is not unattractive, but more unsophisticated than I would like. I belong on a farm somewhere, working the fields, rather than here in Venice, a city of so much culture.

On re-entering the room, I note that Katherine is engrossed in the sketchbook. A woman and a man have just entered and are making a beeline for her. She looks up and frowns, but quickly schools her expression while closing the book.

The woman kisses her cheek while the gentleman takes her hand. I stay put, watching. They sit beside her and I can see she is telling them she is not alone.

Whether I want to or not, I need to join her. Halfway to the table, I nearly lose my nerve. I recognise Lady Diana Saunders from pictures I have seen. This is not a place where I belong.

'Ah, there you are, Sheba.' Katherine smiles. 'Allow me to introduce Lady Diana Saunders and Lord Swindon. They are going to join us for a drink.'

'How do you do?' I say, holding out my hand as I was taught by my mother.

'Lovely to meet you,' Lady Diana says. 'Katherine was just saying that you are an artist from Cornwall.'

'I am.' I look down at my hands, grateful I washed them so thoroughly.

'How lovely,' she says. 'Have you been to the Biennale yet?'

I take my seat beside Katherine. 'I have a ticket for the fifteenth.'

'I wonder what you will make of it.' She smiles warmly at me and I relax a bit.

'How so?' I ask.

'The work on display is varied and not to everyone's taste.'

'Art rarely is.' I pause. 'I grew up in a community of artists.'

'She's met Picasso,' Katherine adds.

'Interesting fellow, I imagine,' says Lord Swindon.

'He is.' I take a sip of my gin as their drinks are brought to the table. How can I move the attention from me and onto someone or something else?

'We've spent a good deal of today at the Accademia. I feel so much better informed.' Katherine picks up a small piece of bread with tomato on it.

'In what way?' asks Lord Swindon.

'I never realised how differently artists can look at things. I've learned so much and will never look at another piece of art the same way.'

'Now that is something.' Lady Diana studies me and it is the most uncomfortable feeling. 'I'm hoping this is a good thing and it's not going to turn your world upside down.'

Katherine looks at her over her glass. 'I find that is always a good thing. One can become so stuck.' She sends her a look I don't understand.

'You two,' says the man. 'Trouble if ever I saw it.' He looks at his watch. 'Drink up. We're due at Peggy's in ten minutes and I must return you to your husband.'

'We can be late,' Lady Diana says.

'We will be already. It always takes longer to reach places here than one thinks.' Lord Swindon rises to his feet.

'That's so dull, but so true.' She finishes her drink and stands. 'You are coming tomorrow night, Katherine?'

'I'm not sure,' Katherine says.

'Just because Forster isn't around doesn't mean you can hide away. Bring Sheba with you. It will be fun, I promise.'

Diana follows Lord Swindon out, and I look to Katherine for interpretation, but she is focused on attracting the waiter's attention.

'We don't need another drink,' I say, longing to head back and spend some time looking through my sketches and thinking about the task in front of me. Katherine is so changeable. I never know what to expect from her or how to capture this quality in her.

'We do. Believe me, we do.'

I sigh and slip the sketchbook behind me. This is a side of Katherine of which I'm uncertain. Forster isn't here and she could just relax. But watching her fidgeting leg, I realise it might take her a while to step back from him and simply enjoy where she is and who she's with.

* * *

Having left the shutters open, I wake with the first light. My head thumps and I see my mother's diary open on the table. Vague memories of showing it to Katherine run through my mind. There was something important that she said, but I can't remember what. And I don't remember going to bed. This is bad. I'm here to work, not to be a drunken companion. To be fair, last night, or what I remember of it, was fun, including seeing Venice shimmering in the dusk as we stumbled home. After that, I recall little.

My brain swims as I sit, and I quickly dress despite my aching head. Dinner at the restaurant was delicious, as was the wine. The nightcap sitting by a canal was a mistake, though. As was the one here. I note the empty glass beside the diary, which is open to 10 June. Today. The word *adventure* comes to mind, followed by *mystery*.

Water and coffee are needed. The palazzo is silent as I head out into the early morning, taking both the diary and my sketchbook. I hope fresh air will bring the rest of the evening into focus. But right in this moment all I can think is that this drinking has to stop. I will speak to her about it today. I can't keep this up and paint.

After wandering for a half-hour, watching shutters open and early churchgoers parade past, I find the café that I was taken to yesterday morning and order a coffee. I can't face food yet, but the caffeine is good. Stepping back out into the campo, I pause to listen to the church bells calling the faithful. Beautifully dressed children tug the hands of their mammas and grandmothers, whose heads are adorned with exquisite lace. The men walk along behind. I glance around for the priest, but heaven alone knows what I would say to anyone, let alone a man of the cloth, when no doubt I still reek of last night's overindulgence. My burps taste of it and I don't very much like myself. I should have put my foot down. I didn't have to go along with it. Katherine could have continued on her own, but in that moment I knew she wouldn't. I don't think she has ever done anything on her own. Yet she is a woman of means and great talent. She could leave Forster. The Great War changed so much.

The church bells slow and a single toll alerts the stragglers to make haste. The heat of the day is growing as I weave my way through calle, not sure where I am heading. The morning sun touches the tops of the buildings lining a narrow canal. I lean against a wall and sketch, capturing the shadows and the light but no real detail. My brain hurts too much for that.

Once I've finished, I move along. In the distance I can see the island where the dead are buried. This morning it is bathed in light and looks the perfect place to leave your mortal remains. Thoughts of death follow me on my way back, despite the beauty of the morning. A door to a church is open and I enter, quickly becoming lost in the darkness. Eventually flickering candles appear and light filters in through windows far above. The scent of incense fills the air. The morbid thoughts and the ones of my mother don't leave, but neither do they chafe against my soul the way they have been recently. The interior of the church is soothing in its darkness.

I perch on the last pew and let my shoulders drop. Slowly the tension leaves me and something akin to peace arrives. I don't believe in God as such, but I do believe there is some sort of higher power. If asked to explain, I wouldn't be able to articulate it. Nor would I be able to draw it. But in this place of silence and fragrance, I feel it.

Here I find the strength to open my mother's diary. What was it Katherine saw last night that I missed? I flip the pages slowly, watching her sketches animate in a weird way, until I come to yesterday's date.

9 June

Today I saw David. For hours I felt his eyes on me, his hunger, his need. It was intoxicating. Something inside me slipped. I transformed under his gaze.

Who was David? Why would him looking at her change her? I rub my temples. It was Venice that changed her, made her normal, not David. What am I missing? My father's name is Francis.

The next entry is about a party she attended. I close the book and resolve to ask Katherine. I hope to begin the painting today, but my head still thumps and now my stomach roils. My body would continually be distracting me, and it's important to be fully present. Something tells me that won't be possible today.

When I step outside again, the sun is high and Venice is full. Working my way through the crowds, I curse myself for lingering so long in the church. I didn't fall asleep, but I almost slipped into a trance, or was it meditation?

'Ah, Miss Kernow.' Father Keeney appears to my right.

'Where have you come from? Mass?' I ask.

'That, and I was visiting a friend over by the Rialto market. You have been sketching again?'

I nod.

'And now you are in a rush?'

'No, not possible.' I gaze at the throngs of people.

He laughed. 'A satisfying morning's work?'

'One sketch.'

'A good one?'

'No, not at all.' I am tempted to show him, but stop. 'I wasn't myself earlier.'

He takes my arm and moves me away from a crowd being led by a woman speaking loudly in French. 'Where are you heading now?'

'The Palazzo Giallo.'

He raises both eyebrows. 'Call me impressed.'

'I'm staying with Katherine Forster and will be painting her portrait.'

'The poet's wife?' he asks.

'You know them?' I hate how Katherine is known as the poet's wife and not as the poet.

'I have met them both. Interesting people.'

That is an evasive answer. So I ask something definite. 'What do you think of his work?'

'The poetry is exquisite.'

'It is.'

He casts me a sideways glance. 'I cannot fault it, quite the opposite, but I must confess that I find it difficult to see him . . . having such insight or feeling.'

I snort.

'You agree. I thought you might.' He smiles. 'We have arrived.'

Part of me is shocked to be here so quickly, and with him. Maybe because I'm still coming to grips with the fact that he knows Katherine. Strangely, I feel they both belong to me separately. I don't want to mix them because I like things when they are clearer or sharper. In my personal life, that is, not my work.

He looks at me like I need to respond. Did I miss something? 'Thanks,' I say. A response that can cover many things.

'Now I know where to find you.'

I open my eyes wide.

'If someone is asking for a recommendation for a portrait.'

'Oh.'

'Is there another reason people would seek you out – other than for your charming personality, of course?' The corner of his mouth lifts.

Something entirely unexpected arrives in me: attraction to a priest.

I shade my eyes and study this puzzle of a man. He has an appeal that is undeniable, and yet he has chosen a celibate life.

The door opens and Katherine stands there blinking. 'Oh my God, there you are, Sheba. We've been concerned.'

'I was out sketching,' I say.

'Good morning, Father Keeney. What brings you to my doorstep?' She covers the space between the door and where we are standing slowly, with her hips swaying just a bit more than usual.

Why should I be surprised? I find him attractive; why wouldn't she? But she is a married woman. And a voice in my head says I am a lesbian. He is a priest. None of this adds up to anything but a mess. My brain is tired from last night and nothing makes sense. Before I can stop myself, I blurt out, 'Katherine, what was it you saw in my mother's diary?'

She blinks at me as if trying to put me in focus. 'Oh, nothing important. It was just why she named you Bathsheba.'

'What?'

She smiles at me like I am a child. 'She must have been a painter's model for King David and Bathsheba. It doesn't take much to put two and two together and realise the model for David was your father.'

'Oh,' is all I can say.

Turning her attention from me to Father Keeney, she says, 'I'm just heading out to meet a friend.' She takes a step towards him. 'Don't suppose you are going my way?'

'I wish I was, but unless you are heading to the university . . .' He softens his words with a big smile. 'I look forward to seeing the portrait. Just make sure she doesn't do what she did to the nuns the other morning.' He bows, and we both watch him walk away.

'Come with me to meet Diana,' Katherine suggests.

'I need to prepare to begin your painting.' I cover my real reason for not wanting to come. Her words. How did she see what I had not? It is so obvious and I am such a fool.

Katherine frowns, but says, 'If you must. What time should I come back?'

'The light should be better at four.'

She nods and walks in the opposite direction to the priest. I close my eyes for a moment. Why am I here? I am not my mother. But I am a painter, and always will be one.

21

4 April 2022

Penzance

Before Rory left with the manuscript, I'd photographed the writing on it. Sitting on the desk in my father's study was a box filled with the contents of two drawers from the study of Harbour House. Tonight, after dinner, I would go through it. The name of the author of the poems wasn't written anywhere on the manuscript, though it did have the date 1940 on one of the pages. Rory had mentioned that Simon's last anthology came out in 1939, and he was never published again. This fitted with what our English teacher had told us years ago. He had a broken heart after losing his wife and daughter in the Blitz in 1941 and was never able to write again. But Rory had also said that his work was rejected in 1946. Had his heart mended, or had he been revisiting works lost in the war? Was this the manuscript that he had lost and been trying to recreate? If it was, I could see the excitement building around the contents of the house. Almost everyone had heard of Simon Forster, and this would help increase interest in my artists. I could feel it in my bones.

But nothing came up in my searches linking them to him in any way. Vivian had met Sheba when she'd travelled to Cornwall for a holiday in 1946 with her sister, Martha, Martha's husband, Jason, and their child. They had stayed with Sheba and Viv had never left. This information I'd gleaned from a short interview Viv had given before an exhibition in Oxford in 1964.

I picked up a letter from the top of the box. There had to be a link. This was the thing I was good at – sensing a connection and then finding it. I owed it to Sheba and Viv.

My mother's voice carried from the garden. She must be on the phone. As much as I longed to solve this puzzle, she came first. Tomorrow I had a meeting with Tash's dad, Jack Thomas – our solicitor. It should be a box-ticking exercise. Of course, he wouldn't know there was no money left.

Before that meeting, Tash and I would head to the office at four in the morning and continue to go through the accounts.

'Bye,' my mother said loudly. Almost immediately, my phone rang. Paul. Had Mum been talking to him again?

'Hello,' I said, walking into the kitchen.

'At last you bother to answer the phone. If it weren't for your mother, you could be dead for all I know.'

I took a deep breath, then said calmly, 'I've tried to ring but you haven't picked up.'

'I've been very busy,' he said.

'So have I.'

'There is nothing more you can do there.' He paused, and I braced myself. 'Come back here now, my love.'

My first instinct was to hang up, but that would make things worse. 'Paul,' I said in my most reasonable voice, 'you know I can't. There is probate involved, and the fact is that Mum isn't . . .' I paused to check she wasn't in hearing distance, 'coping at all, let alone well.'

'You're lying.'

'I'm not.' I rested my head against the cool glass of the window.

Outside, my mother was checking the bird feeder. Daffodils peered back at me. They looked ridiculously happy.

'She tells me she's great and going out every day.'

I laughed bitterly. 'Yes, out the back door then back inside again. She isn't even getting dressed unless Meg or I help her.'

'I don't believe you.'

I sighed. 'You may not, but you're not here to see the truth yourself.'

'I can't be there,' he said, and I pictured the tightness around his mouth from the clipped sound of his words. 'I have work that keeps me here.'

'It's Easter break. You could come.' As I said the words, I knew it was the last thing I wanted.

'You're being selfish expecting me to go somewhere I can't work, and where frankly there is no one and nothing of interest.'

I closed my eyes and counted to ten. We'd been over this ground so many times before. 'Fine, don't come, but . . .' I paused to be sure the words wouldn't be lost, 'I can't come back yet.'

'I don't see why not. You have a solicitor who can do all the necessary things, including selling your mother's and your share of the business.'

He had no idea and I didn't have the energy to explain it to him. The timer on my phone sounded.

'I have to rescue dinner. Bye.' I hung up before he could say another word.

Was he right about my mother? She hobbled back inside and I jumped into action, taking the chicken out of the oven.

'Who were . . . you speaking with?' she asked as she sat down.

'Paul.'

She smiled. 'You are so . . . lucky with him. So clever.'

I didn't reply as I drained the broccoli.

'Make sure you don't mess it up. He makes you better and keeps you stable.'

I swung around. Those were very odd statements. But as I opened my mouth to question them, she winced.

'Are you OK?' I rushed to her side.

She nodded. 'Just a twinge.'

'It looked like more than a twinge.'

She shook her head and her expression said *no more questions*.

I put plates of chicken and veg on the table and sat opposite her. We used to have a good relationship. Not as wonderful as the one I'd had with my father, but good nonetheless. The woman sitting opposite me wasn't like the mother I'd confided in and the one I'd counted as a friend. I wasn't sure if it was her or me who had changed, but we needed to sort this somehow.

I cut into my chicken and watched her try to do the same. That had to be hard. She had been so capable, and yet even this was a monumental task now. I was about to offer to help when she looked up and caught me watching her.

'You won't be here for ever, so I have to do this myself.'

'You're right, I won't be here for ever, but I'm not rushing away.'

'Paul is missing you.'

'I know, but he's capable of lasting a month or two without me.'

'What about your job?' she asked.

'I can do that from anywhere.' The further this conversation went, the more I wanted to know exactly what Paul had been telling my mother and what his motives were.

'He said you needed to be in London.'

'No need. Most things are online these days, and I have friends and colleagues who can check any specific items for me if I need something that's only available in London.'

She looked down, then her head shot up. 'But you're not capable of doing what's needed.'

I blinked. Did she just say what I thought she said? 'Are you implying that I can't catalogue a house?'

She nodded.

My own mother had just called me incompetent. It took everything in me not to walk away and leave her to it. Using the old trick of counting to ten again, I spoke calmly. 'I'd been doing just that with Dad since I was eleven. You know he trained me in the business from a very early age. I'm now thirty and I know a lot more about art and antiques than I did then. I *am* capable.' I sat back, realising what I'd just said. I'd said I was capable and meant it.

'Paul says you need his assistance all the time on your research. He said you wouldn't have a job without his help.'

I ground my teeth, wanting to scream, but instead I asked, 'What else has Paul said?'

'That you'll have another breakdown with all this stress. He said that was why you didn't want to finish your master's.'

'Did he?' There had been nothing I wanted more. That work was so important to me. I'd had so much to say, but he had claimed it wasn't good enough. The argument wasn't strong enough. Was he right about me not being able to handle this? Doubt crept in, swamping my anger.

She stretched out her right hand and put it on mine. 'He also said you haven't been able to conceive. I'm so . . . sorry.'

This was news to me. I was on the pill; I wasn't trying to conceive.

'Thank you,' I said. Now was not the time to set the record straight. I needed to do that directly with Paul.

'So I think it's best if you head back to London and continue trying. You weren't cut out for the pressure of the business world.'

I opened my eyes wide.

'The way you flaked out over your master's . . . after you didn't recognise the Cézanne for what it was and nearly cost the auction house its reputation.'

My shoulders fell. Here we go again. 'Dad agreed with what I'd done.'

'Of course he would. He adored you.'

'And I him.' What I wouldn't do to have him here now.

'But because of that, neither of you could see things the way they were. It's thanks to your uncle's brilliance in the furniture sales that the business is worth anything.'

I had no proof yet, but I had a feeling that my uncle was the cause of the current state of affairs with the empty bank accounts and the dodgy accounting. My mother had no money, and my partner thought I was on the verge of a breakdown and that everything could be sorted out by a solicitor. He was wrong on both counts. This was something I had to fix. My mother needed money, and she had none unless I started selling my parents' art.

The landline rang and I went to answer it.

'Ren, you aren't answering your phone.' Tash sounded breathless.

'Sorry, I put it on silent.'

'I've been going through the info at Companies House.'

'And?' I sank into the chair beside the hall table.

'Barton's hasn't been submitting their full accounts.'

'Is that illegal?'

'No, but it's questionable. Haven't you looked at this stuff before?'

'No.' I pushed my hair back. Here was something else I'd ignored, and I shouldn't have.

'You're listed as a shareholder and director.'

I sighed. 'I should have taken more interest, but let's be honest, no one wanted me near the business.'

'Whether they did or not, you are involved.'

'Shit.' I exhaled. 'OK, are you still up for meeting at four?'

'You bet.'

'So, no detailed accounts. Are they required?'

'Possibly not for a business of this size. And the summary accounts for the last financial year don't have to be filed for months yet.'

I picked up a pen and twirled it through my fingers.

'Could you be wrong?' I scanned the hallway, hoping it would provide me with answers. But all I saw was a gilt mirror, and I didn't like the reflection of the person looking back at me. Tash was right. I did look middle-aged. My hair was neatly pulled back and the small pearl earrings dated me.

'It's a possibility.'

'Have you ever been wrong before?' I asked.

'No.'

'I thought not. See you at four.'

When I walked back into the kitchen, Mum wasn't there. I found her in bed, fully dressed and sound asleep. I pulled a blanket over her and walked back to the kitchen. What the hell was going on? My mother thought I was incapable. And she might be right, but mums were not supposed to think that about their children. Paul was feeding her a bunch of lies. But more pressing was that the business was bust and my father's accounts were empty. How was I going to fix this? Was it even possible?

After I'd cleared up in the kitchen, I went back into the study. The box of letters and diaries beckoned. My brain was spinning over the same things, and at least looking through these might give me something else to think about, otherwise I wouldn't sleep at all.

The first few letters were from Sheba's grandfather. Nothing of great importance, but thanking her for her visit and the gift of the painting of Kensington Gardens. He mentioned missing her company but understanding her need to be in the Hampstead area to be surrounded by other artists.

According to the letters, from 1936 to 1941 she had been living in the Lawn Road Flats, now known as the Isokon Building. This in itself was fascinating. I remembered going to see the building when I was studying the Bauhaus movement. The movement's founder, Walter Gropius, lived there after escaping from Nazi Germany. It had been a haven for leftist thinking, and I seemed to recall something also about Soviet spies. The likes of Henry Moore, Naum Gabo, Ben Nicholson and Barbara Hepworth had frequented the Isobar in the building's ground floor. Sheba had lived in the heart of an artistic colony.

Maybe this was where she did the painting of the roses all those years ago. The area was filled with refugees, and they were very aware of the storm that was threatening Europe and the world. What a life she had lived.

I worked my way through a pile of these letters to Sheba from her grandfather, touched by the close relationship they seemed to have enjoyed. The next few were from a gallery in London. These were important. The history of the sale of her work would help to build up interest and create a better picture of the course of her career.

Picking up a notebook, I saw that inside it was inscribed with Sheba's name, the date 1934 and Venice. It was filled with mostly sketches, but on some pages there were short paragraphs, as though she was talking to someone.

I can only think of you. My hunger for your company is haunting everything I do.

My heart stopped when I saw sketches of a woman. It was the

woman in the painting. Page after page was filled with images of her. I leaned back in my chair. So Sheba clearly knew the woman in the painting, and that alone might explain why she had it. It looked nothing like her work. I studied each page, but none of them were preliminaries of the portrait.

There were quite a few sketches of a priest, a good-looking one. Under one of them, she had written, *Father Keeney intrigues me.*

Keeney was not an Italian name . . . Irish possibly. I typed his name and the year into the search engine. Father Terence Keeney. Catholic priest, Irish American, spy. Born in Boston in 1897, died in London in 1939. Interesting. But it was a rabbit hole I didn't need to go down. I sat back and recalled the photo of Sheba. *TK*. He could have been the photographer.

I closed my laptop and looked at the last sketch in the notebook. It was of a scene in Harry's Bar and done in watercolour. The work was loose, fast and evocative. I was there in the moment, feeling a little bit tipsy. Underneath she had written, *Venice has seduced me but my heart belongs to you.*

Who had her heart? Was it the woman in the painting? It must be. Putting the sketchbook down, I opened another. It was also from 1934. But no longer Venice. The notes in it were sad.

Everywhere despite the sun is grey. Without you there is no joy.

The work was technically good but lacked the vibrancy of the Venice sketches.

I am empty.

Her work changed again when she went to the Slade, and was less inward-looking during this period. There was mention of Martha and Jason and assignments. This must be the Martha who came to Cornwall with Viv. A newspaper cutting was slipped into the last pages. It was a picture of Sheba standing next to the painting that was now in her bedroom. It was entitled *My Love*, and she'd won first prize at the Slade with it that year. According to the article, the painting had been started in Venice, and she told the journalist that her trip to Paris and Venice had been the beginning of her journey to find her style.

I scrolled through the photos on my phone, switching between the one she won the prize for and the portrait. But try as I might, I couldn't see Sheba's hand in the painting of the woman. But the thought wouldn't leave me.

I flipped through another notebook. There I found one of Forster's poems written out in Sheba's handwriting. But it wasn't the version I knew. It began differently.

Your eyes
Seeing what is not visible
Your fingers
Capturing the illusive
Your heart
Holding
Me

Then the words were familiar until the end

I am unmade
Love has disassembled me
To my parts
Only you
Can make me whole

Underneath it was another sketch of the woman from the painting. She was in profile and there was a fur collar about her neck. It was dated 1938. Above the year was the initial K.

I opened my photos again. K's face stared out from my phone screen. Sheba was in love with her, of that I was certain. But it was nothing like Sheba's work. The painting called *My Love* couldn't be of Viv, because they didn't meet until after the war. I believed it was Sheba's portrait of K.

I was on to something. But it would have to wait. Finding these answers would be meaningless if I couldn't save the business.

22

Venice

Katherine turns up at five, very intoxicated. Her eyes are glassy and her breath stinks of garlic and booze. While she's been out, I have set up an easel in her bedroom and the housekeeper has found more sheets to protect the floor. On the canvas I've blocked in the shapes of the room, the window and the chaise.

Her bright blue dress doesn't work with the colours of the drapery.

'Paint me in black,' she slurs. 'Like a widow.'

She goes to her closet and pulls out a black silk dress cut on the bias with a cowl neckline at both front and back.

'Help me out of this.' She looks over her shoulder at me like I'm her maid at her beck and call, but I do as she asks. As we lift the three-quarter-length dress over her head, I stare at her birthmark. It is easier to focus on that and not on the fact that she is standing in only a garter belt and stockings less than six inches from me. The seam heading up the back of her legs directs my eyes to the curves of her behind.

With both of us tugging, the black dress falls into place skimming her shape yet highlighting it. Only two small joins on her shoulders hold the fabric to her body. Every move makes it slip across her skin.

'You don't look like a widow in that,' I manage to say.

'Ha, who says what a widow should look like? Call me a black widow like the poisonous spider.' She takes uneven steps to the chaise. Afternoon sun falls through the window, instantly turning the black into blues and purples. It is electric, and I have to stop myself from immediately painting.

'How do you want me?'

'Sober,' I whisper.

Her eyes open wide. 'No, you definitely don't want that.'

'What are you hiding from? He isn't here.'

She looks directly into my eyes. 'You.'

I take a step back.

'You see me, and I don't want to be seen.'

I watch her lean back on the chaise and turn her shoulders towards the bed without taking her eyes from mine.

'I don't want to see the woman that you see.'

'How do you know what I see?' I ask.

She laughs bitterly. 'I saw those sketches on the train and I have seen your nuns. I also see your hunger.'

My mouth dries.

'I've surprised you.' She continues to look at me, unblinking. 'I see your desire. I feel it. That's what you're afraid of. Your desire for me, a woman.'

I want to look away, but I can't. That is my secret. Once out, the world will change, it will change how I'm viewed and I'll have no control over it. I won't be the artist, the daughter of Francis Kernow. I will be one of those women, a lesbian, and excluded like the artists in Lamorna.

'I've surprised you. You think people don't see you. But they do.'

I shake my head. She sees me, but I am as invisible as a tall, red-haired woman can be. I'm not beautiful, therefore they look and move on. Only recently, here in Venice, have I felt noticed. It could be that nothing about me looks Italian. The men here think they are born to make you feel beautiful, which in me has had the opposite response.

'I see you.' She lifts her arm, pushing her hair back. The silk of her dress slips across her nipples and they rise to a nub.

'So you want me sober.' She laughs. 'I can try, but only if you paint me not as Simon wants me seen.' She draws a breath. 'I challenge you to paint me as you feel me. If you promise to do that, I will be as sober as I can be.'

Our gazes lock. It is a battle. Do I agree? But then I will be visible.

'I can't paint you as I see you and complete the commission.'

'Why not?'

'The painting your husband saw when he asked for a portrait was traditional.' I close my eyes for a moment. 'As I see you, you are colours and shapes, not arms and legs as he would have it.'

'You paint as Picasso.'

'No, different. To him his subjects are more objects, and you are not an object to me. More a feeling.'

'A desire.' She places that word between us and it hangs in the golden light. She is drunk, so speaking plainly, not poetically. Nothing stops her thoughts.

'A desire, an emotion, a movement.'

'A movement of two people pulled together.' She lights a cigarette. Her red lipstick stains the white paper.

'Don't tease me.' It's almost painful to say that.

'I'm not teasing you.'

'Aren't you?'

'God, you are so naïve. Your desire is not one-sided.'

I gasp.

'Now, paint me as you see me, not in blocks of colour and strange shapes but as a woman you want.'

I can't breathe.

'Do you dare?' She tilts her head.

'I don't know.'

'It's time to stop hiding and let yourself shine, be who you are.'

I laugh drily. 'That's easy for you to say when you don't do it yourself.'

'I know I don't, and I drink to forget I don't.'

'If you want me to paint you as I see you, I need you sober.'

Katherine stands. 'I'll cut down to start and let's see how we go.'

I look from her to the canvas. Can I do this? Inside me a voice says, *All you can do is try*. 'If I agree to this, will you write me a poem that you don't give to him?'

A slow smile spreads across her mouth. 'Yes, I will write you a poem that he will not touch.'

* * *

The week has raced by despite me wanting to slow it down. I cling to each moment, trying to make it last. We swim at the Lido, eat gelato every day, are serenaded in gondolas. My world is Katherine's laughter watching a child chasing pigeons, her glance when we spot the same thing, the communication without words and the slightest of touches. I hold them all close and record them each night in my notebook so that I will not lose them.

As I furiously paint the portrait, Katherine is true to her word. In the evenings she will have one cocktail and one glass of wine. When she is not sitting for me, she is writing, or we are looking at art together. We say no more of what I feel, and I begin to wonder if that whole conversation was imagined, until the times when she poses and she drops her guard. There is the woman I love, sober and fully present in the moment. At times I can barely breathe as I work. With every stroke of the brush, I caress her. I know she feels it too, but we do not speak of it.

Although I've seen her writing, she has not given me a poem. I don't push. Each day after I pour my heart into painting her for Forster, but truly for Katherine herself, I take an hour and paint her in colours and shapes. Even in these I haven't quite captured the variable essence of her, someone who can be at ease with a duke and flirt with a priest.

In the distance, the bells chime. She rises from the chaise. 'May I look?'

'No.'

'Simon is back tomorrow.'

'What day is it?' I have lost track of time.

She flips the pages on a diary by her bed. 'It is the thirteenth of June.'

'I have a ticket for the Biennale on the fifteenth.' My world has been so caught up in painting and in Katherine, anything outside of that has ceased to exist.

'Shall I go with you?' she asks.

'If you'd like.' I smile.

She takes my hand in hers. 'I can't imagine anyone I'd want to go with more.'

I look into her eyes, searching. 'Really?'

'Yes.' She leans forward and kisses me.

I can't move. I can't breathe. Just this, this moment that I've dreamed about since our first meeting.

Her mouth moves on mine. I kiss her, tasting her.

The church bells strike the last chime. It is nine. Dinner will soon be ready. Drinks are already on the roof terrace, but time stands still in this moment. I want to remember everything, from the scent of her perfume to the taste of tobacco on her lips.

She pulls back. 'I've so wanted to do that.'

'I . . .'

She places a finger on my mouth. 'Let's go and have our cocktail, or else we will be late for the delicious dinner that has been made for us.'

Lacing her fingers through mine, she leads me out of her bedroom and up the flight of stairs to the roof. The sun is still high, and no breeze lifts the heat of the day. She drops my hand to pour the cocktails. Together we walk to the edge of the roof and look out towards the canal. It is busier now than it was at midday. The stunted shape of the unfinished palazzo jars me less. My mind has become used to it, the shape of it, and the void of what isn't there.

She lifts her glass and locks her gaze to mine. 'To us.'

'To us,' I repeat, not believing it as I'm saying it. But here she is looking at me with such hunger. I don't need the gin; my head is swimming.

She studies me over the rim of her glass. 'Your poem is almost done.'

'Is it?'

'It's the best thing I have written, or it feels that way to me.'

'Why?' I hold my breath, waiting for her answer.

'Because it's honest. It's not written through the haze of drink or drugs.' She laughs. 'Thank you.' She kisses me quickly and moves away before I can respond.

'Dinner is ready.' The man stands by the door to the stairs, and from his expression I think he may have witnessed the kiss.

In the dining room, the air is cooler, being on the north side of the house. Katherine opens the shutters and turns off the chandelier so that the mosquitoes don't come in. They don't seem to reach the roof, but here, if the lights are on, they find their way in once the sun has begun to set.

The first course is a cold tomato soup that is both sweet and spicy. Each flavour sings on my tongue. I look down the length of the table and hate the formality that keeps us apart. Even though the food and wine has never tasted so good, I want none of it. My body is alight with anticipation. She kissed me with intent. I hunger for her with such longing I can barely think.

When the last plate is cleared, I can't sit still. My skin has become so sensitive, it is as if ants are crawling across it. Have I read her actions incorrectly? The looks she sends from the far end of the table are not those of a friend. I may be inexperienced, but my body knows the signs.

Once the servants have gone, Katherine rises to her feet. 'Coffee?'

'No thank you.' I need no more stimulation.

She takes time to select a record for the gramophone. Soon the dulcet tones of Al Bowlly singing 'Guilty' fill the room. Katherine holds her hand out. 'Dance?'

'I don't know how to.' My limbs are heavy.

'I'll teach you.' She smiles with her eyes and I shiver in anticipation. 'Just follow my lead.'

I take her hand and we move together. She whispers, 'I'm guilty.'

I pull back to see her face.

'Of loving you,' she mouths silently.

The song ends.

'Shall we call it a night?' she asks, still holding me in her arms.

'Yes.' I am breathless as she leans in and kisses my lips first, then down my neck.

'Come,' she says, taking my hand. And I do as she asks.

23

5 April 2022

Penzance

Tash jogged on the spot by the office door. It was cold enough for a frost, but thankfully there wasn't one. Our breath clouded as we entered the building. It was dark and silent. This was a relief, because part of me had suspected that my uncle would by now have cottoned onto the fact that his files had been examined.

'I'll put the kettle on and make some decent coffee now that I know where it is,' Tash said, disappearing. I went down the hall to Dad's office and flicked on the lights, forcing myself to breathe. It would take a little time, a month or maybe three, but my life would return. London would wait and I could resolve things with Paul. For the best part of the night, I'd rehearsed what I would say to him later when I called. The key thing to remind myself was that he loved me and was simply trying to protect me. But he didn't need to and that was what I had to make him see. His recent actions with my emails, my Instagram account, his interventions with my uncle all related to how desperate he was for my company. That was clear.

There was a file sitting in the centre of the desk that I hadn't put there. I stared at it. Everything I touched these days seemed to explode in some way, be it my father's empty bank account or Harbour House. Nothing was what it had seemed on the surface. I sank into the chair and looked at the file without opening it.

Valuing the contents of Harbour House should be a doddle and should be done by now. But it wasn't. The poetry manuscript was interesting and the copyright was still in play if it was Simon Forster's work. Today we would finally remove the portrait from the wall, and hopefully its secrets would be revealed. I could do this.

Instead of reading the file, I woke the computer and googled Simon Forster. Poet. Born 1898 and died 1959. Married in 1919, one child, born in 1935. His wife and his daughter both died in the Blitz. His last publication was in 1939 and his best-known poem was published in 1935.

His work was described as romantic and was loosely connected to the Imagist group. Among his contemporaries were T. S. Eliot and W. H. Auden.

I checked my emails. There was nothing from Rory yet, but that wasn't a surprise.

'Here's a decent cup of coffee, which is definitely needed this early.' Tash cradled her mug. The office wasn't exactly warm. 'What do you want me to tackle first?'

'See if you can find more on the company accounts, and I'll go through the correspondence and emails once you get me into his computer again.'

'No problem. What time is your meeting with my dad?'

'Ten o'clock.' I drew a breath. 'I moved it forward because of all this.'

'Sensible.'

'After that, Frank, who helps to fix and hang things around here, will be at Harbour House at one.' I leaned back. 'Aside from finishing up the typing and a bit more research, we should have itemised everything in the house and studios by then.'

'There are some high-priced items, and if you can create a buzz, the sale will result in some good commissions.'

'This we desperately need.' I took a sip of my coffee. 'I don't know what I'm going to do.'

'I get that, but just focus on one thing at a time. And right now, it's reading your uncle's stuff before he comes in.'

I nodded and followed her into his office. She quickly logged me in and then went to check the old filing cabinets.

Scrolling through my uncle's emails had to be up there as one of the most boring things I'd ever done in the name of research, and there had been many. For the past month he'd been going back and forth on a private sale of a large refectory table. Alarm bells began to ring. Why was he selling things privately? To the best of my knowledge, he had never owned a refectory table. For one, it wouldn't fit in his cottage. With dread in my heart, I looked for a similar trail of emails. There were several. He was doing an awful lot of private trading. Never achieving the price he wanted. Somewhere in our records, I'd bet I would find the items he was selling, and this didn't feel good.

'Hey, Ren, come and look at this.'

I went to Tash. She was holding a folder. 'This is weird. Did you know that Barton's have another warehouse-type facility in Hayle?'

'No.' I shook my head, running through everything I'd seen about the business and its assets. A warehouse in Hayle wasn't one of them.

'Thought it would have been common knowledge.'

'No. Does it say when it was purchased?' I asked.

'Yes, it was bought seven and a half years ago.'

I shivered. That was just after the lawsuit. Why on earth would they have bought a warehouse then? The company was really struggling, and it was only in the past few years that things had picked up, with Stephen's furniture sales and the rise in interest in the Cornish artists.

'The more I discover, the more worried I am.' I went back to scrolling through the emails and Tash went back to the files. The first pot of coffee turned into the second as we unearthed more worrying details.

We looked at each other as we heard tyres crunch on the gravel. It was almost nine. Without a word, we flew into action so that by the time the front door opened, we were back in Dad's office, shuffling piles of paper.

My uncle stopped at the door. I needed to keep him chatting long enough for his computer to fully shut down.

'Early,' he said, looking at Tash's feet resting on the desk.

'Catches the worm,' I said, and instantly regretted it. 'So much to do to finish the Harbour House inventory.'

'Nothing worthwhile there.' He turned, and I jumped up and raced after him.

'I don't agree, and we have also found a poetry manuscript that will raise interest in the sale.'

He stopped and turned to look at me. 'Do you think I trust anything you say? Your judgement is hit and miss at best.'

'That may be true,' I countered, rather than saying what I wanted to say. 'But an expert has already agreed with me and has taken it for further verification.'

'It will come to nothing. They were just two old lesbians who had a private income and dabbled in the arts. It wouldn't surprise me if they had written poetry to each other.'

I didn't know how to respond to such an outright dismissive tirade. I might not be worth anything, but these two women were. 'I disagree with you entirely. Both Kernow and Sykes were exceptional artists who have been overlooked purely because they were women.'

'On your hobby horse again.' He snorted. 'I would have thought the mistake you made all those years ago would have taught you something, but clearly not.'

Tash looked like she was about to throw a punch. I had to defuse the situation. 'On another note, I'm seeing the solicitor this morning regarding probate. As you know, Mum's health is not brilliant, and it looks like the best thing for her is for me to sell both our shares.'

He paled.

'I'll know more after I've spoken to him. But are you interested in buying us out?' I smiled hopefully. He turned and walked away.

'That rattled him,' Tash whispered when I walked back to the desk. My legs were shaking. I'd never liked confrontation.

'I shouldn't have said anything.'

'Of course you should have.' She crossed her arms in front of her chest.

'Morning.' Marcia popped her head round the door. 'I see the early elves have been in again. I'm about to make a fresh pot. By the way, I cleaned up your inventory and left a copy on your desk.' She stepped into the office. 'It's right there and you haven't looked at it.'

Tash flipped the folder open; it was empty.

'Now that's odd. I put it there as I was leaving last night.'

Tash and I both looked down the hall.

'He was still here,' Marcia said. 'I'll print off another.'

Stephen appeared at the door. 'With these adjustments.' He handed the paperwork to her. Even from this distance I could see that he'd crossed through *Chippendale* and put in *18th-century bookcase*. I stood and took the list from Marcia.

'I'll go through this first.'

'I'm the senior partner here.'

'You are, but between me and my mother, we control more shares in the business.' I stood straight. 'I may have made a mistake years ago, but I am more than capable of recognising a Chippendale bookcase when its partner is held in the V&A's collection.' Out of the corner of my eye I could see Tash making a face. She was the one who had spotted it, not me, but now was not the time to show weakness.

My uncle looked like thunder as he left. Marcia opened her eyes wide.

The buzzer alerted us to the opening of the front door. Marcia dashed out to welcome whoever had come in. I pushed my hands through my hair. This was crazy. That my uncle had been doing dodgy dealings with the business for years was becoming apparent. It was going to make this morning's meeting with Tash's dad trickier than I'd anticipated.

'She's in the office,' I heard Marcia say. I sent a questioning look to Tash.

'Hello, darling.'

I blinked. Paul stood with a backpack in one hand and a large Longchamp bag in the other.

'Aren't you going to welcome me?' he asked.

Spurred into action, I came round the desk and gave him a kiss.

'I think you can do better than that,' he whispered in my ear, and I shivered; not from excitement, but with something more like fear. I hadn't had this feeling since he had returned to London after the funeral.

He looked across at Tash, who had her arms crossed.

'Never had you pictured as a train enthusiast.' Tash paused. 'So what brings you to the end of the world aside from the Night Riviera?'

'The love of my life who doesn't look at her phone or answer her emails.'

'What a shame,' Tash said, squaring up.

'Look, I must head to my meeting with the solicitor.' I paused, thinking of what to do with Paul. 'Tash, can you run Paul to Mum's and I'll meet you at Harbour House when the meeting is finished?'

'Why don't I just come to the meeting with you? A little extra support.' He smiled, but I didn't trust it. I didn't trust why he was here at all, when every time I'd asked him to come and help me, he'd refused.

'It's OK, I'll be all right on my own.' I didn't want him anywhere near what I had to say to Tash's father.

'Oh, you know, two sets of eyes and two sets of ears always make these sorts of meetings easier. As has been said so much recently, recollections do vary.'

I closed my eyes for a moment. 'Fine.' I handed him the keys. 'Why don't you put your things in the car while I gather the paperwork I need?'

He looked from me to Tash, then turned and left. I stifled a scream. He was the last person I needed here right now, and I would have to find a plausible excuse to prevent him from joining me in the meeting.

'Do you want me to come too?' Tash put her arm round my shoulders.

'Yes, but no. I need you at Harbour House. I also need you to check that no one else has keys but us and the gardener.'

'Why?'

'Let's say a hunch.'

'On it.' She threw her other arm around me and gave me a hug. 'You can do this.'

I drew in a deep breath. 'I sure as hell hope you're right.'

24

_____

Venice

I lie watching Katherine breathe. Her dark hair presses against her cheek. In that moment I know what my painting is missing. Despite the low light, I work swiftly filling in the details from the memory of each touch, each moment of laughter and each second of ecstasy. I don't hear her wake, but when I look up, she is watching me. Her glances aren't veiled and her eyes shine. They don't hide her pain, her genius or her love. It is all there. I work furiously as she moves to the chaise. The rising sun touches her bare skin where I planted kisses not long before. Each brush stroke caresses her now as I touched her, and I relive those moments of passion.

Steps sound on the floor outside the door. I hold my breath. Neither of us has a stitch of clothing on. The person walks on past and I add one last touch of crimson to her mouth. Then I lay down my brush and go and kiss her.

'I must go now.'

She nods, handing me my clothes. She flings on her dressing gown, which only deepens my desire. It is the contrast of the burgundy of the fabric and the fairness of her skin. Once I'm dressed, I pick up the sheet to cover the painting.

'Let me see.'

I stop as she gasps.

'My God.'

'It's you.'

She nods with her hand to her mouth.

'It is you as the world sees you.'

'No, the world sees nothing but a beautiful canvas. You have painted the veneer as well as the complicated person living behind it.' She kisses my cheek. 'Thank you.' She helps me to drape the sheet safely over the painting, making sure that nothing touches the wet surface.

* * *

Forster is due back by four, and Katherine is restless. Only the occasional glance eases my concern that she regrets last night. Focusing on anything other than her is difficult. I can't believe she feels the way I do. The need to talk about us is overwhelming, but she is silent, smoking cigarette after cigarette. By noon I have suggested we head to the Accademia, or go and look at the work on display in a nearby church. But she insists that she must be here when he arrives. Not even the suggestion of Harry's Bar can shift her.

I don't need to be around when he returns. In fact, I'm dreading it. She will alter before my eyes and I'm not sure I'm strong enough. In order to keep sane, I leave the palazzo and seek out the areas the tourists never venture to. There, under clothes lines filled with colourful garments, I work with watercolours. The heat of the day increases my speed, but finally I have to abandon the work. It is too warm to focus. The only places to find cool air are the many churches. I am wary after losing myself and my sense of time in the last one, but I slip through a small door that opens up into a vast space. My eyes adjust and I stroll, admiring the varying saints in ecstasy – and after last night, I understand more of just what that means. Everything inside me is shouting happiness. But then I stop. How can I make this work?

The organ begins playing, startling me. A few painful notes ring out like a runner trying to catch their breath, then the sound transforms to music that transports me elsewhere. I don't recognise the tune, but it fits with the baroque interior.

I sit in a pew to the left side of the church and study the painting of the Ascension of Mary behind the altar. The music and the art blend together in perfection. Closing my eyes, I let myself think about last night. Her touch, her tenderness, her understanding of my lack of experience, and above all, her belief. She believes in me.

Katherine has woven a spell around me. She casts one over everyone except the man who is her husband. He holds such control over her. I open my eyes as fear surges through me. What will he do if he discovers Katherine is my lover? He must not find out and I hope his self-centred nature will blind him. But how do Katherine and I go forward?

The music stops and I wait to see if it will begin again. When it doesn't, I rise to leave the peace of the church and my own disturbing thoughts behind. Sunlight streams through a window, hitting a painting of a biblical scene. My heart stops. Bathsheba and David. My mother is partially draped in a white cloth as she stands by a tub. She is painted in exquisite detail. I can see myself in her features. If only she were here so I could talk to her. My heart aches with longing for her. I need that reassuring touch, the calming voice, the understanding. How do I find my way forward? Grief swamps me and I can't move.

An old woman walks in front of me and I turn away from her scrutiny and study the rest of the painting. My father as David is in profile and stands on a balcony looking down on Bathsheba. My mother's expression is one of innocence, and yet it isn't.

'Is this the painting of your parents?' Father Keeney asks.

I jump. 'Where have you come from?'

'From behind the organ.' He points down the aisle towards the nave.

'Was it you playing?'

He cracks his knuckles. 'It was.'

'Impressive.'

He shrugs. 'You don't have to answer, as I can see for myself how you resemble your mother.'

I flush and look at my mother again. She is delicate where I am awkward, but there is no denying the resemblance.

'The original painting of King David and Bathsheba that was here was sold to pay for repairs to the building. The artist who painted this one gave it to the church. He visits regularly. Would you like to meet him?'

'Yes. That would be wonderful. It would be a way to connect with my mother.'

'Is she lost?'

'She died three years ago.'

He rests a hand on top of mine. 'I'm sorry.'

'Thank you.'

'I'll have a word with Roberto, the artist.' He adjusts the camera hanging around his neck. 'You wouldn't like to be my model for today? I've been given this new camera and I'd love to see what it can do.' His grin is lopsided.

'Well as it happens, I'm free, so I'm happy to oblige.' I haven't been a model in a while. It would be a good change.

'Excellent.'

With one last look at the painting, we head out into the crowded campo, where we dodge crowds. Finally we reach quieter areas and I have lost all sense of where we are. Without warning, we come to the Arsenale. This is an area I have not explored.

'I'll just take a shot or two here.'

Nothing catches my eye, but I am not a photographer.

'If you stand there by the canal.' He points.

The sun is high and it is incredibly hot. There are no shadows to speak of, so I'm at a loss as to his composition. This time of day is not ideal for an artist. Things are flat, but maybe for a photographer it is different.

'The boatyard behind you,' he waves his hand, 'was once the heart of the Venetians' power.'

'That makes sense in view of the water that surrounds them.'

'But their time has passed.' He puts the lens cap back on and takes my arm. The sense of being watched follows me.

Father Keeney's pace picks up as we move through some crowded areas. 'There's been an outbreak of typhus near here, so we'd best be quick.'

'Typhus?'

'Sadly, yes. The poverty in places is astounding, but it is not a side of Venice that many see.'

Even when I arrived, I didn't see the poverty that is in front of me now. Only once we are near the tourist areas does Father Keeney stop.

'There's the Doge's Palace. I think a shot here would be good.'

I pose as asked. He is a most patient man as he waits for crowds and clouds to pass.

The bells ring. Hours have slipped by, and we're now standing with the throngs in St Mark's Square.

'Time to take the classic tourist photograph,' he says.

I laugh as he keeps waving me back until his hand comes up to stop me. While I wait, Katherine and last night fill my thoughts.

'That's it,' he says. 'The film is finished and the last shot is the best. There was something different about it.' He studies me. 'I can't quite place it, but you shone.'

I'm in love, I say silently, but I shrug.

'Shall we have a coffee?'

I look to the clock tower and see the hour. 'Another time.'

'A better offer?' he asks with a smile.

'Maybe,' I say, and take my leave, making my way back towards the palazzo.

My pace slows the nearer I get. I dread my return and long for it in equal measure. These hours being with Father Keeney have been a tonic, but now reality sets in. How am I to behave? If I was in love with a man, I wouldn't have to hide my feelings. People would celebrate young love. No one but Katherine and I will celebrate ours. This isn't fair. I brace myself and enter the palazzo, not sure what will ensue.

The housekeeper informs me that Signor Forster has arrived and that he and the signora are together in the salon, so I avoid it. I have no desire to see him, and I don't have the skill to look him in the eye and lie. I've never been good at lying, which is why I said so little when I left Cornwall. And why I didn't answer my father's questions about why I was going.

I pull out my mother's diary and look at what she was doing on this day twenty-one years before.

> The heat is most oppressive at midday. That is when I, like much of the population, lie in a darkened room and move as little as possible. However, it is when my brain is the most active, as I cannot stop it thinking. The sunlight steals in below and around the shutters and I see shapes and plan paintings in my mind, for it is simply too hot to move.
>
> Last night he walked me back and kissed me. I was changed for ever in that moment. My soul sang. It had found its match. Love changes everything.

I look up. Is that what I felt last night? My mother was twenty-two when she came here. My grandfather didn't want her to come, but she did anyway. When she returned from Venice in December, she was pregnant with me and married to my father. Her life going forward was as normal as the life of an artist could be. There is no normality for me going forward loving Katherine. What do I want more?

I put the diary down and pick up my sketchbook. In a few strokes Katherine is on the page as she was hours ago in bed, with the morning light making her more beautiful. The low rays picked out her hollows and her fullness. After three sketches, I jump up and grab a new canvas. Bright, bold colour touched with light. Sharp, round, undulating. I don't stop to think or to judge. I paint the Katherine of my heart.

I lose track of time and of place.

'Miss Kernow.' Forster stands on the threshold to my room. I didn't hear him knock. He flicks the light on. 'What on earth are you painting?'

My heart stops. It's all there on the canvas. I dash in front of it. He will know. But then I see the distaste in his expression.

'Simply playing with colour,' I say, and watch his Adam's apple move as if he can't quite find his words. He has nicked his neck shaving. There is a spot of dried blood.

'Katherine tells me your portrait of her is finished.'

I nod.

'I want to see it, but she insists you must be there.' His voice is uncertain. This is new. Is it because Katherine has stood up to him?

'The paint is still wet, and until it has dried sufficiently and I can check the balance of the colours in the painting, no one must look at it or move it.'

'I have to look at a covered easel in my bedroom?' He widens his stance.

I stifle laughter, because it was he who chose the location. It is this painting of Katherine that has brought us together. It is his doing. He's made himself a cuckold, if that can happen when your wife sleeps with a woman. Would that trouble him, as he doesn't seem to give women credit for anything? He would be nothing without Katherine.

'Can the easel be moved to another room while the painting dries?' he asks when it's clear I'm not giving ground on this.

I draw in a deep breath, delaying my answer. He is uncomfortable and I'm enjoying it. 'It needs to sit for a week and then it can be placed out of the light, say in the dining room.'

'Hmm.'

'The growing heat in Venice will speed the drying process.'

'If you insist.' He huffs.

'I do.' Behind him I spy Signor Rossi. 'Hello.'

'Signorina Kernow.' He bows slightly and pauses to study my painting. 'This is interesting.'

'Bah, it's a mess,' says Forster.

'No, it is not a mess, it is done with intention and passion.'

'A child with paints could do that.'

Rossi steps closer and examines the brushwork. Then a smile spreads across his face. 'This work is excellent. It is not work I would choose for my home, but it is nevertheless excellent.' He moves back and looks from me to the painting. 'This is a person, no?'

I nod, and fear creeps along my skin.

'I see it, and with the colours you have chosen and the energy, it is clearly a person you care for.'

'Yes,' I say, suddenly uncertain. No one but me can tell that it is Katherine. This I know, but I watch Rossi carefully. A smile plays on his full mouth.

'The painting shows much passion.' He glances at me again.

'Still waters, as they say, can run deeply. I look forward to hearing your reaction to the work at the Biennale.'

'I am so looking forward to experiencing it.'

'Yes, experiencing is the correct term. It leaves you feeling things . . . a bit like your painting here.' He turns from me. 'Come, Simon, Il Duce wishes to see you now. Herr Hitler, the German chancellor, arrives in Venice tomorrow.'

The two men leave my room, and I feel seen and violated. Herr Hitler coming to Venice. My Venice does not have room for fascists, but they are everywhere. I am taking hospitality from one as well as stealing his wife. And that is what I want to do right this minute.

I leave my room, closing the door behind me, and go in search of Katherine. She is pouring gin into a glass. She looks at me and shrugs her shoulders.

'A bit early,' I say.

'He's home.' She taps a pile of pages on the side table before dropping an olive in the glass.

'That bad?'

The front door thuds and the chandelier shivers. I'm worried for Katherine standing under it.

'Take a look for yourself.'

I scan the top page. It is all about a songbird and could have been written by me – someone who has no skill with words at all. In fact, as he said of my painting of Katherine, it could have been done by a child.

She knocks back the drink and pours a second before she gathers the papers together. 'The irony – or maybe not irony, but agony – is that he wants something not just good but brilliant for tomorrow in case he has a chance to talk poetry with Herr Hitler.' She takes a slug. 'Herr Hitler is coming here to meet Mussolini and discuss Austria, among other things, not poetry.'

'Leave him.'

She stares at me. 'Nothing is that simple.'

'You don't need him. Let's leave Venice and head to Cornwall. No one will know you, and no one cares what I do.' I pause, letting a plan take shape in my thoughts. 'Everyone will think we're simply friends. Only we would know the difference. We wouldn't need to live like the fabulous artist Gluck who does so obviously. It might not be as authentic, but we could leave that to our art.'

'That's nothing but a lovely dream.' She smiles, and I can see that the gin in her hand is not her second. She has lost her tolerance while he has been away. 'He controls my money, the money I inherited from my parents. He'd have me declared insane and sent to an asylum.'

I gasp. 'He wouldn't.'

'He tried to once before, but I promised I'd never leave him and he relented.'

This is intolerable. I have to get her away from him. It will destroy her. 'Leave. He won't find you.'

She laughs bitterly. 'How would we survive?'

'Frugally. I'd sell my work.'

She pauses, and I can tell that she is far away. 'Your work is good, but he knows your name.'

'We could stage it so it would appear that we weren't together. I could leave first, or you could, and then he wouldn't know. He'd never give me another thought.'

Sinking onto the sofa, Katherine focuses on me. 'Maybe.' She downs the drink. 'You, my darling, can see the beauty behind the facade, but you cannot see the reality. You haven't lived enough life to know that being who you are can cost you everything.' She rises, kisses me, grabs the papers and leaves.

25

5 April 2022
_____

Penzance

When I sat in the car, I was angrier than I'd ever been. Paul looked like he'd won something, possibly the lottery. I started the engine and gripped the wheel until my knuckles went white. He scrolled through his phone. He'd been reading my emails and replying for me, helping me. I'd stopped that now by changing my passwords. But how long had he been doing it? We'd lived together for eight years, so it could have been quite a while. It was like he didn't trust me. I'd done nothing to make him feel that way. And yet here he was, without warning, coming to a place he despised.

I reversed the car and without a word pulled out into the stream of traffic heading into the centre of town.

'You don't seem happy to see me,' he said, still looking at his phone.

'I'm just surprised.'

'You asked me to come down.'

I bit back my words while I pulled in to let someone pass on a narrow street. 'I did. I asked you and you said you couldn't.' I cast a glance at him before pulling into the little car park near the solicitor's. 'In fact, I asked you not to leave after the funeral. Both times you said no, so that's why I'm a bit surprised to see you here now.'

'I emailed,' he said, 'and you didn't reply, and then I saw you'd changed your passwords.'

How did he know that? But of course his was the backup email if I lost my password. God, why hadn't I remembered that?

I turned into the car park with so many emotions raging inside me. Once the engine was off, I forced my shoulders down to a normal level. I didn't need a fight with Paul right before seeing the solicitor, so I had to play this carefully. 'It's good to see you, but I don't require you in this meeting.' I released my seat belt and grabbed my bag.

He got out of the car. 'You do need me. You're still so wrapped in grief that you won't make the right decisions.'

'Whether they are right or not, they are mine to make.' I smiled at him with as much sweetness as I could muster, which was not a lot.

'What about your mother's point of view?' he countered.

I opened my mouth, then shut it, pausing before saying, 'I am the executor of my father's estate.'

'You are making decisions for your mother and she hasn't given you that power.'

I was about to ask him how he knew, but then I remembered he'd been on the phone to her every day. It was becoming clear he hadn't simply been checking she was OK, but much more.

'This is my meeting about my father's estate. I'm going in alone.'

'You don't have the experience for this and you'll get things wrong. You know you will. You become flustered when under pressure.'

'Paul, I've told you I'm going to this meeting on my own.' I looked at him across the car bonnet. My legs were shaking but he couldn't see that.

'Fine. I'll sit in the waiting room.'

'OK,' I said, but it wasn't. Had Paul always been so interfering? Why hadn't I seen it?

I locked the car and we headed into the offices. I was relieved when I was ushered straight through to Mr Thomas, because it didn't give Paul any further time to argue with me and wear me down. I had enough doubts about my abilities without him adding to them.

'Ah, Kerensa.' Jack Thomas stood and came around the desk. He opened his arms and gave me a hug, one that was much needed. I'd known this man for a long time.

'Right, you requested this meeting,' he said, settling back into his chair.

'I did.' I sat down. 'I moved it forward because things at the auction house and my father's affairs are not what you think they are.'

'Go on?' he prompted.

I blew out all the air that had built up within me. 'My father's current account is overdrawn. The savings accounts are empty, as are the investment accounts.'

'Really?' His eyebrows drew together.

'Sadly, yes. I'm still trying to get to the bottom of it. What's clear is that he's been feeding money somewhere on a regular basis.'

'Does your mother know?' he asked.

'She's just figured it out. We've raided her Premium Bonds to pay for Meg Pascoe. All of this came to light when Meg's standing order didn't go through.'

'Not good. Can you take a loan from the business for the interim?'

I snorted. 'No. I think the business accounts are in a similar condition to my father's personal accounts.'

'That seems odd. Have you spoken to your uncle?' He picked up a pen.

I put my hands up. 'Not yet, other than to ask if he was in a position to buy Mum and me out.'

'How did he react?'

'He walked away.' Telling the bare facts like this was hard. It felt like it was all my fault.

'Kerensa, this doesn't sound good at all. I'll need to see the bank statements, and you'll need to consult with your uncle.'

'I know.' Dread filled me at the thought. I paused. 'All of this will affect probate, won't it?'

'Yes and no. As the bulk of the estate goes to your mother, that part should be fairly straightforward.'

'The house, and the non-existent value of the company?'

'It still has its good name.' He tented his fingers.

'But with Dad dead, its resident expert in Cornish art is gone. We'll just become a house clearance operation.'

'You bring skill to the table.'

I laughed.

'Seriously, you do. Tash has told me about all the work you do behind the scenes on *Fake or Fabulous*. You make the experts look good.'

'They're the experts, though, and I'm just the researcher.'

'As I've told you almost as many times as I've told Tash, believe in yourself.' He came around the desk and gave me another hug. 'Let me know if we can help with your mother.'

'Thanks.' I could have stayed there safely for ever. But Paul was waiting on the other side of the door.

'Since her diagnosis with vascular dementia, I know things have become harder.'

I froze. 'What?'

Jack sat on his desk and took my hands in his. 'You didn't know?'

I shook my head. 'When? How? Why?'

'After her stroke. Your father came in with her and did all the paperwork giving him lasting power of attorney. And we will need to do that with you now, as soon as possible, while she still can.'

I tried to form coherent sentences, but none came. My mother had dementia. That explained some things, but not why I didn't know.

'I recall her saying she was going to tell you,' Jack said.

I thought of Paul, sitting in the outer office. He knew, I realised, and he was the reason why I didn't. He was trying to protect me, but instead he'd made things far worse. I'd lost my father, and now I was losing my mother too.

My phone buzzed. It had better not be Paul telling me to hurry up.

It was Tash. Rory was at Harbour House. His trip to Exeter had been quick.

I scrolled through my emails, and sure enough there was one from Paul. There was one from Rory too, saying he had verified the work and would be back today. That email had arrived about ten last night. Paul had taken the train shortly thereafter. Something told me that was why he was here. And that he still had access to my emails. Alarm bells went off inside me. I would need to tread carefully.

'I'm here for any legal advice you need, and also as a sounding board.' Jack's expression showed concern. Tash looked so much like him.

His kindness nearly had me weeping, but then I thought of Paul and squared my shoulders. Many things were uncertain, but

I needed to fix things for my mother, confront my uncle and, if I could, honour my two artists. One fact was vital for my sanity at this moment, and that was Paul and how he made me feel. I had to face him, and I couldn't let him railroad my mother into what he thought was best for her.

'One more question. Tash mentioned that you remembered there being wills for Sheba Kernow and Viv Sykes.'

Jack nodded. 'Yes. I recall filing them.'

'The contents?'

'Unfortunately I didn't read them. It always becomes complicated when people die intestate, or apparently so.'

'And without the wills, the estate will pass to the great-nephews?'

'Sadly, I can't say. But ask around, because people do remember things.'

In the outer office, I saw Paul perched on the edge of his chair. Although the night on the train had left him a little less groomed than normal, he was still good-looking and poised. He scrolled continuously through his phone, possibly checking my emails and messages. He would know that Rory was at Harbour House. Had I become so incompetent that he had stepped into the void?

He glanced up, frowning. It was a split second before his expression changed and he was all smiles again. 'Good meeting?'

He might have overheard it sitting so close to Jack's office, but he wouldn't hear the details from me.

'Yes.' I waved at the receptionist and headed out the door.

Paul caught up with me. 'The coffee and pastry they offered on the train really didn't do it for me. Can we go and get something to eat?'

It was nearly twelve. 'Sure.' Rather than head to the car, I walked to a café around the corner.

It was obvious he wanted to talk, but I ignored him, squinting in the sunlight and wishing I'd remembered my sunglasses. At four this morning they hadn't seemed essential.

Inside the café there was a happy buzz, and I tried to let it soothe me.

'What can I get you?' Paul asked.

'Just a black coffee, thanks.' I took a seat.

He sent me a sharp look. 'Have you been eating? You've lost weight, which looks great, but you need to eat.'

'What?' That whole statement didn't make sense. I looked great but I needed to eat. 'I have been eating.'

He made his way to the counter, and returned with the coffees. 'I'm worried about you.'

'Thank you.' I gave him a smile. His face lit up and my heart jumped, reminding me how I felt about him. He was my dream. Clever, good-looking and devoted. I never worried that there was someone else. He was always either by my side or working. I couldn't want a more loyal partner. He was here even though he hated it. This was all good. I was overplaying his interference. It came from a place of concern.

He picked up my hand. 'I'm here for you. I'm sorry I haven't come before now.' He gave it a squeeze. 'It was wrong of me. I didn't see all you were trying to carry. There is no need for you to do this on your own.'

I took a deep breath and made myself relax. I'd been overreacting earlier.

'That's better. I can see my girl again.'

'Thanks.' It would be good to share my worries. 'It's been hard.'

'Tell me all about it.'

'There is no money.'

He blinked.

'None. We've had to raid Mum's Premium Bonds to pay her carer.'

'She won't need a carer for long.'

'Seriously, Paul, Mum talks a great game.' I stopped. She didn't talk well, which I now realised was not simply the stroke but the dementia too. That also explained some of her odd comments. 'That's not the right expression. Her speech is better, but she isn't doing well, as the fall last week showed. She will need a carer long-term, especially because of the dementia.' I stared at him and he looked down at his hand holding mine. I waited to see if he would say anything. Maybe he didn't know? That was possible.

'Surely she'll get one through the health services.'

I cleared my throat. 'That will take time, and up until now it hasn't been necessary, but with Dad . . .'

'Yes, I see where you're going with this. But she will rally.'

'I wish you were right, but she won't. It's past that now, and as much as I don't want to accept that, I'm going to have to.'

'Look, I'm sure you're just emotional at the moment and your vision is clouded.' He looked up. Two plates of food were making their way towards us. One was a salad and the other was a big fat cream bun. My mouth watered at the sight of the salad, and I couldn't believe how thoughtful he'd been to get me something even though I'd said I only wanted coffee.

He indicated to the waiter, who gave him the salad and put the cream bun in front of me. I froze.

Once he had left, Paul smiled at me. 'You looked like you needed a treat.' He started to tuck into his salad and I glanced at the bun. My stomach gurgled loudly. He looked up. 'See, I was right, you haven't been eating.'

I couldn't deny that meals hadn't been regular, but I ate when I was hungry, and right now my stomach was making its thoughts about the bun clear. I picked up the cutlery. Just a small piece of it would tame the animal within, and I would have a sandwich with some nutrition in it later.

'That's better,' he said as he watched me try to cut into it. 'Why don't you just pick it up and eat it all. You know you want it. You don't have to pretend with me.'

I cast him a furious glance and continued trying to ease my way through the bun. The knife was little more than a straight edge.

'Being here has not done you any favours. You need to finish up and come back to London. We'll find a place to put your mother into and all will be well. Cornwall is not good for either of you.'

I stopped trying to cut the bun and stared at him.

'In fact, I've spoken to your mother about this.'

'What?'

'Yes, she's been worried about the stress this is putting you under. She's noticed that you've lost weight and even mentioned that you were drunk one night.'

I pushed the knife down hard, and cream shot out and hit him. I sat back, stifling my laughter. From the horror on his face, you'd think he was covered in blood. His bright blue cashmere jumper looked like it had fluffy clouds all over it. I handed him my napkin.

'That's no bloody good. No bloody good at all.' He stood and went to the counter. The man there ushered him into a back room, and he returned with his jumper damp but clean. I schooled my features into a straight face. All I wanted to do in that moment was tell Tash.

'I've paid the bill. We're leaving now.' He took my arm and marched me out of the café.

The walk to the car was accomplished at speed. I needed to be at the house when that painting came off the wall. There was just enough time to drop him at my mother's house, but I didn't want to leave them alone together after what he had just said.

'You could apologise.' He glared at me.

I opened my eyes wide despite the bright April sunshine.

'You nearly ruined my jumper.'

'I didn't ask for a cream bun.' I unlocked the car and opened my door. He hadn't replied, and it crossed my mind that I could drop him at the train station, but I knew that wouldn't solve my problem. He'd simply call my mother and take a taxi there. There was only one thing I could do. I would bring him to Harbour House, then later have a long-overdue face-to-face chat.

26

Venice

The contrast between the phthalo-blue sky and the terracotta of the walls is sharp, almost tart in its vividness. None of the lingering mists of the past few mornings soften the day. The tension in the air is almost unbearable despite the fact that we're outside for breakfast. The table is shaded from the sun by an awning and the scent of the roses is cloying. Katherine hasn't said a word other than to ask for more coffee, while Forster talks non-stop about Il Duce and his brilliant new poems, which he waves about. He doesn't mention the large painting still dominating his room. From Katherine's appearance, she hasn't slept at all. Rather than come to the Biennale with me today, she should go to bed.

'Serafino tells me the Biennale is filled with works like your painting,' Forster says, flipping over the newspaper he is reading.

Katherine looks at me. 'Painting?'

'Yes, the one in her room that looks like a child has been given a box of paints.' He lifts his coffee cup. 'But Serafino saw something of merit in it, even if he wouldn't want it hanging on his wall.'

'You haven't shown me.' Katherine eyes me across the table.

'I painted it yesterday.' I smile when I long to reach out and touch her, give her some reassurance.

Her head moves up and down, but it is more like she is about to nod off than in any sort of communication.

'I understand Ben Nicholson is one of the artists representing Great Britain. Do you know him?' Forster helps himself to tea.

'I do, and also Winifred Nicholson, who has paintings there as well.' It is not quite a month since I last saw her. Then I was searching for a miracle cure to become normal so I could fit into life in St Ives, and now I'm searching for a way forward with Katherine. We must make our love work somehow. It would mean that I couldn't go home to St Ives. Nellie made it plain that there is no place for me there as a freak. But now I know love and I am complete with Katherine, I will sacrifice the dream of a normal life with a family and acceptance in St Ives. My life with Katherine would be too difficult there. I couldn't be me and I couldn't subject her to that type of scrutiny. Now, thinking of the isolation of Lamorna, I see the appeal. There would be no need to hide who I am. I would be free to be an artist and a lesbian.

Forster clears his throat. 'His work is very odd.'

I blink, refocusing on him. 'It's striking and innovative,' I place my hands flat on the table. 'And Winifred's is a breath of fresh air.'

'It looks like child's work as well, but at least I know what was being painted.' He butters a piece of toast. 'Now the painting you did of the urchin, that was perfection.'

There is only one way to see the world, his. I reach for the strawberry jam, longing to throw it at him.

'I trust your painting of Katherine is up to that standard. It irks me no end that I can't look at it.'

'You mustn't.' Katherine looks up from her plate.

'I don't see why not.' He takes a bite of toast and my stomach turns. How has she stayed with him? He is unbearable in every way.

'Aside from me, do you want others to see your poems before they are ready?' Katherine challenges him, and I'm relieved to see the fight back in her.

'Well, if you put it that way.' He presses the newspaper flat.

'I do.' She reaches across the table and places her hand on his. It takes everything in me not to knock it away. So I eat my egg and look at the beautiful mosaic work on the table.

'What time shall we leave?' asks Katherine.

'In half an hour.' I send her a questioning look.

She stands. 'I had better dress properly.'

'Herr Hitler arrives today.' Simon leans back in his chair and looks as if he's won an award. 'I will be with Conte Volpi, taking him to the Biennale. I'm pleased that you and Katherine will witness this historic moment.'

Katherine stops still and looks over her shoulder at me, then her husband. With her smile fixed in place, she says, 'That will be wonderful, darling.'

He grins, and my heart sinks. Our day alone enjoying art is to be doubly ruined.

* * *

The crowds are light as we arrive, and I try to push to the back of my mind the fact that Forster and Herr Hitler are coming to this place of joy. The range of art on display is truly inspiring, and ideas bubble within me. The use of line, shape, form and colour is so varied. Before we left, I didn't have time to show Katherine the painting of her that he had dismissed. When I looked at it again last night, it helped to fill some of the space left empty inside me without her by my side. I'm consumed by jealousy. He has the pleasure to be with her. But she told me that she had spent the night working on his words.

On the vaporetto journey to Giardini, she nodded off. If she would take my advice, we could find a peaceful spot for her to take a nap. With her arm through mine, she says, 'I don't want to miss a moment of this day with you.'

'This is hard,' I say.

'Incredibly. All I want is to be with you, but we must make the most of the moments we have.'

I can't argue, and I'm worried about her. The dark shadows under her eyes do not detract from her beauty but strangely make it more compelling. But she is being ripped apart and I'm part of the cause.

'With any luck we will be in the wrong pavilion when Simon appears, and we won't have to see him at all.'

'We can hope.' I sigh. The beauty around us is great but there is also a sense of dread following us. What can I do to shake it off? 'We haven't visited the British pavilion yet. I'm longing to see it after what your husband said.' I regret my words as soon as I've uttered them.

'Please don't remind me he's my husband. Call him Simon or Forster, but not my husband.'

'As you wish.'

'I do fervently wish.' She smiles. 'I've been thinking about what you said.'

My heart clenches. 'Yes?'

'It might work.' She squeezes my arm and holds me close to her side. I'm grinning, wanting to dance and sing and shout. Instead we walk sedately past beautifully dressed people of all nationalities. They take no notice of us, but surely our happiness must be visible.

'It will take some careful planning.'

My heart races. This will happen. We will be together. I calm my thoughts and say, 'Of course.'

'It also can't be rushed.' She pauses. 'We need to build up your name so that when you return to England, people will seek you as a portrait painter.'

My shoulders fall.

'What's wrong?' She studies my face.

'That's not really what I do.' It's clear where she is heading with this. Sacrifices will have to be made.

'We will need something to live on, and if you paint portraits for the wealthy, you will then have the means to indulge your real passion.'

'True.' I know this, for I watched my parents paint for the visitors and then for themselves. It is part of survival.

'I don't know yet what I can do to bring in money, but I'll start hiding my jewels. We will be able to sell them as necessary, and the same with some of my clothes.'

'You've been thinking about this.' Excitement bubbles in me like the fountain in the distance with Cupid at the top.

'Freedom.' She is almost breathless as she says the word. The expression on her face is one of longing. 'Do you have an address that I can send things to for storage?'

I consider my father but know that wouldn't work with the harridan there. My grandfather would do it for me, though. 'Yes.'

'Good.' She brings her free hand to mine and holds it for a moment. Need for her surges through me.

'It will take time so that things don't seem to fit together,' she says, squinting in the bright sun.

'I agree.' The air about us is sweet with the scent of jasmine. We are in a paradise now, but we will create a new one together.

'I want you to know I haven't felt this hopeful in years.' Tears glisten in her eyes. I want to kiss her, but instead I take my hankie and dab her eyes. 'Simon is safe. I understand our relationship.'

'A prison is safe.'

'True.' She stays my hand. 'Our plan is reckless. Is it really what you want?'

I nod.

'You'll be forced to paint to sell, not to express your talent. You won't be able to hide your work.'

'I know.'

'You know, but do you understand? And what will your father say? Will you be able to go home?'

I take a deep breath. 'I don't know how he will react. I know that my friends will not accept me. But I cannot accept myself without you.'

'Are you sure? You are young, you may have a change of heart.'

I close my eyes. She's trying to make sure I know the risks and what it all means. I came to Venice to find a cure, but instead I found love, and discovered that to be fully me, I need to accept who I love, who I am and what I am. For that, I will risk exclusion, I will hide our love so that only we know it. There will be a safe place in Cornwall where I am not known and where we can live as friends to the outside world. It will work. 'I am sure. I have found my home in you.'

Another tear slips down her cheek. 'I felt that once, but love can break and die.'

'Do you love me?' Jealousy for what she felt for the man she loved before threatens to swamp me.

She smiles. 'I do, but I don't know if love is enough for the price we will have to pay.'

I take her hand in mine. 'It is.'

'There you are,' Forster's voice booms across the garden.

We drop hands and step back. Our hope of not seeing him is destroyed.

'Darling,' Katherine says.

'Allow me to introduce you to Conte Volpi.'

Volpi kisses Katherine's hand. 'Enchanting.'

'And this, my darling, is Herr Hitler.' Forster's chest is puffed out as I catch sight of a short man who looks like the many photographs I have seen. His eyes remind me of a rodent. He is dressed rather drably in a dark suit. From the papers, I know he is here to discuss the fate of Austria with Mussolini.

Katherine gives a stunning performance, with her face lighting up with a smile. 'Herr Hitler, what an honour it is to meet you.' A man I hadn't noticed translates her words.

Hitler's reply is lost to me, but the man again translates. 'Herr Forster has spoken of your appreciation of my work,' he says.

'I'm so pleased he has.' She beams at Hitler, but it doesn't reach her eyes. Thankfully no one notices. She transforms from the real woman I love to an award-winning actress wooing her audience. The vile man begins to smile. I don't like the way he looks at her. I prefer Volpi's open admiration.

Hitler turns to the aide, who says to me, 'And you are?'

'An artist, Bathsheba Kernow.' Forster steps closer to me. Hitler frowns as he appraises my attire and Forster's expression matches his. My stomach turns.

Hitler stares openly as he stands in front of me. We are eye to eye. I don't offer my hand. Again he speaks to the aide, who says, 'We are about to enter the British pavilion. Accompany us.'

It is an order. I want to refuse, so I hold back. This is wrong. I'm not a fascist and I don't have to pander to them. Katherine's glance pleads with me, so I follow the party inside. Immediately I spot Winifred's work. Her presence is here, and I relax.

'Herr Hitler, what do you make of the work?' Simon asks in hesitant German, which the translator rephrases after asking Simon in English what he was trying to say.

Hitler stands in front of a work of Ben Nicholson. It was all white with cut-out shapes. His voice is loud and unpleasant, and even without the translation that follows, his opinion is clear.

'Herr Hitler finds this work very unsatisfying. He says he is an artist, and this,' the aide waves his hand, 'does not offer anything to the viewer. It is nothing.'

Anger rises in me. He had no right to say it offers the viewer nothing. Each viewer is different. 'It challenges the viewer to see things a different way,' I say.

Simon bashes my arm. The aide translates and Hitler speaks quickly.

'Your mind is ill formed if you see anything in this,' the aide declares while Hitler studies my features, looking for something. Whatever he finds, he does not like it, and he walks away. I don't follow.

Katherine rests a hand on mine. I am torn, but I will not continue with them. Simon takes her arm, leading her on. Before long, they are out of sight. I take a seat, and slowly the rage inside me dies. The sooner Katherine and I leave, the better. I will find a way to earn enough money for us to live on. She could tutor children, or maybe there is something else.

Coming out of my thoughts, the first painting I see is one of Winifred's. Her life has been turned upside down, but she is thriving. Katherine will do the same. Maybe then she could write and publish under her name.

I stop. Not her own name, because then he would find her. It would have to be a pseudonym. She would never be able to appear in public. My shoulders sink. She will never receive the accolades she deserves for her work. This is wrong, and yet I can't see a way that we could fix it, unless he dies. My breath catches. Murder is not in me, even though it would solve everything.

'I'm so glad you stayed here and I found you,' Katherine says. She places a hand on my arm.

I look behind her to make sure she is alone. 'What have you done with them?'

'I left them when Herr Hitler refused the painting he was offered because it wasn't right, and then took another that met with his approval.' She shivers. 'He was so unpleasant.'

'How did you escape?' I drink her in, relieved she is with me again. It pushes my worries away.

She smiles. 'I pleaded a headache from a late night.' She gives a bitter laugh. 'Simon couldn't say anything to that, as it was for his sake that I was up all night.'

'You do look exhausted.' The strain of the encounter with Hitler and the acting it required shows on her beautiful face.

'Thank you.' She touches her cheek.

'I didn't mean it that way.'

'I know.' She takes my arm. 'Let's find a cup of tea, or something stronger.'

I send her a look.

'It has to appear to Simon that everything is the same, until it isn't.'

I can't argue with that, but I can hope we will find tea before alcohol. But maybe a gin will help me to forget that rude man.

27

5 April 2022

———————————

Newlyn

I took the coast road and turned on Radio 4. There was an upcoming programme on the role of muses in art that sounded good. An expert was talking about how women had always been overlooked in the arts. This was a subject close to my heart, and I was thrilled that others had taken on the challenge of redressing the balance.

Paul shut the radio off.

'That was interesting.' I turned it back on, hearing a male voice that made the hair on my arms stand up. Before I could place the voice, Paul turned it off again.

'She's simply trying to sell her book.'

'That's fair, but you know it's a subject that's important to me.' I could listen to it later. I didn't need to fight this battle now. My energy was needed for other things.

'You couldn't find enough evidence to back it up.'

We'd been around this a thousand times. Paul had pointed out every single flaw in my thesis, and I'd dug deeper and deeper until I gave up and accepted defeat. According to him, I couldn't construct a strong enough argument, but clearly someone else had.

Rather than go through it all again, I pressed the button for Radio Cornwall. Secretly I knew this would annoy him, as he hated all local stations. The song playing took me back to just before I'd met him. The world had been mine then, unlike now. However, today the sky was blue and the poetry manuscript had been verified. But this bothered me. I didn't think the work could be Forster's. If he had written those poems in the first place, why would he produce pale comparisons after the war? I thought about the pen and paper on the chaise longue. The woman in the portrait was a writer.

Paul put up his window as we neared the harbour. The smell of fish was strong, and out of the corner of my eye I could see his hand covering his nose. He sent a pointed look to my open window. It was easy to ignore him as I manoeuvred through the busy area. Besides, this was life on the edge of the water – beautiful and at times fragrant.

The road twisted onwards and I swung into Harbour House's drive.

'Nice spot. Shame about the garden,' Paul said as he climbed out.

The garden was a joyous riot of spring colour. Early bluebells vied with the late daffodils and camellias. It was glorious but not ordered in any way. His comment didn't deserve a reply, so I didn't look at him as I walked to the open front door. In the hallway stood Tash, Rory and the handyman. He was holding on to two ladders.

'I made it in time.'

Tash turned. 'You did, and from what Frank's been saying, we might just need all of us to bring her down safely.' She glared at Paul.

He, however, smiled and held out his hand to Rory. 'I haven't seen you since the conference in Manchester, or maybe it was the last time you popped into the art history department.'

Rory took his hand and looked from me to Paul.

'Yes, Ren is my partner,' Paul proclaimed. I wanted to deny it, but it was the truth.

'You'll be interested in this house and the work it contains,' Rory said, letting go of Paul's hand. 'I'd say it chimes with your work.'

'I'll be the judge of that,' Paul cut in, and I was embarrassed at his rudeness. Rory took a step back, then glanced at me.

In that moment, I was certain that was why Paul was here – Rory. Never had I given him reason to doubt my devotion, but he was acting like a cat trying to mark his territory. Speaking of cats, Bastard walked in and rubbed against both Rory and Tash, but avoided Paul. Tash would say the cat had sense and I didn't.

'Thanks for coming, Frank,' I said, nodding at the ladders. 'I knew you'd be the right person to bring our lady down.'

'The way you say "our lady" makes me want to bless myself.' Frank chuckled.

Tash frowned.

'Years of Catholic school.' He looked up. 'She is a beauty.'

'A bit over the top,' Paul said. 'The artist overdid the work, it's too fawning.'

'Don't know about that, but I'd be certain that the painter had a thing for her.' Frank carried his ladders towards the stairs. He propped one against the base and took the other one to the landing.

Tash turned to Paul, 'Why don't you make yourself useful and put the kettle on. You can make everyone some tea.'

Paul appeared to be about to argue, but then disappeared. I imagined he didn't complain because of his curiosity to see the rest of the house.

Tash was sent to the landing to hold one ladder in place, and I was tasked with holding the other on the ground floor, effectively forming a scaffold-like feature. The two men progressed carefully towards the painting.

'They didn't want it falling off the wall, that's for sure,' Frank said to no one in particular.

Between them they managed to lift the painting off the many hooks holding it.

'Been a long time since I've handled a frame as heavy as this,' Frank said.

They brought it safely down and Tash darted to the back of the painting. 'Nothing. Not a mark of any sort.'

'The gold leaf on the frame is very fine.' Frank stroked it carefully before coughing from the dust he'd raised. 'I imagine it's worth as much as the painting.'

'No,' said Rory, transfixed. 'She is priceless.'

'Nonsense,' said Paul, who was trapped behind the ladder and unable to come through. Of course, I could tell him to venture up the back staircase, but I felt the tiniest of victories at his exclusion. 'I can tell even from a distance that it is the work of a student at best.'

With care I picked my way upstairs, drawn to the painting. The closer I was to her, the more I knew Paul was wrong. This was a special painting that transcended the ordinary. Silence fell on the four of us as we took in the beauty of the work.

'Hey, is anyone going to come and drink the tea I made?'

Tash laughed, sending me a glance. 'We'll be down in a moment,' she called, sounding like a mother with an unruly child.

I reached the top step and saw the painting up close. It was glorious. Whoever the artist was, they had been well trained. The brushwork, the use of colour and the perspective were faultless. In fact I struggled to find anything wrong with it. It had the touch of a Sargent and none of the sweetness of de László. There was an edge to it that I couldn't put my finger on.

'The artist was in love with her,' Rory said as he turned to me. I nodded.

'His brushwork is outstanding.'

I raised an eyebrow. 'Why do you say *his*?'

'Sorry.' He smiled. 'I fell prey to an easy and sloppy assumption that the artist was a man.'

'Well, it could be, but I'd say it was a woman.' Tash stepped closer to the canvas.

'Why?' I asked.

'Well, look at the way the fabric of her dress falls.' She pointed to the woman's stomach. 'It's like the . . . what cats have, the . . .'

'Primordial pouch.' Rory said, and I was impressed with his knowledge. As if on cue, Bastard sauntered by with her paunch on display.

'Men either ignore a woman's stomach or they do a Lucian Freud on her and all you see is the baggy belly and saggy tits. I would argue that this painter knows a woman's body well because she had one of her own.' Tash smiled.

'That's utter tosh,' Paul said from below. I had almost forgotten he was there.

'I know what you mean,' said Rory, ignoring him. 'Now that you've said it, I can see it.'

'Well, be it a man or a woman who painted her, I'd swear they'd just had their leg over. That's my two pence worth.' Frank began gathering his ladders from the top down. 'Need anything else shifted, Ren?'

'No, that's all, thanks, Frank.'

'I'll be off then.'

Tash gave him a hand with the first ladder, leaving Paul stuck behind the other one for another few minutes. Meanwhile Rory helped me in placing the painting securely in the master bedroom.

'I don't care who painted it, but it's clear they were in love with her, and she loved them back.' His voice was filled with awe.

I stood back from the painting. 'Yes, you're right. You know, it reminds me of one of Forster's poems.'

'Of course it does.' Rory paused, then said, '*I am unmade / Love has disassembled me / To my parts / Only you / Can make me whole.*'

I swallowed.

Longing like I'd never known filled me.

Our eyes met.

Connection.

Trembling, I looked down. The last thing I needed was for Paul to see my attraction to Rory, or worse, to see the flash of what I thought I had just seen in Rory's eyes. It had been so long since anyone had looked at me that way, I could be wrong. Maybe it was just how he was feeling about the painting.

I turned from him and studied the canvas. The paper and pen on the chaise by her left hand were clear. I crouched to read what was written there. My breath caught. The words of the poem he'd just recited were visible.

'Look.' I pointed.

Rory kneeled beside me. He mouthed the words, then turned to me.

'Are you thinking what I'm thinking?' I asked.

He swallowed and nodded. 'I'm not sure how it can be, but yes.'

For a moment I longed to be someone else. Someone who hadn't failed, who wasn't in a relationship, someone who was free to lean in and kiss this man. But I wasn't any of those things, so I rose and dashed downstairs, to find Tash and Paul in a stand-off.

'Thank you so much for helping Ren, but you won't be needed now that I'm here.'

Tash laughed good and loud before she replied. 'You have never been a help but have done everything in your power to hinder her.'

'How dare you say that!' Paul replied. 'You're just jealous that she loves me and not you.'

'The only thing I'm jealous about is the great wallop of cream you have in your hair that she didn't bother to tell you about. It makes you look . . . not distinguished academic but more circus clown.' Tash pushed past him towards the kitchen.

Paul's face was puce and he did look like a clown. I bit my lip as I prepared myself for the tirade that was about to explode.

'How could you?' he whispered.

I didn't say a word, for if I did, there would be hell to pay later.

In the kitchen, I laughed when I saw Paul's version of making tea. The teapot was on the counter. The box of tea bags was vaguely close to it and the kettle had been filled.

'The man is useless,' Tash said through gritted teeth.

I couldn't argue with that.

'Please tell me he is at least good in bed. There has to be some redeeming quality.'

I didn't reply.

'Christ, Ren, what the hell are you with him for when the likes of that hot hunk of manhood Rory has eyes for you?' She almost spat the words into my ear as she poured boiling water on the tea bags in the pot.

Rory entered the kitchen. 'Can I give you a hand?' He picked up a tray from beside the cabinet and began stacking mugs and the milk onto it. 'Anyone take sugar?' he asked.

'Paul,' I said.

'Such a shame Frank had the last of it.' Tash grinned. 'If he needs sweetness, he could look inside himself, or try a biscuit.'

I shrugged. She knew that the half a teaspoon Paul took in his tea was the only sugar he had. There had been an incident when

I'd begun dating Paul, and Tash had cooked a big dinner for the four of us to get to know each other. It was a disaster from start to finish. She had cured a piece of salmon but had done so with sugar. The main course had included sugar-glazed carrots, and the pudding was a trifle with crystallised sugar on the top. Paul had picked through his food to the point of being rude. She had worked so hard, and he had eaten only the chicken breast and drunk far too much wine. It had not been a good start. He had explained that sugar depressed him, but at the end of his meal when he demanded tea with precisely half a spoonful, it was a wonder that Tash hadn't thrown the rest of the trifle at him.

I turned away and started looking in the kitchen drawers for the right tools to take the canvas of the woman out of the frame. There had to be some clue on the back to the artist, if not the sitter. From Sheba's sketchbook, I knew the woman was K and she was in love with her. But how had Viv felt?

My phone beeped. It was a message from my uncle.

The great-nephews have been in touch and wish to come to the house. Need to provide the keys.

No, was my first thought. If they came here, they would need to be accompanied. A bad feeling was lingering in my gut, and I couldn't explain it, but I had to protect the reputations of these women. I would not have their work stolen or dismissed. It was important.

I replied.

Will discuss later when I return to the office.

I needed to speak to the court-appointed administrator to understand exactly what rights the great-nephews had to access the property. I stopped moving. Of course, that was if they'd actually made the request in the first place. It could be my uncle, and I didn't trust him.

I followed the others out of the kitchen. Paul was on the

landing, facing off with Bastard. From the blood on his hand, it appeared that Bastard had won.

'Who does that cat belong to?' he asked. 'And is there a first aid kit around?'

'Bastard belongs to the house, and yes, I have one in my car.' Tash put the teapot down on a table. 'Follow me . . . and you should know better than to approach a cat.'

'I didn't. I was approaching the painting.'

Rory sent me a glance as they walked out to Tash's car and we went into the study.

'So, Paul is your partner.'

I nodded.

'He's a huge advocate for women artists, but it's funny he doesn't seem to be able to see what is here.' He put the tray down. 'This house is full to the brim of some of the best work of the mid twentieth century I've seen, and yet I've never heard of either artist.'

'It's a disgrace, but it could be partially of their own choosing.'

'In what way?'

'They lived a quiet life and rarely held exhibitions, and although my father knew of them, they were barely on his radar, yet he knew the work of Sheba's parents well.' I walked to a painting above the fireplace. 'This painting of St Ives Bay was done by her father in 1941.' I swung around and pointed to the small Albert Wallis on the wall by the window. 'Wallis's work has been widely praised, but although Sheba's mother's work was well known during her lifetime, that recognition disappeared after her death. She barely receives a footnote in the history of the St Ives School, although during her life she was a main figure.'

'This is wrong,' he said, pouring the tea.

'I agree. But leaving that aside, you rushed back for a reason, I assume.'

'Yes, Tim Pearce is certain the manuscript is Forster's work as I mentioned in my email.'

'I don't agree.'

'The painting?' He handed me a cup.

'That just confirmed it for me.' I took a sip of tea. 'I've been going through the correspondence, and I've seen the handwriting of the person who annotated the poems.'

'Do you have a name?'

I added a splash more milk to my tea. 'Only the initial K.'

'Can you show me?'

'The originals are at my mother's, as I've been going through them at night. But I took a photo of this one.' I opened my phone and handed it to him.

Please protect these. They were written for you and written for her. He must not have them. It is only since having Isabella that my eyes have truly been opened. Thank you for seeing me through the haze of drink and drugs in Venice. Thank you for loving me and reminding me I am worthy, worthy of love and worthy of credit for my words, which is why I've sent these to you.

He stole your poem from me. I am so sorry. It was meant for you alone, but maybe it is the payment we equally share for me breaking my marriage vows. Each word is yours and I am sorry you must share them with the world. Please hold the enclosed close to you. He must never know what happened to them.

I love you.

K

He stared at the screen for a long time. When he looked up, his eyes held tears. 'Do you think K is Simon's wife Katherine?'

'The wife who died in the Blitz?' I asked.

'Yes.' He handed the phone back to me. 'Before this letter and seeing the poem in the portrait, I would have bet my career on those poems being Simon's work, but even the syntax in the letter leans to it.'

'Bet your career on what?' Paul asked, coming into the room. 'That I'm right about the painting upstairs?'

I cast Rory a stern look and prayed he'd understand that what I'd just shared with him was confidential.

Tash glanced between us as she joined us in the study. The tension in the air was thick, giving me some idea that words had been said outside while Tash wielded her first aid kit. Paul probably had more scars now than he did from Bastard.

The cat sat elegantly on the windowsill watching us, and I decided the best thing to do would be to pour the rest of the tea and give everyone a biscuit in the hopes of salvaging the day, or what was left of it. I needed to head back to the office, but first the frame needed to come off the painting.

I signalled to Tash and she followed me out of the room. K's words to Sheba stayed in my mind.

Grabbing the tools from the kitchen, we made quick work of loosening the painting from the frame. The canvas sides revealed nothing other than a few stray blobs of paint. Lifting it so that the afternoon light lit it, I studied it again.

'I think Sheba painted this.'

Tash stepped back to study the whole painting. 'It's nothing like her style.'

'Her later style.' Placing the painting securely down in the master bedroom, I raced down through the house and out to the studio. Once I'd located the key, I went to the far corner, where there were a few canvases I hadn't attributed to her. Looking closely now, however, there was something about them. They were landscapes, and I brought them outside into the bright daylight to see if there were any markings or signature. In the rocks on the beach on one there appeared to be two Bs.

'I can see where you are going with this.' Tash walked out of the kitchen with a fresh packet of biscuits in her hand.

'Yes, but if there is a signature, it's BB.' I tilted the painting back and forth so that the sheen on the painting revealed the brushwork.

'Where?' She squinted at it. I pointed to the rocks.

'Got it.' She went into the studio and picked up one of the other canvases. Coming outside, she said, 'Here it is again.'

They were not dated, so I had nothing to guide me in that way. But I stopped. One of the paintings of St Ives didn't seem right. It was a watercolour sketch of the frontage of the Broadway Kinema. I did a quick search on my phone. The cinema was built in 1920 and was renamed the Regal in the thirties. This must have been painted before the name change. Sheba would have been a young teenager at the time.

Tash had been looking over my shoulder, but now she dashed away. I followed her, locking the studio, double-checking it was secure.

Paul met me in the hallway. 'You need to tell Tash that she isn't needed. She isn't qualified, and I am, and I love you.' He stroked my arm. I had to remind myself that this was a sign of love. But it seemed possessive rather than loving.

'Come and look,' Tash shouted.

I raced upstairs to find her lying on the floor with her nose almost touching the canvas. Even I had to admit she looked ridiculous.

'Ren, she *has* signed it. Look at the shoes.'

Down on all fours, I examined them. On one buckle was a clear *BB*. 'This is good. But it doesn't prove yet that it was Kernow.'

Paul stood at the top of the stairs. 'I've been looking at Kernow's artwork and how she signs her paintings "Sheba", so BB wouldn't be her.'

I couldn't argue with his logic, although I wanted to. BB. Her full name was Bathsheba Kernow. No matter who it was, it was the same artist as the three paintings in the studio.

Tonight, when I had time, I'd do more research.

Back on my feet, I said, 'I need to go and meet with my uncle. Tash, can you lock up and drop off the key with me either at the office or at Mum's.'

Rory came out of the study. 'I have to be over at Helwyn House. For the next few days I'll be working on the prep work for next year's Hebe Courtenay prize for historical fiction.' He picked up his jacket and handed me the manuscript. 'I suggest that this goes into a safe.'

'Good idea.' I took it from him.

'You know how to reach me, and if you find anything further, let me know.'

As Rory left, Paul stood with his arms across his chest.

'Don't mind me,' he said.

'I can drop you at Mum's.' She was out playing mahjong and shouldn't be back until six. Hopefully this would mean he wouldn't have any more private conversations with her.

28

Venice

We are on the roof terrace and the gramophone is filling the air with Noël Coward singing 'Mad Dogs and Englishmen'. Rossi is laughing. He has such a kind face. I find it hard to think of him with those leaders.

'Il Duce did not think much of Herr Hitler,' he says to Forster.

'This is not true. The two men are aligned in thought.'

Rossi sends him a look. 'They disagreed about as much as they agreed on.' He like me seems to distrust Forster's ability to read people. Forster is so self-obsessed that he notices little around him. How can people believe he writes such emotive poetry? They are fools. Katherine, however, misses nothing, even when like tonight she is full of gin and, I suspect, cocaine. Her eyes are overbright and she is restless.

'That's just normal political negotiations.'

'You were there when they said farewell.' Rossi puts his glass down and raises both hands. 'It was positively, how do you say, icy.'

'Frigid.' Katherine stands and pours another gin.

'Not at all. It was simply for the cameras.' Simon holds out his glass for a refill.

'When I asked Il Duce what he thought of Herr Hitler, he called him . . . a mad little clown I think is how it translates.'

'Il Duce would never be so rude!'

But Il Duce spoke the truth for once, and it fits with my own evaluation of Herr Hitler. They are both terrible, and looking at Rossi right now, I wonder what he really thinks. He strikes me as a man who does what is expedient. Currently he is a fascist, but if things would work better for him if he changed his views, he would do so without another thought. Forster, however, is in love with fascism. He is wedded to every aspect of it. He even praises the brutality of the Blackshirts. They've been out in numbers these past two days.

'Let us not disagree about this.' Forster turns to me. 'When will we see Katherine's portrait? I am bored of looking at a sheet in my room.'

'It can be moved to the dining room tomorrow.' I wave my hand and decline a refill.

'This is ridiculous. I am housing you, and paying a good price for this painting – which, if it's at all like the portrait of the street urchin, will have you swamped with commissions.'

'Simon, darling, this is wonderful, and you do love launching careers, but normally you wouldn't witness the waiting period. It would be tucked away in an artist's studio. Patience is required, especially for genius to bloom.'

'Hmm.'

She strokes his arm and I look away. She is protecting me, but I don't want her to touch him at all. Their relationship is finished and ours has begun. Yet I know we must play a game.

'I do pick geniuses, and I can see the potential in you, Miss Kernow.' He pauses. 'But of course, it will be key that you don't fulfil the role of a true woman and have a child. If you do that, you will lose your gift. It is the need for children that makes women creative, and when they can't have them, they put their energies into creating art.'

I open my mouth to shout at him.

'Darling, that is a cruel thing to say.' Katherine puts her glass down with a thump.

'It is the truth. Think of your friend Hilda Doolittle.'

'H. D. is still writing.'

'But it's just not as good now she has taken up with this Bryher.'

'Bryher is a lovely person.'

'You mean woman. This trend for women to take on men's names and dress like them . . . Signs of perversion.'

Katherine sends me a look.

'Take Miss Kernow in her trousers all the time.' He waves a hand at me.

'It's practical for her work.'

'Hmm.' He paces and Rossi steps aside. I am concerned that Rossi has seen the looks between Katherine and me. 'Enough of this, we are due at the Volpis'.' Forster looks at me. 'If you dressed like a woman, one could bring you out into society.' He walks away and I am left standing with my mouth open.

'There is one thing he is correct in,' says Rossi. 'Your work is genius.' He bows and follows Katherine off the terrace. I turn to the view. Across the Grand Canal sits the Palazzo Venier dei Leoni, and in this moment I long to see it finished.

* * *

I'm standing by the entrance to the Accademia, waiting for Father Keeney so we can visit the artist who painted my mother. As I left, Forster reminded me that he wanted the painting out of the bedroom. Katherine was nowhere to be seen. I heard them come home as the bells were chiming three. How can he expect her to be creative when the life he is asking her to live is so draining? Katherine and I have a plan partially in place. Time alone to work out the finer details is elusive. Forster is ever present, and I hate it. He must know how I feel about him, but then maybe not, for he seems oblivious to so many things.

Before long, the tall priest appears through the throngs of tourists. He smiles broadly as he reaches me. 'So many people, it's a wonder the city doesn't sink.' He takes my arm and leads me away from the crowds. We amble through calle after calle and over small bridges, finally coming to an empty campo.

'I love these quiet spaces,' I say, noting the almost sleepy feel to the square.

'I do too. In the past, the campos used to be fields of sorts.'

'Really?'

'So they say.' He shrugs. 'Roberto's studio is just over there.' He leads the way through a gate and a small garden, and up two flights of stairs. He taps on the door, and we enter a room with three large north-facing windows.

'*Buongiorno*,' says a small man with a deeply lined face. His grey eyes appear huge and look like they have seen all the world. I warm to him. 'I am sorry to hear that your mother has died.' His gaze doesn't leave my face. 'She was a bright thing.' He pauses for a moment. 'Climbing so quickly in her art.' His hands rise to the sky, then he points to a painting hanging on the wall behind me. It's one of my mother's. Even twenty-one years ago, her style was established.

'It's beautiful.'

'Like she.' He spreads charcoal sketches out on the table. They depict my mother in many poses, including one where it is clear she is pregnant with me. Grief hits. I am winded by it. Father Keeney rests a hand on my arm.

'Your parents were very much in love.' Roberto hands me a hankie and I dab my eyes. 'How is your father?' He opens another folder, which contains sketches of him.

'He has found love again.' As I say the words, a joy for him fills me along with a longing to see him. He will be a father again any time now. With distance I can see how hard it must have been for them to have a proper life with me moping around all the time. It still stings, but not as badly.

'Padre tells me that you too are an artist.' Roberto gathers the sketches.

'I am.' The painting of Katherine that Forster hates comes to mind.

'Would you like to come and work here with me?'

'Yes!'

He smiles. 'I hear you are staying with your subject but you have finished the commission.'

I look at Father Keeney. How does he know that?

'There is a small room.' Roberto points to a door to the left. 'You may use it if that would work for you.'

A choice is in front of me. Return to the pensione by the Ponte delle Tette, or come here. 'I would like that very much.'

'*Bene*.' He claps his hands.

'How do I contact you?' I ask.

He nods. 'Just come when you are ready.'

'Thank you so much.' I glance at his work, which is classical in every way. So very different to mine, but there will be much he can teach me. Excitement vies with the thought of not being so close to Katherine. But I will need to move on soon, and this is the way to do it.

'Thank you, Roberto. We will leave you to your work and I will see you soon.'

'*Sì. Ciao*.' He waves, and we descend to the garden in silence.

The sketches of my mother and father run through my mind. What were her thoughts on falling in love? Her journals begin to tail off once things had picked up with my father. She only captured the first sparks of love and didn't enlighten me on what came next. The journals were never meant for me, or possibly anyone but her. I came here expecting one thing, and instead found love, in the most inconvenient place. Falling in love is hard enough, but falling in love with a married woman is even worse.

'Shall we go and have some lunch?' Father Keeney asks as he opens the gate.

'That would be lovely.'

'I know of a little place.'

'Of course you do.' He seems to know far too much of everything. This worries me. Surely he doesn't mix in social circles with Katherine. But what do I know. Little, it is becoming apparent.

'You're very quiet. Seeing the images of your mother was hard.'

'Grief doesn't go away.' I search for the words to express my feelings. 'They were beautiful. What surprised me was the desire to see my father.'

'That's a surprise?'

'I left, or rather I was pushed out by my stepmother.' And by Nellie, if I'm honest. They know what I am and what that would mean in our small community.

'I see.'

Again I'm afraid he might. Maybe I shouldn't spend time with him. He might work out that I'm in love with Katherine, but perhaps he has already. It strikes me just how foolish this is. If Forster figures out what is happening under his nose, he will be furious.

'Here we are,' Father Keeney says, opening a door to a small restaurant, where he is greeted warmly. After a fast exchange in Italian, we are seated by a window.

'I have taken the liberty and ordered.'

I raise an eyebrow.

'Well, in truth I was told what we are having.'

I laugh as two glasses of white wine appear, along with a bottle of mineral water.

'Now, my young friend, tell me what you have been up to now that the portrait is complete.'

I send him a sideways glance.

'Simon Forster chewed my ear off the other night about the indignity of having to look at it covered in sheets.'

I relax. His knowledge is innocent, even if I'm not. This kind man in front of me would not understand who and what I am. No amount of confessing and forgiveness would change it. I know this in my bones. My mother was different to me, and looking at this handsome man opposite me, I do not feel the attraction or the fascination I feel with Katherine and have felt towards other women. This has huge ramifications for my life and for Katherine's as we go forward. I believe that for us both to be comfortable, we will have to pass as normal, simply two friends living companionably.

'I've lost you.'

I blink. 'Sorry. A lot on my mind.'

'I can see you are worried about something. I thought it might be about where to go now that the commission is finished.'

'That is a concern.' I take a sip of the cool, sharp wine. 'But the opportunity to work with Roberto is wonderful.'

'Hmm.' He looks like he is about to say more when steaming bowls of pasta arrive. 'Spaghetti vongole. My favourite.'

'I've not tried this yet.' I'm used to seafood, but these do not look like razor clams. 'Before my arrival here, I'd never had pasta.'

He expertly rolls the spaghetti around his fork. 'Ah, thanks to many Italian immigrants to the United States, pasta is well known there, although it is considered foreign food by the Irish side of my family.'

'I'm sure you can find pasta in London, but it hasn't made its way to Cornwall just yet.' I copy his twirling and taste the pasta. 'This is heaven.'

'Possibly close,' he says. 'But you were about to tell me your concerns.'

'Was I?' I focus on the pasta. It would be too easy to talk to him. I miss the ease of the friendship I had with Nellie before things changed between us.

Now my life has altered beyond what I could have imagined months ago, before I set off to find a cure. But like my mother, I have found love. My time in Venice is nearing its natural conclusion much faster than planned. Unlike her, I am not going to return married and pregnant. But I will return full of joy and hope. Away from Simon, Katherine will flourish, and so will I in her love.

'You were. I'm wondering if by being focused on this commission you are stifling the learning you should be enjoying.'

I laugh. 'The commission has been a learning process.'

'I'm sure it has, but it will not have created anything as original as your nuns.'

I stop twirling my pasta and look at him fully. 'How do you know? You have not seen the painting.'

'True, I haven't, but if you have managed to incorporate that burst of insight into it, I will be delighted.'

'This afternoon I will move it from their bedroom. At least that way it won't trouble Forster, except when he chooses to eat at home, which these days is rare.'

'Excellent.' He pauses and studies me. If I could run and hide

I would. 'You have changed since the first time I met you. You have the look of a woman in love.'

My throat tightens. This is the last thing I want, but I can't stop the love showing.

'I wonder who has captured your heart.' He takes a sip of wine. 'I could make some guesses.'

How do I stop this? I begin to reply when a woman comes from the kitchen and speaks with her hands flying.

'I must leave immediately.' Father Keeney stands. 'I'm sorry.' He is gone before I can even comment.

The waiter brings me a glass of red wine and what looks like veal. I don't want to eat on my own, but it would be rude to waste it. At least with only my own company I can work through the next step of the plan to be with Katherine now that I have a place to move into.

* * *

With the help of Signora Bocca, I move the canvas then the easel into the dining room. Only once it is placed securely do I take another look.

The housekeeper gasps. '*Bellissimo.*'

'*Grazie.*' I smile. Signora Bocca takes a longer look, then leaves.

Katherine gazes out from the painting with such hunger and love it is powerful. I have no idea what Forster will make of it, but that really doesn't matter any more. It is far better than the one of the boy. The surface, although still tacky, is drying fast in the heat. I can only hope that it won't crack. I prepared the paints correctly, but I have never experienced such sustained heat before. But people have been creating great works of art here for ever, and those paints have stood the test of time.

Katherine enters as I'm covering it again.

'Do you have to hide it?' Her voice catches.

'I don't think it's a good idea if he sees it.'

'Yes, but it reminds me of who I can be.' She sighs and looks around to make sure we are alone. 'This is harder than I thought.'

It is easier for me because I don't have to pretend, but she does.

'Simon is so different right now. He's changed in ways I can't say.'

I watch the play of emotions across her face. She is tired, and the strain is taking its toll. Guilt grips me.

'Have you changed your mind?' We haven't had any time together since Forster returned. She has had to be with him for various social events. I've spent my time painting, creating an array of portraits that could be used to entice clients. I can lie with my brush and flatter the most unlikely sitter. None of these works are like this painting, and if Katherine needs to see this to give her strength, then I can risk leaving it uncovered. Simon is going away again soon, before the poetry exhibition begins in a few weeks' time.

I put the sheet down. 'He doesn't come in here too often.'

She shakes her head. 'Breakfast is now outside or with his new friends, and we are out every night.' She yawns.

'The air flow will be good for the drying process.'

'Is it really me?' she asks.

'It is truly you.' I glance from her to the painting. She is more radiant on the canvas than the tired woman before me. But the true her is reflected in the painting. Her soul shines in person and in paint.

'No, it's the me that you see, and you see me differently from anyone else.'

'Maybe I do.' I hesitate. 'But to see what I truly see, you need to follow me.'

We walk to my room. The other painting of her rests against the wall.

She stares at it. 'That's me?'

'Yes, that's you.' I bend down and lift it onto the easel.

She slips her hands into her pockets. For the longest time she doesn't say anything.

'Do you like it?' Fear gnaws my insides. This type of exposure is hard. This painting is as much a reflection of me as it is of her.

'I love it.' She turns to me. 'I like that I'm there in shape and colour and movement.' She pauses. 'It's so different, and yet . . .' she walks closer, 'it's the same.'

I laugh. She pulls her hand out of her pocket and hands me a folded sheet of paper. 'I've finished your poem.'

'I thought it was finished before.'

'There were two phrases that didn't work.' She opens my sketchbook. There are pages and pages of her. 'It's a bit like you doing all these preliminary sketches and then you do a painting.' She glances at the canvas again.

'I understand.' It makes sense looking at it like that.

The sound of Signora Bocca greeting Forster below alerts us. Katherine quickly leans in and kisses me before racing downstairs. I remind myself that this is all necessary, but it may drive me mad in the process. Creeping past the salon to the dining room, I debate covering the painting after all. As I gaze at it, pride and desire fill me. I lift the sheet from the floor.

'I insist,' I hear Forster say, then the door swings open.

With his chest puffed out, he stops and stares. 'It is not a disappointment like that silly work you did the other day.' With that pronouncement, he leaves.

Katherine mouths *sorry* and follows him. I study the painting again, grateful that he doesn't see what is there.

29

Penzance

My head was spinning as I drove to the office. Tash had taken me aside and told me she had now been through all the information on the Companies House website and it didn't make for happy reading. No professional accounts or audits had been done for seven years. She imagined that this had been a cost saving. So the only way I was going to discover exactly what was happening was to hear it directly from my uncle.

Vying with the financial problems was my mother, I still couldn't believe that she had dementia. And what was worse was that no one had told me, not even my father. One good thing was that Tash was babysitting Paul, having insisted I had enough to do. She would drop him off, but she had a few errands to run first. I wouldn't be surprised if he found himself in Devon.

The car park was empty except for Marcia and my uncle's cars. This was a relief. Before entering, I took a few deep breaths and calmed my nerves. I wouldn't be asking for anything I didn't have a right to.

Marcia was on the phone and she waved as I passed. I didn't stop at my father's office but went straight to Stephen's, pushing the door open without knocking. He looked up. His hair was a mess and he was ashen-faced.

'You have some explaining to do.' I stood in front of his desk.

There was a flash of defiance in his eyes. 'I don't owe you anything.'

Anger made speaking both harder and yet easier. 'You do, on so many counts, but we can stick to the simplest. Between us, my mother and I own the majority of this business, such as it is.'

He laughed bitterly. 'Not that you cared about it before now.'

I stared at him. 'You were the one who told me to leave.'

He looked down.

'Well, I'm back and the business finances are in a mess, so you had better tell me everything.'

He placed his head in his hands. Old-fashioned ledgers covered his desk. He had done a business studies degree, whereas Dad had been allowed to do an art history one. Being the elder brother, Dad was always first in line, and he knew that. It was why he went out of his way to praise Stephen, to counter the guilt he felt.

Both Stephen and I could be stubborn, but I cracked first. 'Shall I simply notify the authorities of your illegal activities?'

His head shot up. 'I don't know where to begin.'

'The truth from the start would be best.' I pulled out a chair and sat. 'First, though, was it really the great-nephews who asked for the keys?' I stared at him without blinking.

He shook his head.

'I'm guessing that you planned to remove the Chippendale pieces and sell them privately.'

'Yes.' His eyes were bloodshot and I thought he might have been crying.

'That's theft.'

'Don't you think I know that.'

I remained silent this time. My father's clock chimed seven times. It was ten minutes to four. If he didn't begin soon, we could be here a long time. This needed resolving now. I had my mother to protect.

'I'm sorry,' he said eventually. I waited, but he didn't say anything else.

'Thank you, but I need to know exactly what you are sorry for, in full detail.'

'All payments to our clients have been made.'

I drew a deep breath. This was worse than I'd imagined if payments to clients were in question. 'Good.'

'The business is overdrawn,' he stated flatly.

I nodded. 'And you have a warehouse full of pieces of furniture you can't sell unless you've altered them substantially so that no one would recognise them.'

'Yes.' He glanced at me with fear and resentment in his eyes.

'How long has this been going on?' I summoned all the patience I could find. Behind him was a picture of my grandfather laying the first concrete block for the extension of this building. It was all coming to an end here.

'Since you missed the Cézanne,' he said flatly.

'Right, it always comes back to that.' I pulled my shoulders back.

'Well, yes. I tried to build the business up again.' He puffed out his chest. 'And I did.'

'By inflating the bidding, shill bidding.'

He nodded.

'But sometimes you were stuck being the buyer.'

I looked at the inkwell on his desk. It had belonged to my grandfather. Its only value was sentimental. The business was gone. I couldn't explain how gutted I felt now that what I had feared was true.

'You recouped the company's reputation. Why keep going?' I knew this thanks to Tash's investigations.

He clasped his fingers together but didn't say anything. He was uncomfortable and he should be. What he'd done was illegal. As I thought about it, it became clear.

'Did it become like gambling?'

He lifted his eyes and met mine, then nodded.

'When did my father discover what you were doing?' But I knew the answer. He'd been paying out money from his personal accounts to try and shore up the business. No doubt more guilt, but this time not because of me.

'A payment bounced.' He placed his hands on the desk. Part of me felt for him, but only part.

'So, a year ago.' Everything began to fall into place.

'Yes.' His shoulders dropped lower and he looked suddenly far older than his years.

'No wonder Dad was on his bike. He had to have some way to relieve his stress.'

My poor father. Between Mum's diagnosis and Stephen's illegal activity, his stress levels must have been unbearable. Who could he confide in? It should have been me. I should have been here for him. My heart stopped in that moment. He never would have spoken to Paul about it. He was never as sold on him as I'd wanted. He'd brushed away my worries about his lack of enthusiasm with 'No one will ever be good enough for my girl.' Well, I *was* his girl, and I was going to fight for Mum.

I squared my shoulders. 'Who else knows the situation?'

'No one.' Stephen studied his hands.

Throttling him, which was what I wanted to do, wouldn't help, but pressing on might. 'Do we put up a bankruptcy sign?'

He stared at me wide-eyed.

'I don't see we have any other choice.' I silently apologised to my grandfather and my father. I'd begun the downfall and my uncle had finished it.

He cleared his throat. 'I will put my house on the market.' He spoke so quietly I wasn't immediately sure what I'd heard.

I opened my mouth to say no, but stopped. Even if I let the business fold, I had to think of my mother. She needed the money. He had taken a wreck of a house above one of the most beautiful coves in Cornwall and remade it into something special. 'OK. What's its value?'

'It should be at least one point five.' He dared to meet my glance.

'And your mortgage?'

'Fifty.'

I released the air I was holding. It might cover it. 'I suggest you call your preferred agent and list it immediately.'

'We can't pay salaries.' He leaned back in his chair.

I stood. 'Marcia has been with this firm my whole life. She needs to know what is happening. It will be her choice if she stays. As for the men, we'll speak to them together and give them a choice.'

'I'm sorry.'

I placed my hands on the desk and looked directly at him. 'Sometimes, as you know, sorry doesn't make things better. I forgive you for myself, but I can't forgive you for the stress you put my father under, nor for the dangerous financial state you have put my mother in.'

'I know, I know.' He placed his head in his hands again.

'Pull yourself together. I'm going to get Marcia, and then afterwards we will speak to Jack Thomas.'

He nodded.

'I need to hear your confirmation.'

'Yes, to all of it.'

'Fine, then call the estate agent now. It's spring, your house is beautiful. It should go quickly.'

As I walk away, I wonder who that woman who just spoke was. I didn't recognise her, but something inside of me did.

* * *

By the time I left the office, I had Marcia on side. She offered me a loan to pay the men, feeling it was best for the moment to keep the state of things private. She pointed out that news tended to snowball. Stephen had already spoken to an estate agent, who felt offers over one million seven hundred thousand pounds would be right for the four-bedroom cottage with sea views and direct access to the coastal path. Part of me felt sorry for my uncle. That cottage was his joy, and I suspected he'd had very little of that in his life since his plan to save the reputation of the firm had gone so disastrously wrong.

I pulled into the drive, dreading seeing Paul. He would want to know everything, but with Marcia's words still fresh in my mind, I wouldn't tell him a thing. His behaviour back at Harbour House, trying to make Tash go away, had bothered me. And he'd been downright rude to Rory, who was not only an expert but a colleague of his. It was all very unprofessional.

After Mum went to bed, we would have to have a heart-to-heart. I was convinced he'd known about her illness, and he hadn't told me. The sense of betrayal I felt was incredibly strong. He would say I was overreacting, but if this relationship was going to continue, he had to change. No more checking my emails, no more going behind my back to my family or my colleagues.

The front door opened as I reached it, and Meg came out.

'How was today?' I asked, adjusting the bags in my hands.

'Excellent, she seemed much brighter.'

'I only found out today about her dementia diagnosis. I'm sorry if anything I've said or done . . .'

'I did wonder if you knew, but I thought you must.'

I shook my head.

'It's a lot to take on, dear.' She gave me a hug. 'Be kind to yourself and remember she loves you.'

'She hasn't gone so far that she doesn't know me.'

'No, dear, she hasn't. She's still competent. In fact, before mahjong, she had me take her to see the assisted living apartments.'

'What?'

'She's thinking ahead. So she is still very much with it.'

'Oh.'

Meg hugged me again. 'This is a good thing, even if it's overwhelming. She's thinking of you and your man.'

My shoulders dropped. Everything was racing forward. We would need to do a new lasting power of attorney. It was something we couldn't delay. In fact, if Tash hadn't delivered Paul here yet, I would tackle the subject with Mum right now.

'I'll be in at half eight tomorrow,' Meg said.

I thanked her and walked into the house. There was no sign of Paul.

'Is that you . . . love?' Mum called from the sitting room.

'Yes, Mum, I'm home.'

'I'm glad you're here. I had an odd phone call from Paul saying he was trapped in St Ives.'

I swallowed a smile. Not quite Devon, but unless Paul wanted to take a bus, he was stuck there until Tash saw fit to bring him back. I couldn't love her more.

Sitting in the chair beside my mother, I knew I couldn't put this discussion off. 'Mum, why didn't you tell me about your illness?'

She looked down at her hands. 'Did Paul tell you?'

'No, Jack Thomas did.'

She turned away. 'Oh.'

'You shouldn't have kept it from me.'

She sighed and looked at me. 'Your father wanted to tell you, but I told him I would.'

'But you didn't.'

'Paul thought it would break you.'

I closed my eyes. 'He was wrong.'

'I can see that. You've been dealing with everything.' She reached out and put her right hand over mine. The memory of all the times in my childhood when I had taken comfort from the touch of her hand nearly undid me. 'Thank you,' she said. 'Did you hear him on the radio today talking about muses and women painters?'

'What?'

'It was on Radio 4. I heard it when Meg took me out in her car.'

I closed my eyes. He hadn't wanted me to hear him.

'What he was saying sounded an awful lot like what you used to say.' She paused. 'It took me a while to remember where I had seen your thesis recently. But then I recalled it was in the box in your room.'

I nodded. I'd seen it there too. So much work I thought had gone to waste, but someone else had made use of it. A tsunami of rage was swelling inside me. He'd stolen my work. How had I not seen this?

'I suppose if Paul is in St Ives . . . he'll be back soon. Best to have dinner ready.'

So I could throw it at him, I thought but didn't say aloud.

The mother in front of me right now wouldn't understand. The mother who had raised me to be strong, fierce and kind would. Yes, as Meg said, she was still competent, but only just. I rose and hugged her tight, then went to listen to the programme while I cooked.

30

30 June 1934

Venice

The painting, only just touch-dry, has been moved to the salon. This is not what I wanted, but I know it will help with the future, my future with Katherine. This doesn't stop how uneasy I feel as guests begin to arrive for the great unveiling. Katherine tried to stop Forster creating this big event, but he would have none of it. In his words, 'I'm launching an artist's career, and this is how it's done. I shall also do a poetry reading to entice people to accept the invitation.'

Dread fills me. I don't doubt my work, but I can't predict people's reaction. I rub my sweaty palms down the side of the dress I'm wearing. He could not have a woman in trousers at such an event in his home. I'm tempted to point out that the villa is not actually his, but I bite my tongue. Something I do constantly in his presence.

The gown is the one I wore that night on the train, Katherine's, and I look like a peacock. The bird that represents sinful pride. I am proud of my work, and I am sinful too, so maybe it is apt. Unlike the female, the peahen, which is more restrained in its plumage, this dress has the full bravado of the male. I do not have that confidence, but I must find it.

'Sheba.' Katherine stands in the doorway. Her eyes are glassy. This reveals her concerns about this evening more than words can. I glance at my packed things. I leave tomorrow morning. Forster has paid me handsomely. But of course he spends freely, as it's not his money, but hers.

Once I'm beside her, she takes my hand for a moment. I shiver. Our plan is set. She must stay put for the poetry competition, then she will head back to London as if nothing has changed between her and Forster. I will follow in August and find us a place to live in Cornwall. Once I've done that, she will leave him. He will never make the connection, and she will be free. The money he has paid for the portrait will take me home and pay the rent for a year. All things being well, I should be able to continue to earn enough to support us. That is why tonight is important. This painting will launch my career. Not the one I envisioned, but one that will allow me to be with the woman I love.

'Ready?' she asks with a tremor in her voice.

'Yes,' I say, with more confidence than I feel. The painting is good, but what will people see? That is my concern. I can only hope it is simply Katherine's beauty.

Together we enter the salon. The first face I see is that of Father Keeney. His smile eases some of my tension, but also increases it. He is perceptive.

Forster clears his throat. 'Lords, ladies and gentlemen. My wife Katherine and the artist Bathsheba Kernow.'

I try not to wince at his use of my full name.

'You all know of my appreciation of the arts, and when we met this struggling young artist on the train, I knew immediately that I would help her on her way. Tonight we will see the portrait she has painted of my beautiful wife, which I commissioned after seeing her painting of a street urchin.' He pauses and walks to the covered painting on the easel. 'I think you will be astounded by the finished piece.' With a great flourish, he pulls the sheet off.

There is silence.

Waiting for a reaction, I'm unable to breathe or move. I appear ghostly in the mottled glass of the mirrors in the salon.

Finally, applause. I relax. Forster puffs up more. He hasn't properly studied the painting yet. He engages in conversation with Lady Diana Saunders while sipping champagne. Katherine introduces me to Conte Volpi again.

'You have an exquisite talent,' he says, his glance resting on the curves of Katherine's shoulders.

'Thank you,' I reply, noting Father Keeney studying the painting. The priest looks from me to Katherine and then to the tools of her trade, which I impulsively added when I signed it last week. He knows. I can only hope that he is the only one so observant.

Forster joins me beside Volpi. He looks over his shoulder at the portrait.

'You've captured her beauty to perfection.' He smiles like a proud parent. Does he notice the paper and pen on the end of the chaise? Does he even know how to read a painting? It was a reckless act but part of the style of the work.

Katherine pulls me away and introduces me to more people. The numbers have swelled, and guests drift out onto the lawn, their attention moving from the painting to the evening parade of gondolas on the Grand Canal. I take a moment to breathe, but the air is heavy and scented with jasmine.

Father Keeney hands me a glass of champagne. 'That is a very brave painting.'

I accept the glass but don't meet his eyes, because I'm afraid what I'll see there. His judgement means more to me than anyone apart from Katherine.

'It is exquisite, and every person in the room will have been moved by it.'

'Thank you,' I mumble, still not meeting his gaze.

He leans closer to me and whispers, 'Be careful. He may not have noticed yet, but he will, and I believe he can be very cruel.'

I look up.

'It's not you I am concerned for.' He looks out at the garden, where Katherine is laughing with some guests. 'I won't enter into a moral discussion, but you may have crossed a line publicly, and you have also answered a question regarding the poetry.' He pauses. 'Be careful. This is not a game.'

He leaves me looking at my work as people pause and appraise it. He is right. I have been reckless.

* * *

It is near midnight when Rossi arrives, full of apologies for missing the unveiling. Il Duce needed him. Guests have begun to leave, and I am beginning to breathe normally after Father Keeney's comments. The night has been spent listening to people talk of politics and art. Herr Hitler's recent visit is still fresh in everyone's minds. Father Keeney comes to say goodbye. His gaze is following Rossi.

'Do you not like him?' I whisper.

He smiles. 'Rossi is a shrewd man who fixes things for people, and he has made a career of being in the right place at the right time. But . . .' he pauses, 'if you need a steady friend who is always there for you, I would not choose him.'

I tilt my head and assess Rossi again.

'I've surprised you?'

'He has been nothing but kind to me.'

'You are young.' He softens his words with a smile. 'Rossi

looks after himself. If he finds you are no use to him, or could in any way be detrimental, then he will be ruthless.' He bows slightly. 'I must be off, but do take care, Sheba. You move in interesting circles, but they have no patience or tolerance for those who are different to themselves.' He walks to Katherine to make his farewells.

'Have you enjoyed your time in our city?' Conte Volpi asks me.

'Very much.'

'It attracts many talented painters like yourself.' He glances over his shoulder at the portrait. 'And what do you think of our leader? I could tell you do not approve of Mr Hitler.'

I must learn to hide my feelings. Both leaders care little for the lives of women, especially those who choose not to fit into what they see as our role. 'I have not had the honour of meeting Il Duce.'

He laughed. 'Very diplomatic. I look forward to seeing more of your work. I believe my wife might be interested in sitting for you.'

'That would be an honour.'

'We will be in touch.' He walks off and I breathe again. This will all work. People are not seeing anything other than a beautiful woman.

Across the room, Katherine is laughing. She is drunk. I miss the Katherine who wasn't intoxicated on anything but life. The one who showed me the real her. The one who is still a broken eighteen-year-old having lost the man she loved and her child. Before she'd revealed this, I was fascinated, bewitched even, but now my feelings have grown so much more. Because of those feelings and my respect for her work, I accept the Katherine who moves across the salon to speak with a guest. Her smile is overdone, her gaze flirtatious. Forster comes to her side and places a possessive hand on her back. It says to all, *she is mine*, but it lies.

I long for tonight to be over. It has been exhausting, and I feel exposed in this peacock dress and with my work on display. Each nerve ending is raw, and I am jumpy. Too much champagne and dull conversation. Thankfully, more people leave, and Forster escorts them through the gate in the garden to the quay. Gondolas move swiftly with their lanterns swaying, casting shadows against the walls and leaving light reflections in the water. Everything feels unbalanced. I walk back to the salon, wondering if I can simply retreat to my room. Once tonight is over, a new phase begins.

Rossi walks up to me holding out a glass. Out of politeness, I accept it. He stares with admiration at the painting, then turns to me.

'I haven't had time to study this work yet.'

'It is the style that Forster wished for.'

'It is indeed. You have fulfilled the request and yet . . . gone beyond.' He steps closer to the canvas. My heart skips as his eyes rest on the paper and pen. 'Harking back to the tradition of painting the sitter with their tools, so to speak.' He takes a sip of his champagne. 'This is indeed a remarkable painting. In it you have revealed so much.' He looks at me. 'You have shown what a fool Simon has made of us all.'

Bloods drains from my face as I realise what he has said. I grab the back of a chair so I don't fall over.

'Very remarkable, for it speaks of the artist as much as the sitter.' His glance narrows and he steps closer to me. I am aware of Father Keeney's words from earlier. There is no one around us, but the buzz of conversation has faded away and only a ringing of warning remains in my ears. How can I stop Rossi saying anything further? I have shown him to be a fool, and he knows he has made Mussolini look a fool as well.

'So much talent in such a twisted mind. I hadn't seen that in you.'

I want to say something but don't know what. Dread mixes with the realisation that we aren't alone. Forster is standing and staring at the portrait. Rossi mustn't talk to him. I must act. I've been so reckless. I open my mouth to speak.

'Only a person in love could have created such a painting,' Rossi says to me as Forster arrives at his side.

The expression on Forster's face changes. It is clear he heard.

'Excuse us, Serafino. It has been a long evening. Shall we meet for breakfast?'

Rossi bows. 'Of course, and again my apologies for my late arrival.'

Forster sees him out and Katherine sways towards me. She has no idea what has just happened.

'Katherine . . .' I begin.

Forster storms back into the room. I have never seen such rage. His face is distorted with it. He looks between Katherine and me, then to the painting.

'Deviants, both of you.' He moves towards it, but Katherine steps between him and the canvas.

He stops, his hands in fists, his wild-eyed glance darting between us. I flinch. 'Leave this house immediately and take that wretched work of filth out of my sight.'

I grab the painting as best I can.

'Out of my house!' he shouts.

'She can't leave tonight.' I hear the plea in Katherine's voice.

'What do you know, you . . . you whore!'

I'm frozen, wanting to run yet desperate to stay and protect her.

'I will not have a woman put out on the street tonight. She will leave tomorrow.' Katherine speaks slowly, and I can see she is sobering up.

'You are damn right she will.'

She turns to me. 'Go.'

I flee with the painting and take it through to the dining room, hoping it will be safe there for the night. Then I race to my room and bolt the door. My heart is thumping so loudly I can't hear. What will he do now? I pull off the gown and get dressed ready to leave. There is no way I can sleep, but Katherine is right, I can't set off in the middle of the night.

I take a deep breath to slow my heart rate, and that is when I hear the shouting. Then silence. I'm more worried when I can't hear them.

What have I done? Below, their bedroom door slams, then I hear their voices as clearly as if they were in the room with me.

'Be reasonable, Simon,' Katherine pleads.

I pace the floor.

'Reasonable,' he shouts. 'You don't know the meaning of the word.'

I hear a thwack. I race to the window and peer over the small balcony. But I can see nothing.

Katherine sobs. 'Simon, I love you. It was just a distraction.'

'You debased creature.'

Another thwack. I hear her cry out, and I race downstairs to their bedroom.

Katherine yells in pain and I try to open the door. It's locked. Her screams pierce through me and I pound on the door until I can do so no longer. My throat is raw from shouting.

He hasn't stopped. His voice changes to groans of pleasure. Katherine sobs.

These sounds will never leave me. I am useless. Nothing I can do will save her. Slowly I return to my room, closing the windows to deaden the sound. I am such a fool.

PART THREE

We read the past by the light of the present, and forms vary as the shadows fall, or as the point of vision alters.

James Anthony Froude

31

1 August 1935

London

The skies are heavy with rain and I have no energy to move. My grandfather hasn't asked any questions about my unannounced return in July last year. I haven't seen Katherine again. All I wanted to do was return in the night and kill Forster. He is a beast, but the law is on his side. She is his wife, his property. There is nothing I can do.

The August sun lacks the warmth I need to feel alive. My days are endless and the nights are hell. I hear her cries, feel my anger and impotence. I cannot save her. She must save herself, but I fear she will slowly die with the drugs she takes to numb the emptiness he creates in her life. Looking in the mirror, I see that my skin is the pallor of the skies above. I have forced myself outdoors daily to make my grandfather feel better. He asks questions about my future that I can't answer. I have no idea what I will do. Returning to Cornwall doesn't appeal. I have a new brother, a stepmother who doesn't want me around, and I haven't changed. If anything, I'm more certain of who I am. How can I keep that inside and hidden without love to make it worthwhile?

The portrait arrived here yesterday, sent on by Father Keeney along with the rest of my things. He apologised again for the delay. He was called to Rome and left Venice shortly after I did, and it was only last month that he was able to return. His letter was full of news, but none I wanted to hear. He knew what I needed to know, and as many times as I read the letter, it didn't appear.

The day after the unveiling of the portrait, he found me sitting in the church in which the painting of my mother and father as Bathsheba and David hung. Thinking logically had proved impossible. What I'd heard, and had been powerless to do anything about, wouldn't leave me. I confided in Father Keeney. There was too much anger and horror to keep it all inside me. He listened, letting me pour out my fears and worries. His anger was visible, but when he spoke, it wasn't what I wanted to hear. He cautioned me against intervening between a husband and wife. He left me with the promise that he would speak to her.

It was a week later before I heard from him. He said she was managing, and that her message to me was that she was OK and I should go home and stay away.

It nearly killed me. Leaving Venice was a relief and a torment. While I was there, she was near, but now I know nothing of her. The not knowing eats away at me. I left La Serenissima a different person. Despite Father Keeney's encouragement, my heart has not healed. Seeing the portrait here brings the pain sharply into focus. Katherine's beauty haunts me. My grandfather adores it, and he sees what it says. But he loves me, and for that I am grateful.

For the millionth time, I read the poem Katherine wrote for me, but the words don't bring comfort. They speak of a love that burns too brightly. Nothing can hold it. It is not like the phoenix that will be reborn. There are days when it is all too much. If my grandfather didn't exist, I wouldn't. He watches me so closely.

Father Keeney also sent the photograph he took of me in St Mark's Square. The day was glorious. The world, and Katherine's love, was mine. I was full of joy. Everything was perfect, but perfect doesn't last. Days later, it was all gone and I'd learned just how soul-destroying life could be.

I head outside and follow my usual route through the park, passing children and prams. Their joyful calls should lift me, but they don't. Nothing does. I haven't touched my work. Grandfather has suggested I go to the Slade, or at least take some courses. He insists it would be sinful if I didn't use my talent. He, bless him, has no idea of how sinful I am. Of the Seven Deadly Sins, pride and lust ruled me until wrath slipped in. I envied Forster his position in Katherine's life and I was certain we could beat him. In my rush to be with her, I didn't take the risks on board. I was, and still am, a fool. I'm twenty-one. I can't live with my grandfather for ever. He is right, I must find the strength to work again, and attending classes might help me find a way back.

Rain begins to fall in big fat drops as I near the Prince Albert Memorial. I haven't thought to bring an umbrella with me. Before I even leave the park, I'm soaked through. Shivering starts, and by the time I'm at the door, my teeth are chattering. The housekeeper makes a fuss and I spend a long time immersed in hot water. I could just sink down and let it cover me and then be no more. It tempts me.

'Here's some more hot water,' Mrs Smith says, bringing a full kettle in.

'Thank you.'

'We don't need you becoming sick. Your grandfather is worried enough with the news from Cornwall.'

'What news?' I sit up, but sink back down as the cold air hits my skin.

'Oh, I wasn't supposed to say.' She looks at me, then away.

'Well, you've started now.'

'It's just that the woman your father took up with has gone and left him with the baby.'

'What?' I ask.

'Yes, she ran off with another artist from what I gather.' She tuts.

'How is my father?' I ask, my heart tightening.

'From what your grandfather said, quite distressed.'

I climb out of the bath. 'I should go to him.'

She grabs a towel. 'He'll need someone to look after the baby.'

I laugh. 'No, that will not be me.'

She sends me a look and leaves the room. I have descended very low in her esteem. In her eyes it is the role of women to take care of children, but there is no reason why I should be the one to look after my half-brother. My father will find someone. I have my career to think about, and I have to find a means to pay my own way.

* * *

Before I set off to Cornwall, I confirm my place to study at the Slade. This will ensure that I won't be expected to look after the child. But doubts set in as I step off the train in St Ives and walk through the familiar lanes to my father's studio. The cry of the gulls, the smell of the sea. Familiar faces smile in greeting. This was my home, but it isn't any more. I'm not the same Sheba who left here in search of a miracle.

I hear my half-brother before I see him. His cries are loud and angry. I push the door open carefully to spy a big ginger cat squaring off with the small child who is clutching his hand. The cat has won despite the marmalade-coloured fur in the toddler's grasp.

An older woman walks from the kitchen. 'Can I help you?'

'I'm here to see my father.' I smile encouragingly at her.

She sends me a queer look. Perhaps she is unaware that my father has another child. She is unfamiliar to me, so is probably not local.

'He's painting on the quay.' She picks up my brother and takes him to the kitchen. 'I told you, Tommy, leave the cat alone.'

Sensible advice. However, I offer my hand to the cat to sniff before I scratch between its ears. It appears that Marmalade remembers me, and a loud purr confirms this.

The cat follows me out of the house and down to the quay. It is easy to pick out my father in his paint-splattered fishing smock. He is engrossed in capturing the scene. The tide is out and the boats lie at awkward angles waiting for the return of the water. The colourful hulls shimmer and reflect off the damp sand. Gulls hover hopefully while a few men clear the barnacles off their boats' hulls. This scene has not changed while I was gone, and I'm relieved in a way, yet at the same time I'm not. I want it to be different, like me somehow. Several tourists stand watching my father. He is oblivious to them.

As I come closer, I see the canvas. His style has altered a little, but it is still his, simply looser. Broad sweeps of colour and small, swift marks bring the scene to life. It is good.

Once at his side, I let him work on, although I long to say something. He doesn't notice me until I cast a shadow on his canvas and he glances up ready to tell me off.

'My God, Baba!' He flings his arms about me. 'How wonderful.'

There are tears in his eyes when he lets go of me. It is then I see that he's aged during the time I've been away.

'Let me pack this up and then we can talk properly.'

Without a word I fall into the old routines that I learned at my parents' side. The easel is folded and paints stored. He glances at his watch. 'Mrs Sweeting will stay until six thirty. Shall we stop for a drink at the Sloop Inn?'

That answers one of the questions I wanted to ask. *Who is the woman with my brother?*

'That sounds wonderful.'

I'm tired, but seeing him fills me with love. His eyes are so like mine, and he is trying to read me. 'I have a thousand questions,' he says, 'but they can wait until I've ordered.'

I sit on a stool outside, letting the place settle about me. Nellie walks past with a child in her arms, one holding her hand and another dragging a stick along the ground.

'Nellie.' I wave, and a smile spreads across her face.

She walks over. 'Well look at you.'

I hold out my hands and take the babe from her arms. 'Who is this?'

'Mary.'

'She's a beauty.' The child is the image of her mother, with her umber eyes flecked with viridian.

'Are you all right?' Nellie asks, studying me.

I smile.

'That's not an answer. You're too thin, and you shine less than you did when you left.' She stares at me. 'Your heart's been broken.'

I swallow a lump.

'They do heal.' She puts her hand on my arm.

'Not so sure.' I know my heart can't heal because of the damage I've done. That reality walks with me continuously, along with the not knowing if she is OK.

'Oh Baba. You will mend. I promise.'

I hide my emotions in her daughter's neck.

'I'm sorry about the things I said before you left.'

I look at her.

'You're different, and that makes things hard, but it doesn't mean we can't be friends.'

I swallow. That's something.

She puts her hand over mine. 'I've missed you.'

'Ma.' Her son tugs her hand.

'It's feeding time. Come and see me.' She takes the child from my arms and I watch them continue along the harbour, then turn up Fish Street.

My father returns with a pint for himself and a half for me. 'Tell me everything.'

'Before I begin, I need to ask a few questions.'

He nods, then takes a sip of his beer.

'What happened?'

He shakes his head slowly. 'I was so blinded, by grief, by need, that I didn't see things correctly. I'm sorry.'

'Did you love Mum?' I have to ask, because he was so quick to take up with the harridan.

He takes my hand in his. 'With my whole heart. I was your mother's only lover.' He lets go and picks up his beer again. 'She wasn't mine, though. I thought diversity fed my art.' He snorts. 'Instead, it stole things away.'

'Mum knew.' I take a sip. The cider is cool and crisp.

'I know. I was open about it. I never loved anyone else, but I did need others.'

'I see.' His hair is now more grey than brown at his temples. He is still ridiculously handsome.

'Do you? You have grown up.' He laughs. 'The funniest thing is now that I'm looking after Tommy, I have no energy or even need for that.'

I raise an eyebrow, not believing his words.

'Her departure changed me. It was like someone had removed very dark glasses.' He turns the pint in his hands. 'She told me what she said to you. I'm so sorry. I wish you had come to me at the time. Is that why you left?'

'One of the reasons.'

'Oh Baba.' His eyes are so sad.

'It was time for me to go and it was good that I did.' That at least is partly true.

'But you came back sooner than you planned.' He studies me and I hope I'm giving nothing away.

'Things changed.' I run my finger along the side of the glass with memories of Katherine and her cool skin in my thoughts.

'So now you're off to the Slade.'

'Yes.' I smile. 'I'll live with Grandpa.'

'I haven't seen your work. Has it changed?'

Never again will I paint like I did in Venice. Never again will I do another portrait like that. People can read them too easily. 'Yes, quite a bit. I think . . . I think I've found my style.'

'Good.'

'It is.' I pause. 'I don't think you'd know my work if you saw it, though.'

'Then I look forward to seeing it.' He grins. 'Are you here long enough to paint with me?'

'A week.' The sun is low in the sky, and I squint. The colours of the fishing boats almost pulse in intensity.

'You can tell me all about your travels. I know you were on a pilgrimage of sorts.'

I turn back to him. Katherine used that same word. 'I was, and I certainly found what I wasn't looking for.' This is true.

'Are you OK?' he asks.

I look at my glass, then up at him. He is my father and I can tell him. 'I lost my heart and had it broken.'

'I see.' He reaches for my hand again.

'I don't think you can.'

'I know you better than you think.' He pushes a piece of hair off my face. 'You fell in love with someone who wasn't free to love you.'

'This is true.'

'She chose the life she knew.' He places a finger under my chin. My head flies up. How long has he known?

'Whether you knew or not, both your mother and I saw.'

'Does it upset you? Did she . . .'

'Baba, we love you. Love is love. Sadly, not all of society feels this way, but if you loved someone, no matter who it was, I would love them too.'

'Thank you.'

'You will find love again.'

I shake my head.

'You will.' He smiles. 'It will catch you unawares, and you will wonder how.'

'Have you found someone else?' I ask, almost afraid of the answer.

'Like I said, no energy, but I do know that even though I am forty-five, it may yet find me again.'

'I hope it does, but I think I may be better off without it.' The pain of hurting someone else chills me.

'I'd like to say don't fall in love with someone who belongs to someone else, but life is never that easy.' He finishes his pint. 'Best drink up. Mrs Sweeting doesn't take too well to me being late.' We bring our glasses to the bar and walk into the September evening.

32

5 April 2022

——————————

Penzance

The programme on art had just finished. I was fuming. Everything that had come out of Paul's mouth had sounded like the words I'd written that hadn't been good enough. The arguments he'd used were mine. Once dinner was in the oven, I went into the bedroom to find the box with my thesis. Maybe I was misremembering.

Opening the lid, I found the last printout covered in Paul's notes. The red pen was blinding, but when I looked past it and saw my words, I screamed into my pillow. My words and arguments *had* been good enough, good enough for Paul to be using them on Radio 4 years later. I dropped the paper on top of the box and accepted it was all in the past. There was no going back. I'd believed him and he'd used me for his own gain. I felt for the locket around my neck that he'd given me, promising his love, promising he'd look after me, have my back, be my one and only. I pulled it off, breaking the delicate chain, and threw it in the box.

After a walk through the garden, I was back in control of my emotions. Paul was something I would deal with later. Right now, Mum and the business came first. Paul could head back to London, and then once things were sorted here, I would finish with him. I froze. How did I have a life without him? It was all I'd known for ages.

I heard a car pull in and braced myself. If I remained cool and didn't rise to anything, it would all be easier. I slapped a smile on my face and turned as Tash escorted Paul into the house.

'That smells divine. I'd love to stay for dinner.' Tash grinned and Paul sent me a look. I ignored him and laid another place at the table. Without asking, he went to my father's wine rack and selected the best bottle he could find. Before he could open it, Tash said, 'That doesn't go with roast chicken.' She removed the bottle and the corkscrew from his hands.

I took a bottle of Gavi out of the fridge, hiding my smile. Tash dared to go where no one else did.

Paul stalked off and returned with a large whisky.

'That looks lovely, Paul. May I have one?' Mum asked.

'Ren can get one for you.' He took a large sip.

Mum frowned at him. 'She's sorting the dinner.'

He looked at her, then put his drink down and left the kitchen.

'Is he often this tetchy?' she asked me.

I was about to say no, but to be honest, he was. 'Yes.'

'Why do you put up with it, dear?'

Tash walked into the room. 'That's a very good question.'

I didn't answer as Paul returned carrying a small whisky for my mother. An awkward silence filled the kitchen, but he took no notice of it as he sat down. Meanwhile, Tash brought the salad to the table, saying, 'Paul, why don't you carve the chicken?'

'Ren can.' He glanced at my mother.

'She's mashing the potatoes right now and you mentioned repeatedly in the car how hungry you were.' Tash looked intently at him. 'You'll eat sooner if you help.'

I pounded the potatoes wondering why I hadn't seen this before. He was about to push back, but instead he rose and set about carving the bird. I refused to look at him directly. Tash would have kept his feathers ruffled all afternoon.

What I wanted more than anything was to sit quietly and think things through. How was I going to make sure my mother had enough money for her care? Did we have to report the state of the business? The one thing I was grateful for was that my uncle hadn't been about to mortgage the buildings. Dad and I would have had to agree to it. So if his house didn't sell, money from the sale of the business property should cover most of what my father had loaned him. But I couldn't see any future for Barton's. This saddened me, and that was a surprise. I'd enjoyed working with Tash on Harbour House and I wanted Sheba and Viv's work to receive the accolades it richly deserved. There were still so many questions. Why had neither of them had an exhibition until the 1960s as my research unearthed? Tomorrow I would pin down Tilly, the gardener. She would be able to answer some of it, I was certain.

'I forgot to mention, Ren, your uncle called,' Mum said.

'He hasn't returned my calls,' Paul muttered.

'You have business with him?' Tash asked, taking the green beans to the table.

He sent her a filthy look when she came for the plate of chicken. She ignored him and helped my mother with her food. The mashed potatoes were done, and I noted that Paul had finished his whisky and poured himself a healthy glass of wine and a small glass for my mother. Nothing, not even an offer, for Tash or me. Not that I minded. I was too tired and it wouldn't help me to think clearly.

Dinner passed in silence and Paul finished the bottle of wine. Tash raised an eyebrow but for once kept her silence. However, my mother didn't.

'Paul, that's a bit much.'

His face was a picture as he stopped himself from his first response. 'It's been a hard day.'

Tash rolled her eyes, and I thought how if his had been hard, mine had been a disaster. Part of me wanted to laugh, but I held back. The day wasn't over yet. Tash rose and told Paul to help her clear. Reluctantly he joined her, and she made him wash up while I helped Mum, who wanted to go straight to bed. All this news had exhausted her. Our pace was slow, but once in her room, I helped her to change and get into bed.

As I bent to kiss her, she said, 'Darling, when we can arrange it, I think it's best if I go into a home.'

I sank down on the side of the bed.

'Things will only become harder. Your father and I discussed this, and we should have told you.'

'You should have.'

'I'm sorry. I think I haven't seen things clearly.' She sighed. 'You've spent so little time with us.'

I closed my eyes for a moment. 'It was wrong. I should have been here more.'

'Is Paul always this rude?' she asked. 'I don't remember him being so, but then things are slipping.'

I was unable to reply. Tears threatened. I nodded. It was the truth, and I was only just seeing it clearly now. I kissed her again and headed back to the kitchen.

Tash was on her own, standing at the sink. He had crossed the line with her. It was clear on her face.

'I know you love him, but I don't understand why. He's destroying you and it's killing me.'

'Tash—'

'No, you don't see what he's made you. He's taken away the gorgeous girl who was going to take on the world. He's starved you of love, the right type of love, the type that builds you up, not pulls you down. He's a thug, he's underhand, devious, and he's poisoned the people around you so he has you to himself.' She drew in a breath. 'I know you don't want to hear these words, but he controls you.'

'No.'

'Yes. Normal people don't hack into their partner's emails. They don't go behind their back. He's changed you, and not for the better.'

I shook my head back and forth, not wanting to hear what she was saying. It hit home, though, and I agreed with every word she said.

'Find your inner strength and leave him. Please. Because watching this happen to you is soul-destroying. I love you. You are a wonderful, intelligent woman, and you'll shine again once he is out of your life.'

I simply stood still. Out of the corner of my eye I saw Paul pouring himself another whisky. Tash had spoken quietly, in such a measured tone that it made her words more penetrating. There was no reply I could make to it. It was an ultimatum of sorts.

She dried her hands on a tea towel. 'I'll meet you at Harbour House tomorrow at ten.' She leaned in and hugged me. 'I love you and I believe in you.'

She peered into the sitting room. 'Will you be OK? He's beyond angry.'

I swallowed. Part of me wanted her to stay but I needed to talk to Paul, and that wouldn't happen if she was here. It had to be alone. 'I'll be fine.'

'He's never been violent, has he?'

I shook my head. He'd come close once, but that was five years ago, when he thought I was flirting with a colleague. He'd promised never to do it again. Thus far he'd kept that promise.

She stared at me. 'I'm just a call away.'

'Thanks.' I walked her to the door and watched her drive away with my heart sinking. All I wanted to do was crawl into bed and sleep. Instead I went into the sitting room. Paul glared at me over the rim of his glass. This was not a good start. He was drunk and I was filled with anger. Tash was right. Now was the time. I called a taxi.

'A taxi is booked and will be here in a few minutes.'

He glared at me. 'I'm not leaving.' He knocked back the rest of his whisky.

'You are.'

He laughed and rose to his feet. 'I will do what I want.'

'You've been doing that all along. Like stealing my work.' I braced myself.

'So what?' He swayed a bit. 'You didn't need it.'

'What? That makes no sense.' I stepped back from him.

'You had me. You didn't need your work and I did.'

The look in his eyes worried me.

'You are worth nothing without me.' He was slurring his words. 'You can't even recognise an original painting.' He took a step closer.

'There is nothing wrong with caution.'

'Ah yes, caution. I keep you safe and protected. You owe me.' There was hate in his expression. I'd seen it once before, when he verbally abused a museum curator who had misattributed a reference. By the end, the man was broken. But I would not be.

'I don't owe you anything.'

'Oh, you do. You were a wreck eight years ago and I took pity on you, protected you.'

'You stole my work, my words, and you continue to use it.'

'So what? No one knows. You don't need it doing your little job.'

I drew in a deep breath and regretted it. The smell of stale booze coming off him was repulsive. His calm veneer gone along with the control he normally had over himself.

'You are a cow, a stupid lazy cow and you are lucky I look after you.'

'No, I can see I'm not lucky at all. You have lied to my parents, lied to my uncle, and God knows who else. You have hacked into my emails and tried to control my life.'

'Tried? I am your life. Without me you are nothing, nothing at all.'

'Well, then I will just have to find that out myself. You are going now. You can take the sleeper back to London and be glad I'm not reporting you to the university.'

He didn't move. His eyes narrowed. I prayed my mother couldn't hear this. He took another step towards me. On the table was a bronze of a nude. I picked it up. 'Come any closer and I will use this.'

He laughed.

The doorbell rang.

'Your taxi.' Still clutching the bronze, I fled to the hallway and opened the door.

The driver took one look at my face and mouthed, 'Are you OK?'

I nodded.

He picked up Paul's bag and walked to the sitting room. 'Come on, mate.'

Paul looked from me to the driver. He wouldn't make a scene. Not in front of someone else. His demeanour changed and he became all charm. 'Just coming,' he said, grabbing his backpack. It was then that I noticed the papers stuffed in there. My thesis.

Acting faster than I'd thought I could, I grabbed them as he was stepping out the door. He didn't notice, as he was telling the driver to take him to the station. I closed and locked the door, then sank to the floor and began to shake.

When I looked up, my mother was standing there in her nightdress. 'Oh my darling girl.'

'He's gone.'

She stroked my head with her right hand. 'I'm so proud of you,' she said.

She held out her hand. I took it and stood. Then she wrapped me in her arms, and I cried for the lost years.

33

16 September 1935

London

In my last look at the studio before I left Cornwall, I saw Mum's work back on display and the world felt better, which I hadn't thought would happen without Katherine by my side. But time with my father and my brother filled a little of the hole she'd left. I'm looking forward to beginning a new direction at the Slade. I can't live off my grandfather's generosity for ever, and my father reminded me that selling my work isn't a bad thing. He cautioned me not to become too high and mighty, saying, 'Humility is good, and you still create art even when you do it with a view to paying the rent.'

New-school nerves play havoc with my stomach, but I've worked alongside some of the greatest artists living and that is a good grounding to go into this year at the Slade. Besides, I'll meet new people. My grandfather is a delight, but his friends are not. How can he be so forward-thinking and still be friends with many who aren't? It doesn't make sense to me.

Entering the large studio space for my first class, I take the spot furthest away from other people. A shyness I've never felt before overcomes me. Just as the tutor is about to begin, a large woman dashes in and takes the space beside me. She mouths *sorry*, and there is something delightful about her giant presence.

The hours fly by, and after the initial sketch, I don't think about the room, who is there or anything other than the work. Not even hunger interrupts the burst of creative energy that rules my day. I look up from the paper surprised that the class has ended.

As I leave the studio, the woman who was next to me all day catches up. 'Hello, I'm Martha Sykes.'

'Sheba Kernow,' I say.

Her glance narrows. 'Your mother is an artist.'

'Was. She died a few years ago.'

'I'm sorry.' She doesn't look away but continues to study me.

'Thank you.'

'Look, I've really put my foot in it. I'm from Manchester and I don't know a soul here, and, well, you looked approachable.' She wipes her palms down her trousers.

I feel her nerves. 'Is it the red hair?'

'Possibly.' She grins. 'Do you have time for a drink?'

'I know just the place,' I say.

We walk in silence to the Fitzroy Tavern.

Once we are inside, Martha asks, 'What can I get you?'

'As the weather is warm, a cider would be good.' Because of the dark wood interior and the smoke, I grab a table by the window for some light and watch my new acquaintance. She is strongly built, and her brown hair is contained in a low knot on the back of her head.

'Here we go.' She places the half-pints on the table. 'God, I need this after today.'

I frown. Nothing about today surprised me or, for that matter, really pushed me.

'I hate drawing,' she confesses.

I blink. 'Hate?'

'Yup, give me a slab of rock and let me go.'

'A sculptor, then.'

She nods, and her eyes sparkle. 'It's in the family. Both my parents are, as is my younger sister, Viv.'

'Can I ask why you are here then?' The pub is warm and the cider is cool. I relax into the space, enjoying the black and white tiled floor and the effect it has on my tired mind.

'My parents thought it would strengthen my work if I went back to basics, to be forced to draw properly and to learn something about perspective. They do despair.'

'That bad?'

'Bad doesn't cover it.' She takes a sip of her cider, and I notice the strength of her hands and assess again how powerfully she is built. 'But you, surely with parents who are artists who would have taught you . . .'

'I needed . . . something.'

'If you say so.'

My father was surprised by the way my painting had evolved. I no longer feel the need to capture what is in front of me. I am pulled now by the essence of what I see. 'I'm at a crossroads, I think, and going back to the basics, which I absorbed rather than learned, seems like a . . . a way forward.'

'That sounds like it's more about life than art.' She casts me a sideways glance.

'It might just be.'

'New ways are always good.' She raises her glass. 'Here's to new ways forward and to new beginnings.'

'New beginnings.' Maybe my father is right. There is a future ahead.

'Hello, you two were in the class today.' A lanky man with unkempt hair walks towards us. I draw back into my seat, but Martha beams.

'Hello. Join us.' She taps the stool beside her. I eye the newcomer over the rim of my glass.

'I'm Jason Sewell.'

'I'm Martha Sykes, and this is Sheba Kernow.'

'Kernow. Relation of Francis Kernow?'

'Daughter.'

'He's a member of the St Ives Society of Artists?'

I nod and look down at my cider.

Martha whistles. 'No pressure then, with that pedigree.' She smiles and the atmosphere lightens.

'State your goal, Jason Sewell,' she says.

'To become the best artist of the twentieth century.'

She snorts into her glass. 'Nothing like a man who thinks big.'

We both join in her laughter.

'And for that bravado, the next round is on you.' Martha pushes him towards the bar.

28 January 1936

My head hums painfully all day while we work on perspective. No matter how I try, I can't get it right. The day doesn't want to end, but I do. I can barely keep my eyes open. I would have thought my time in Venice would have prepared me for drinking with students, but between the cider and the terrible red wine that followed, I want to die. Neither Martha nor Jason shows any ill-effects. I can't decide if I hate them or think they are the best things to happen to me.

Both of them live in Hampstead, and they want me there too. I might just do that. My grandfather is wonderful and is supporting me, but recently he has taken up with a widow and I am distinctly in the way. So tonight I will raise the idea with him, if Martha and Jason don't distract me with the pub at the end of the day.

Stepping back from the work, I can see that my perspective is off. But rather than erase or start again, I madly transform it into how I feel. Nothing is where it should be and this has transferred to the paper. After an intense half-hour, I step away ready to go back to the task at hand.

The tutor comes up and assesses what I've done. I'm prepared to be booted off the course.

'Your work is much stronger when you aren't constrained by convention. Your perspective in this is terrible, unlike your previous technically perfect pieces. However, there is feeling here, passion even, that takes the distorted lines and makes them glorious.' He pauses. 'Now put that aside and do the work I asked.' He says the latter with a smile.

Martha leans over. 'You dodged a bullet there, and that's the best thing I've seen you do.'

Jason is on my other side. 'Bloody teacher's pet. If I didn't know better, I'd swear you're sleeping with him. But since you refused me and I'm irresistible, I know which way you swing.' He grins.

'I am simply the second choice,' Martha whispers.

'Not second, equal first. I wanted you both at the same time.' He laughs.

I roll my eyes, thankful for their friendship, and focus on the task at hand.

11 May 1936

Kensington Gardens should be a safe place. I'm working fast on the play of the vibrant spring greens when a dog dashes towards me and knocks over my easel.

'Damn.' I'm silently cursing the person who let their dog loose when my breath stops. Katherine stands in front of me with a broken dog lead. She looks little different than the last day I saw her in Venice, almost two years ago now.

'Sheba.' Her voice comes out dry and raspy.

'Katherine.' I look around her for evidence of Forster.

'He's not with me,' she says, reading my mind, and I relax a little.

'I'm sorry.' I need to say so much more, but I don't know how to begin.

'There is no need. I walked into loving you with my eyes wide open.'

I gasp.

She smiles sadly.

'Do you . . .' I can't say any more.

'Yes.'

'Then now, this moment . . .' My voice trails away.

She smiles sadly, placing her hand on her heart. 'I would, but there is one I love more, who is my whole heart and soul.'

I lean against the tree. She has found someone else. I can't breathe as pain sears through me.

'Isabella is thirteen months old. She is the product of that brutal night.'

I close my eyes, trying to process her words. She has a daughter.

'My beautiful girl stayed the course and brings me joy.'

I exhale, feeling colour return to my face. 'Oh Katherine, that's wonderful.' I take her hand in mine. The feel of her cool skin sets everything inside alight. I'm home. 'Where is she?'

'She's napping with the nanny.' The spaniel comes bounding up and Katherine catches him by the collar. 'I came out to get some fresh air.' She looks down at the dog. 'I'm sorry.'

I'm puzzled by her apology. 'I was the one at fault.' Awkward silence fills the space between us. 'Are you well?' I ask, though there are a thousand other things I really want to know.

'Yes, fine.' She doesn't meet my glance when she speaks.

'And him . . .'

She ignores my question. 'You look well.'

I grit my teeth for a moment. She knows what I want to know. 'Thank you. And is Forster pleased about the child?'

She laughs bitterly. 'What was it he said . . . that having children uses all women's creative energy?'

I notice the hint of a bruise just above her wrist.

'I must be off. Isabella will be waking soon.'

We stand a foot apart, but the whole world is between us.

'I didn't mean to . . .' she begins. 'Please forgive me. If she hadn't arrived . . .'

'I know.' There is pain in her eyes and I feel it physically. Does she think I don't understand how much having a child means to her? 'Has anything changed with him?'

She turns away. 'I'm just so sorry.'

'You don't need to apologise to me. Of course you have to stay with him now you have a child.'

She is about to speak, but stops. Then she says, 'Please, please know that it wasn't my choice.'

I frown, not understanding. 'Can I see you again? Do you live here in Kensington?'

'No, and maybe.' She fixes the lead and leaves without looking at me again. I sink onto the wet grass and stare at my ruined work. The bright greens have gone muddy.

* * *

Martha holds open a book of poetry. 'Have you seen this? I picked it up at Hatchards on Saturday, and my goodness, this man is talented. Such longing, especially this poem. "Venetian Vespers".'

My heart stills at the title. It can't be. Her words. It is her voice that reads them to me as we lie side by side. Her hand resting on my waist. Her mouth near my ear so that each syllable stirs my hair and my desire.

> *The ringing of the Angelus*
> *The touch of your hand*
> *The taste of you*
> *Have become my faith*
> *My reason*
> *Light plays in your hands*
> *Setting fire to the chosen path*
> *Love is alchemical*
> *I am lost*
> *Combined with you*

I find my voice to stop her. 'Who is the poet?'

'Simon Forster,' she says. 'I've read his work before, but this collection is his best by far.' She taps the page of a different one. 'But it's this poem in particular.'

I catch sight of the page but I don't need to read the words. They are scratched onto my heart. How did he get the poem? Katherine must have given it to him. Now I know what she was saying sorry for . . . for betraying me, us, our love.

As I scan the page, my body contracts. These are *my* words. They were written for me, about me. They are not his, they don't belong to him, they don't belong to others. But now they do. One thing jars. The fourth line, it's not right. It was the reason she didn't give me the poem right away. She wasn't happy with that phrase. Did she change her mind again?

'Isn't it fabulous. I was lost to the words when I read it last night.'

I close my eyes. I mustn't respond. Martha isn't to know, and I can never say, although I have in Katherine's portrait. The opening of the poem is on display to any keen observer, but even I know that it's her beauty that draws the eye, not those small details. So they can't know that it was Katherine, not Simon, who wrote those words, for me and me alone. Like the portrait that was painted for Katherine even though Forster commissioned it. But that painting, newly framed by my grandfather, sits in my room. Nothing is as it should be.

'Are you OK? You've gone white?' Martha takes the book from my shaking hands.

'Didn't sleep well last night,' I lie. 'I think I'll head home now.'

'Not a bad idea. Rest up. We have the exhibition in a week's time, and you haven't finished yet.'

11 June 1936

'You're a dark horse. How could you not tell us?' Martha looks at the abstract portrait of Katherine. I've been tempted to paint it again, but I could never capture the raw emotion of the original. The rest of my works on display are shadows of that piece, and it has won the prize. It is cheating, although I have added to it, but it feels right somehow. Katherine's words about me are now public, so my painting of her is public. So public in fact that it will be in tomorrow's *Times*. Many people will not understand or like it. But to me it is everything. Despite her betrayal of giving my poem to Simon, I still love her.

I haunt the park at all hours. Not once have I spotted her or her dog. But each time I hold a small bit of hope in me that I will at least catch sight of her. Even the smallest glimpse could fill some of the ache in my heart.

Both Jason and Martha have noticed the change in me and have done their best to jolly me, but it doesn't work. I need to know why she gave it to him. Part of me understands that she must have needed to, maybe to protect her and Isabella. But I want to hear that from her. To be honest, I want to hear from her about anything, anything at all.

My grandfather makes his way across the room to me. 'This is the same woman as the other portrait?'

'Yes.'

'I prefer the other, but I understand this one, which I didn't think I would. I am too old for these new ways.' He glances about the room. 'Your mother tried to push the boundaries of her work, but in the end she found she fitted in a different place.'

The flowing yet harsh landscapes of West Penwith fill my thoughts. There is one of her paintings that I love more than I can express. It is simply of the sea and Godrevy lighthouse.

'She would be so proud of you.' He walks closer to the painting. 'So very proud.'

My father enters the room. My little brother, Tommy, is with my grandfather's housekeeper. She is not pleased but understands he cannot attend the opening.

'My darling Baba, you have found your style and it is magnificent. Such passion!' He hugs me. I feel a fraud, as this work was painted two years ago. My more recent work doesn't have the same energy or heart. It's not bad, but it is not the same. Somehow if I am to succeed, I must find this in myself again. Part of me wonders if it is because I am here in London. No matter how hard I try, it doesn't stir me the same way. Kensington is lovely, but there is nothing wild or raw or seductive about it.

Martha walks up to my father. 'I'm Martha Sykes and your daughter is brilliant.'

'Sykes? Related to Brian Sykes, the sculptor?'

'He's my father and he's here.' She points to the other side of the room.

'Haven't seen him in years.' He bows his head, saying, 'If you'll excuse me.'

Martha stands beside me as we watch our fathers greet each other. 'We are so lucky to have had the backgrounds we had. We grew up living and breathing all things art. We both could draw before we could talk, I imagine.'

I smile.

'But I look at what Jason has achieved in this year, and I am astounded.'

'That is true.' Guilt floods me, as he came second to me.

'We need to celebrate, and we need to discuss how you must share in the studio we are about to rent in Hampstead and you must leave the comfort of Kensington to suffer for your art like the rest of us.'

I cast her a sideways glance.

'Two reasons actually. One, you need to leave your lovely grandfather, and two, we can't afford it without you.'

I laugh.

'I'll take that as a yes.'

I've sold four paintings and two more commissions have come in, so I can do this. Maybe it is time to stop haunting the park looking for what I can't have and instead look to the future.

34

7 April 2022

Penzance

I opened the list of counsellors that Tash's husband, Gareth, had sent me. As soon as I began to blame myself, he told me I was not at fault. He recommended that I talk with a professional who could help me work through my feelings. I would ring them all later today. Gareth suggested I talk to each of them and see who I felt most at ease with. It was all overwhelming.

The front door opened and Tash came in. She handed me a coffee. 'Thought the caffeine might help.'

'Thanks.' I blew on the surface. 'Not sure a double or even quadruple espresso could take away the exhaustion I feel.'

'Take the day off.'

'Tash, I can't take another day off.'

Both of us were exhausted. Mum had called Tash when she'd heard what was happening. Tash had arrived minutes after Paul had gone. She had stayed up with me unpicking my life from his. This had meant extracting my money from the joint accounts and changing the backup email addresses to hers.

Yesterday we'd driven to London, where Gareth met us. Thankfully, Paul was out, so we removed my stuff from the flat.

There were a few pieces of artwork, the most important being the Laura Knight sketch that my father had given me for my twenty-first birthday, the Jaunty Blythe painting of the boat, the Maddie Hollis painting of Kynance and the Elise Tremayne portrait of my great-grandmother. In under four hours, my life with Paul was erased and we were back on the road to Cornwall. To be honest, it was like I had a bit of whiplash, and I didn't know what to think, let alone feel. The funny thing was, aside from a few shadow spots on the walls, the flat looked little altered without my things.

'Then tell me what you need, and I'll bring it to you here,' Tash said.

We faced each other off. I wasn't going to win when she looked like that; I knew this of old.

'Fine, the full files on Harbour House, and Dad's iMac.'

'Consider it done. And you will put your feet up until I'm back.'

'No, I'm going to go through some more of the correspondence and write a news release.'

She sighed. 'Rory will be coming by in a bit. He wanted to go through a few things with you.'

I put a hand to my hair.

'You look fine, just a bit tired.' She smiled. 'Please try and rest, and if you can't do that, then set the world alight with the genius of Sheba and Viv. And also, I think you should talk to someone at *The West Briton* about our lady in the portrait. It could be Katherine Forster, but without a photo of her, we have nothing to go on. Maybe if you get an article in the local paper, the nationals will pick it up.' She paused. 'Personally, I agree with you that she wrote the poems, and even Rory agrees.'

'What do I agree?' He stood by the study door. Mum smiled at me. Rory had charmed her, and I wasn't surprised. She had been addicted to his series.

'The lines of poetry on the page in the painting.'

'That's why I'm here. Tash left me the key and I spent yesterday going through all the paperwork that you didn't have here. And I found this.' He held out a yellowed and folded sheet of paper. With a hand not quite steady, I took it and opened it. In a beautiful handwritten script was the poem, but better. The addition of the seven lines at the start, the ones on the portrait written in Katherine's hand, gave me shivers. I looked up at him.

'I know.' His glance was full of kindness and something more. Maybe it was pity, but my heart said it wasn't.

'Good, I'm off. The two of you can work together here.' Tash dashed out the door. If I didn't know better, I'd swear she was doing this on purpose.

'Is that OK with you?' Rory asked.

'Of course.'

He looked concerned. 'I'm sorry about what happened to you.'

A lump the size of a melon arrived in my throat.

'For what it's worth, I never liked Paul, and he's not well thought of by half of the faculty, but he plays the game well.'

I looked down. It didn't reflect well on me that I had stayed with someone who was so . . . I couldn't even find the word I wanted. Rory touched my hand. His glance was filled with understanding when I couldn't understand it all myself. It was difficult seeing it in someone else.

He touched the paper with the poem. 'So I do believe your theory is correct: that Simon's wife, Katherine, was the actual poet.'

'Does this often happen?' I sat back.

'Sadly there are many instances, like the early work of Colette.'

I let this sink in. 'What do we do now?'

'We obtain all the evidence we can to prove it.' He lifted a cardboard box from the floor to the desktop.

'OK. This is the type of work I love.' I smiled.

'Good.'

My stomach growled so loudly I had to acknowledge it. It was the first time in days I'd had any desire for food. 'Sorry about that.' I looked at my watch. It was almost noon. 'Can I offer you a sandwich.'

'Yes please. I didn't have breakfast this morning, but *my* stomach was being polite.'

I sent him a smile as I left him. My mother was playing cards with Meg in the garden in the sunshine. In all of this I had to remember what I was here to do. I needed to arrange the return of my parents' money so that my mother could be looked after properly going forward. I wanted this so much. Seeing her struggling with words and other things was hard, and it must have been even harder for my father.

In the kitchen, I raided the leftover chicken from that fateful night and made chicken salad sandwiches. Rootling about in the cupboard, I found a packet of crisps. The last of Dad's secret stash. I hesitated. Once they were finished, it was like another bit of evidence that he had been here was gone. I stopped myself heading down that line of thinking. Instead I needed to believe that every time I had ready-salted crisps, he was sitting with me and we were sharing.

Adding crisps to both plates, I put them on a tray with glasses and a jug of water.

Mum came into the kitchen. 'That looks good.' She stole a crisp. 'That Rory . . .'

'Mum.' I sent her a look.

'I may be old and losing my mind, but he is one fine specimen.'

I glanced over my shoulder and hoped that Rory hadn't heard her.

'I want to say again how sorry I am that I thought Paul was saying true things. Your father never quite believed him, whereas I did. I was wrong.'

I put the tray down and gave her a big hug. 'Apology accepted. I believed him too.'

'Oh my darling.' She stepped back. 'That is the saddest bit.' She blew her nose. 'Now go and feed that divine man.'

I envied her ability to switch her thoughts so quickly. Mine were not clear and were slow-moving. Mostly I was waiting for the backlash. Paul couldn't reach me, I told myself, but I knew that wasn't true. He knew where I was. He could say vile and untrue things about me. He knew the state of the business, and if that went public, fixing things would be impossible.

In the study, Rory was on his feet, pacing. His face was thunderous and I couldn't imagine what had set this off in him. I put the tray down and he looked at me.

'Is this yours?' he asked in a voice that was quiet and measured.

'Is what mine?' Only when I stepped closer did I see that he was holding my thesis. 'Yes, it's mine.' All the hours I had put in, and then Paul had made me believe it wasn't good enough. That was what he had done to me. He'd taken away my confidence, my belief in myself.

Rory held out a sheet. 'Are these Paul's notes on it?'

I nodded. 'He was trying to help me bring it up to a good enough level to submit for my master's, but sadly he convinced me it would never make the grade.' I laughed bitterly. 'It wasn't until I listened to him on Radio 4 that I realised he'd taken my work.'

'He told you it wasn't good enough?' His voice was very soft.

'Yes, hence you've found it here and not registered at the uni.'

'I saw Paul give this paper at a conference almost word for word, and then it was published.'

'What?'

'He stole your work and put his own name to it.'

'He published it?' I sank into a chair.

He nodded. 'It was so good, he was given tenure on the back of it, and with your permission he will be fired because of it.'

'What?'

'This is outright plagiarism, and he was working for the university when he took advantage of a student he was in a relationship with.'

I swallowed. It was all there in front of me, and I felt so grubby. I couldn't meet Rory's gaze.

He kneeled beside me. 'This isn't your fault.'

I shook my head. 'It is. I let it happen.'

'No, he *made* it happen, and it makes me so angry. He used his position of power to steal your work.'

So many thoughts ran through my mind. Most were the mistakes I'd made, but some of that was overridden by anger. Rory just stayed quietly by my side. Eventually I asked, 'What does this mean?'

'Once I hand this over, he will lose his position and should never be hired by another university again.' He put the paperwork down. 'This makes sense of his odd behaviour at Harbour House. He is no champion of women artists. He is simply a thief and so much more that I won't say.'

'I thought he loved me.' Once the words were out of my mouth, I felt pathetic.

'He made you think that.' He sighed. 'People like him love only themselves and think only of themselves.'

I looked at the floor, letting the words sink in. It wasn't my fault. Paul had used me.

'Thank you for helping. Knowing that he will face consequences for what he's done makes me feel better.' I sighed. 'I wouldn't want him to do this to anyone else.'

'Nor would I.' He picked up a letter. 'Shall we begin to set this record straight for Katherine Forster?'

'Yes please.' It was more important than ever to make sure that Katherine received the credit for her work. My heart went out to her.

35

Penzance

Finally back in the office a few days later, I had the complete inventory of Harbour House ready to send. But before I did that, I had a meeting arranged with Tilly, the gardener. She was due in five minutes. Every time I'd been to the house this week to check things and look for other paperwork, she had been just leaving. Bastard was behaving oddly. She wouldn't leave me alone, and eventually I would end up following her to the main bedroom, where she would sit down, paw the carpet and stare at the corner. The same conversation would take place.

'What do you want, Bastard?' I'd give her a scratch and wait. She'd continue to stare at the corner. 'I don't understand,' I'd tell her. Then I would head back downstairs, none the wiser.

Tash, Rory and I had been through every piece of paper in the house. Thankfully we had found Sheba's journal from Venice, which provided evidence that Katherine had written the poetry. Rory was putting together the case for a major programme to prove that she was the real author of Simon Forster's work. But despite the presence of the poem on the chaise, we still didn't know whether the woman in the painting was Katherine. It could be, and my gut said it was, but without proof we were stuck.

Marcia escorted Tilly into the office.

'Cup of tea?' she asked.

'Yes please,' we both replied in unison.

Tilly's eyes were wide as she looked about. 'Bet it's hard sitting in your father's chair.'

'Terribly,' I said, longing for his company. Being here brought it home that he was never coming back, and my heart ached with that knowledge.

She sat down. 'Thank you for doing right by my ladies.'

'I feel like they're mine too, but we're not quite there yet.'

Marcia came in with two mugs and a packet of biscuits. 'You haven't had any lunch, Ren. You need something.'

I raised an eyebrow. 'Jaffa Cakes don't offer much in the way of nutrition.'

'This is true, but it was all I had, and they were your father's favourites.'

'Thank you.' I smiled and looked to his picture, which I'd propped up on the desk. Somehow I was going to make this all work out, but I wasn't sure how yet.

'Tilly, we have turned out every cupboard and catalogued every piece of art, but we haven't found the wills. Jack Thomas remembers that originals were lodged with the firm he trained at, but everything was lost in a fire fifteen years ago. Did Sheba or Viv say anything to you?'

'Not something we would talk about.' Tilly sipped her tea.

'OK, the other thing: was there a child living at the house at one point?'

'Oh yes. Sheba and Viv both spoke with great sadness about Isabella.'

'Isabella?'

'She was Sheba's.' She put her mug down.

'But Sheba never married.'

'No, she never did. Viv was the love of her life.'

'Do you know what happened?' I asked.

'It was before my time, but there was some falling-out, I think.' She drew a breath as her glance darted about the room. 'They never said.'

'Do you know when?'

She shook her head. 'I came to work for them in 1980, and I had the feeling that it was quite a while before then.'

I wasn't hopeful about this, but I had to ask. 'Did they ever tell you who the woman in the portrait was?'

'That was Sheba's other love, according to Viv.' Tilly laughed. 'Would have driven me mad to have a former lover hanging on the wall, but Viv was the least jealous soul I ever knew.'

'Yes, I don't think I'd care for it either.' I took a sip of tea, making a note about a daughter. Why had no one mentioned her? It wasn't really my place to become involved in this. Barton's had been hired to do a job. But this was all part of the story, and that made it crucial.

'What's happening to the house and their things?' Tilly asked.

I'd arranged an extension for the sale due to what we had discovered about the manuscript. I'd also highlighted a few pieces that could be sold quickly if required. But it was all complicated by the lack of wills. Jack had explained to me in great detail the ins and outs of two people living together unmarried and dying within a month of each other without wills. I glanced up. Tilly was watching me. I hadn't answered her question.

'I don't know,' I said.

'I think they would have left it to charity over the great-nephews. The first time I ever saw either of them was at the funeral.'

'Thank you for this. Now that I know about Isabella, I will

try and find out more about her. Sadly I can't use the censuses as they aren't released for that period so I'll have to find some other way.'

'Thank you for caring.' Tilly drained her mug, took a biscuit, and left without another word.

The online records told me that Sheba bought Harbour House in 1941, for cash. But there was nothing else I could search without more detail as Isabella Kernow brought up nothing but a bunch of social media profiles. If Isabella was still alive, she would be in her late eighties. I don't think she was on TikTok.

Who might have known them?

I ate a biscuit, then picked up my bag to reapply my lip gloss. In the bag was my new phone with a new number. Paul had been bombarding me with messages alternating between conciliation and threats. It had been constant, and one of the ways he had kept me on edge. Changing numbers caused so much extra work, but it was worth it for the peace.

Gloss applied, my next task was at Harbour House where I was meeting the team from the local BBC to talk about the painting and Sheba and Viv.

* * *

Bastard greeted me on arrival, but then returned to the study, where Rory was hard at work. He looked up and grinned. 'Camera-ready, I see.'

I rubbed my sweaty palms down the sides of my skirt. 'I don't see why you couldn't do this.' I paused. 'You know how to be in front of a camera.'

'There are many reasons, the most important one being that this is your story to tell.'

'Fair, but . . .'

'You'll be wonderful.'

I made a face at him, then went to Francis Kernow's painting hanging in the study. I hadn't really paid attention to the inscription on the back when I'd catalogued it.

My dearest Baba,

This little painting of the lighthouse is to remind you, as you look out from the windows of your new home with its new perspective, that this is where you are from. It is good to see your past as you step into a new life.

Baba, you aren't a black sheep, but an artist of true talent. Your mother would be so proud. She would also apologise for your name. But I won't. I love the artist and woman you have become. It is time as you embark on your new life here in Newlyn to leave the BB behind and emerge as you.

Dad

When I'd first seen this, it hadn't made sense, but now it was clear. BB was definitely Sheba when she'd signed her early work.

I spotted a cameraman walking past the door. 'Must go and do this, as you won't,' I said.

Rory laughed, and I went out into the hall.

'Thank you for coming.' I said, stopping by the portrait, which was sitting on one of Sheba's easels. 'You're here about this.'

The reporter didn't reply; just stared at the portrait. 'Wow!'

'I know. She is magnificent, but we're not certain who she is, although we have a theory.'

'Right. We'll take a few shots of the outside of the house and then talk about the missing wills.'

'And apparently there was a daughter, Isabella.' The hand-made bear still on the bed upstairs came to mind.

'Ooh, this is intriguing,' he said. He looked about. 'Anything else we should know?'

'It was all in the email except for the bit about Isabella; that I only discovered today.'

Rory walked out of the study. 'Daughter?'

'Isabella Kernow. I think she might have been born in the 1930s.'

He shook his head and took me into the study. There was a photo album on the desk. 'This can't be a coincidence.'

I frowned.

He opened the album. There was a picture of a young girl on Sennen beach. Long hair, aged about ten, and facing out to sea. I picked it up to study it more closely.

'Katherine and Simon had a daughter named Isabella, born in 1935,' Rory said.

I put the album down. 'Katherine and her daughter died in the Blitz.'

'So it was reported at the time.'

'Are you saying that Viv was Katherine?' I stepped back. This didn't make sense. Viv's information was too sound.

'No, Katherine was fourteen years older than Sheba.' He paced. 'It *can't* be a coincidence. Both women couldn't have given birth to a daughter in the same year and called her Isabella.'

'Well, it's possible, but I agree it's unlikely. Sheba was gay and in love with Katherine, from what her diary says.'

'Sorry to interrupt, but we are ready to film you.'

'Right, coming.' I sent a look to Rory, then headed to the hall and stood beside the portrait. I hated being in front of the camera, or a crowd for that matter, but now I had no choice. It was for Sheba, and also for the business. What I felt inside didn't matter at this point.

36

10 March 1941

London

Hyde Park looks so different. The railings are gone and vegetables are growing. It is still an oasis of beauty, but I'm so exhausted it no longer refreshes me. By night I drive ambulances and by day I try to keep painting. My life in Hampstead is good, though. I've met so many artists, writers and interesting people who keep my mind off other things. Martha and Jason married before he joined the navy. She is a ball of nerves and she's thinking of moving back to Manchester to be with her family. With all the bombs falling in London, I hope Katherine is no longer here. One of those nightly raids killed my grandfather, and today I'm allowed to pick through the rubble with my first cousin, Moira, to take whatever is salvageable.

This war has taken a terrible toll, but hope still lives. Dad has asked if I want to come home to Cornwall, and I do, especially now. Without my grandfather here, and with Martha going back home, I've no reason to stay. Now that I've inherited a substantial amount from him, I will be able to buy my own home, and with frugal living I will be fine. My grandfather would be pleased.

Lamorna calls to me. It will become my home in Cornwall, away from prying eyes so I can be me.

The thought of fresh air and green fields pleases me. I hunger for it in a way I can't explain. Even my latest work has been created from memory rather than what exists in front of me, and I confess this is not good. My painting is always better when I work from the immediate.

Outside the remains of my grandfather's house, I'm greeted by my cousin. We embrace, then enter the half of the house that is still standing. It is like a surrealist painting. Reality versus nightmare.

'How do we do this?' Moira asks.

I shrug. The task is beyond my understanding, yet it is repeated by others every single day in this city.

'Is there anything you want or need?' I note the almost untouched drawing room. His books still on the shelves and flowers scattered on the floor with shards of the broken vase.

'Not really,' she says, picking up a photograph with the glass smashed. 'I have a full house.' She puts it down and picks up his pipe. 'What about you?'

'Possibly the furniture, and I love his books. I'm going to see if any of my things have survived.'

'Go carefully.' She sinks onto the sofa and stares at the painting by Turner still hanging on the wall.

I climb the stairs, holding the railing in case the steps give way. Parts of the wall are missing and patches of blue appear through the gaps. The carpet on the landing is thick with ash and plaster dust, dulling its jewel-bright colours. The door to my old room is wide open, and the first thing I see is the portrait. It is not on the wall but lying on the floor. However, it is intact. Nothing else matters. With care I pick it up and make my way downstairs to meet the man we've hired to help us. This is such a sad task, but at least my grandfather lived a long life. That is what I need to keep at the front of my thoughts.

* * *

I take one last look at the house as I stand on the pavement. It has taken two days, but everything worth saving has been removed and divided between Moira and myself. The postman greets me.

'I'm so sorry for your loss.' He hands me a letter. 'I hoped I'd see you today, as this is addressed to you.'

The writing is familiar and my hand shakes as I flip the package over, looking for a return address, but there is none. It was posted days ago.

'I'll keep an eye out for post and forward it on to your grandfather's solicitors.'

'Thank you.' I smile. 'That's kind.'

He nods and continues his rounds. Leaning against the trunk of a plane tree, I open the envelope, unable to breathe. I have waited so long to hear from Katherine that this seems almost cruel now that I have made a life without her. There is a sheaf of papers that I realise is a manuscript held together by string, with a letter on top. But there is also another folded note. I read that first.

My dearest Sheba,

I think of you every day as I walk in the park hoping to see you. I still dream of the escape we had planned. Have you returned to Cornwall? I am writing to you at your grandfather's address, the one you gave me in Venice. I pray this reaches you, although with this awful war . . .

347

I had hoped that having a child would perhaps mellow Simon, even if it could not change him. This has not been the case. I'll keep this brief, for there is too much to say. But I need to act. Can you meet me in Kensington Gardens? I walk there with my daughter every day from three until four.

K xxx

I fold the letter and race to the gardens. It is a quarter to four.

I am breathless and I don't know where to search for her. I spin around fighting tears. She needs me.

'Sheba?'

My heart stops. Two feet in front of me is Katherine, holding a child's hand.

'It's you!' She's real and not simply conjured from my thoughts. Her face is pale, dark shadows hollow under her eyes. The little girl holding her hand doesn't appear much better. I rush to embrace Katherine, and when I pull back, I see the outline of a bruise below the collar of her dress. When I look directly in her eyes, she doesn't look away.

'You must leave him.'

'I know.' She glances down at her daughter.

'Not her too?' I say.

'I have managed to stop him so far.' She draws a breath. 'You see, I haven't been able to write, or more correctly, I have been writing but I haven't given it to him. He stole your poem. I'm so sorry.' Her eyes fill.

'It doesn't matter. You and Isabella do.'

She reaches for my hand and spots her work clutched under my arm. I meet her gaze.

'Mumma,' the child says. Katherine strokes her daughter's

head while the little girl studies me. I crouch down to her level and say, 'Hello, Isabella, I'm your mother's friend, Sheba.'

She leans into Katherine's side and hides before giving me a cheeky smile.

I stand. 'Leave him.'

'How can I do that?'

'Because of the bombing. Tell him you are going to Cornwall, or to family somewhere.'

She closes her eyes for a moment. 'You are right, of course. I could tell him I'm taking Isabella to friends, and that I will return so that I can write without her distracting me.'

'And you?' My heart is racing.

'On the pretext of checking on her, I will leave and never return.' The corners of her mouth lift and her eyes shine with the thought.

'This will work.' I pause, quickly pulling ideas together. 'I'm leaving London tomorrow and I plan to buy a house.'

'How can you afford that?' she asks.

'Sadly, my grandfather . . .'

She takes my hand in hers. 'I'm so sorry.'

'Thank you.'

I pull out a piece of paper and a pencil from my pocket and write down my father's details. 'I will be here. Do not delay.'

'I'll be as swift as I can. Thank you.' She leans forward and kisses my cheek. She still wears the same perfume. Rose, jasmine and vanilla.

2 June 1941

Newlyn

It has taken more time than I imagined to find a house that will be suitable to have a child living in it too. This fact ruled out

Lamorna for its remoteness, so I have bought a place on the edge of Newlyn. It is a fine house with a good garden and two outbuildings. But it is full of damp, so Dad is working with me to clean every inch with vinegar and, where necessary, bleach. Thankfully the weather is fine and every window is open.

'Remind me again why you need a house this large?' he asks, scrubbing the salt off the sitting room window.

It feels like forever since I saw Katherine in the park. I've received one note, which said only:

It is taking time, but it will happen.

K xx

'I told you that a friend and her daughter would be joining me.'
He pauses and looks at me. 'Are you certain?'
I laugh bitterly. 'There is no certainty in anything now.'
'Only death.' We both pause, then continue with the windows without saying another word. My thoughts circle around my anticipation for Katherine's arrival and fear that they won't come.

When we stop to eat, my father hands me an envelope. My heart sinks as I recognise Katherine's handwriting. Is she not coming? I open it in haste and quickly read.

We had a near miss. The house three down from us was destroyed. He has given his blessing.

K xx

'Whatever you have read has made you smile,' my father says. I nod and relax in the sunshine. She will make it here. Things take time and I must be patient. Below us, the harbour is busy with both fishing boats and smaller military boats. Even here in Cornwall the war is ever present.

'Which of the outbuildings will you make your studio?' he asks.

'The one closer to the water, I think.' It is a wonderful space to work in. New windows and skylights will need to be added in due course. Although I want everything done now, there is time ahead to make things perfect.

'Good choice. More tea?'

I nod, and while I listen to him in the kitchen, I hold the note close to my heart, closing my eyes for a moment.

'Sheba.' Katherine stands above me, blocking the sun. I blink, then jump to my feet.

'You made it!' I fling my arms around her and breathe her in. Part of me comes back to life.

'We did,' she says, grinning.

Over her shoulder I see my brother, Tommy, deep in discussion with Isabella.

I take Katherine's hands in mine.

'Your father is lovely.' She watches him chat to the children.

'He is,' I say, wanting not to talk but to hold her. We can't now, but maybe later, when the others have left us. Days ago, I washed all the linen and made the beds. Fate has been kind with Harbour House. The dear woman who lived here died in her sleep, and her son didn't want the house or anything in it. The purchase was quick.

'I have so many questions.' I study her. Tiredness pours off her.

'I have answers, but the one you will want to know first is that I have a week before I must return for a bit.'

I swallow.

'He would only let me take her away with the promise of poetry.' She sighs.

'But he doesn't know where you are, so you don't have to go back.'

'No, he didn't even ask where I was taking her.' She shakes her head. 'For a man who claimed he wanted children . . .'

'He only wanted your talent.'

'I see that now.' She draws a breath. 'In fact, so much is clear. He didn't discourage my excess when I was pregnant before. He enabled it. He didn't want that child, and he only wanted this one so that I would be tied to him.'

'Oh Katherine.'

She shrugs. 'But I do have to return briefly, for there are things I couldn't take without drawing attention to them. I will only go back for them, and then never again.'

I squeeze her hand. My dream is here and now.

37

12 April 2022

Penzance

Stephen was down with flu and I had to run the auction tomorrow. It was too late to bring someone else in. I hadn't done this in years. My stomach was in knots. I would stutter and fail, I was certain. My father calmly looked out at me from a photo.

'Dad, this isn't fair. I can't do this.' His clock chimed five and I laughed. It was ten to three. I scrolled through the emails that had flooded in after the BBC piece on Sheba and Viv. Nothing that would help, but plenty of good stories about them and their quiet involvement in the community.

'Ren, there's someone here who would like a word.' Marcia stepped aside, and a silver-haired woman with a cane walked into the room.

I stood and came around the desk, pulling out a chair. She smiled, and I shivered. There was something in her smile that was familiar.

Once she'd sat down, I studied her face again, telling myself my eyes were lying.

'You're Isabella,' I said.

She nodded.

'Tea or coffee?' Marcia asked.

'Tea, please,' Isabella said. 'Milk, no sugar.'

Marcia disappeared and I sat in my father's chair, shaking a bit.

'I'm Ren Barton.'

'I saw you on the news last night.' She tucked her cane safely against the arm of the chair.

'And you are Isabella Kernow, daughter of . . .'

She looked at me but didn't say anything.

With Rory's certainty in mind, I said, 'Katherine and Simon Forster.'

'Yes.' She clasped her hands together. 'It's strange to acknowledge it.'

'Have you never told anyone?'

'Only my late husband, and he said it's simply something in the past.' She smiled.

'He's right, of course, but there's a story here and I only have parts of it.'

'You may have more of it than I.' Her eyes were clear, and conveyed humour and intelligence.

I had a thousand questions, but I couldn't rush them. 'You live in Penzance?'

'Bryher in the Isles of Scilly. Well, at least for a little while longer.'

'How wonderful.'

'It is, but I'm here looking at an easier place to live, since I'm not getting any younger.' She tapped her cane.

Marcia came in with the tea, then left again.

'I was shocked to see the portrait and to hear of Sheba and Viv.'

'Did you not know they'd died?' I asked.

'I assumed they had, given their ages. I also assumed they had changed their wills.'

'You were the beneficiary?'

'I was, but that was years ago, before I left.' She played with the silver bangle on her right arm.

'When exactly was that?'

'I was headstrong, to say the least, and fell in love at seventeen.' She had a faraway look on her face. 'He was nineteen and in a band.'

I had a feeling I knew where this was going.

'Needless to say, Sheba wasn't keen, and I said some terrible things.'

I sent her an encouraging look.

'The young can be very cruel, and I was wanting to hurt her.' She turned the bangle on her wrist. 'Then two years later the band wanted to go to Europe.' She looked at me. 'I didn't have a passport.'

Rory came to the door. 'Oh, sorry, I don't mean to intrude.'

I stood. 'Rory, I'd like you to meet Isabella Kernow.'

His eyes opened wide and he held out his hand. 'I'm Rory Crown.'

'You're the dishy professor from the telly.'

I laughed, and he flushed.

I pulled up another chair for him.

'Isabella,' I began.

'Bella Stedman now.'

'Bella, I think Rory should hear what you have to say, because he's been working on your mother's poetry.'

'My mother's?' She frowned, looking between us.

'Yes, the poems thought to be the work of your father, Simon Forster, are actually Katherine's.'

She leaned back in her chair. 'That explains a lot.' She was quiet for a moment. 'I found my birth certificate, and I was furious when I discovered that my father was alive and Sheba and Viv had kept this from me.' She paused. 'Looking back now, I can see why, but at the time I was young and angry and trapped, or so I thought.'

'What did you do?' Rory asked.

She laughed. 'Like all children, I knew where things were kept, even though I wasn't supposed to.' She looked at both of us. 'So I went to the secret hiding place. First I found their wills, and that was when I discovered that my name wasn't Isabella Kernow but Isabella Forster.'

'That must have been . . .' I struggled to find a word. 'Unsettling.'

'Sheba had told me that my parents had both died in the Blitz. I never doubted it. She also said she had adopted me, which I never questioned, and I don't think anyone else did either.'

'Do you remember your parents?' I asked. She had been six when she came to Cornwall, and many of my own strongest early memories were from that time.

'Vaguely. I remember my mother, but that might be because of the portrait.'

'The war caused so much destruction,' Rory said. 'So many documents lost to bombing, and so many displaced people.'

'What happened after you found the birth certificate?' I asked.

'I took it, stormed out and caught the first train out of Penzance.' She picked up the mug and turned it in her hands. 'Foolish. Viv caught me as I was leaving and tried to talk me down. She told me the whole story of my mother and Sheba's plan to escape my father, but I didn't want to believe her. Viv was so good, so kind.'

'When did she arrive?' Rory asked.

Bella smiled. 'After the war, in forty-six. She came for a holiday and never left.' She twisted the bangle on her wrist again. 'The war years were hard, with me and Sheba muddling our way through.' She looked up. 'Viv brought joy with her, and as a family unit we did pretty well until the teenage years.' She laughed drily. 'I wasn't easy.' She lifted her wrist and showed me the rough-hewn bracelet. 'Viv made this for me. It was to remind me of love, which has no beginning and no end.' She dropped her arm to her lap. 'They were both good women and wanted the best for me. I was their focus – not their art, not anything else.'

'So you know why you came to Cornwall?' I asked.

She nodded. 'My mother loved Sheba, and at first I thought that was why I ended up there, but no.' She took a sip of tea. 'Viv told me my father was abusive. Sheba wouldn't even say his name.' She rubbed her left knee. 'He was still alive when I found him. Never had I encountered someone so bitter, so twisted.'

I walked around the desk and kneeled beside her, taking her hand.

'He told me I couldn't be the daughter of the whore who had been his wife. That they had both died in the Blitz.' She drew a breath. 'But he knew I hadn't been in the house when my mother was killed. I confronted him with the truth. He denied it.' Her shoulders dropped. 'I showed him my birth certificate and he tried to destroy it, saying all I was after was the money.'

'Oh Bella.' What that must have felt like, I couldn't imagine.

'I called him all sorts of things because it was clear he could at least have looked for me, wanted me. I was his child. Instead he had lied and said I'd been with my mother.' She closed her eyes and my heart went out to her. That rejection would cut so deeply.

'The sad thing was, I'd said such unforgivable things to Sheba.' She turned the bangle once again. 'I knew that with those words I'd destroyed all the love I'd been given.'

'They couldn't have been that bad.' Memories of my own battles with my mother during my teen years ran through my mind. So much shouting on my part and calmness on hers.

'I told her I hated her. That she had wrecked my parents' marriage and that she had been a terrible mother replacement.' She drew a breath. 'I was incredibly broken afterwards and fell into heavy drug use . . . anything to get away from the thoughts in my head.' She slid the bangle up and down her arm. 'I was too ashamed to contact her.'

She closed her eyes and her chest rose and fell rapidly. When she opened her eyes, tears pooled in them. 'Even now I'm ashamed, even after finding love myself and ending up so close, having married a man from Bryher.'

'Being so near must have been hard,' Rory said.

'It was. But I knew from having seen snippets in the papers that they were both working and fine, and I couldn't disrupt their lives again now that they were living them rather than putting everything on hold for me.' She swallowed. 'Because that was what they'd done. They were both brilliant artists, but because of me, they didn't exhibit, and they rarely sold any work. The risk was too great if they became known. Questions would have been asked about me.'

She placed both hands on her knees and clenched them. 'You see, I couldn't forgive myself, so how could they forgive me? Being so close was my personal pain, but even so, I somehow missed the reports of their deaths. Probably lost in the chaos when my husband passed.'

Her glance met mine. There were so many emotions playing across her face. I had to do something. Her poor heart.

I stood. 'Do you want to see the house?'

'I want to see the painting of my mother,' she said.

'Of course. I am so happy to be able to show it to you.' I looked to Rory and met his gaze. There were tears in his eyes.

38

Newlyn

Rory helped Bella out of the car while Tash opened the front door of Harbour House. Bastard dashed in as Bella stopped and stared at the facade.

'It hasn't changed, except the wisteria is bigger.' She walked towards the door. 'It will be glorious in a few weeks. I remember the smell.'

Inside the house, she stopped in front of the portrait. Her hand reached out to her mother's. 'I've missed her.' She turned to me. 'How did you get her down?'

'With difficulty.' I glanced up at the screws still in the wall where the painting had hung.

She laughed. 'I tried to climb up to kiss her once and nearly killed myself, but the painting survived unscathed.' She lifted her fringe and showed me a scar. 'Some things fade but never leave you.'

I shivered, thinking of Paul. But then reminded myself that that applied to love as well. Dad was gone, but his love was always with me.

Bella looked around, then went into the sitting room, where an old gramophone sat in the far corner. She found a record and cranked the machine, and the sound of Noël Coward's voice warbled out. 'It still works.' She closed her eyes. 'One of my last memories of my mother was of her and Sheba dancing to this in here.' She scanned the room. 'Not much has changed.'

Bastard sauntered in and stared at her.

'What a magnificent cat.' She bent, leaning heavily on her cane, and held her hand out. Bastard sniffed it, then allowed Bella to give her a scratch.

'Bastard owns the place,' I said.

'I can see that, and I would guess that Sheba named the animal.' She straightened.

I frowned. 'Why would you say that?'

'"Poor bastard" was a favourite expression of hers.'

Rory came into the room. 'Tash has gone to make tea.'

'Wonderful. I would like to go to my room, if you would give me a hand, Rory. I'm not brilliant with stairs, which is why I'm leaving my beloved Bryher.'

'Of course,' he said, taking her arm.

I looked out of the window. It was good that we could bring Bella here, but it still didn't resolve everything. Bastard snaked through my legs, then pawed them before taking a few steps towards the door. When I didn't follow, she complained. I knew the routine, so I let her lead me her upstairs. I heard Rory and Bella chatting in the little room as I entered the master bedroom. Bastard sat in the same spot and stared at the wall.

'Look, Bastard, we've been through this before. There is nothing there but a dead electrical socket. Tash checked and I believe her.'

She didn't move when Bella and Rory came into the room.

'Cat marks the spot,' Bella said.

'What?' I asked.

'Bastard is sitting on the floorboard under which Sheba kept all the important documents, such as birth certificates and the deeds to the house.'

I looked at Rory, and then at Tash, who had just joined us. Bastard stepped off the edge of the carpet where she had been sitting and I lifted the corner. It was hard to see which board it was, but Bella came over and tapped with her cane. It wouldn't lift, though, and Rory got down beside me to assist.

'As it hasn't been opened in a while, I'll go and grab a screwdriver.' Tash dashed out.

Bella sat on the bed. 'I always loved this room. Sheba would read to me here.' She pointed to the low nursing-style chair in the corner. 'I would sit on her lap and peer out the window.' She blew her nose. 'I hadn't expected this old place would stir so much inside me.'

I went to her side. 'It's hard.'

'It is, harder than I thought, and I'm as tough as old boots. But it appears I've gone leaky.' She wiped her face.

'This should do the trick.' Tash wielded a long chisel and in moments had prised the floorboard up. Rory extracted a black metal box. He opened it, revealing documents and a sketchbook. Turning to Bella, he asked, 'May I?'

She nodded, and in moments we were looking at the wills of both women. Everything went to Bella.

'I'll give Dad a call and he can deal with it,' Tash said.

'But—'

She interrupted me. 'You have enough on your plate. No argument.'

I knew she was right. This was something I could leave in other people's hands. I glanced up and saw my favourite painting of Sheba's, the one she had won the award for. Even if I couldn't bring these women the respect they deserved for their work, I'd at least been a part of making sure their wishes were fulfilled.

'I see you're looking at the painting of my mother,' Bella said, rising to her feet. 'Sheba told me it was Mum.' She paused. 'It's beautiful, but I always preferred the other one.'

I suddenly saw the painting in a new light. No wonder it always filled me with joy when I looked at it. It was all the colours of love.

Bella tapped the sketchpad in my hand. 'I remember that. Each month Sheba had me sit for her. May I?'

I handed it to her, and as she opened it, a sheet of paper fell out. I scooped it up recognising Katherine's writing. 'It's from your mother.' I held it out to her.

'Can you read it to me? These are not the best reading glasses.'

'Of course,' I said, opening the folded sheet to the first page.

My love,

These past ten days in London have been dreadful, and it's not the bombs. They are terrible, but I bless them too. Every night we end up in the shelter at Simon's insistence, which saves me from enduring his presence in my bed. Being far from you and Isabella is hell, but at least I know you are both safe. Today I booked the train, and I am counting the hours until I can be with the two most important people in my life.

In preparation this week, I have sold some jewellery and wired the money to you. He has no idea, and this lifts me more than it should. I've written some half-hearted poems to appease him. He hasn't been impressed, but I told him that I am like a rusty machine that needs oiling! He believes it. The thought of you has words singing in me, but he will not have them.

I have sent things ahead. They may arrive before me. I wish I were with them and on my way already. This morning I visited my parents' solicitor and checked the details of their wills and the trust. With me and Isabella gone, he only has use of the funds while he is alive. If there is anything left, it will go to the charities my parents supported. The solicitor thought my questions odd, but I explained them away in light of the heavy bombing of late.

I can't explain this feeling of freedom and joy. It is better than any drug and it's hard work to keep my happiness hidden. To keep sane these past few days, I have relived our week together. Isabella's joy as we took her to the beach. Her face as her toes dug in the sand and she paddled for the first time. We swam, we sunbathed, and as the sun kissed my skin, I felt your lips and knew that come the evening I would be lying beside you, wrapped in your love.

I turned the page over and saw Rory watching me.

Even as I write these words, I feel your caress. Each stroke confirms your love, your need, and mine matches it. Every atom, every particle of my being calls to you. I am only whole with you. You make me better, a better human, a better mother and a better poet. Your love has grown inside of me and altered my very make-up.

I paused. 'Maybe I should stop.'
'No,' they all said in unison.

*Oh, these silly words mean little when I am not with
you. I remind myself it is only hours until I board
an overcrowded train that will lead me to you and
Isabella. Then and only then can my life truly be
complete. You, me and Isabella, our perfect family.*

*I love you with all my heart. Thank you for
seeing beyond the image to the real woman, the one
who was locked inside full of fear and self-loathing.*

I paused again, and my glance met Rory's.

*Kiss my darling girl. In two nights I will be in
your arms, dancing with you, knowing I'm only
guilty of love, but this time it's entirely right.*

Yours forever,

K xxx

Silence filled the room. Tash blew her nose, and I gulped.
Bella had tears in her eyes while Rory stood with his eyes closed.
Outside, the sound of the sea became louder as the words sank in.

'I am devastated for Katherine and Sheba,' said Tash. 'And
even more devastated for you, Bella. So much love, so much
talent lost.'

Bella smiled sadly. 'Thanks to all of you, not lost, but found.'
She blew her nose too, then looked at her watch. 'I have an
appointment. I don't suppose one of you could drop me off?
Sadly it's too late to cancel it.'

'Rory,' I said. 'Would you mind?'

He took Bella's arm. 'Not at all.' They left the room, and I
heard her cane tapping on the stairs.

Bastard sat smugly on the bed. I looked at her. 'OK, you were right all along, Bastard, and I wasn't clever enough.'

She licked a paw and proceeded to clean her face. That told me.

Tash cleared her throat as she looked up from her phone. 'Marcia just messaged me. Hot off the press, there's a bidding war going on right this very minute for Stephen's house. They are asking for sealed bids.'

'What?' I sank onto the nursing chair.

'With that money, he can pay your mother back and repay the company.'

I nodded, letting the news sink in. We weren't out of the woods yet, though. There was all the furniture he'd accumulated illegally sitting the warehouse, and what to do next. Tash perched beside me on the arm of the chair.

'It will be OK.'

'Really?' I shook my head, not seeing how it could be.

'Yes, you're actually good at this stuff and always have been, plus you were shit-hot in front of the camera.'

'I was not.' I cringed just thinking about it. There was nothing worse than seeing and hearing yourself on film.

'Rory said he was impressed.' She raised an expressive eyebrow.

'No.'

'Yes he did. He likes you, and not in he wants to be your best friend.' She fixed her intense stare on me, pinning me to the spot.

'Don't even go there. It's wrong, I'm wrong.' I put my hands up.

'I'll let you have "it's not the right time", but that man likes you, and he's in no rush.' She paused, looking about the room. 'He's looking for a place down here.'

'What?' That couldn't be right.

'He wants to live down here and needs good transport links.'

It was my turn to raise an eyebrow. 'One main road in and out, one train line, a small airport . . .'

She hit my arm. 'And you'll be here.'

'Will I?' But as I asked that question, I knew she was right. I wasn't returning to London. My mother and Barton's needed me. And if Rory was in town, that could prove to be a good distraction in the future. Not now, but maybe soon.

Epilogue

6 May 2024

Tash carried in a tray of glasses, Gareth followed with champagne and Annabelle brought popcorn. My mother, Bella, Marcia, Meg and Stephen were already sitting in front of the large television in the sitting room of Harbour House. Also with us were Lucy and Kit Williams and their three children over from Helwyn House. During the past two years Lucy had become a friend as I spent more and more time with Rory.

Rory was organising the champagne while I stepped outside, calling Bastard and waving a treat to get her attention. It was a stand-off but the programme on Katherine Forster was on in three minutes, and even for Bastard I wasn't going to miss it. Of course, I'd seen snippets already and watched other parts being recorded, plus I was in it. It had been a whirlwind.

I caught sight of the glimmer of a golden eye under a rose bush. Opening the disgusting tube of cat yoghurt, I bent low to waft the foul scent closer to the wild beast. Reluctantly Bastard was drawn to the lure of the treat, and I scooped her up before she could complain.

Once I was back in the sitting room, we managed a quick group picture with glasses held aloft in a toast to Katherine, Sheba and Viv before we settled in to watch the hour-long programme, which had us all sniffling at the end. Rory's final words spoke of the journey he'd been on and the importance of getting the story right. He referenced his previous programme on Simon Forster and emphasised that mistakes could easily be made. He drew attention to the fact that Anonymous was often a woman who couldn't write as herself, as Virginia Woolf had said. Then he added that it was a sad fact that women chose to operate anonymously, but that this was better than having a man taking credit for the words or the painting or the work in general. He cautioned everyone, especially himself, to look carefully, not to jump to conclusions like he had. Only then, he said, might we be lucky enough to actually see what was in front of us and hear the story properly.

'That was fabulous.' Bella stood. 'Thank you all for setting the record straight.' She laughed. 'Or should I say setting it queer, as my mother was definitely bi and Sheba was gay.'

Tash raised her glass. 'Here's to using our words more carefully.'

We all toasted.

'Time to get these two home,' said Marcia. 'Don't want to be told off for bringing them back drunk.' She kissed my cheek before bundling my mother and Bella into the car to take them back to the assisted living facility where they were neighbours.

Lucy moved across to sit next to me. 'Tonight was a triumph in so many ways.'

'It was. I'm so proud of what Rory has done in . . . correcting the record.'

She looked at me. 'He said he never would have seen what was right in front of his eyes if it weren't for you and your intuition.'

I laughed. 'He would have seen it eventually.'

'You're good for him.' She got up and began to collect empty glasses.

'He's good for me.' I caught Rory's glance from across the room, where he and Gareth were chatting.

'Rory's greatest strength is his loyalty.' She tucked an empty bottle under her arm. 'And for a while I thought it would be his undoing.'

I grabbed a few glasses. 'I don't understand.'

'He loved my aunt, and until you, I didn't think he'd ever allow love into his life again.'

'Oh.' I looked across at the profile of the man who had been so patient with me.

'Thank you for bringing him out of his grief and back to life.'

My heart was filled with love, and when he turned and sent me a half-smile, I could barely breathe. 'I think it might be the other way around.'

Lucy laughed. 'Well, that works too. I love having him this close. Bella told me tonight how happy she is that he bought the house.'

'She has no family and she really wanted it to go to someone who would love it.' She had even given him the portrait of Katherine because she said it belonged here at the house and was far too big for her new flat.

Lucy looked around the room, which still contained the sculpture of Bastard and many of the original furnishings and paintings, but now also held new things, like the large-screen TV and a sound system more up to date than the old gramophone in the corner.

On evening and weekends, we had between us sanded, repaired and repainted every corner of the house and the studios. Stephen had been a star with the furniture. He really did have a knack for restoring. Harbour House had a new lease of life, with Bastard still ruling over it despite her advancing years.

'Now I need to get my lot home, as the kids have a sailing

lesson in the morning.' Lucy headed off to round up her family. I took the empties to the kitchen, where Tash joined me.

'Well, Kerensa Barton, this all looks pretty good to me.' She nodded towards a picture of me that Rory had stuck on the fridge.

'Yes, it's good.' A glow of happiness began inside me.

'Hmm, you need to trust me when I say a man fancies you.'

I laughed. 'Maybe.'

'Well I'll take that, because I'm thrilled to have my bestie back in town!'

'Me too.' I hugged her.

Gareth walked into the kitchen holding his daughter's hand. 'This one has had a sugar high and is about to collapse. It's time to go.'

'Sorry to leave you with this.' Tash waved her hand.

'No worries. It was a great celebration.'

'It was.' She raised her glass, which still had a sip in it. 'To Katherine, Sheba and Viv.' She knocked it back.

'It's a good thing I'm driving,' Gareth said, giving Tash a kiss.

Rory walked with me out to the drive to see them off. Bastard came and sat beside us. 'Is there any fizz left?' he asked.

'Hmm, a good half-bottle.' I said, tucking my arm in his as we walked back into the house.

'Shall we sit outside and enjoy the night?'

'Good plan.' We collected the fizz and two glasses. Bastard joined us as we stood in the darkness fragranced with roses and jasmine.

Lights along the coast gleamed, and the sky was full of stars. Rory stood by the stone wall and I joined him.

'Magic,' he said.

'It is.' I poured the champagne and handed him a glass.

'Thank you.'

I leaned into his side, enjoying his warmth.

'I could say the same.' His breath caressed my temple.

I turned to him and looked him directly in the eyes. 'After all that happened, I didn't think I could be this happy.'

'I didn't think I could love again.'

I gasped.

'I love you and have from the minute I saw you.' He took my champagne from my hand and put both glasses down on the wall. 'From that moment all I could think about was you.'

'It was pretty much the same for me, though it shouldn't have been.'

He ran his thumb across my cheek, sending shivers through me. 'I'm not going to even address that.'

I kissed him. 'I love you too, and thank you for being patient with me.'

He laughed. 'Trying to get you to say yes to a date was worse than getting a racehorse into a starting gate.'

'You know all about racehorses?' Under my hand I felt his heart beating.

'As a matter of fact . . .'

I kissed him again. 'Show-off.'

He dug in his pocket and pulled out a box. 'I saw this when I was in London last week and hoped I'd find the right time . . .'

I couldn't breathe as he opened the box. In the moonlight the art deco diamond ring shimmered.

'But I think now might be good.' He paused, getting down on one knee. 'I am unmade, love has disassembled me, to parts, only you can make me whole.' His eyes met mine.

Katherine's words to Sheba coming from Rory. I couldn't breathe.

'Will you marry me?'

'Yes.'

He took my hand in his and slipped the ring on my finger.

'My father always said that every object has a story to tell.'

'Did he?' Rory asked, rising to his feet.

'He did. What story does this ring have to tell?' I asked.

'I don't know its past, but I hope it will tell of a future filled with love.' He kissed me.

'Me too,' I said, feeling breathless.

'Kerensa, my love, you have my heart.'

'You have mine,' I whispered. 'Always.'

Bastard yowled as she sat on the wall, watching us with something like a smile on her face.

Acknowledgements

My first thanks go to my readers. I appreciate each and every one of you. Your enjoyment spurs me onwards to write the next story.

This book wouldn't be what it is without the support of Mr Liz AKA my husband Chris. He has been on every research trip, double-checked facts, read and reread each draft of this book. He has listening to me rant, rage and despair when the story wasn't working. Through it all he reminds me that I can tell stories and I try hard to believe him. Huge thanks to my children Sasha, Dom, Andrew, and Annabel plus the loving purrs of Sooty and Ziggy. And yes Bastard is based on Sooty.

The book is dedicated to Brigid Coady who has been my writing soulmate since we met twenty years ago. Together we have pounded the keyboards as unpublished to published writers, finding our way to the stories we needed to tell. I think she knows my writing process better than I do and she certainly understands my stories better than me much of the time. I am so grateful she is in my life making me laugh, reminding me of my process and just being the best of buddies.

Brigid is one third of The Blessing of Writers. Deborah Harkness is the other third. Her arrival into Brigid's and my writing world has not only been a blessing but it has been a challenge to make both Brigid and I better writers. As a group we are stronger together and I am so grateful for this.

In the course of research in Venice, I would have been lost without Gwen Hammond. She is also a trusted early reader, ploughing through the story when I need to know if it works. Her input is invaluable.

To make sure I had Sheba's thinking as an artist correct, Sarah Wimperis kindly read Sheba's story. Caroline Lay helped me with my research into auction houses, allowing me to make Barton's as real as possible but it is not Lay's Auctioneers and is purely from my imagination. However the story of Tutankhamen's cat is true. The Italian was checked by my dear friend Roberta Bortolami and my daughter Sasha checked Ren's timeline for me. Any mistakes are mine.

Books don't publish themselves; they require the skill and expertise of so many. Huge thanks to Luigi and Alison Bonomi, Kate Mills, Rachael Nazarko, Jane Selley, Anne O'Brien plus the marketing, sales and production teams at HQ.

Author's Note

For eagle-eyed readers of previous books, you will have noted that Jaunty Blythe (*A Cornish Stranger*), Maddie Hollis (*The Cornish House*) and Elise Tremayne (*The Secret Shore*) are mentioned along with real Cornish artists. It was great fun to 'visit' with them again.

Hitler did meet Mussolini in person for the first time in Venice in 1934. When I discovered that Mussolini considered himself a poet and likewise Hitler an artist, I had to choose June 1934 to set Sheba's and Katherine's story. The words that Rossi utters are a translation of what Mussolini said about Hitler after their meeting. It is also true that Hitler was offered a painting but refused it and took one he preferred.

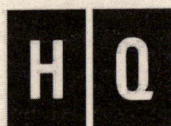

ONE PLACE. MANY STORIES

Bold, innovative and
empowering publishing.

FOLLOW US ON:

@HQStories